mys

· THE OXFORD SHERLOCK HOLMES ·

General Editor
Owen Dudley Edwards

The Valley of Fear

ARTHUR CONAN DOYLE

The Valley of Fear

Edited with an Introduction by
Owen Dudley Edwards

NOV   1997

Oxford   New York
OXFORD UNIVERSITY PRESS
1993

Oxford University Press, Walton Street, Oxford OX2 6DP

Oxford New York Toronto
Delhi Bombay Calcutta Madras Karachi
Kuala Lumpur Singapore Hong Kong Tokyo
Nairobi Dar es Salaam Cape Town
Melbourne Auckland Madrid
and associated companies in
Berlin Ibadan

Oxford is a trade mark of Oxford University Press

British Library Cataloguing in Publication Data
Data available

Library of Congress Cataloging in Publication Data
Data available

ISBN 0-19-212314-9
ISBN 0-19-212329-7 (set)

1 3 5 7 9 10 8 6 4 2

Typeset by Pure Tech Corporation, Pondicherry, India
Printed in Great Britain by
BPCC Paperbacks Ltd
Aylesbury, Bucks

CONTENTS

ACKNOWLEDGEMENTS

I N the preparation of the present text much of the value of my work is due to American and Irish historians who have aided me in the remote and recent past. The late Maureen Wall, *née* Maureen McGeehin, foremost historian of Irish Catholic life in the eighteenth century, laid the foundations of my knowledge of Irish agrarianism (and that of Wayne G. Broehl). I owe so much also to my valued colleague Rhodri Jeffreys-Jones in his studies and guidance on the history of American labour violence. My grateful thanks are also due to the wisdom and kindness of so many friends in the historical profession in the United States who have taught me so much so well: Monsignor John Tracy Ellis, Professors Charles A. Barker, C. Vann Woodward, Waldo H. Heinrichs, John Appel, the late Kenneth Wiggins Porter, Edwin A. Bingham, Robert W. Smith, Sydney V. James, Robert L. Peterson, Willie Lee Rose, Robin W. Winks, James M. McPherson, Clarke L. Wilhelm, Sara Jean Wilhelm, Lynn H. Parsons, Alan M. Smith, Vincent P. De Santis, David Montgomery, Eric S. Foner, Thomas N. Brown, Henry Nash Smith, the late Lawrence Eric Goldman, the later John Christopher Farrell, Bertram Wyatt-Brown, James V. Compton, John Tricamo, Robert B. Patterson, Mark H. Freeman, William H. A. Williams, Benjamin F. Hull, James P. Barefield, J. B. Crooks, Charles B. Dew, Daniel J. O'Sullivan, Robert S. Dill, Gennaro R. Falconeri, Harold Bauman; and to Elizabeth Lewandowski of Birdsboro, PA., the late Daniel W. Hamm of Allentown, PA, and the late Mike and Pat Farrell of State College, PA, all of whom make Pennsylvania a sacred memory for me.

Finally, I owe a word of thanks to ACD's fellow-townsman Sean Connery, for his thoughtful and thought-provoking performance as Black Jack Kehoe in the film *The Molly Maguires* (1970).

GENERAL EDITOR'S PREFACE
TO THE SERIES

ARTHUR CONAN DOYLE told his *Strand* editor, Herbert Greenhough Smith (1855–1935), that 'A story always comes to me as an organic thing and I never can recast it without the Life going out of it.'[1]

On the whole, this certainly seems to describe Conan Doyle's method with the Sherlock Holmes stories, long and short. Such manuscript evidence as survives (approximately half the stories) generally bears this out: there is remarkably little revision. Sketches or scenarios are another matter. Conan Doyle was no more bound by these at the end of his literary life than at the beginning, whence scraps of paper survive to tell us of 221B Upper Baker Street where lived Ormond Sacker and J. Sherrinford Holmes. But very little such evidence is currently available for analysis.

Conan Doyle's relationship with his most famous creation was far from the silly label 'The Man Who Hated Sherlock Holmes': equally, there was no indulgence in it. Though the somewhat too liberal Puritan Micah Clarke was perhaps dearer to him than Holmes, Micah proved unable to sustain a sequel to the eponymous novel of 1889. By contrast, 'Sherlock' (as his creator irreverently alluded to him when not creating him) proved his capacity for renewal 59 times (which Conan Doyle called 'a striking example of the patience and loyalty of the British public'). He dropped Holmes in 1893, apparently into the Reichenbach Falls, as a matter of literary integrity: he did not intend to be written off as 'the Holmes man'. But public clamour turned Holmes into an economic asset that could not be ignored. Even so, Conan Doyle could not have continued to write about

---

[1] Undated letter, quoted by Cameron Hollyer, 'Author to Editor', *ACD— The Journal of the Arthur Conan Doyle Society*, 3 (1992), 19–20. Conan Doyle's remark was probably *à propos* 'The Red Circle' (*His Last Bow*).

Holmes without taking some pleasure in the activity, or indeed without becoming quietly proud of him.

Such Sherlock Holmes manuscripts as survive are frequently in private keeping, and very few have remained in Britain. In this series we have made the most of two recent facsimiles, of 'The Dying Detective' and 'The Lion's Mane'. In general, manuscript evidence shows Conan Doyle consistently underpunctuating, and to show the implications of this 'The Dying Detective' (*His Last Bow*) has been printed from the manuscript. 'The Lion's Mane', however, offers the one case known to us of drastic alterations in the surviving manuscript, from which it is clear from deletions that the story was entirely altered, and Holmes's role transformed, in the process of its creation.

Given Conan Doyle's general lack of close supervision of the Holmes texts, it is not always easy to determine his final wishes. In one case, it is clear that 'His Last Bow', as a deliberate contribution to war propaganda, underwent a ruthless revision at proof stage—although (as we note for the first time) this was carried out on the magazine text and lost when published in book form. But nothing comparable exists elsewhere.

In general, American texts of the stories are closer to the magazine texts than British book texts. Textual discrepancies, in many instances, may simply result from the conflicts of sub-editors. Undoubtedly, Conan Doyle did some re-reading, especially when returning to Holmes after an absence; but on the whole he showed little interest in the constitution of his texts. In his correspondence with editors he seldom alluded to proofs, discouraged ideas for revision, and raised few—if any—objections to editorial changes. For instance, we know that the *Strand*'s preference for 'Halloa' was not Conan Doyle's original usage, and in this case we have restored the original orthography. On the other hand, we also know that the *Strand* texts consistently eliminated anything (mostly expletives) of an apparently blasphemous character, but in the absence of manuscript confirmation we have normally been unable to restore what were probably stronger original versions. (In any case, it is perfectly possible that Conan Doyle, the consummate professional, may have come to exercise self-censorship in the certain knowledge that editorial changes would be imposed.)

Throughout the series we have corrected any obvious errors, though these are comparatively few: the instances are at all times noted. (For a medical man, Conan Doyle's handwriting was commendably legible, though his 'o' could look like an 'a'.) Regarding the order of individual stories, internal evidence makes it clear that 'A Case of Identity' (*Adventures*) was written before 'The Red-Headed League' and was intended to be so printed; but the 'League' was the stronger story and the *Strand*, in its own infancy, may have wanted the series of Holmes stories established as quickly as possible (at this point the future of both the Holmes series and the magazine was uncertain). Surviving letters show that the composition of 'The Solitary Cyclist' (*Return*) preceded that of 'The Dancing Men' (with the exception of the former's first paragraph, which was rewritten later); consequently, the order of these stories has been reversed. Similarly, the stories in *His Last Bow* and *The Case-Book of Sherlock Holmes* have been rearranged in their original order of publication, which—as far as is known—reflects the order of composition. The intention has been to allow readers to follow the fictional evolution of Sherlock Holmes over the forty years of his existence.

The one exception to this principle will be found in *His Last Bow*, where the final and eponymous story was actually written and published after *The Valley of Fear*, which takes its place in the Holmes canon directly after the magazine publication of the other stories in *His Last Bow*; but the removal of the title story to the beginning of the *Case-Book* would have been too radically pedantic and would have made *His Last Bow* ludicrously short. Readers will note that we have already reduced the extent of *His Last Bow* by returning 'The Cardboard Box' to its original location in the *Memoirs of Sherlock Holmes* (after 'Silver Blaze' and before 'The Yellow Face'). The removal of 'The Cardboard Box' from the original sequence led to the inclusion of its introductory passage in 'The Resident Patient': this, too, has been returned to its original position and the proper opening of 'The Resident Patient' restored. Generally, texts have been derived from first book publication collated with magazine texts and, where possible, manuscripts; in the case of 'The Cardboard Box' and 'The Resident Patient', however, we have employed the *Strand* texts, partly because of the restoration of the latter's opening, partly to give readers a flavour of the magazine in which the Holmes stories made their first, vital conquests.

In all textual decisions the overriding desire has been to meet the author's wishes, so far as these can be legitimately ascertained from documentary evidence or application of the rule of reason.

One final plea. If you come to these stories for the first time, proceed now to the texts themselves, putting the introductions and explanatory notes temporarily aside. Our introductions are not meant to introduce: Dr Watson will perform that duty, and no one could do it better. Then, when you have mastered the stories, and they have mastered you, come back to us.

OWEN DUDLEY EDWARDS

University of Edinburgh

INTRODUCTION

I

IN *THE VALLEY*:
THE STAGE-MANAGEMENT OF FEAR

'O where are you going?' said reader to rider,
'That valley is fatal when furnaces burn,
Yonder's the midden whose odours will madden,
That Gap is the grave where the tall return.'

W. H. Auden, 'Five Songs', V (Oct. 1931)

*T*HE *Valley of Fear* occupies a unique place amongst
Arthur Conan Doyle's Sherlock Holmes stories; to
appreciate this it is necessary not to read this introduction,
or the Explanatory Notes, before reading the story. The
same prohibition is offered in the general editorial preface
as advice for reading all the stories; but with this work alone
it becomes a command, on pain of severe loss: stay away,
until you know the book.

Almost every one of the other fifty-nine stories are detective stories in that they are literally stories about a detective.
There are thrills to be obtained by the first discovery of who
did what and why, but they are subordinate to the main
delight, the progress of the story. We are to watch Holmes
in action, and to question him, through the medium of
Watson. We do not challenge him or, still more absurdly,
have him challenge us. These are not puzzles; they are, as
the first series of short stories insisted, adventures. Their
author was a story-teller in the way that Homer or Shakespeare or Defoe or Swift or Scott or Tolstoy were. The *Iliad*
and the *Odyssey* were meant to be heard again and again,
Hamlet and *Macbeth* to be seen time after time, *Robinson Crusoe*
and *Gulliver's Travels* perpetually ready to be invoked into
island enchantment, *Waverley* and *War and Peace* eternally to
be questioned on their location over History's frontiers. We
do not mind that we know how they eventuated, or that the

stories are told so memorably we have no chance of forgetting who did what and their probable motives. Reading the
Sherlock Holmes canon works on the same principle. Can
we recall stopping to enquire why in 'Silver Blaze' (*Memoirs*)
Holmes singled out the curious incident of the dog in the
night-time, or did we simply rub our hands, and gleefully
await the next words of our author? Of course we can read
the stories as puzzles (more or less as the lady in 'The
Macbeth Murder Mystery' of James Thurber (1894–1961)
proved the murderer could not be Macbeth) and thus find
additional means of entertainment; but the main point of
the stories is that they are stories.

The Valley of Fear is also a story, but the puzzle element is
exceptionally important. Holmes is begirt with rivals from
the start: a provoked Watson traps his friend in the third
sentence he completes; MacDonald and White Mason make
comments on the mystery far above the professional norm;
Moriarty broods over all, still invincible; and, as Holmes
discovers, the chief architect of the deceit, whom he must
defeat, is probably the greatest American detective of their
time. So for this story, the enjoyment of rereading partially
turns on the memory of our first bewilderment as it built up
successively in the two parts, to say nothing of the coda
resolving the first problem to confront the reader then
apparently forgotten: Moriarty's interest in the case.

Must the rereading therefore be slightly flat, as the
rereading of a conventional detective story tends to be? *The
Valley of Fear* has never attained the popularity of the other
three long stories. The second part has been criticized as
being mere flashback, a device otherwise limited to Conan
Doyle's nonage (in *A Study in Scarlet* and *The Sign of the Four*)
when he was still drawing heavily on the works of Émile
Gaboriau (1833–73). Howard Haycraft, whose *Murder for
Pleasure: The Life and Times of the Detective Story* (1942) was
for many years the sole history of its subject believed
'posterity will pronounce' *The Valley of Fear* 'sadly inferior
to anything else in the saga', and found flashback 'used
without apology . . . embarrassingly in the manner of Bertha

M. Clay at her worst' (pp. 51, 54). And Haycraft treated the Holmes saga with general respect, although 'by modern standards the tales must often be pronounced better fiction than detection', a pronunciation inviting greater respect than he may have intended. Haycraft's most impressive successor as the historian of detective fiction, Julian Symons, seems in his *Portrait of an Artist: Conan Doyle* to agree about *The Valley*, feeling it 'give[s] up detection part of the way through, to deal with life . . . in a miners' settlement' (pp. 85–6).

The book has had many friends, certainly, headed by John Dickson Carr, who considered it 'his last and best detective-novel' (*Life*, p. 279). 'Let aesthetic critics', snarled Carr 'devote themselves to *A Study in Scarlet* or *The Sign of the Four*, which really did have uncertain handling. But let them refrain from talking nonsense about *The Valley of Fear*' (p. 283). God protect it from its friends, but he had a point. What we find in the book is there by design, and is a different matter from earlier use. Even the mathematics of the matter is suggestive. All the other works keep non-Holmes matter to a minimum—thus Holmes is off-stage in only five of *A Study in Scarlet*'s fourteen chapters, in none in *The Sign*, in four of *The Hound*'s fifteen—but in *The Valley* he finds n place in eight of the fifteen chapters (including 'The Tragedy of Birlstone', the scene-setting chapter 3 of Part 1). For every seven pages he inhabits, he is absent from eight.

This was evidently the author's intention from the outset. Herbert Greenhough Smith (1855–1935), editor of the *Strand*, must have been startled as well as delighted when informed in January 1914 that Conan Doyle offered the *Strand* a new Sherlock Holmes novel now in the process of composition. 'The Dying Detective', later published in *His Last Bow* (1917), had been blazoned in triumph by the *Strand* for its December 1913 number, but its predecessor, 'The Disappearance of Lady Frances Carfax,' had been published in December 1911. Now the sporadic offerings were suddenly speeding up, and this Holmes novel would be the first since the immensely profitable *Hound of the Baskervilles*, which sent *Strand* sales soaring in August 1901. The *Strand* was to commission its first colour illustration for the opening instalment published in September 1914, showing Holmes wrestling with Porlock's cipher, embattled with pipe and in the resplendent armour of a red dressing-gown. (Unable to call on the artistry of Holmes's iconographic immortalizer in the *Strand*, Sidney Paget (1860–1908), Greenhough Smith would employ Frank Wiles.) But from the first the editor had been itching for any information he could get on this most unexpected bonus. On 6 February 1914 Conan Doyle replied to a tentative query:

The *Strand* are paying so high a price for this story that I should be churlish indeed if I refused any possible information.

The name, I think, will be *The Valley of Fear*. Speaking from what seem the present probabilities it should run to not less than 50,000 words. I have done nearly 25,000, I reckon roughly. With luck I should finish before the end of March.

As in the *Study in Scarlet* the plot goes to America for *at least* half the book while it recounts the events which led up to the crime in England which has engaged Holmes's services . . . But of course in this long stretch we abandon Holmes. That is necessary. (Lancelyn Green, *Uncollected Sherlock Holmes*, 134–7.)

A week or two later the author told the editor that his method of writing had been to do two opening Holmes chapters and then, contrary to what he had designed as the publication order, had embarked on the American part. On the schedule given there, by 6 February he had completed what we now know as Part 1, Chapters 1 and 2, and Part 2, Chapters 1, 2, and probably some part of 3; that is 'The Warning', 'Mr Sherlock Holmes Discourses', 'The Man', 'The Bodymaster', and part of 'Lodge 341, Vermissa'. For want of contradicting information, it can be assumed that he went on to finish the American part (he must have been into Chapter 4 by the date he informed Greenhough Smith of his composition order); that this was followed by Chapter 3 of Part 1 (in which Holmes is absent); and that the remaining four chapters (which Holmes dominates) and the Epilogue were the last to be written. Conscious of how much would be written without Holmes, the author dropped Watson as narrator for the first time since the unexplained third-person narrative in Part 2 of *A Study in Scarlet*, and for the first time ever a Holmes story was intended to be completely third-person in the telling. The final manuscript as sent to the *Strand* was still written in that form, but whether on his own reappraisal, or at the urging of Jean, Lady Conan Doyle, Greenhough Smith, or an American editor, or possibly Alfred H. Wood, ACD's secretary, Part 1, Chapters 1, 2, 5, 6, 7, and the Epilogue were made Dr Watson's narrative, with appropriate light changes to the same effect in Chapter 4 and a brief introductory paragraph for Chapter 3. But whether Watson was narrating or not, the narrator in both parts was anything but 'omniscient'. The only character whose mind is visible to the reader is Watson (apart from the brief exception of Josiah H. Dunn immediately before his own murder).

Watson remained vital to the story. He was Holmes's foil, and, as Holmes acknowledges by quoting from foil-fencing's most famous passage in literature, he was if anything hyperactive during their *tête-à-tête* moments in this story (Part 1, Chapters 1 and 6). His personal observation is vital on matters of interest to readers who are not professional detectives. In *The Valley of Fear* Watson was needed to see and hear what the professionals would not be in a position to notice. And he was essential to explain the origins of Part 2, although we never discover how much its present form is his work or that of John Douglas—an ambiguity that seems highly deliberate.

There is no reason to assume that Conan Doyle made more than one draft of the story; indeed the schedule of writing suggests that he did not. January saw its inception, February the completion of at least half the text as well as public agitation on a variety of issues, including reform of the Divorce Law and the need for a Channel tunnel; engagement with public issues—including a new crusade against the importation of animal skins and bird plumage—continued into March, by which time *The Valley* was nearly complete. In mid-April he completed both *The Valley* and the short story 'Danger!' (on the perils of national famine resulting from enemy submarine attacks); in the middle of the following month he worked on the proofs of 'Danger!' and departed with his wife for North America, which they toured from 27 May to 1 July (possibly at the same time revising the American text of *The Valley* or supervising editorial changes). After their return Conan Doyle was embroiled with a renewal of the Home Rule controversy. Thus there seems to have been very little time to supervise final revisions in proof at the end of July, the last possible date, although the change from a complete third-person narrative may well have been made that month, if not when he was in America. After the outbreak of war Conan Doyle looked on *The Valley of Fear* as an *enfant terrible* distracting public attention from the gravity of the conflict. Locked into serialization plans, the *Strand* went ahead with its September number, coloured frontispiece and all. Conan Doyle wrote to Greenhough Smith on 11 September 1914 (Metropolitan Toronto Library, MSS) deploring 'rank bad luck' for the editor to be lumbered with what must be a work of so little benefit to the magazine in present circumstances. In fact, *The Valley of Fear* must have been a great advantage to the *Strand* when the public desperately needed some relief from war, especially as the long, hard winter of trench warfare fastened its hold. The attrition among so many of the *Strand*'s rivals was in marked contrast with what was still Sherlock Holmes's magazine.

Let us look at the development of the story as Conan Doyle wrote it. We begin with what might be termed the Moriarty Prologue, in which the Napoleonic master criminal is proved to have knowledge of, and probably intention of, danger to one Douglas at Birlstone; Douglas is then reported as having been murdered. This necessitated some violence to the existing canon. In 'The Final Problem' (*Memoirs*) Watson had never heard of Moriarty up to two weeks before the professor's actual death, and Holmes's presumed one, at the Reichenbach Falls on 4 May 1891. When *The Valley* opens, Moriarty is very much alive and an old topic, and

Holmes is rapidly reaching a state of acute frustration at his inability to convince the police of the professor's depravity. He jokes, a little woodenly for him, about Watson's vulnerability to an action brought by Moriarty for defamation; but it is Holmes himself who is endangered by Moriarty's unassailable reputation. Slander actions may be illusory; a loss of credibility with the authorities, hitherto accustomed to refer problem cases to the 'consulting detective', is an unpleasant likelihood. This may be connected with the weeks of sterility preceding *The Valley*'s opening, and is based on governmental indifference to Conan Doyle's pleas of injustice in the cases of George Edalji and Oscar Slater.

Why the violence to the canon? The recent creator of Culverton Smith ('The Dying Detective', *His Last Bow*) or the future creator of Baron Adelbert Gruner ('The Illustrious Client', *Case-Book*) was in no need of old villains for want of new. Martin Priestman in his *Detective Fiction and Literature: The Figure on The Carpet* (1990) suggests that Moriarty's ultimate victory in the story is to reassure the public that British criminals succeed where the American variety so conspicuously fail, but Conan Doyle, author of Holmes's derisive 'His reverence is our own home-made article' ('The Solitary Cyclist', *Return*), hardly seems to revel in criminological chauvinism. Moriarty is here because his name is as great a guarantee of efficiency to the reader as to the criminal (for, as the Epilogue proclaims, he is as truly a consulting criminal as Holmes a consulting detective). We have to receive wholly credible assurance at the outset that Douglas is in danger from an outside threat. It does not eliminate Cecil Barker and Ivy Douglas as suspects in Part I: they could always have consulted Moriarty themselves. And while John Douglas's resurrection will exonerate them, their relationship towards one another remains ambiguous to the end of the book. But Moriarty with his 'Dear me!' will give a final assurance that Ivy Douglas is innocent of the ultimate actual murder of her husband. There are enough intentional ambiguities without leaving unintentional ones open. I suppose few readers doubt that Barker will console

Ivy Douglas and that they, at least, will live happily ever after; but any such assertion would now be an anticlimax. They are themselves only afterthoughts in the tragedy of Birdy Edwards. And that tragedy creates the overriding necessity for Moriarty. McMurdo/Edwards/Douglas is doomed. Moriarty in the Prologue is proof that the author had determined on that doom from the first.

Moriarty as a creation retains his great force of invisibility. P. G. Wodehouse (1881–1975) wrote of him some years later (*Performing Flea*, 1953), quoting his letter to William Townend of 23 July 1923):

A villain ought to be a sort of scarcely human invulnerable figure. The reader ought to be in a constant state of panic, saying to himself, 'How the devil *is* this superman to be foiled?' The only person capable of hurting him should be the hero. . . .

Taking Moriarty as the pattern villain, don't you see how much stronger he is by being an inscrutable figure and how much he would have been weakened if Conan Doyle had switched off to a chapter showing his thoughts? A villain ought to be a sort of malevolent force, not an intelligible person at all.

In the present context Porlock plays the part of unleashing apprehension as to what else we do not know, apart from what Holmes can decipher. We can concede Priestman a comparative point, if not on chauvinistic grounds: no moment spent among the Scowrers projects fear equal in intensity to that which Moriarty summons from Porlock. The benevolence of Moriarty described by MacDonald throws the unknown context of Porlock's terror into even starker relief. The germ of the effect may be simple enough: a Jesuit instructor with one face as a disciplinarian, another displaying public benevolence; an Edinburgh professor advising a fashionable client in a manner that is in total contrast to his oral examination of a student. But having learned fear in these experiences, Conan Doyle turned it to results beyond the reach of his fellow-victims. *The Valley*'s Prologue is the book's first lesson in the stage-management of fear.

Conan Doyle then got to work on his American material. The Odyssey in the company of Jack McMurdo commenced.

Its first achievement was the establishment of a rhythm to condition the audience. In general, a Holmesian audience was taught its business by Watson; sometimes, in non-Holmes stories such as 'The Little Square Box', 'The Heiress of Glenmahowley', or 'The Man from Archangel', there is a narrator whom the audience knows to be ludicrous. Watson may be a little dim on occasion, but ethically he is generally a dependable guide, whereas the absurdities of the narrators in some of the non-Holmes stories are rooted in false ethics. McMurdo is not the narrator, but Conan Doyle invites his readers to give him some moral support, for the virtues of courage, chivalry, charm he exhibits. He appears to fall in love with a worthy young lady, and despite his dubieties he provides a contrast with the repulsive bravo Ted Baldwin. McMurdo is a white knight in tarnished armour—a flawed hero, but an improvement on most of those around him.

Nevertheless, the tension in the story has everything to do with McMurdo's ethical ambiguity. There are several Watson figures—Scanlan, Morris, Ettie Shafter, even old Shafter—and their liking for McMurdo encourages us to sympathize with him. In all four cases (Scanlan most belatedly and uncertainly), they exhibit repugnance for the Scowrers' conduct; at best, all they derive from McMurdo is the cold comfort of his tactical dissent from the Scowrers, while being apparently in full agreement with their underlying strategic principles. Yet they love and admire him. Ettie has not only to worry about his associates and his participation, to whatever extent, in their outrages; she learns also that beneath his outward demeanour lurk secrets of apparently far greater menace and horror; Shafter's hard-earned knowledge that the Scowrers are all for one, one for all, cannot follow the obvious logic of forbidding McMurdo the house after terminating his tenancy; Morris risks his life simply to confront McMurdo with realities which might make a better man of him; Scanlan loses faith in the Scowrers but not in the one with whom he has the most recent acquaintance, McMurdo.

In the formal shape of *The Valley* Morris, Scanlan, and the Shafters are four tempters, and like Eliot's Fourth Tempter in his markedly Holmesian *Murder in the Cathedral,* their temptations lie in the direction in which the hero actually intends to go. They want him to serve Good, which in fact he seeks to do, but cannot do if he declares his true identity. At the moment of truth, therefore, there is a presumption of shame at our previous misgivings about McMurdo, which we share with the Shafters, Morris, and—probably—Scanlan.

But the problem of McMurdo is that he not only disguises himself as one of the Scowrers; in certain respects he strengthens them. Evil as they are (and there is no ambiguity on that point), he makes them worse. He scoffs at moderation and seems to take pleasure in bucking any prevailing trend, contradicting any expressed sentiment; thus, like the famous 'trimmer' Halifax (1633–95), he trims against the norm. It helps him gain attention, and gives weight to his opinions; but there is a self-indulgence, even self-fulfilment, in it. It is an interesting question as to how a principled spy is to obtain emotional release. But while McMurdo can claim to have held Baldwin's hand from killing James Stanger, he is quick to pressurize Scanlan and Morris into justifying murder. Here we are on the verge of a question directly confronted by Kurt Vonnegut in *Mother Night* (1961): Howard W. Campbell Jr. broadcasts incendiary anti-Jewish Nazi propaganda in order to send the Americans coded messages vital for their victory in the Second World War; is he thereby exonerated from guilt for any evil caused or exacerbated by his camouflage?

With the American part concluded, Conan Doyle went back to create a country-house murder that is finally explained with the discovery of the living John Douglas, hitherto presumed killed. His appearance is a perfect curtain-call, as is McMurdo's self-unmasking as Birdy Edwards. His first action is to hand Watson a manuscript—not necessarily the same which forms Part 2 but a symbolic assertion that the stage-management of both parts has the same architect. In both cases self-revelation quietens fears which concealment has exacerbated: McMurdo is not the successor but the accuser of McGinty; Cecil Barker is not the murderer but the protector of Douglas. In both a new fear will commence: Douglas must become a fugitive like McMurdo. But Part 1's conclusion throws a rather more sinister light on Part 2.

If McMurdo/Edwards/Douglas is the theatre illusionist, born of Conan Doyle's stage successes, Holmes is the critic— the critic as artist ('Watson insists that I am the dramatist in real life'), but pre-eminently the critic. He is a busy and censorious critic in the Birlstone investigation, owing a little to that other critic-dramatist George Bernard Shaw (1856–1950), with whom ACD had walked in their days as neighbours at Hindhead. Conan Doyle could expect his audience to be alert, at least subconsciously, to the better-known Holmesian dicta; and the dog that does not bark in the night, in *The Valley of Fear*, is the absence of any expression of acceptance by Holmes of Douglas's Birlstone story. Other cases abound with generous concluding expressions of conviction and absolution. Conan Doyle has more space here, but there is not a word from Holmes, nor even a ceremonial handshake, to suggest any acceptance of Douglas's account of the Birlstone killing. The handshake is pointedly given to architects of the deception Holmes has unravelled, and given twice, in 'The Missing Three-Quarter' and 'The Abbey Grange' (*Return*). It is denied to the libertine King in 'A Scandal in Bohemia' (*Adventures*) and to the blackmailing Charles Augustus Milverton (*Return*). But its absence here is a strange judgemental Limbo, almost as though Douglas is not in Holmes's world. The transparency of Douglas's story is asserted when he says

'I got a glimpse of a man in the street . . . It was the worst enemy I had among them all . . . I knew there was trouble coming, and I came home and made ready for it. I guessed I'd fight through it all right on my own . . .

'I was on my guard all that next day . . . After the bridge was up . . . I put the thing clear out of my head.'

As a strategist of fiction, Conan Doyle was fond of the baited trap: it had its own ethical satisfaction, the hunter becoming the quarry. Both Holmes and McMurdo use it, the one making the bait the threat of disclosure of the weighted bundle in the drained moat, the other the trapping of Birdy Edwards. What McMurdo did, Douglas would naturally do again, once more with the same bait. Baldwin walked into a trap and had his head blown off. It was not self-defence in the eyes of the law—whence Holmes's silence, since in this story he is tied inescapably to the police—but, morally speaking, it certainly was. As Auden puts it in his mid-1930s 'Detective Story':

> Yet, on the last page, a lingering doubt:
> The verdict, was it just?

But with these two successive architectures of lies, the supposed solutions of 'the tragedy of Birlstone', what becomes of McMurdo's credibility in Part 2, now asserted to be an edifice built, with or without elaboration by Watson, on his own composition? What lies are here? The self-evident point is McMurdo's own rise in the Scowrers' organization. It is easy enough to see that McGinty, facing the rising ambition of Baldwin, welcomes Baldwin's forceful rival: but that in itself is a long way from making him an heir apparent after three months. The Scowrers were hardly likely to make a Bodymaster of an unknown newcomer simply because of his enthusiastic involvement in their affairs, or his being an object of dislike to Captain Marvin. The suggestive passage is that ending Chapter 5, when a list of victims is prefaced by 'Why should these pages be stained by further crimes?' The device ensures that no word needs to be said of McMurdo's implication in the crimes in question. Conan Doyle clearly intended the Scowrers to be seen as irretrievably guilty as hell, McGinty's corruption is grossly palpable: 'year by year, Boss McGinty's diamond pins became more obtrusive, his gold chains more weighty across a more gorgeous vest, and his saloon stretched farther and farther, until it threatened to absorb one whole side of the Market Square'. One can almost see the Bodymaster's body expanding beneath our eyes. (The cartoons of Thomas Nast (1840–1902) against the leaders of Tammany Hall seem a probable inspiration.) The sadistic Baldwin, the ferocious Cormac, and the incorruptible Harraway are unquestionable instruments of populistic terrorism; but all the more would they have needed stronger proof of McMurdo for the succession than botched attempts on the life of Chester Wilcox.

Douglas's inevitable death is a shock, a seemingly unnecessary cruelty; but within this context it makes perfect sense. McMurdo/Edwards/Douglas is a benefactor who has released the valley from its fear. But in doing so he has become accursed himself, marked out for slaughter, a Cain in his own time whose crime was to eradicate crime but who must still pay his penalty. His situation is more ambiguous than that of the avenger who turns pirate to kill the murderer of his wife and sons ('How Copley Banks Slew Captain Sharkey', *Pearson's Magazine*, May 1897, reprinted in *The Green Flag*) but their situations have comparable features: ' ". . . You are my man now, and I have bought you at a price, for I have given all that a man can give here below, and I have given my soul as well. To reach you I have had to sink to your level. For two years I strove against it, hoping that some other way might come, but I learnt that there was no other way. I've robbed and I have murdered—worse still, I have laughed and lived with you—and all for the one end . . ." ' Perhaps here, more than anywhere in *The Sign of the Four*, we see the influence of Wilkie Collins's *The Moonstone*—that final scene when the priests who have restored their religion's lost icon thereby become isolated wanderers on the face of the earth. So Douglas is exiled from Barker, the closest friend he has ever made and the colleague-in-contrivance whose capacity for conspiracy is never plumbed. Holmes will not write to Douglas but gives instructions to his wife: and for Holmes to choose a wife rather than a husband as a target of confidence is to proclaim the world turned upside-down.

It leaves McMurdo/Edwards/Douglas as a tragic figure. Underneath all the contrivance Birlstone has been the scene of a genuine tragedy, if not the one that first appeared. And in keeping with Tragedy's high traditions, the hero is likeable:

it is the one certain point about him, other than his courage. The butler thinks of him as 'a kind and considerate employer—not quite what Ames was used to, perhaps, but one can't have everything'. The Englishman Cecil Barker is prepared to lie himself into the dock for his Irish-American friend. Watson's first reaction to Douglas is centred on his 'remarkable face—bold grey eyes . . . and a humorous smile'. The last is important: McMurdo/Edwards/Douglas has enjoyed his theatricals. But in the end Douglas ceases to be the author of his own script. Holmes's judgement on his death is his epitaph: 'Well, I've no doubt it was well stage-managed.'

II
HOW GREEN WAS HIS *VALLEY*?
THE IRISHNESS OF CONAN DOYLE

I will show you fear in a handful of dust.
> *Frisch weht der Wind*
> *Der Heimat zu*
> *Mein Irisch Kind*
> *Wo weilest du?*
>> T. S. Eliot, *The Waste Land* (1922)[1]

In July 1881 Conan Doyle was staying at Ballygally, Lismore, Co. Waterford, in the valley of the great Munster Blackwater, where his maternal cousin Richard Foley had the salmon rights (and made £1,000 a year from it). It was probably his first visit, and he thought it paradise, though the great Land League was at its height. Richard, as a considerable landlord, had marched, sea-booted, into a local meeting, subsequently telling his relative (a decade his junior) how he had expressed his regret that the League had not one neck on which he could put his foot. The League was an open organization, wose national president was Charles

---

[1] Eliot was quoting from Wagner's *Tristan und Isolde* (first performed in London in 1882), I. i. 5-8:

> Fresh blows the wind
> To the homeland—
> My Irish child
> Where do you live?

Stewart Parnell, MP (1846–91); landlords readily assumed
that secret agrarian bands, oath-bound to Captain Moon-
light, included many of the League members. The League
preached non-violent action, successfully initiated in its campaign against Captain Charles Cunningham Boycott (1832–
97); but when the Cork cattle show was boycotted, Conan
Doyle and his Foley cousins decided on point of principle to
attend it, armed, in order to exhibit a token cow in defiance of
what they were sure would be violent reprisals. For all of his
bold front, Richard Foley was jumpy enough: his youthful
cousin made a late-night window entry after a dance, only to
be greeted by his host with a double-barrelled gun which he
was on the verge of firing. Conan Doyle made light of it in
writing to friends, but it might have ended disastrously.[2]

So the very first discernible origin of *The Valley of Fear*
comes from Ireland over thirty years before the writing. It
gives us the owner–intruder encounter (significantly, with
the owner as ambusher) and the author's experience of
intimidation, extortion, and an atmosphere of incipient
violence. But in one respect the Foley brothers were not
typical landlords: they were of Catholic stock, and it was
their own ethnic group against whom they armed themselves. If Conan Doyle made any researches on the origins
of agrarian agitation in the district, he would have found
plenty of stories. About 50 miles to the east there was land
his paternal ancestors had come from, and at the beginning
of the nineteenth century the populist agrarian secret society
in those parts called itself 'Moll Doyle's Children'. In spite
of—and because of—his loathing for them, the Scowrers
were flesh of his flesh and bone of his bone. *The Valley of Fear*
luxuriates in Irish cadences, nowhere more so than in
the speech of that improbably surnamed Irishman Birdy
Edwards. Conan Doyle actually made more use of Scottish
than Irish material in his first decade as writer of fiction in
the 1880s, but Irish themes flicker through some early stories.

[2] ACD to Amy, Mrs Reginald Ratcliff Hoare, of Birmingham, n.d.
(July–Aug. 1881), New York Public Library, Berg Collection.

'That Little Square Box' (*London Society*, Christmas Number 1881), the earliest story he was subsequently prepared to keep in print, was a satire on anti-Irish scare stories: during his Irish visit Home Secretary Sir William Harcourt (1827–1904) announced that clockwork-rigged barrels of dynamite, disguised as cement, had been discovered in Liverpool on the *Malta* and on the *Bavarian*; Conan Doyle's story light-heartedly described how a poltroon on board the *Spartan* discovers what are thought to be German-Irish terrorist devices which prove to be boxes for racing-pigeons. 'The Heiress of Glenmahowley' (*Temple Bar*, Jan. 1884) came closer in its opening to the stories of agrarian outrage with which his Foley cousins had filled his ears, but the purpose was again satirical, its target being once more the prevalent anti-Irish sentiment. The story was pro-landlord propaganda, certainly, in the vein and style of Synge's *Playboy of the Western World* over twenty years later; but as with Synge it had bigger game afoot. It lampoons the absurdities of English fortune-hunters rather than reworking the familiar theme of homicidal Irish shiftlessness. But the theme is taken up again in *The Valley of Fear*, though the humour has gone.

Between 'Glenmahowley' and *The Valley of Fear* lay Conan Doyle's Irish masterpiece in miniature, 'The Green Flag', first published in the *Pall Mall Magazine* for June 1893 and given pride of place in the short-story collection of the same name in 1900. Its action lay about the time of his Irish visit, or a year or two thereafter, and it had language in common with *The Valley*, but its tone was more compassionate than hitherto. The plot turns on a mutiny in the Sudan among British troops during the rise of the Mahdi: it ends, movingly, with the massacre of the mutineers who have repudiated Queen Victoria but who rally her breaking troops in defence of their own green flag (the story's last, throat-catching words being the tribute of the victorious Arab leader). The mutineers denounce the royal widow of Windsor in rejection of the pleas of Captain Foley: 'It was the Impire laid my groanin' mother by the wayside. Her son will rot before he upholds it, and ye can put that in the charge-sheet in the next coort-martial.'

There is authenticity here, enough to indicate that in his little forays with his Foley cousins they met some plain speech in the Blackwater valley. It is the residue of sympathy in the telling, the touch of mourning over the motives, which, however weakened by the evil of the Scowrer cases and the intervening rise in Conan Doyle's social status, give reality to the progenitors of the rank and file in *The Valley of Fear*. The high point of fear in *The Valley* may well be the attractiveness and youth of the assassins—not Baldwin and Cormac, but Wilson who is chosen to be blooded at the Rae killing, or the frank-faced lad Andrews who murders Dunn—or the courtesy of the older killer Lawler apologizing for his reticence concerning the 'commission' he has been sent to carry out while declaring readiness to speak of past deeds 'till the cows come home' (words redolent more of the Blackwater valley than of Schuylkill or Vermissa). The homicidal rage of the 'Green Flag' mutineers ultimately finding its outlet against the Arabs goes on as a way of life in *The Valley of Fear*.

'The Green Flag' suggests a decade of rather fuller study and reflection on Ireland than the visit of 1881 had initially induced. Formally, Conan Doyle read the lessons of the Parnellite Home Rule party's involvement in Land League agitation to the point of breaking with Doyle family Liberal and Irish devolutionary traditions. On 6 July 1886 he wrote to the Portsmouth *Evening News* giving among his reasons for voting Unionist in reply to Gladstone's conversion to Irish Home Rule:

1 That since the year 1881 the agitation in Ireland has been characterised by a long succession of crimes against life and property.
2 That these murders and maimings have never been heartily denounced by any member of the Irish Parliamentary party.
3 That politicians who could allow such deeds to be done without raising their voices against them cannot be men of high political morality—and are, therefore, however talented, unfit to be trusted with the destinies of a country.

Hence he would have closely followed the special commission to investigate *The Times*'s charges, made in 1887, connecting 'Parnellism and crime', including the exposure of the forgeries which constituted the pivot of the newspaper's case. But he also saw the evidence in February 1889 of the secret agent Thomas Billis Beach (1841–94), who as Major Henri Le Caron had infiltrated Irish-American revolutionary organizations and held their confidence unquestioned for over twenty years. Le Caron's *Twenty-five Years in the Secret Service* was published in 1892; he died on 1 April 1894 and was buried in the cemetery at Norwood (where the Conan Doyles were then living), having been guarded by the authorities for five years. Le Caron's boss at the Home Office, Sir Robert Anderson (1841–1918), also the author of a somewhat acid appreciation of the Holmes stories,[3] wrote about his famous spy on several occasions; one of these, in *Blackwood's Edinburgh Magazine* (Apr. 1910), led to an acrimonious debate in the House of Commons.

An account of Le Caron's death appeared in *The Times*, which Conan Doyle usually read:

There is something almost superhuman in this spectacle of a man who could devote his life to so terrible a duty, keeping his secret locked up from all companions . . . The self suppression which enabled him to come through such a life-long ordeal would alone entitle him to respect. . . . the risks he ran were not ended by his return to this country. From the moment he took his place in the witness box he was liable to become the object of a murderous conspiracy, and the danger arising from this cause could only be evaded by a further life of secrecy.[4]

It becomes easy to see how the spy who found real security only as a corpse in a cemetery near Conan Doyle at Norwood might inspire the fictional creation of a comparable spy as a supposed corpse in a country house near Conan Doyle at Crowborough.

Land League Ireland in 1881, Le Caron quick in 1889, or Le Caron dead in 1894 (followed by rumours that the death notice was a fraud to throw off pursuit, April Fools' Day

---

[3] 'Sherlock Holmes as seen by Scotland Yard', *T.P.'s Weekly*, 2 Oct. 1903.
[4] Quoted in J. A. Cole, *Prince of Spies: Henri Le Caron* (1984), 202–3.

being an all too appropriate death-day): why should these memories suddenly inspire *The Valley of Fear* in 1914? They had been fodder for Conan Doyle's Unionism; he was now a Home Ruler. On 26 March 1912, for instance, he fired off a characteristic defence of the country of his ancestors to the *Daily Express* in rejoinder to its sneers of 'Peaceful Ireland':

I observe that you use the above heading in an ironical sense whenever you have to chronicle any disorder in Ireland. But if the two islands be compared, is it not true in its lost literal sense?

Where in Ireland is there evidence of that syndicalism among men . . . which has convulsed this country?

If disorder be an argument against fitness for self-government, then Ireland is surely the fitter of the two.

Within eighteen months Dublin was locked in the most serious labour confrontation in Irish history; syndicalism was being preached by Big Jim Larkin (1876–1947) and hammered out in the press by James Connolly (1868–1916). The former was born in Liverpool; the latter, like ACD, was from Edinburgh but no less eager than he to declare the future of Ireland. There were bitter and bloody clashes between the Dublin police and the locked-out workers and strikers: 'The Dublin Cossack!' Larkin thundered in Edinburgh of the club-wielding police.

It had seemed that Conan Doyle might at last find reconciliation with his dead father over the Home Rule issue which had divided them in the 1880s, along with religion and other issues on which no reconciliation was possible. And now the reassurance and peace Ireland had seemed to offer him crumbled. The colleague in his crusade against oppression in the Belgian Congo and who had converted him to Home Rule, Sir Roger Casement (1864–1916), on whom he had drawn for Lord John Roxton in *The Lost World* (1912) and *The Poison Belt* (1913), now seemed to be moving towards Anglophobia. Casement responded to Conan Doyle's 'Germany and the Next War' (*Fortnightly Review*, Feb. 1913), which counselled Britain to prepare against German aggression, with his 'Ireland, Germany and the Next War', predicting that German victory over Britain would be 'great gain to Ireland' (*Irish Review*, July 1913). Suddenly the great ancestral fount of reassurance in a disintegrating world was becoming the greatest harbinger of fear. Somehow Conan Doyle had to confront and exorcize the devils from his own past; they were not, as he had thought, dead or even sleeping. As it happened, syndicalism, the very doctrine from which he had thought a Home Rule Ireland so providentially immune, became the focus of his action. Between his optimistic chaffing of the *Daily Express* and the Dublin clashes, Conan Doyle had been visited by a self-styled expert on American syndicalism who was, of all things, a detective. William John Burns (1861–1932) arrived at Windlesham, Crowborough in April 1913 to pay noisy obeisance to Sherlock Holmes.

Whatever Conan Doyle might have been prepared to say about Holmes, he was unlikely to want much time to do it, which was as well, as Burns naturally progressed to the time-consuming topic of himself, his life and works. He was bursting with his own recent venture into print, *The Masked War: The Story of a Peril that Threatened the United States by the Man who Uncovered the Dynamite Conspirators and Sent Them to Jail* (1913), recently published by Conan Doyle's own American publishers, the George H. Doran Company. He was later to attempt collaborative detective fiction, and his first intention may have been to suggest a little collaboration with Conan Doyle—perhaps even involving Sherlock Holmes. After all, Holmes had taken a Pinkerton detective as a colleague in 'The Red Circle' (published in the *Strand* in March and April 1911); why could not Conan Doyle do the same with a graduate of Pinkerton's—now triumphantly on his own, fearless, intrepid, full of the latest scientific theory, dauntless in the face of attempts on his life (Chapter 2 of *The Masked War* is entitled 'Attempts to Kill Burns'), ready to defy his assassins with a nerve superior to theirs:

He told me that when he conducted the San Francisco prosecutions he was told he would be shot in court. Upon which he gave instructions that in that case his men should kill all the lawyers and witnesses on the other side. 'I would be dead, Sir Arthur; and so it would be all the same to me' (quoted in Carr, *Conan Doyle*, 278).

Was it at this point that Conan Doyle was seized by the idea of the murder of an American private detective in a house rather like Windlesham?

Conan Doyle drew his guest out on American detective feats of the past. Naturally, Burns had much to say of the most famous labour violence case of the end of the last century—the Molly Maguires of Schuylkill County, Pennsylvania. The name could be traced back to early-nineteenth-century mid-Ulster, and was contemporary with Moll Doyle's Children in east Munster and south-west Leinster. Unionists used it as a term of reproach for the Ancient Order of Hibernians, a quasi-Masonic Catholic movement of uncertain American antecedents. Had Conan Doyle read the syndical-ist writings of his fellow-Edinburgher, James Connolly, he would have found a similar hostility to the Hibernians. At what point some mental label silently affixed by host on guest as 'Wordy Burns' may have become Birdy Edwards, in so far as he did, we do not know, nor are we entitled to say categorically that that was the inspirational spoonerism: but Conan Doyle certainly invented a detective who is wholly unable to talk about his own achievements while engaged in them or writing about them, since his story of the past concealed his identity and his story in the present concealed his existence.

Conan Doyle wrote *The Valley of Fear* out of an intensely personal reaction to questions of national identity. But he grasped the material at hand in the Molly Maguire story, and was ready enough to build an impressive landscape in his Vermissa Valley. Dennis Porter in *The Pursuit of Crime: Art and Ideology in Detective Fiction* (1981) judges that 'Probably nowhere else in the genre is there such an effort to combine in a single work the antithetical landscapes of the country house and the chaotic city' (p. 191). In the end it becomes a metaphor for Ireland and the kingdoms its children found: the Tammany Hall empires that Boss McGinty symbolizes by his power, cruelty, and corruption, as well as his geniality and confidence in the hold of kinship and tradition; the perpetuation of hatred and murder as ways of life, though their origins are forgotten, and the survival of increasingly meaningless rituals; and the husk of a country house asserting Irish conquest of English seats of power—now capable only of accommodating marriages built without mutual confidence and proving no more than a hiding-place grimly akin to a tomb. Birlstone, with its suspicions and charades, is Conan Doyle's *Heartbreak House*; Vermissa Valley, with its inheritance of Irish conspiracy, murder, and endless espionage, is his *Long Day's Journey into Night*.

In his preface to *Sherlock Holmes: The Complete Long Stories* (1929) Conan Doyle stated: '*The Valley of Fear* . . . had its origin through my reading a graphic account of the Molly McQuire [*sic*] outrages in the coalfields of Pennsylvania, when a young detective drawn from Pinkerton's Agency acted exactly as the hero is represented as doing.' The 'account' is agreed to have been Allan Pinkerton (1819–84), *The Mollie Maguires and the Detectives* (1877). But its inflated, self-congratulatory pomposities were far from sufficient for Conan Doyle's needs: one simply has to look at Pinkerton's patronizing and synthetic Irish-American sentences in contrast to Conan Doyle's sinewy Irish prose to see the author's judgements on his source. In any case, despite the Holmesian elements, the novel in its American part is virtually historical, and Conan Doyle's method in writing historical fiction was indiscriminate mastery of all the available sources. He seems to have read as widely as possible on the Molly Maguires on the same principle.

Yet there was no wide range of alternatives to Pinkerton and his ghost-writers; two or three detailed accounts were available in Britain, but even newspaper comment at the time had been sparse. Pinkerton included a major speech, with a detailed if bitterly partisan history of the Mollies, by the Reading Railroad president Franklin Benjamin Gowen (1836–89), who hired the Pinkertons and led the court counsel for prosecution in the trials (he later committed suicide).

But Conan Doyle's researches leave in their wake further mysteries. Today the two leading accounts of the Mollies are Wayne G. Broehl Jr., *The Molly Maguires*, and Arthur H. Lewis, *Lament for the Molly Maguires*, both appearing by coincidence in 1965. Both are admirably judicious, defending neither the Mollies nor their many enemies. They complement one another admirably: Broehl carried out extensive research in Ireland and made the most of access to Pinkerton, Reading, and official reports; Lewis conducted interviews, examined folk traditions, and talked with families in Schuylkill county itself. It can be concluded that Conan Doyle somehow gained access to material otherwise unavailable until the appearance of these works in 1965. For instance, Burns may have been the cause of his getting in touch with the former 'young detective' James McParlan (1844–1919) who still flourished as a Pinkerton executive in Denver, Colorado. Some of *The Valley*'s material seems too close to things Lewis picked up from McParlan's reminiscences, preserved in Pennsylvania, for Conan Doyle not to have tapped this or a comparable source. It seems impossible for Conan Doyle to have visited Schuylkill county: he had no time on his 1894 tour (so admirably charted by Christopher Redmond), and the North American tour of 1914 was undertaken after he had completed *The Valley of Fear*.

This in turn raises another mystery. Allan Pinkerton had been dead for thirty years when Conan Doyle was writing *The Valley of Fear*, but his son William (1846–1923) was in firm control of the family business and obviously interested in any fictional version of his father's agency. James D. Horan, the firm's historian, has the following quotation in his book *The Pinkertons: The Detective Dynasty that Made History* (1967), from his 1948 interview with Pinkerton manager Ralph Dudley, concerning the appearance of *The Valley of Fear*:

W. A. P. raised the roof when he saw the book. At first he talked of bringing a suit against Doyle but then dropped that after he had cooled off. What made him angry was the fact that even if Doyle was fictionizing the story, he didn't have the courtesy to ask his permission to use a confidential discussion for his work. They had been good friends before but from that day on their relationship was strained. Mr Doyle sent several notes trying to soothe things over and while W. A. P. sent him courteous replies he never regarded Mr Doyle with the same warmth (p. 499).

The problem is that the confidences were supposedly exchanged during 'a transatlantic cruise', according to a letter from William Pinkerton to his harassed New York superintendent, George D. Bangs Jr., which Horan does not date or locate. But if so, when? 1894 seems too early to make sense, 1914 too late. And what could young Pinkerton have told Conan Doyle that was not in the published family history? It was McParlan—or some other direct testimony—that he needed, not the view from the board room. If Pinkerton opened files to Conan Doyle, that would have been another matter, or if he, too, had facilitated introductions, all the better; but nothing is said of that. All one can say is that there may have been implications in William Pinkerton's anger that must remain unknown, failing light being shed on the matter by further research into the Pinkerton archives.

In any case, the Pinkertons were far less in control of the Molly Maguire investigation than they pretended. Allan Pinkerton had innumerable improving maxims about his operatives not drinking on the job, but even by his account McParlan commenced his investigations by drinking himself blind. The archives seem to have preserved nothing concerning his earliest months on the case, and like a sensible man his admissions were to the point. If he acted as *agent provocateur*, or if he participated in any deeds of violence to maintain his cover (both extremely likely), he took pains that the records protected him. He was a remarkable man, with an extensive memory, an ability for assimilating written records, excellent acting talent, and a remarkable capacity for roistering in general and consuming alcohol of every available kind in particular. The last quality was particularly necessary since most of the Mollies were publicans: had McParlan (alias McKenna) observed Pinkerton's prohibition he would have remained as ignorant of the Mollies as his masters.

But he was no Jack McMurdo. The Explanatory Notes to this edition indicate where *The Valley of Fear* drew on the Odyssey of James McParlan/McKenna for Jack McMurdo's story, but there is a great gulf between McMurdo's austere, dignified, essentially chivalric figure and the boozing, promiscuous McKenna. But McParlan/McKenna is far from being a despicable figure: his courage and resource were admirable, and he was more ready than McMurdo to acknowledge his own uglier aspects. It is clear that McKenna liked many of the men he met, and that they liked him: that was their tragedy. McMurdo likes none of the men he meets, except perhaps Barker: that is his.

Finally, Conan Doyle's choice of name for his detective-spy is significant. Douglas is noble. Edwards is probably a joke. McMurdo, an unusual name in either Ireland or Scotland, is found in Ireland much more frequently as 'Murtagh'. It means 'Mac Muircheartaigh', the son of 'Muircheartach', a name known in pre-Norman history among the strongest of the Irish kings. (This may account for Conan Doyle's original use of it—for a prize-fighter in the *The Sign of the Four*.) But in one sense it has to be a faithless king. It is to McKenna, not to McMurdo, that one might apply Tennyson's description of Lancelot:

> His honour rooted in dishonour stood,
> And faith unfaithful kept him falsely true.

Bodymaster McGinty's expiring 'You blasted traitor!' is an empty execration: betrayal is inevitable in such a criminal hierarchy. As McMurdo in his one moment of complete frankness (in his Douglas persona) tells Ivy, McGinty was never master of his body: McKenna could not have made such a claim for some of *his* McGintys. If McMurdo betrayed anyone, it was people who had no faith in him, people who expected the worst from him as a Scowrer on the make, and were not disappointed. Even so, we are to believe that he caused as little hurt as he could.

But Conan Doyle's loss of his Catholic faith led him to deny McMurdo one of McKenna's strongest characteristics.

It had been essential for Pinkerton to select a Roman Catholic to infiltrate the Molly Maguires; but while McParlan accepted that, as McKenna, he would have to live excommunicated from Catholicism (because Archbishop James Frederic Wood (1813–83) of Philadelphia and his clergy had withheld the sacraments from the Molly Maguires), and while, theologically, he knew he had not committed their sin within his heart, he yearned for his formal return to the Church. The Mollies, however, were by no means all of the same level of conviction as McParlan, and many were strongly anti-clerical. Some priests who spoke out against the Mollies, as so many did, were knocked around and threatened with worse: in response the Mollies were denounced even more strongly. Conan Doyle would have found himself in full sympathy with the priests' incessant reminders of the evil inherent in what the Mollies did; yet he would also have recoiled at the psychological bullying by the clerics, however good the cause. Ironically, the Molly Maguires claimed the same freedom of mind he had insisted on for himself. So Jack McMurdo is deprived of a religion. To the end he remains alone and uncomforted: in the fullest sense, uncomfortable.

III
DREAMERS OF THE BONES:
CARR, HAMMETT, WODEHOUSE.

The hand of the LORD was upon me, and carried me out in the spirit of the LORD, and set me down in the midst of the valley which was full of bones . . .

Again he said unto me, Prophesy upon these bones, and say unto them, O ye dry bones, hear the word of the LORD . . .

So I prophesied as he commanded me, and the breath came into them, and they lived, and stood up upon their feet, an exceeding great army (Ezekiel 37: 1, 4, 10).

John Dickson Carr (1906–77) was, in the main, a fine detective-story writer: perhaps that helped to make him a bad biographer, with his invented conversations and distorted situations. But whatever the limits of his *Life of Sir Arthur Conan Doyle*, the judgement of one detective-story writer on another must always lend it a particular value. It is the value of its period, the self-proclaimed 'Golden Age' of detective fiction, with its rules and its snobberies, its generic 'Cheese-cake Manor' and 'Mayhem Parva', 'Sergeant Beef' and 'Crawly Worme Explains' (to purloin the respective acidities of Raymond Chandler, Colin Watson, Leo Bruce, and Philip MacDonald). It is, unintentionally, patronizing, but that is because it hails a progenitor; and in filial piety, Baby wants to be taller than Father.

Carr was born in Uniontown, Pennsylvania, but—or should it be hence?—his interest in *The Valley of Fear* centres not in his native state so much as in ' "The Tragedy of Birlstone" . . . a very nearly perfect piece of detective-story writing.'

From the opening chapter, with its noble Holmes–Watson dialogue, to the solution of the crime in the study, the reader is told every vital clue. These clues are emphasized, flourished, underlined. More than this, it is our clearest example of Conan Doyle's contribution to the detective story. . . .

. . . Conan Doyle . . . invented the enigmatic clue. We find it running far back through the stories, notably . . .:

'Is there any point to which you would wish to draw my attention?'

'To the curious incident of the dog in the night-time.'

'The dog did nothing in the night-time.'

'That was the curious incident.'

Call this 'Sherlockismus'; call if by any fancy name; the fact remains that it is a clue, and a thundering good clue at that. It is the trick by which the detective—while giving you perfectly fair opportunity to guess—nevertheless makes you wonder what in sanity's name he is talking about. The creator of Sherlock Holmes invented it; and nobody except the great G. K. Chesterton, whose Father Brown stories were so greatly influenced by the device, has ever done it half so well.

Now the missing dumb-bell, if anything, is better than the dog in the night-time (pp. 282–3).

Thus the Golden Age worshipped its gods, and the passage explains in what form Conan Doyle's influence made itself felt when market economics turned detective fiction from short story to novel. *The Valley of Fear*, the sole Holmes long story ready even to play at puzzle rather than whole-hearted simple adventure mingled with demonstrations, was the exemplar. But the 'Sherlockismus' may be most valuable not in what it withholds but in what it tells: that one must look at negative evidence, that the commonplace may convey symptoms more truly than the exceptional—and it does so by an epigram not easily forgotten. The Golden Age detective implied omniscience; Sherlock Holmes was the product of an age in pursuit of enquiry. Julian Symons would write of Carr, 'Since the whole story is written around the puzzle there is no room for characterization . . . what one remembers . . . is never the people, but only the puzzle' (*Bloody Murder*, ch. 9).

The Valley of Fear, parent of the puzzle genre, may seem subject to its limitations, for the exceptional lightness of all characters other than the alleged corpse: but it takes a rereading to pursue very different quests. Why was 'the faithful Ames' 'by no means whole hearted about Barker'? Why was Ivy Douglas laughing with Barker and why was she amused about the absence of her husband's ring on the corpse? Conan Doyle once proclaimed himself so much under the influence of Henry James that he wrote 'A Physiologist's Wife' with an inexplicably bigamous heroine whom he called 'Mrs O'James'. The Golden Age regarded ambiguity of that kind as a blemish. In embracing Holmes it was in danger of sinking him, like his dumb-bell, in the eyes of less rigidly formulaic critics.

Raymond Chandler, in a backhanded compliment to the English detective story, applauded its 'sense of background, as if Cheesecake Manor really existed all around and not just the part the camera sees'. For this *The Valley of Fear* bears responsibility, for Birlstone is partly inspired by the cinema set. Conan Doyle was very interested in the development of cinema, and also in its falsehoods. A few years later, in 'The Nightmare Room', he posed a triangle turning on a draw for suicide between an American husband and the English lover of another ambiguous lady, ending in the sudden epiphany of a stranger saying to the three of them, 'Rotten! . . . Rotten!

We'll take the whole reel once more to-morrow!' *The Valley of Fear* itself was filmed closer to publication than any other Holmes story, being released by Samuelson Film (with the experienced stage Holmes performer H. A. Saintsbury) in 1916. (Arthur Wontner and Christopher Lee successively played Holmes in the novel's 'talkie' adaptations: the Wontner version (1935) rendered Ted Baldwin as 'Balding', presumably for fear of offending the incumbent prime minister.)

As Dennis Porter puts it, the Gothic supernatural shadow cast by the ancestral home is dispelled at the novel's denouement, where the second part turns out to be all too real. 'The material of the "valley of fear" is that of Hammett, down to political graft, police corruption, beatings, murders, and bombings. In this part, therefore, the relationship between language and crime is sympathetic, whereas in the first it turns out to be ironic' (p. 192). Samuel Dashiell Hammett (1894–1961), like Conan Doyle a defector from childhood Catholicism, devoured all kinds of mystery fiction as a boy in Baltimore. His papers and juvenilia are not known to have survived, but Holmes would have been unavoidable, up to and including *The Valley of Fear*, serialized in the Baltimore *Sun* in 1915, the year Hammett entered the Pinkerton detective agency which supplied *The Valley*'s background. And as Porter observes, Hammett's first novel, *Red Harvest* (1929), is virtually the fate of a township such as Vermissa (although translated to Montana) after the cleanup by the Pinkertons. The name 'Vermissa' (so close to 'vermin') seems a direct inspiration for the first words of *Red Harvest*: 'I first heard Personville called Poisonville'. The strategy of the protagonist in each case is similar: accompanying thugs to the scene of an outrage; limited, if any, intervention; judicious tactical secret alerts; an evident policy of covert exacerbation of conflict. Hammett lets the reader taste more of the protagonist's mental revulsion than Conan Doyle's structure enables him to do: we know his narrator is a detective; we do not know what McMurdo is. But they are the same breed, unscrupulous to the level of frightening their closest associates.

Conan Doyle was the pathfinder, the writer who took American crime fiction from Pinkerton's pompous kitsch and pulp thrillers in general. 'When I reached this place I learned that I was wrong and that it wasn't a dime novel after all': McMurdo speaks for his creator, and for the type in which he is fashioned. The Continental Op. learns the same thing in Poisonville; so did his maker. Priestman acknowledges that the two paragraphs and line of speech covering the murders of Dunn and Menzies form a direct line to Hammett, save for Dunn's 'presentiment of death'. Hammett seems to have docketed that presentiment for his own detective's use: 'I lit a cigarette and wondered why I felt the way I did, wondered if I were getting psychic, wondered whether there was anything in this presentiment business or whether my nerves were just ragged.' The Dunn murder was inspired by the Sanger-Uren killing (see Explanatory Notes, p. 220); but Conan Doyle isolates everyone. His assassins are silent; Dunn apparently dies without knowing Menzies will stand by him; Menzies makes his sacrifice equally alone (Uren, Sanger's friend, was at his side throughout and they died in comradeship). Similarly, McMurdo and the Op. may find oases of human kindness, especially with women; but they have no ability to end their own isolation. Having created an exemplar of comradeship in Watson's interpretation of Holmes, Conan Doyle now launched the solitary operative in McMurdo, whose want of the warmth of personal narration gives an iciness to his role, psychologically as well as ethically, only paralleled in Hammett by the figure of Sam Spade. But *The Valley of Fear* gave birth to other children.

'Before you are through with that', nods John Douglas in the direction of the papers he has given Watson which become Part 2, 'you will say I've brought you something fresh'. The words appeared in the *Strand* for January 1915. Later in the same issue was 'The Romance of an Ugly Policeman' by P. G. Wodehouse, at the time resident in New York. Later in the same year he produced the first story of his Blandings Castle saga: he entitled it *Something Fresh*.

('Fresh' meaning what it does in American, it had to be rendered in the USA as *Something New*.) Wodehouse would see the charm of a hardboiled detective handing Watson a manuscript so different in character and perspective from the Holmesian canon. *Something Fresh* was indeed the great Wodehousian breakthrough: the words seem to have summoned him into the field he would make so pre-eminently his own. Hitherto his work had been school stories and sketches, sometimes extended to book length. This set him on his road as the supreme artist in English comedy in the twentieth century.

On the face of it, *The Valley of Fear* and *Something Fresh* seem worlds away from one another, but close analysis of the texts yields many parallels and oppositions. Wodehouse even begins with a hero (Ashe Marson) shackled to the production of pulp detective fiction and resenting it as bitterly as Conan Doyle might about his inescapable Holmes; but when Marson solves the mystery of the missing scarab his miserable imitation of Holmes, Gridley Quayle (*sic*), provides him, in answer to appropriate citation of the stories, with the Birdy Edwards moment 'I write them'. A variant of the misinterpretation of Porlock's cipher ('Mahratta'/'Government'/'pigs'-bristles') turns up with a code an empire-builder expects his loved one to read from the words 'Meredith elephant kangaroo'. The bogus murder at Birlstone becomes the Efficient Baxter's confusion of cold tongue in the darkness with a corpse, and the arousal of Blandings Castle by Lord Emsworth's revolver is the polar opposite of the silence at Birlstone. The imposter servants Ashe Marson and Joan Valentine desperately trying to pass for the real thing in the almost incomprehensible rituals of the servants' hall derive from McMurdo as a Scowrer (and the lowest servant would be a [pot-]scourer, whence the idea); and what a galaxy of Wodehouse imposters were to follow them down the saga! Ashe Marson first gets his chance by half-charming, half-bullying the millionaire Peters after the manner of McMurdo to McGinty, but defers as McMurdo does over a matter of proper address. Even the male chauvinism explicit in Baldwin's, and implicit in McMurdo's, relationship with Ettie is thrust fully into the open: the empire-builder George Emerson finally wins Aline Peters only by revealing his vulnerability, probably a good critical comment on Ettie's ultimate acceptance of McMurdo—and both of those romances end with the disguised departure of the lovers by train. The precautionary Morris–McMurdo alibi of an employment offer is followed in Peters's device to give Marson a story in burgling the Blandings Museum. Baxter's dream of accompanying Peters in a bomb attack on Blandings from the air turning into his view from inside Blandings of the bomb as it falls, is McMurdo both bombing Chester Wilcox and warning him against the bomb.

The use of the name McMurdo had to wait a decade more when Wodehouse introduced in 'Those in Peril on the Tee' (*Strand*, June 1927) Sidney McMurdo who so acutely reminded the detective-story writer John Gooch of the Human Gorilla in his novel *The Mystery of the Severed Ear* (see 'The Cardboard Box', *Memoirs*):

> 'For two pins' said Sidney McMurdo, displaying a more mercenary spirit than the Human Gorilla, who had required no cash payment for his crimes, 'I would tear you into shreds.'
>
> 'Me?' said John Gooch, blankly.
>
> 'Yes, you . . .' He rose; and, striding to the mantelpiece, broke off a corner of it and crumbled it in his fingers.

Clearly just the friend Tiger Cormac needed. The crumbled mantelpiece is presumably an act of homage to Dr Grimesby Roylott's exercises on the poker ('The Speckled Band, *Adventures*).

The critical factor here is not, of course, name, or even variation on situation, but that *The Valley of Fear* proved the final match to the train of powder building up in Wodehouse partly through Conan Doyle's earlier influence. The next stage would be the birth and development of Jeeves and Wooster, the greatest of all variations on Holmes and Watson.

But it was because *The Valley of Fear* was born of such pain that its children have given so much pleasure.

NOTE ON THE TEXT

The text is based on the first US edition, published in New York by George H. Doran Company on 27 February 1915, save where preferable readings obtain from the text as printed in the *Strand* magazine, (September 1914–May 1915), from British book publication by Smith, Elder & Co. of London on 3 June 1915, from the *Complete Sherlock Holmes Long Stories* published by John Murray of London on 14 September 1929, and from the *Complete Sherlock Holmes* published by Garden City Publishing Co. of Garden City, NY in 1936 in succession to Doubleday Doran incorporating Doran. Alternative readings are included in the Explanatory Notes, and the editions are discussed at their commencement. Punctuation variations between *Strand* and Doran have been determined by the rule of reason.

SELECT BIBLIOGRAPHY

1. A. CONAN DOYLE: PRINCIPAL WORKS

(a) *Fiction*

A Study in Scarlet (Ward, Lock, & Co., 1888)
The Mystery of Cloomber (Ward & Downey, 1888)
Micah Clarke (Longmans, Green, & Co., 1889)
The Captain of the Pole-Star and Other Tales (Longmans, Green, & Co., 1890)
The Sign of the Four (Spencer Blackett, 1890)
The Firm of Girdlestone (Chatto & Windus, 1890)
The White Company (Smith, Elder, & Co., 1891)
The Adventures of Sherlock Holmes (George Newnes, 1892)
The Great Shadow (Arrowsmith, 1892)
The Refugees (Longmans, Green, & Co., 1893)
The Memoirs of Sherlock Holmes (George Newnes, 1893)
Round the Red Lamp (Methuen & Co., 1894)
The Stark Munro Letters (Longmans, Green, & Co., 1895)
The Exploits of Brigadier Gerard (George Newnes, 1896)
Rodney Stone (Smith, Elder, & Co., 1896)
Uncle Bernac (Smith, Elder, & Co., 1897)
The Tragedy of the Korosko (Smith, Elder, & Co., 1898)
A Duet With an Occasional Chorus (Grant Richards, 1899)
The Green Flag and Other Stories of War and Sport (Smith, Elder, & Co., 1900)
The Hound of the Baskervilles (George Newnes, 1902)
Adventures of Gerard (George Newnes, 1903)
The Return of Sherlock Holmes (George Newnes, 1905)
Sir Nigel (Smith, Elder, & Co., 1906)
Round the Fire Stories (Smith, Elder, & Co., 1908)
The Last Galley (Smith, Elder, & Co., 1911)
The Lost World (Hodder & Stoughton, 1912)
The Poison Belt (Hodder & Stoughton, 1913)
The Valley of Fear (Smith, Elder, & Co., 1915)
His Last Bow (John Murray, 1917)
Danger! and Other Stories (John Murray, 1918)
The Land of Mist (Hutchinson & Co., 1926)
The Case-Book of Sherlock Holmes (John Murray, 1927)
The Maracot Deep and Other Stories (John Murray, 1929)

The Complete Sherlock Holmes Short Stories (John Murray, 1928)
The Conan Doyle Stories (John Murray, 1929)
The Complete Sherlock Holmes Long Stories (John Murray, 1929)

(b) *Non-fiction*

The Great Boer War (Smith, Elder, & Co., 1900)
The Story of Mr George Edalji (T. Harrison Roberts, 1907)
Through the Magic Door (Smith, Elder, & Co., 1907)
The Crime of the Congo (Hutchinson & Co., 1909)
The Case of Oscar Slater (Hodder & Stoughton, 1912)
The German War (Hodder & Stoughton, 1914)
The British Campaign in France and Flanders (Hodder & Stoughton, 6 vols., 1916–20)
The Poems of Arthur Conan Doyle (John Murray, 1922)
Memories and Adventures (Hodder & Stoughton, 1924; revised edn., 1930)
The History of Spiritualism (Cassell & Co., 1926)

2. MISCELLANEOUS

A Bibliography of A. Conan Doyle (Soho Bibliographies 23: Oxford, 1983) by Richard Lancelyn Green and John Michael Gibson, with a foreword by Graham Greene, is the standard—and indispensable—source of bibliographical information, and of much else besides. Green and Gibson have also assembled and introduced *The Unknown Conan Doyle*, comprising *Uncollected Stories* (those never previously published in book form); *Essays in Photography* (documenting a little-known enthusiasm of Conan Doyle's during his time as a student and young doctor), both published in 1982; and *Letters to the Press* (1986). Alone, Richard Lancelyn Green has compiled (1) *The Uncollected Sherlock Holmes* (1983), an impressive assemblage of Holmesiana, containing almost all Conan Doyle's writing about his creation (other than the stories themselves) together with related material by Joseph Bell, J. M. Barrie, and Beverley Nichols; (2) *The Further Adventures of Sherlock Holmes* (1985), a selection of eleven apocryphal Holmes adventures by various authors, all diplomatically introduced; (3) *The Sherlock Holmes Letters* (1986), a collection of noteworthy public correspondence on Holmes and Holmesiana and far more valuable than its title suggests; and (4) *Letters to Sherlock Holmes* (1984), a powerful testimony to the power of the Holmes stories.

Though much of Conan Doyle's work is now readily available there are still gaps. Some of his very earliest fiction now only survives in rare piracies (apart, that is, from the magazines in which they were first published), including items of intrinsic genre interest such as 'The Gully of Bluemansdyke' (1881) and its sequel 'My Friend the Murderer' (1882), which both turn on the theme of the murderer-informer (handled very differently—and far better— in the Holmes story of 'The Resident Patient' (*Memoirs*)): both of these were used as book-titles for the same pirate collection first issued as *Mysteries and Adventures* (1889). Other stories achieved book publication only after severe pruning—for example, 'The Surgeon of Gaster Fell', reprinted in *Danger!* many years after magazine publication (1890). Some items given initial book publication were not included in the collected edition of *The Conan Doyle Stories*. Particularly deplorable losses were 'John Barrington Cowles' (1884: included subsequently in *Edinburgh Stories of Arthur Conan Doyle* (1981)), 'A Foreign Office Romance' (1894), 'The Club-Footed Grocer' (1898), 'A Shadow Before' (1898), and 'Danger!' (1914). Three of these may have been post-war casualties, as seeming to deal too lightheartedly with the outbreak of other wars; 'John Barrington Cowles' may have been dismissed as juvenile work; but why Conan Doyle discarded a story as good as 'The Club-Footed Grocer' would baffle even Holmes.

At the other end of his life, Conan Doyle's tidying impaired the survival of his most recent work, some of which well merited lasting recognition. *The Maracot Deep and Other Stories* appeared in 1929, a little over a month after *The Conan Doyle Stories*; 'Maracot' itself found a separate paperback life as a short novel; the two Professor Challenger stories, 'The Disintegration Machine' and 'When the World Screamed', were naturally included in John Murray's *The Professor Challenger Stories* (1952); but the fourth item, 'The Story of Spedegue's Dropper', passed beyond the ken of most of Conan Doyle's readers. These three stories show the author, in his seventieth year, still at the height of his powers.

In 1980 Gaslight Publications, of Bloomington, Ind., reprinted *The Mystery of Cloomber, The Firm of Girdlestone, The Doings of Raffles Haw* (1892), *Beyond the City* (1893), *The Parasite* (1894; also reprinted in *Edinburgh Stories of Arthur Conan Doyle*), *The Stark Munro Letters, The Tragedy of the Korosko*, and *A Duet. Memories and Adventures*, Conan Doyle's enthralling but impressionistic recollections, are best read in the revised (1930) edition. *Through the Magic Door* remains the best introduction to the literary mind of Conan Doyle, whilst some of his volumes on Spiritualism have autobiographical material of literary significance.

ACD: The Journal of the Arthur Conan Doyle Society (ed. Christopher Roden, David Stuart Davies [to 1991], and Barbara Roden [from 1992]), together with its newsletter, *The Parish Magazine*, is a useful source of critical and biographical material on Conan Doyle. The enormous body of 'Sherlockiana' is best pursued in *The Baker Street Journal*, published by Fordham University Press, or in the *Sherlock Holmes Journal* (Sherlock Holmes Society of London), itemized up to 1974 in the colossal *World Bibliography of Sherlock Holmes and Doctor Watson* (1974) by Ronald Burt De Waal (see also De Waal, *The International Sherlock Holmes* (1980)) and digested in *The Annotated Sherlock Holmes* (2 vols., 1968) by William S. Baring-Gould, whose industry has been invaluable for the Oxford Sherlock Holmes editors. Jack Tracy, *The Encyclopaedia Sherlockiana* (1979) is a very helpful compilation of relevant data. Those who can nerve themselves to consult it despite its title will benefit greatly from Christopher Redmond, *In Bed With Sherlock Holmes* (1984). The classic 'Sherlockian' work is Ronald A. Knox, 'Studies in the Literature of Sherlock Holmes', first published in *The Blue Book* (July 1912) and reprinted in his *Essays in Satire* (1928).

The serious student of Conan Doyle may perhaps deplore the vast extent of 'Sherlockian' literature, even though the size of this output is testimony in itself to the scale and nature of Conan Doyle's achievement. But there is undoubtedly some wheat amongst the chaff. At the head stands Dorothy L. Sayers, *Unpopular Opinions* (1946); also of some interest are T. S. Blakeney, *Sherlock Holmes: Fact or Fiction* (1932), H. W. Bell, *Sherlock Holmes and Dr Watson* (1932), Vincent Starrett, *The Private Life of Sherlock Holmes* (1934), Gavin Brend, *My Dear Holmes* (1951), S. C. Roberts, *Holmes and Watson* (1953) and Roberts's introduction to *Sherlock Holmes: Selected Stories* (Oxford: The World's Classics, 1951), James E. Holroyd, *Baker Street Byways* (1959), Ian McQueen, *Sherlock Holmes Detected* (1974), and Trevor H. Hall, *Sherlock Holmes and his Creator* (1978). One Sherlockian item certainly falls into the category of the genuinely essential: D. Martin Dakin, *A Sherlock Holmes Commentary* (1972), to which all the editors of the present series are indebted.

Michael Pointer, *The Public Life of Sherlock Holmes* (1975) contains invaluable information concerning dramatizations of the Sherlock Holmes stories for radio, stage, and the cinema; of complementary interest are Chris Steinbrunner and Norman Michaels, *The Films of Sherlock Holmes* (1978) and David Stuart Davies, *Holmes of the Movies* (1976), whilst Philip Weller with Christopher Roden, *The Life and Times of Sherlock Holmes* (1992) summarizes a great deal of useful information concerning Conan Doyle's life and Holmes's cases, and in addition is delightfully illustrated. The more concrete products of the Holmes industry are dealt with in Charles Hall, *The Sherlock Holmes Collection* (1987). For a useful retrospective view, Allen Eyles, *Sherlock Holmes: A Centenary Celebration* (1986) rises to the occasion. Both useful and engaging are Peter Haining, *The Sherlock Holmes Scrapbook* (1973) and Charles Viney, *Sherlock Holmes in London* (1989).

Of the many anthologies of Holmesiana, P. A. Shreffler (ed.), *The Baker Street Reader* (1984) is exceptionally useful. D. A. Redmond, *Sherlock Holmes: A Study in Sources* (1982) is similarly indispensable. Michael Hardwick, *The Complete Guide to Sherlock Holmes* (1986) is both reliable and entertaining; Michael Harrison, *In the Footsteps of Sherlock Holmes* (1958) is occasionally helpful.

For more general studies of the detective story, the standard history is Julian Symons, *Bloody Murder* (1972, 1985, 1992). Necessary but a great deal less satisfactory is Howard Haycraft, *Murder for Pleasure* (1942); of more value is Haycraft's critical anthology *The Art of the Mystery Story* (1946), which contains many choice period items. Both R. F. Stewart, *... And Always a Detective* (1980) and Colin Watson, *Snobbery with Violence* (1971) are occasionally useful. Dorothy Sayers's pioneering introduction to *Great Short Stories of Detection, Mystery and Horror* (First Series, 1928), despite some inspired howlers, is essential reading; Raymond Chandler's riposte, 'The Simple Art of Murder' (1944), is reprinted in Haycraft, *The Art of the Mystery Story* (see above). Less well known than Sayers's essay but with an equal claim to poineer status is E. M. Wrong's introduction to *Crime and Detection*, First Series (Oxford: The World's Classics, 1926). See also Michael Cox (ed.), *Victorian Tales of Mystery and Detection: An Oxford Anthology* (1992).

Amongst biographical studies of Conan Doyle one of the most distinguished is Jon L. Lellenberg's survey, *The Quest for Sir Arthur Conan Doyle* (1987), with a Foreword by Dame Jean Conan Doyle (much the best piece of writing on ACD by any member of his family). The four earliest biographers—the Revd John Lamond (1931), Hesketh Pearson (1943), John Dickson Carr (1949), and Pierre Nordon (1964)—all had access to the family archives, subsequently closed to researchers following a lawsuit; hence all four biographies contain valuable documentary material, though Nordon handles the evidence best (the French text is fuller than the English version, published in 1966). Of the others, Lamond seems only to have made little use of the material available to him;

Pearson is irreverent and wildly careless with dates; Dickson Carr has a strong fictionalizing element. Both he and Nordon paid a price for their access to the Conan Doyle papers by deferring to the far from impartial editorial demands of Adrian Conan Doyle; Nordon nevertheless remains the best available biography. The best short sketch is Julian Symons, *Conan Doyle* (1979) (and for the late Victorian milieu of the Holmes cycle some of Symons's own fiction, such as *The Blackheath Poisonings* and *The Detling Secret*, can be thoroughly recommended). Harold Orel (ed.), *Critical Essays on Sir Arthur Conan Doyle* (1992) is a good and varied collection, whilst Robin Winks, *The Historian as Detective* (1969) contains many insights and examples applicable to the Holmes corpus; Winks's *Detective Fiction: A Collection of Critical Essays* (1980) is an admirable working handbook, with a useful critical bibliography. Edmund Wilson's famous essay 'Mr Holmes, they were the footprints of a gigantic hound' (1944) may be found in his *Classics and Commercials: A Literary Chronicle of the Forties* (1950).

Specialized biographical areas are covered in Owen Dudley Edwards, *The Quest for Sherlock Holmes: A Biographical Study of Arthur Conan Doyle* (1982) and in Geoffrey Stavert, *A Study in Southsea: The Unrevealed Life of Dr Arthur Conan Doyle* (1987), which respectively assess the significance of the years up to 1882, and from 1882 to 1890. Alvin E. Rodin and Jack D. Key provide a thorough study of Conan Doyle's medical career and its literary implications in *Medical Casebook of Dr Arthur Conan Doyle* (1984). Peter Costello, in *The Real World of Sherlock Holmes: The True Crimes Investigated by Arthur Conan Doyle* (1991) claims too much, but it is useful to be reminded of events that came within Conan Doyle's orbit, even if they are sometimes tangential or even irrelevant. Christopher Redmond, *Welcome to America, Mr Sherlock Holmes* (1987) is a thorough account of Conan Doyle's tour of North America in 1894.

Other than Baring-Gould (see above), the only serious attempt to annotate the nine volumes of the Holmes cycle has been in the Longman Heritage of Literature series (1979–80), to which the present editors are also indebted. Of introductions to individual texts, H. R. F. Keating's to the *Adventures* and *The Hound of the Baskervilles* (published in one volume under the dubious title *The Best of Sherlock Holmes* (1992)) is worthy of particular mention.

A CHRONOLOGY OF
ARTHUR CONAN DOYLE

1855   Charles Altamont Doyle, youngest son of the political cartoonist John Doyle ('HB'), and Mary Foley, his Irish landlady's daughter, marry in Edinburgh on 31 July.

1859   Arthur Ignatius Conan Doyle, third child and elder son of ten siblings, born at 11 Picardy Place, Edinburgh, on 22 May and baptized into the Roman Catholic religion of his parents.

1868–75   ACD commences two years' education under the Jesuits at Hodder, followed by five years at its senior sister college, Stonyhurst, both in the Ribble Valley, Lancashire; becomes a popular storyteller amongst his fellow pupils, writes verses, edits a school paper, and makes one close friend, James Ryan of Glasgow and Ceylon. Doyle family resides at 3 Sciennes Hill Place, Edinburgh.

1875–6   ACD passes London Matriculation Examination at Stonyhurst and studies for a year in the Jesuit college at Feldkirch, Austria.

1876–7   ACD becomes a student of medicine at Edinburgh University on the advice of Bryan Charles Waller, now lodging with the Doyle family at 2 Argyle Park Terrace.

1877–80   Waller leases 23 George Square, Edinburgh as a 'consulting pathologist', with all the Doyles as residents. ACD continues medical studies, becoming surgeon's clerk to Joseph Bell at Edinburgh; also takes temporary medical assistantships at Sheffield, Ruyton (Salop), and Birmingham, the last leading to a close friendship with his employer's family, the Hoares. First story published, 'The Mystery of Sasassa Valley', in *Chambers's Journal* (6 Sept. 1879); first non-fiction published—'Gelseminum as a Poison', *British Medical Journal* (20 Sept. 1879). Sometime previously ACD sends 'The Haunted Grange of Goresthorpe' to *Blackwood's Edinburgh Magazine*, but it is filed and forgotten.

1

1880   (Feb.–Sept.) ACD serves as surgeon on the Greenland whaler *Hope* of Peterhead.

1881   ACD graduates MB, CM (Edin.); Waller and the Doyles living at 15 Lonsdale Terrace, Edinburgh.

1881–2 (Oct.–Jan.) ACD serves as surgeon on the steamer *Mayumba* to West Africa, spending three days with US Minister to Liberia, Henry Highland Garnet, black abolitionist leader, then dying. (July–Aug.) Visits Foley relatives in Lismore, Co. Waterford.

1882   Ill-fated partnership with George Turnavine Budd in Plymouth. ACD moves to Southsea, Portsmouth, in June. ACD published in *London Society*, *All the Year Round*, *Lancet*, and *British Journal of Photography*. Over the next eight years ACD becomes an increasingly successful general practitioner at Southsea.

1882–3 Breakup of the Doyle family in Edinburgh. Charles Altamont Doyle henceforth confined because of alcoholism and epilepsy. Mary Foley Doyle resident in Masongill Cottage on the Waller estate at Masongill, Yorkshire. Innes Doyle (b. 1873) resident with ACD as schoolboy and surgery page from Sept. 1882.

1883   'The Captain of the *Pole-Star*' published (*Temple Bar*, Jan.), as well as a steady stream of minor pieces. Works on *The Mystery of Cloomber*.

1884   ACD publishes 'J. Habakuk Jephson's Statement' (*Cornhill Magazine*, Jan.), 'The Heiress of Glenmahowley' (*Temple Bar*, Jan.), 'The Cabman's Story' (*Cassell's Saturday Journal*, May); working on *The Firm of Girdlestone*.

1885   Publishes 'The Man from Archangel' (*London Society*, Jan.). Jack Hawkins, briefly a resident patient with ACD, dies of cerebral meningitis. Louisa Hawkins, his sister, marries ACD. (Aug.) Travels in Ireland for honeymoon. Awarded Edinburgh MD.

1886   Writing *A Study in Scarlet*.

1887   *A Study in Scarlet* published in *Beeton's Christmas Annual*.

1888   (July) First book edition of *A Study in Scarlet* published by Ward, Lock; (Dec.) *The Mystery of Cloomber* published.

1889   (Feb.) *Micah Clarke* (ACD's novel of the Monmouth Rebellion of 1685) published. Mary Louise Conan

Doyle, ACD's eldest child, born. Unauthorized publication of *Mysteries and Adventures* (published later as *The Gully of Bluemansdyke* and *My Friend the Murderer*). *The Sign of the Four* and Oscar Wilde's *The Picture of Dorian Gray* commissioned by Lippincott's.

1890   (Jan.) 'Mr [R. L.] Stevenson's Methods in Fiction' published in the *National Review*. (Feb.) *The Sign of the Four* published in *Lippincott's Monthly Magazine*; (Mar.) First authorized short-story collection, *The Captain of the Pole-Star and Other Tales*, published; (Apr.) *The Firm of Girdlestone* published; (Oct.) first book edition of the *Sign* published by Spencer Blackett.

1891   ACD sets up as an eye specialist in 2 Upper Wimpole Street, off Harley Street, while living at Montague Place. Moves to South Norwood. (July–Dec.) The first six 'Adventures of Sherlock Holmes' published in George Newnes's *Strand Magazine*. (Oct.) *The White Company* published; *Beyond the City* first published in *Good Cheer*, the special Christmas number of *Good Words*.

1892   (Jan.–June) Six more Holmes stories published in the *Strand*, with another in Dec. (Mar.) *The Doings of Raffles Haw* published (first serialized in Alfred Harmsworth's penny paper *Answers*, Dec. 1891–Feb. 1892). (14 Oct.) *The Adventures of Sherlock Holmes* published by Newnes. (31 Oct.) Waterloo story *The Great Shadow* published. Alleyne Kingsley Conan Doyle born. Newnes republishes the *Sign*.

1893   'Adventures of Sherlock Holmes' (second series) continues in the *Strand*, to be published by Newnes as *The Memoirs of Sherlock Holmes* (Dec.), minus 'The Cardboard Box'. Holmes apparently killed in 'The Final Problem' (Dec.) to free ACD for 'more serious literary work'. (May) *The Refugees* published. *Jane Annie: or, the Good Conduct Prize* (musical comedy co-written with J. M. Barrie) fails at the Savoy Theatre. (10 Oct.) Charles Altamont Doyle dies.

1894   (Oct.) *Round the Red Lamp*, a collection of medical short stories, published, several for the first time. *The Stark Munro Letters*, a fictionalized autobiography, begun, to be concluded the following year. ACD on US lecture tour with Innes Doyle. (Dec.) *The Parasite* published; 'The Medal of Brigadier Gerard' published in the *Strand*.

1895   'The Exploits of Brigadier Gerard' published in the *Strand*.

1896   (Feb.) *The Exploits of Brigadier Gerard* published by Newnes. ACD settles at Hindhead, Surrey, to minimize effects of his wife's tuberculosis. (Nov.) *Rodney Stone*, a pre-Regency mystery, published. Self-pastiche, 'The Field Bazaar', appears in the Edinburgh University *Student* (20 Nov.).

1897   (May) Napoleonic novel *Uncle Bernac* published; three 'Captain Sharkey' pirate stories published in *Pearson's Magazine* (Jan., Mar., May). Home at Undershaw, Hindhead.

1898   (Feb.) *The Tragedy of the Korosko* published. (June) Publishes *Songs of Action*, a verse collection. (June–Dec.) Begins to publish 'Round the Fire Stories' in the *Strand*—'The Beetle Hunter', 'The Man with the Watches', 'The Lost Special', 'The Sealed Room', 'The Black Doctor', 'The Club-Footed Grocer', and 'The Brazilian Cat'. Ernest William Hornung (ACD's brother-in-law) creates A. J. Raffles and in 1899 dedicates the first stories to ACD.

1899   (Jan.–May) Concludes 'Round the Fire' series in the *Strand* with 'The Japanned Box', 'The Jew's Breast-Plate', 'B. 24', 'The Latin Tutor', and 'The Brown Hand'. (Mar.) Publishes *A Duet with an Occasional Chorus*, a version of his own romance. (Oct.–Dec.) 'The Croxley Master', a boxing story, published in the *Strand*. William Gillette begins 33 years starring in *Sherlock Holmes*, a play by Gillette and ACD.

1900   Accompanies volunteer-staffed Langman hospital as unofficial supervisor to support British forces in the Boer War. (Mar.) Publishes short-story collection, *The Green Flag and Other Stories of War and Sport*. (Oct.) *The Great Boer War* published. Unsuccessful Liberal Unionist parliamentary candidate for Edinburgh Central.

1901   (Aug.) 'The Hound of the Baskervilles' begins serialization in the *Strand*, subtitled 'Another Adventure of Sherlock Holmes'.

1902   (Jan.) *The War in South Africa: Its Cause and Conduct* published. 'Sherlockian' higher criticism begun by Frank

Sidgwick in the *Cambridge Review* (23 Jan.). (Mar.) *The Hound of the Baskervilles* published by Newnes. ACD accepts knighthood with reluctance.

1903   (Sept.) *Adventures of Gerard* published by Newnes (previously serialized in the *Strand*). (Oct.) 'The Return of Sherlock Holmes' begins in the *Strand*. Author's Edition of ACD's major works published in twelve volumes by Smith, Elder and thirteen by D. Appleton & Co. of New York, with prefaces by ACD; many titles omitted.

1904   'Return of Sherlock Holmes' continues in the *Strand*; series designed to conclude with 'The Abbey Grange' (Sept.), but ACD develops earlier allusions and produces 'The Second Stain' (Dec.).

1905   (Mar.) *The Return of Sherlock Holmes* published by Newnes. (Dec.) Serialization of 'Sir Nigel' begun in the *Strand* (concluded Dec. 1906).

1906   (Nov.) Book publication of *Sir Nigel*. ACD defeated as Unionist candidate for Hawick District in general election. (4 July) Death of Louisa ('Touie'), Lady Conan Doyle. ACD deeply affected.

1907   ACD clears the name of George Edalji (convicted in 1903 of cattle-maiming). (18 Sept.) Marries Jean Leckie. (Nov.) Publishes *Through the Magic Door*, a celebration of his literary mentors (earlier version serialized in *Great Thoughts*, 1894).

1908   Moves to Windlesham, Crowborough, Sussex. (Jan.) Death of Sidney Paget. (Sept.) *Round the Fire Stories* published, including some not in earlier *Strand* series. (Sept.–Oct.) 'The Singular Experience of Mr John Scott Eccles' (later retitled as 'The Adventure of Wisteria Lodge') begins occasional series of Holmes stories in the *Strand*.

1909   ACD becomes President of the Divorce Law Reform Union (until 1919). Denis Percy Stewart Conan Doyle born. Takes up agitation against Belgian oppression in the Congo.

1910   (Sept.) 'The Marriage of the Brigadier', the last Gerard story, published in the *Strand*, and (Dec.) the Holmes story of 'The Devil's Foot'. ACD takes six-month lease on Adelphi Theatre; the play *The Speckled Band* opens there, eventually running to 346 performances. Adrian Malcolm Conan Doyle born.

1911 (Apr.) *The Last Galley* (short stories, mostly historical) published. Two more Holmes stories appear in the *Strand*: 'The Red Circle' (Mar., Apr.) and 'The Disappearance of Lady Frances Carfax' (Dec.). ACD declares for Irish Home Rule, under the influence of Sir Roger Casement.

1912 (Apr.–Nov.) The first Professor Challenger story, *The Lost World*, published in the *Strand*, book publication in Oct. Jean Lena Annette Conan Doyle (afterwards Air Commandant Dame Jean Conan Doyle, Lady Bromet) born.

1913 (Feb.) Writes 'Great Britain and the Next War' (*Fortnightly Review*). (Aug.) Second Challenger story, *The Poison Belt*, published. (Dec.) 'The Dying Detective' published in the *Strand*. ACD campaigns for a channel tunnel.

1914 (July) 'Danger!', warning of the dangers of a war-time blockade of Britain, published in the *Strand*. (4 Aug.) Britain declares war on Germany; ACD forms local volunteer force.

1914–15 (Sept.) *The Valley of Fear* begins serialization in the *Strand* (concluding May 1915).

1915 (27 Feb.) *The Valley of Fear* published by George H. Doran in New York. (June) *The Valley of Fear* published in London by Smith, Elder (transferred with rest of ACD stock to John Murray when the firm is sold on the death of Reginald Smith). Five Holmes films released in Germany (ten more during the war).

1916 (Apr., May) First instalments of *The British Campaign in France and Flanders 1914* appear in the *Strand*. (Aug.) *A Visit to Three Fronts* published. Sir Roger Casement convicted of high treason after Dublin Easter Week Rising and executed despite appeals for clemency by ACD and others.

1917 War censor interdicts ACD's history of the 1916 campaigns in the *Strand*. (Sept.) 'His Last Bow' published in the *Strand*. (Oct.) *His Last Bow* published by John Murray (includes 'The Cardboard Box').

1918 (Apr.) ACD publishes *The New Revelation*, proclaiming himself a Spiritualist. (Dec.) *Danger! and Other Stories* published. Permitted to resume accounts of 1916 and 1917 campaigns in the *Strand*, but that for 1918 never serialized. Death of eldest son, Captain Kingsley Conan Doyle, from influenza aggravated by war wounds.

1919   Death of Brigadier-General Innes Doyle, from post-war pneumonia.

1920–30   ACD engaged in world-wide crusade for Spiritualism.

1921–2   ACD's one-act play, *The Crown Diamond*, tours with Dennis Neilson-Terry as Holmes.

1921   (Oct.) 'The Mazarin Stone' (apparently based on *The Crown Diamond*) published in the *Strand*. Death of mother, Mary Foley Doyle.

1922   (Feb.–Mar.) 'The Problem of Thor Bridge' in the *Strand*. (July) John Murray publishes a collected edition of the non-Holmes short stories in six volumes: *Tales of the Ring and the Camp*, *Tales of Pirates and Blue Water*, *Tales of Terror and Mystery*, *Tales of Twilight and the Unseen*, *Tales of Adventure and Medical Life*, and (Nov.) *Tales of Long Ago*. (Sept.) Collected edition of ACD's *Poems* published by Murray.

1923   (Mar.) 'The Creeping Man' published in the *Strand*.

1924   (Jan.) 'The Sussex Vampire' appears in the *Strand*. (June) 'How Watson Learned the Trick', ACD's own Holmes pastiche, appears in *The Book of the Queen's Dolls' House Library*. (Sept.) *Memories and Adventures* published (reprinted with additions and deletions 1930).

1925   (Jan.) 'The Three Garridebs' and (Feb.–Mar.) 'The Illustrious Client' published in the *Strand*. (July) *The Land of Mist*, a Spiritualist novel featuring Challenger, begins serialization in the *Strand*.

1926   (Mar.) *The Land of Mist* published. *Strand* publishes 'The Three Gables' (Oct.), 'The Blanched Soldier' (Nov.), and 'The Lion's Mane' (Dec.).

1927   *Strand* publishes 'The Retired Colourman' (Jan.), 'The Veiled Lodger' (Feb.), and 'Shoscombe Old Place' (Apr.). (June) Murray publishes *The Case-Book of Sherlock Holmes*.

1928   (Oct.) *The Complete Sherlock Holmes Short Stories* published by Murray.

1929   (June) *The Conan Doyle Stories* (containing the six separate volumes issued by Murray in 1922) published. (July) *The Maracot Deep and Other Stories*, ACD's last collection of his fictional work.

1930   (7 July, 8.30 a.m.) Death of Arthur Conan Doyle. 'Education never ends, Watson. It is a series of lessons with the greatest for the last' ('The Red Circle').

The Valley of Fear

PART 1

The Tragedy of Birlstone

· CHAPTER 1 ·

The Warning

'I AM inclined to think—' said I.

'I should do so,' Sherlock Holmes remarked, impatiently.

I believe that I am one of the most long-suffering of mortals, but I admit that I was annoyed at the sardonic interruption.

'Really, Holmes,' said I, severely, 'you are a little trying at times.'

He was too much absorbed with his own thoughts to give any immediate answer to my remonstrance.* He leaned upon his hand, with his untasted breakfast* before him, and he stared at the slip of paper which he had just drawn from its envelope. Then he took the envelope itself, held it up to the light, and very carefully studied both the exterior and the flap.

'It is Porlock's* writing,' said he, thoughtfully. 'I can hardly doubt that it is Porlock's writing, though I have only seen it twice before. The Greek "e"* with the peculiar top flourish is distinctive. But if it is from Porlock, then it must be something of the very first importance.'

He was speaking to himself rather than to me, but my vexation disappeared in the interest which the words awakened.

'Who, then, is Porlock?' I asked.

'Porlock, Watson, is a *nom de plume*,* a mere identification mark, but behind it lies a shifty and evasive personality. In a former letter he frankly informed me that the name was not his own, and defied me ever to trace him among the teeming millions of this great city. Porlock is important, not for himself, but for the great man with whom he is in touch. Picture to yourself the pilot-fish with the shark, the jackal with the lion—anything that is insignificant in companionship

5

with what is formidable. Not only formidable, Watson, but sinister—in the highest degree sinister. That is where he comes within my purview. You have heard me speak of Professor Moriarty?'*

'The famous scientific criminal, as famous among crooks as—'

'My blushes,* Watson,' Holmes murmured, in a deprecating voice.

'I was about to say "as he is unknown to the public".'

'A touch*—a distinct touch!' cried Holmes. 'You are developing a certain unexpected vein of pawky* humour, Watson, against which I must learn to guard myself. But in calling Moriarty a criminal you are uttering libel* in the eyes of the law, and there lies* the glory and the wonder of it.* The greatest schemer of all time, the organizer of every devilry, the controlling brain of the underworld—a brain which might have made or marred the destiny of nations. That's the man. But so aloof is he from general suspicion—so immune from criticism—so admirable in his management and self-effacement, that for those very words that you have uttered he could hale you to a court and emerge with your year's pension* as a solatium* for his wounded character. Is he not the celebrated author of *The Dynamics of an Asteroid*—a book which ascends to such rarefied heights of pure mathematics that it is said that there was no man in the scientific press capable of criticizing it? Is this a man to traduce? Foul-mouthed doctor and slandered* professor—such would be your respective *rôles*. That's genius, Watson. But if I am spared by lesser men our day will surely come.'*

'May I be there to see!'* I exclaimed, devoutly. 'But you were speaking of this man Porlock.'

'Ah, yes—the so-called Porlock is a link in the chain some little way from its great attachment. Porlock is not quite a sound link, between ourselves. He is the only flaw in that chain so far as I have been able to test it.'

'But no chain is stronger than its weakest link.'

'Exactly, my dear Watson. Hence the extreme importance of Porlock. Led on by some rudimentary aspirations towards right, and encouraged by the judicious stimulation of an occasional ten-pound note sent to him by devious methods, he has once or twice given me advance information which has been of value—that highest value which anticipates and prevents rather than avenges crime. I cannot doubt that if we had the cipher we should find that this communication is of the nature that I indicate.'

Again Holmes flattened out the paper upon his unused plate.* I rose and, leaning over him, stared down at the curious inscription, which ran as follows:

534 C2 13 127 36 31 4 17 21 41
DOUGLAS* 109 293 5 37 BIRLSTONE*
26 BIRLSTONE 9 127 171

'What do you make of it, Holmes?'

'It is obviously an attempt to convey secret information.'

'But what is the use of a cipher message without the cipher?'

'In this instance, none at all.'

'Why do you say "in this instance"?'

'Because there are many ciphers which I would read as easily as I do the apocrypha of the agony column.* Such crude devices amuse the intelligence without fatiguing it. But this is different. It is clearly a reference to the words in a page of some book. Until I am told which page and which book I am powerless.'

'But why "Douglas" and "Birlstone"?'

'Clearly because those are words which were not contained in the page in question.'

'Then why has he not indicated the book?'

'Your native shrewdness, my dear Watson, that innate cunning which is the delight of your friends, would surely prevent you from enclosing cipher and message in the same envelope. Should it miscarry you are undone. As it is, both have to go wrong before any harm comes from it. Our second post is now overdue, and I shall be surprised if it does not bring us either a further letter of explanation or, as is more probable, the very volume to which these figures refer.'

Holmes's calculation was fulfilled within a very few minutes by the appearance of Billy, the page,* with the very letter which we were expecting.

'The same writing,' remarked Holmes, as he opened the envelope, 'and actually signed,' he added, in an exultant voice, as he unfolded the epistle. 'Come, we are getting on, Watson.'

His brow clouded, however, as he glanced over the contents.

'Dear me,* this is very disappointing! I fear, Watson, that all our expectations come to nothing. I trust that the man Porlock will come to no harm.

' "Dear Mr Holmes," he says, "I will go no further in this matter.* It is too dangerous. He suspects me. I can see that he suspects me. He came to me quite unexpectedly after I had actually addressed this envelope with the intention of sending you the key to the cipher. I was able to cover it up. If he had seen it, it would have gone hard with me. But I read suspicion in his eyes.* Please burn the cipher message, which can now be of no use to you.—Fred* Porlock." '

Holmes sat for some little time twisting this letter between his fingers, and frowning, as he stared into the fire.

'After all,' he said at last, 'there may be nothing in it. It may be only his guilty conscience. Knowing himself to be a traitor, he may have read the accusation in the other's eyes.'

'The other being, I presume, Professor Moriarty?'

'No less. When any of that party talk about "he", you know whom they mean. There is one predominant "he" for all of them.'

'But what can he do?'

'Hum! That's a large question. When you have one of the first brains of Europe up against you and all the powers of darkness* at his back, there are infinite possibilities. Anyhow, friend Porlock is evidently scared out of his senses. Kindly compare the writing in the note with that upon its envelope, which was done, he tells us, before this ill-omened visit. The one is clear and firm; the other hardly legible.'

'Why did he write at all? Why did he not simply drop it?'

'Because he feared I would make some inquiry after him in that case, and possibly bring trouble on him.'

'No doubt,' said I. 'Of course'—I had picked up the original cipher message and was bending my brows over it—'it's pretty maddening to think that an important secret may lie here on this slip of paper, and that it is beyond human power to penetrate it.'

Sherlock Holmes had pushed away his untasted breakfast and lit the unsavoury pipe which was the companion of his deepest meditations.

'I wonder!' said he, leaning back and staring at the ceiling. 'Perhaps there are points which have escaped your Machiavellian* intellect. Let us consider the problem in the light of pure reason. This man's reference is to a book. That is our point of departure.'

'A somewhat vague one.'

'Let us see, then, if we can narrow it down. As I focus my mind upon it, it seems rather less impenetrable. What indications have we as to this book?'

'None.'

'Well, well, it is surely not quite so bad as that. The cipher message begins with a large 534,* does it not? We may take it as a working hypothesis that 534 is the particular page to which the cipher refers. So our book has already become a *large* book, which is surely something gained. What other indications have we as to the nature of this large book? The next sign is C2. What do you make of that, Watson?'

'Chapter the second, no doubt.'

'Hardly that, Watson. You will, I am sure, agree with me that if the page be given, the number of the chapter is immaterial. Also that if page 534 only finds us in the second chapter, the length of the first one must have been really intolerable.'

'Column!' I cried.

'Brilliant, Watson. You are scintillating this morning. If it is not column, then I am very much deceived. So now, you see, we begin to visualize a large book, printed in double columns, which are each of a considerable length, since one

9

of the words is numbered in the document as the two hundred and ninety-third. Have we reached the limits of what reason can supply?'

'I fear that we have.'

'Surely you do yourself an injustice. One more coruscation, my dear Watson. Yet another brain-wave. Had the volume been an unusual one he would have sent it to me. Instead of that he had intended, before his plans were nipped, to send me the clue in this envelope. He says so in his note. This would seem to indicate that the book is one which he thought that I would have no difficulty in finding for myself. He had it, and he imagined that I would have it too. In short, Watson, it is a very common book.'

'What you say certainly sounds plausible.'

'So we have contracted our field of search to a large book, printed in double columns and in common use.'

'The Bible!' I cried, triumphantly.

'Good, Watson, good! But not, if I may say so, quite good enough. Even if I accepted the compliment for myself, I could hardly name any volume which would be less likely to lie at the elbow of one of Moriarty's associates. Besides, the editions of Holy Writ are so numerous* that he could hardly suppose that two copies would have the same pagination. This is clearly a book which is standardized. He knows for certain that his page 534 will exactly agree with my page 534.'

'But very few books would correspond with that.'

'Exactly. Therein lies our salvation. Our search is narrowed down to standardized books which any one may be supposed to possess.'

'Bradshaw!'*

'There are difficulties, Watson. The vocabulary of *Bradshaw* is nervous and terse, but limited. The selection of words would hardly lend itself to the sending of general messages. We will eliminate *Bradshaw*. The dictionary* is, I fear, inadmissible for the same reason. What, then, is left?'

'An almanack.'

'Excellent, Watson! I am very much mistaken if you have not touched the spot. An almanack! Let us consider the claims of *Whitaker's Almanack.** It is in common use. It has the requisite number of pages. It is in double columns. Though reserved in its earlier vocabulary, it becomes, if I remember right, quite garrulous towards the end.' He picked up the volume from his desk. 'Here is page 534, column two, a substantial block of print dealing, I perceive, with the trade and resources of British India. Jot down the words, Watson. Number thirteen is "Mahratta". Not, I fear, a very auspicious beginning. Number one hundred and twenty-seven is "Government", which at least makes sense, though somewhat irrelevant to ourselves and Professor Moriarty. Now let us try again. What does the Mahratta Government do? Alas! the next word is "pigs'-bristles". We are undone,* my good Watson! It is finished.'*

He had spoken in jesting vein, but the twitching of his bushy eyebrows bespoke his disappointment and irritation. I sat helpless and unhappy, staring into the fire. A long silence was broken by a sudden exclamation from Holmes, who dashed at a cupboard, from which he emerged with a second yellow-covered volume in his hand.

'We pay the price, Watson, for being too up-to-date,' he cried. 'We are before our time, and suffer the usual penalties. Being the seventh of January, we have very properly laid in the new almanack. It is more than likely that Porlock took his message from the old one. No doubt he would have told us so had his letter of explanation been written. Now let us see what page 534 has in store for us. Number thirteen is "There", which is much more promising. Number one hundred and twenty-seven is "is"—"There is" '—Holmes's eyes were gleaming with excitement, and his thin, nervous fingers twitched as he counted the words—' "danger". Ha! ha! Capital!* Put that down, Watson. "There is danger—may—come—very—soon—one". Then we have the name "Douglas"—"rich—country—now—at—Birlstone—House—Birlstone—confidence—is—pressing". There, Watson! what do you think of pure reason and its fruits? If the greengrocer had such a thing as a laurel-wreath I should send Billy round for it.'

I was staring at the strange message which I had scrawled, as he deciphered it, upon a sheet of foolscap on my knee.

'What a queer, scrambling way of expressing his meaning!' said I.

'On the contrary, he has done quite remarkably well,' said Holmes. 'When you search a single column for words with which to express your meaning, you can hardly expect to get everything you want. You are bound to leave something to the intelligence of your correspondent. The purport is perfectly clear. Some devilry is intended against one Douglas, whoever he may be, residing as stated, a rich country gentleman. He is sure—"confidence" was as near as he could get to "confident"—that it is pressing. There is our result, and a very workmanlike little bit of analysis it was.'

Holmes had the impersonal joy of the true artist in his better work, even as he mourned darkly when it fell below the high level to which he aspired. He was still chuckling over his success when Billy swung open the door and Inspector MacDonald* of Scotland Yard* was ushered into the room.

Those were the early days at the end of the 'eighties, when Alec MacDonald was far from having attained the national fame which he has now achieved. He was a young but trusted member of the detective force, who had distinguished himself in several cases which had been entrusted to him. His tall, bony figure gave promise of exceptional physical strength, while his great cranium and deep-set, lustrous eyes spoke no less clearly of the keen intelligence which twinkled out from behind his bushy eyebrows. He was a silent, precise man, with a dour nature and a hard Aberdonian accent.* Twice already in his career had Holmes helped him to attain success, his own sole reward being the intellectual joy of the problem. For this reason the affection and respect of the Scotchman for his amateur colleague were profound, and he showed them by the frankness with which he consulted Holmes in every difficulty. Mediocrity

knows nothing higher than itself, but talent instantly recognizes genius, and MacDonald had talent enough for his
profession to enable him to perceive that there was no
humiliation in seeking the assistance of one who already
stood alone in Europe, both in his gifts and in his experience. Holmes was not prone to friendship, but he was
tolerant of the big Scotchman, and smiled at the sight of
him.

'You are an early bird, Mr Mac,' said he. 'I wish you luck
with your worm. I fear this means that there is some
mischief afoot.'

'If you said "hope" instead of "fear" it would be nearer
the truth, I'm thinking, Mr Holmes,' the inspector answered,
with a knowing grin. 'Well, maybe a wee nip* would keep
out the raw morning chill. No, I won't smoke, I thank you.
I'll have to be pushing on my way, for the early hours of a
case are the precious ones, as no man knows better than
your own self. But—but—'

The inspector had stopped suddenly, and was staring with
a look of absolute amazement at a paper upon the table. It
was the sheet upon which I had scrawled the enigmatic
message.

'Douglas!' he stammered. 'Birlstone! What's this, Mr
Holmes? Man, it's witchcraft! Where in the name of all that
is wonderful did you get those names?'

'It is a cipher that Dr Watson and I have had occasion to
solve. But why—what's amiss with the names?'

The inspector looked from one to the other of us in dazed
astonishment.

'Just this,' said he, 'that Mr Douglas, of Birlstone Manor
House, was horribly murdered this morning.'*

· CHAPTER 2 ·

Mr Sherlock Holmes Discourses

IT was one of those dramatic moments for which my friend existed. It would be an over-statement to say that he was shocked or even excited by the amazing announcement. Without having a tinge of cruelty in his singular composition, he was undoubtedly callous from long over-stimulation. Yet, if his emotions were dulled, his intellectual perceptions were exceedingly active. There was no trace then of the horror which I had myself felt at this curt declaration, but his face showed rather the quiet and interested composure of the chemist who sees the crystals falling into position from his over-saturated solution.

'Remarkable!' said he; 'remarkable!'

'You don't seem surprised.'

'Interested, Mr Mac, but hardly surprised. Why should I be surprised? I receive an anonymous communication from a quarter which I know to be important, warning me that danger threatens a certain person. Within an hour I learn that this danger has actually materialized, and that the person is dead. I am interested, but, as you observe, I am not surprised.'

In a few short sentences he explained to the inspector the facts about the letter and the cipher. MacDonald sat with his chin on his hands, and his great sandy eyebrows bunched into a yellow tangle.

'I was going down to Birlstone this morning,' said he. 'I had come to ask you if you cared to come with me—you and your friend here. But from what you say we might perhaps be doing better work in London.'

'I rather think not,' said Holmes.

'Hang it all, Mr Holmes!' cried the inspector. 'The papers will be full of the Birlstone Mystery in a day or two, but

14

where's the mystery if there is a man in London who prophesied the crime before ever it occurred? We have only to lay our hands on that man and the rest will follow.'

'No doubt, Mr Mac. But how did you propose to lay your hands on the so-called Porlock?'

MacDonald turned over the letter which Holmes had handed him.

'Posted in Camberwell—that doesn't help us much. Name, you say, is assumed. Not much to go on, certainly. Didn't you say that you have sent him money?'

'Twice.'

'And how?'

'In notes to Camberwell post-office.'

'Did you never trouble to see who called for them?'

'No.'

The inspector looked surprised and a little shocked.

'Why not?'

'Because I always keep faith. I had promised when he first wrote that I would not try to trace him.'

'You think there is some one behind him?'

'I *know* there is.'

'This Professor that I have heard you mention?'

'Exactly.'

Inspector MacDonald smiled, and his eyelid quivered as he glanced towards me.

'I won't conceal from you, Mr Holmes, that we think in the CID that you have a wee bit of a bee in your bonnet* over this Professor. I made some inquiries myself about the matter. He seems to be a very respectable, learned, and talented sort of man.'

'I'm glad you've got as far as to recognize the talent.'

'Man, you can't but recognize it. After I heard your view, I made it my business to see him. I had a chat with him on eclipses—how the talk got that way I canna think—but he had out a reflector lantern and a globe and made it all clear in a minute. He lent me a book, but I don't mind saying that it was a bit above my head, though I had a good Aberdeen upbringing. He'd have made a grand meenister,* with his thin face and grey hair and solemn-like way of talking. When he put his hand on my shoulder as we were parting, it was like a father's blessing before you go out into the cold, cruel world.'

Holmes chuckled and rubbed his hands.

'Great!' he cried; 'great! Tell me, friend MacDonald; this pleasing and touching interview was, I suppose, in the Professor's study?'

'That's so.'

'A fine room, is it not?'

'Very fine—very handsome indeed, Mr Holmes.'

'You sat in front of his writing-desk?'

'Just so.'

'Sun in your eyes and his face in the shadow?'

'Well, it was evening, but I mind that the lamp was turned on my face.'

'It would be. Did you happen to observe a picture over the Professor's head?'

'I don't miss much, Mr Holmes. Maybe I learned that from you. Yes, I saw the picture—a young woman with her head on her hands, keeking at you sideways.'*

'That painting was by Jean Baptiste Greuze.'*

The inspector endeavoured to look interested.

'Jean Baptiste Greuze', Holmes continued, joining his fingertips and leaning well back in his chair, 'was a French artist who flourished between the years 1750 and 1800. I allude, of course, to his working career. Modern criticism has more than endorsed the high opinion formed of him by his contemporaries.'

The inspector's eyes grew abstracted.

'Hadn't we better—' he said.

'We are doing so,' Holmes interrupted. 'All that I am saying has a very direct and vital bearing upon what you have called the Birlstone Mystery. In fact, it may in a sense be called the very centre of it.'

MacDonald smiled feebly, and looked appealingly to me.

'Your thoughts move a bit too quick for me, Mr Holmes. You leave out a link or two, and I can't get over the gap.

What in the whole wide world can be the connection between this dead painting man and the affair at Birlstone?'

'All knowledge comes useful to the detective,' remarked Holmes. 'Even the trivial fact that in the year 1865 a picture by Greuze, entitled "La Jeune Fille à l'agneau", fetched not less than four thousand pounds*—at the Portalis sale—may start a train of reflection in your mind.'

It was clear that it did. The inspector looked honestly interested.

'I may remind you,' Holmes continued, 'that the Professor's salary can be ascertained in several trustworthy books of reference. It is seven hundred a year.'*

'Then how could he buy—'

'Quite so. How could he?'

'Aye, that's remarkable,' said the inspector, thoughtfully. 'Talk away, Mr Holmes. I'm just loving it. It's fine.'

Holmes smiled. He was always warmed by genuine admiration—the characteristic of the real artist.

'What about Birlstone?' he asked.

'We've time yet,' said the inspector, glancing at his watch. 'I've a cab at the door, and it won't take us twenty minutes to Victoria. But about this picture—I thought you told me once, Mr Holmes, that you had never met Professor Moriarty.'

'No, I never have.'

'Then how do you know about his rooms?'

'Ah, that's another matter. I have been three times in his rooms, twice waiting for him under different pretexts and leaving before he came. Once—well, I can hardly tell about the once to an official detective. It was on the last occasion that I took the liberty of running over his papers, with the most unexpected results.'

'You found something compromising?'

'Absolutely nothing. That was what amazed me. However, you have now seen the point of the picture. It shows him to be a very wealthy man. How did he acquire wealth? He is unmarried. His younger brother is a station-master* in the West of England. His chair is worth seven hundred a year. And he owns a Greuze.'

17

'Well?'

'Surely the inference is plain.'

'You mean that he has a great income, and that he must earn it in an illegal fashion?'

'Exactly. Of course, I have other reasons for thinking so—dozens of exiguous threads which lead vaguely up towards the centre of the web where the poisonous motionless creature is lurking. I only mention the Greuze because it brings the matter within the range of your own observation.'

'Well, Mr Holmes, I admit that what you say is interesting. It's more than interesting—it's just wonderful. But let us have it a little clearer if you can. Is it forgery, coining, burglary? Where does the money come from?'

'Have you ever read of Jonathan Wild?'

'Well, the name has a familiar sound. Some one in a novel, was he not? I don't take much stock of detectives in novels—chaps that do things and never let you see how they do them. That's just inspiration, not business.'

'Jonathan Wild wasn't a detective, and he wasn't in a novel.* He was a master criminal, and he lived last century—1750 or thereabouts.'

'Then he's no use to me. I'm a practical man.'

'Mr Mac, the most practical thing that ever you did in your life would be to shut yourself up for three months and read twelve hours a day at the annals of crime. Everything comes in circles, even Professor Moriarty. Jonathan Wild was the hidden force of the London criminals, to whom he sold his brains and his organization on a fifteen per cent commission. The old wheel turns* and the same spoke comes up. It's all been done before and will be again. I'll tell you one or two things about Moriarty which may interest you.'

'You'll interest me right enough.'

'I happen to know who is the first link in his chain—a chain with this Napoleon-gone-wrong at one end and a hundred broken fighting men, pickpockets, blackmailers, and card-sharpers at the other, with every sort of crime in between. His chief of the staff is Colonel Sebastian Moran,* as aloof and guarded and inaccessible to the law as himself. What do you think he pays him?'

'I'd like to hear.'

'Six thousand a year. That's paying for brains, you see—the American business principle. I learned that detail quite by chance. It's more than the Prime Minister gets.* That gives you an idea of Moriarty's gains and of the scale on which he works. Another point. I made it my business to hunt down some of Moriarty's cheques lately—just common innocent cheques that he pays his household bills with. They were drawn on six different banks. Does that make any impression on your mind?'

'Queer, certainly. But what do you gather from it?'

'That he wanted no gossip about his wealth. No single man should know what he had. I have no doubt that he has twenty banking accounts—the bulk of his fortune abroad in the Deutsche Bank or the Crédit Lyonnais as likely as not. Some time when you have a year or two to spare I commend to you the study of Professor Moriarty.'

Inspector MacDonald had grown steadily more impressed as the conversation proceeded. He had lost himself in his interest. Now his practical Scotch intelligence brought him back with a snap to the matter in hand.

'He can keep, anyhow,' said he. 'You've got us side-tracked with your interesting anecdotes, Mr Holmes. What really counts is your remark that there is some connection between the Professor and the crime. That you get from the warning received through the man Porlock. Can we for our present practical needs get any farther than that?'

'We may form some conception as to the motives of the crime. It is, as I gather from your original remarks, an inexplicable, or at least an unexplained, murder. Now, presuming that the source of the crime is as we suspect it to be, there might be two different motives. In the first place, I may tell you that Moriarty rules with a rod of iron over his people. His discipline is tremendous. There is only one punishment in his code. It is death. Now, we might suppose that this murdered man—this Douglas, whose approaching

fate was known by one of the arch-criminal's subordinates—
had in some way betrayed the chief. His punishment followed and would be known to all, if only to put the fear of
death into them.

'Well, that is one suggestion, Mr Holmes.'

'The other is that it has been engineered by Moriarty in
the ordinary course of business. Was there any robbery?'

'I have not heard.'

'If so it would, of course, be against the first hypothesis
and in favour of the second. Moriarty may have been
engaged to engineer it on a promise of part spoils, or he may
have been paid so much down to manage it. Either is
possible. But, whichever it may be, or if it is some third
combination, it is down at Birlstone that we must seek the
solution. I know our man too well to suppose that he has left
anything up here which may lead us to him.'

'Then to Birlstone we must go!' cried MacDonald, jump-
ing from his chair. 'My word! it's later than I thought. I can
give you gentlemen five minutes for preparation, and that is
all.'

'And ample for us both,' said Holmes, as he sprang up
and hastened to change from his dressing-gown to his coat.
'While we are on our way, Mr Mac, I will ask you to be
good enough to tell me all about it.'

'All about it' proved to be disappointingly little, and yet
there was enough to assure us that the case before us might
well be worthy of the expert's closest attention. He brightened and rubbed his thin hands together as he listened to
the meagre but remarkable details. A long series of sterile
weeks* lay behind us, and here, at last, there was a fitting
object for those remarkable powers which, like all special
gifts, become irksome to their owner when they are not in use.
That razor brain blunted and rusted with inaction. Sherlock
Holmes's eyes glistened, his pale cheeks took a warmer hue,
and his whole eager face shone with an inward light when
the call for work reached him. Leaning forward in the cab,
he listened intently to MacDonald's short sketch of the
problem which awaited us in Sussex. The inspector was

himself dependent, as he explained to us, upon a scribbled account forwarded to him by the milk train in the early hours of the morning. White Mason,* the local officer, was a personal friend, and hence MacDonald had been notified very much more promptly than is usual at Scotland Yard when provincials need their assistance. It is a very cold scent upon which the Metropolitan expert is generally asked to run.

'Dear Inspector MacDonald,' said the letter which he read to us, 'official requisition for your services is in separate envelope. This is for your private eye. Wire me what train in the morning you can get for Birlstone, and I will meet it—or have it met if I am too occupied. This case is a snorter. Don't waste a moment in getting started. If you can bring Mr Holmes, please do so, for he will find something after his own heart. You would think the whole thing had been fixed up for theatrical effect, if there wasn't a dead man in the middle of it. My word, it *is* a snorter!'

'Your friend seems to be no fool,'* remarked Holmes.

'No sir; White Mason is a very live man, if I am any judge.'

'Well, have you anything more?'

'Only that he will give us every detail when we meet.'

'Then how did you get at Mr Douglas and the fact that he had been horribly murdered?'

'That was in the enclosed official report. It didn't say "horrible". That's not a recognized official term.* It gave the name John Douglas. It mentioned that his injuries had been in the head, from the discharge of a shot-gun. It also mentioned the hour of the alarm, which was close on to midnight last night. It added that the case was undoubtedly one of murder, but that no arrest had been made, and that the case was one which presented some very perplexing and extraordinary features. That's absolutely all we have at present, Mr Holmes.'

'Then, with your permission, we will leave it at that, Mr Mac. The temptation to form premature theories upon insufficient data is the bane of our profession. I can only see two things for certain at present: a great brain in London and a dead man in Sussex. It's the chain between that we are going to trace.'

· CHAPTER 3 ·

The Tragedy of Birlstone

AND now for a moment I will ask leave to remove my own insignificant personality* and to describe events which occured before we arrived upon the scene by the light of knowledge which came to us afterwards. Only in this way can I make the reader appreciate the people concerned and the strange setting in which their fate was cast.

The village of Birlstone is a small and very ancient cluster of half-timbered cottages on the northern border of the country of Sussex. For centuries it had remained unchanged, but within the last few years its picturesque appearance and situation have attracted a number of well-to-do residents, whose villas peep out from the woods around. These woods are locally supposed to be the extreme fringe of the great Weald forest, which thins away until it reaches the northern chalk downs. A number of small shops have come into being to meet the wants of the increased population, so that there seems some prospect that Birlstone may soon grow from an ancient village into a modern town. It is the centre for a considerable area of country, since Tunbridge Wells, the nearest place of importance, is ten or twelve miles to the eastward,* over the borders of Kent.

About half a mile from the town, standing in an old park famous for its huge beech trees, is the ancient Manor House of Birlstone. Part of this venerable building dates back to the time of the first Crusade,* when Hugo de Capus* built a fortalice in the centre of the estate, which had been granted to him by the Red King.* This was destroyed by fire in 1543,

22

and some of its smoke-blackened corner-stones were used when, in Jacobean times, a brick country house rose upon the ruins of the feudal castle. The Manor House, with its many gables and its small, diamond-paned windows, was still much as the builder had left it in the early seventeenth century. Of the double moats which had guarded its more warlike predecessor the outer had been allowed to dry up, and served the humble function of a kitchen garden. The inner one was still there, and lay, forty feet in breadth, though now only a few feet in depth, round the whole house. A small stream fed it and continued beyond it, so that the sheet of water, though turbid, was never ditch-like or unhealthy. The groundfloor windows were within a foot of the surface of the water. The only approach to the house was over a drawbridge, the chains and windlass of which had long been rusted and broken. The latest tenants of the Manor House had, however, with characteristic energy, set this right, and the drawbridge was not only capable of being raised, but actually was raised every evening and lowered every morning. By thus renewing the custom of the old feudal days the Manor House was converted into an island during the night—a fact which had a very direct bearing upon the mystery which was soon to engage the attention of all England.

The house had been untenanted for some years, and was threatening to moulder into a picturesque decay when the Douglases took possession of it. This family consisted of only two individuals, John Douglas and his wife. Douglas was a remarkable man both in character and in person; in age he may have been about fifty, with a strong-jawed, rugged face, a grizzling moustache, peculiarly keen grey eyes, and a wiry, vigorous figure which had lost nothing of the strength and activity of youth. He was cheery and genial to all, but somewhat offhand in his manners, giving the impression that he had seen life in social strata on some far lower horizon* than the county society of Sussex. Yet, though looked at with some curiosity and reserve by his more cultivated neighbours, he soon acquired a great popularity among the villagers, subscribing handsomely to all local objects, and attending their smoking concerts and other functions, where, having a remarkably rich tenor voice, he was always ready to oblige with an excellent song.* He appeared to have plenty of money, which was said to have been gained in the Californian gold-fields, and it was clear from his own talk and that of his wife that he had spent a part of his life in America. The good impression which had been produced by his generosity and by his democratic manners was increased by a reputation gained for utter indifference to danger. Though a wretched rider, he turned out at every meet, and took the most amazing falls in his determination to hold his own with the best. When the vicarage caught fire he distinguished himself also by the fearlessness with which he re-entered the building to save property, after the local fire brigade had given it up as impossible. Thus it came about that John Douglas, of the Manor House, had within five years won himself quite a reputation in Birlstone.

His wife, too, was popular with those who had made her acquaintance, though, after the English fashion,* the callers upon a stranger who settled in the county without introductions were few and far between. This mattered less to her as she was retiring by disposition and very much absorbed, to all appearance, in her husband and her domestic duties. It was known that she was an English lady who had met Mr Douglas in London, he being at that time a widower. She was a beautiful woman, tall, dark, and slender, some twenty years younger than her husband, a disparity which seemed in no wise to mar the contentment of their family life. It was remarked sometimes, however, by those who knew them best that the confidence between the two did not appear to be complete, since the wife was either very reticent about her husband's past life or else, as seemed more likely, was very imperfectly informed about it. It had also been noted and commented upon by a few observant people that there were signs sometimes of some nerve-strain upon the part of Mrs Douglas, and that she would display acute uneasiness if her absent husband should ever be particularly late in his return.

On a quiet countryside, where all gossip is welcome, this weakness of the lady of the Manor House did not pass without remark, and it bulked larger upon people's memory when the events arose which gave it a very special significance.

There was yet another individual whose residence under that roof was, it is true, only an intermittent one, but whose presence at the time of the strange happenings which will now be narrated brought his name prominently before the public. This was Cecil James Barker, of Hales Lodge, Hampstead. Cecil Barker's tall, loose-jointed figure was a familiar one in the main street of Birlstone village, for he was a frequent and welcome visitor at the Manor House. He was the more noticed as being the only friend of the past unknown life of Mr Douglas who was ever seen in his new English surroundings. Barker was himself an undoubted Englishman, but by his remarks it was clear that he had first known Douglas in America, and had there lived on intimate terms with him. He appeared to be a man of considerable wealth, and was reputed to be a bachelor. In age he was rather younger than Douglas, forty-five at the most, a tall, straight, broad-chested fellow, with a clean-shaven, prize-fighter face, thick, strong, black eyebrows, and a pair of masterful black eyes which might, even without the aid of his very capable hands, clear a way for him through a hostile crowd. He neither rode nor shot, but spent his days in wandering round the old village with his pipe in his mouth, or in driving with his host, or in his absence with his hostess, over the beautiful countryside. 'An easy-going, free-handed gentleman,' said Ames, the butler. 'But, my word, I had rather not be the man that crossed him.' He was cordial and intimate with Douglas, and he was no less friendly with his wife, a friendship which more than once seemed to cause some irritation to the husband, so that even the servants were able to perceive his annoyance. Such was the third person who was one of the family when the catastrophe occurred. As to the other denizens of the old building, it will suffice out of a large household to mention the prim, respectable, and capable Ames and Mrs Allen, a buxom and cheerful person, who relieved the lady of some of her household cares. The other six servants in the house bear no relation to the events of the night of January 6th.

It was at eleven forty-five that the first alarm reached the small local police-station in the charge of Sergeant Wilson, of the Sussex Constabulary. Mr Cecil Barker, much excited, had rushed up to the door and pealed furiously upon the bell. A terrible tragedy had occurred at the Manor House, and Mr John Douglas had been murdered. That was the breathless burden of his message. He had hurried back to the house, followed within a few minutes by the police-sergeant, who arrived at the scene of the crime a little past twelve o'clock, after taking prompt steps to warn the county authorities that something serious was afoot.

On reaching the Manor House the sergeant had found the drawbridge down, the windows lighted up, and the whole household in a state of wild confusion and alarm. The white-faced servants were huddling together in the hall, with the frightened butler wringing his hands in the doorway. Only Cecil Barker seemed to be master of himself and his emotions. He had opened the door which was nearest to the entrance, and had beckoned to the sergeant to follow him. At that moment there arrived Dr Wood,* a brisk and capable general practitioner from the village. The three men entered the fatal room together, while the horror-stricken butler followed at their heels, closing the door behind him to shut out the terrible scene from the maid-servants.

The dead man lay upon his back, sprawling with out-stretched limbs in the centre of the room. He was clad only in a pink dressing-gown, which covered his night clothes. There were carpet slippers upon his bare feet. The doctor knelt beside him, and held down the hand-lamp which had stood on the table. One glance at the victim was enough to show the healer that his presence could be dispensed with. The man had been horribly injured. Lying across his chest was a curious weapon, a shot-gun with the barrel sawn off a foot in front of the triggers. It was clear that this had been fired at close range, and that he had received the whole charge in the face, blowing his head almost to pieces. The triggers had been wired together, so as to make the simultaneous discharge more destructive.

The country policeman was unnerved and troubled by the tremendous responsibility which had come so suddenly upon him.

'We will touch nothing until my superiors arrive,' he said, in a hushed voice, staring in horror at the dreadful head.

'Nothing has been touched up to now,' said Cecil Barker. 'I'll answer for that. You see it all exactly as I found it.'

'When was that?' The sergeant had drawn out his notebook.

'It was just half-past eleven. I had not begun to undress, and I was sitting by the fire in my bedroom, when I heard the report. It was not very loud—it seemed to be muffled. I rushed down. I don't suppose it was thirty seconds before I was in the room.'

'Was the door open?'

'Yes, it was open. Poor Douglas was lying as you see him. His bedroom candle was burning on the table. It was I who lit the lamp some minutes afterwards.'

'Did you see no one?'

'No. I heard Mrs Douglas coming down the stair behind me, and I rushed out to prevent her from seeing this dreadful sight. Mrs Allen, the housekeeper, came and took her away. Ames had arrived, and we ran back into the room once more.'

'But surely I have heard that the drawbridge is kept up all night.'

'Yes, it was up until I lowered it.'

'Then how could any murderer have got away? It is out of the question. Mr Douglas must have shot himself.'

'That was our first idea. But see.' Barker drew aside the curtain, and showed that the long, diamond-paned window was open to its full extent. 'And look at this!' He held the lamp down and illuminated a smudge of blood like the mark of a boot-sole upon the wooden sill. 'Some one has stood there in getting out.'

'You mean that some one waded across the moat?'

'Exactly.'

'Then, if you were in the room within half a minute of the crime, he must have been in the water at that very moment.'

'I have not a doubt of it. I wish to Heaven that I had rushed to the window. But the curtain screened it, as you can see, and so it never occurred to me. Then I heard the step of Mrs Douglas, and I could not let her enter the room. It would have been too horrible.'

'Horrible enough!' said the doctor, looking at the shattered head and the terrible marks which surrounded it. 'I've never seen such injuries since the Birlstone railway smash.'

'But, I say,' remarked the police-sergeant, whose slow, bucolic common sense was still pondering over the open window. 'It's all very well your saying that a man escaped by wading this moat, but what I ask you is—how did he ever get into the house at all if the bridge was up?'

'Ah, that's the question,' said Barker.

'At what o'clock was it raised?'

'It was nearly six o'clock,' said Ames, the butler.

'I've heard,' said the sergeant, 'that it was usually raised at sunset. That would be nearer half-past four than six at this time of year.'

'Mrs Douglas had visitors to tea,' said Ames. 'I couldn't raise it until they went. Then I wound it up myself.'

'Then it comes to this,' said the sergeant. 'If anyone came from outside—*if* they did—they must have got in across the bridge before six and been in hiding ever since, until Mr Douglas came into the room after eleven.'

'That is so. Mr Douglas went round the house every night the last thing before he turned in to see that the lights were right. That brought him in here. The man was waiting, and shot him. Then he got away through the window and left his gun behind him. That's how I read it—for nothing else will fit the facts.'

The sergeant picked up a card which lay beside the dead man upon the floor. The initials V.V., and under it the number 341, were rudely scrawled in ink upon it.

'What's this?' he asked, holding it up.

Barker looked at it with curiosity.

'I never noticed it before,' he said. 'The murderer must have left it behind him.'

' "V.V. 341." I can make no sense of that.'

The sergeant kept turning it over in his big fingers.

'What's V.V.? Somebody's initials, maybe. What have you got there, Dr Wood?'

It was a good-sized hammer which had been lying upon the rug in front of the fireplace—a substantial, workmanlike hammer. Cecil Barker pointed to a box of brass-headed nails upon the mantelpiece.

'Mr Douglas was altering the pictures yesterday,' he said. 'I saw him myself standing upon that chair and fixing the big picture above it. That accounts for the hammer.'

'We'd best put it back on the rug where we found it,' said the sergeant, scratching his puzzled head in his perplexity. 'It will want the best brains in the force to get to the bottom of this thing. It will be a London job before it is finished.' He raised the hand-lamp and walked slowly round the room. 'Hullo!' he cried, excitedly, drawing the window curtain to one side. 'What o'clock were those curtains drawn?'

'When the lamps were lit,' said the butler. 'It would be shortly after four.'

'Some one has been hiding here, sure enough.' He held down the light, and the marks of muddy boots were very visible in the corner. 'I'm bound to say this bears out your theory, Mr Barker. It looks as if the man got into the house after four, when the curtains were drawn, and before six, when the bridge was raised. He slipped into this room because it was the first that he saw. There was no other place where he could hide, so he popped in behind this curtain. That all seems clear enough. It is likely that his main idea was to burgle the house, but Mr Douglas chanced to come upon him, so he murdered him and escaped.'

'That's how I read it,' said Barker. 'But, I say, aren't we wasting precious time? Couldn't we start out and scour the country before the fellow gets away?'

The sergeant considered for a moment.

'There are no trains before six in the morning, so he can't get away by rail. If he goes by road with his legs all dripping, it's odds that some one will notice him. Anyhow, I can't leave here myself until I am relieved. But I think none of you should go until we see more clearly how we all stand.'

The doctor had taken the lamp and was narrowly scrutinizing the body.

'What's this mark?' he asked. 'Could this have any connection with the crime?'

The dead man's right arm was thrust out from his dressing-gown and exposed as high as the elbow. About halfway up the forearm was a curious brown design, a triangle inside a circle, standing out in vivid relief upon the lard-coloured skin.

'It's not tattooed,' said the doctor, peering through his glasses. 'I never saw anything like it. The man has been branded at some time, as they brand cattle.* What is the meaning of this?'

'I don't profess to know the meaning of it,' said Cecil Barker; 'but I've seen the mark on Douglas any time this last ten years.'

'And so have I,' said the butler. 'Many a time when the master has rolled up his sleeves I have noticed that very mark. I've often wondered what it could be.'

'Then it has nothing to do with the crime, anyhow,' said the sergeant. 'But it's a rum thing all the same. Everything about this case is rum. Well, what is it now?'

The butler had given an exclamation of astonishment, and was pointing at the dead man's outstretched hand.

'They've taken his wedding-ring!' he gasped.

'What!'

'Yes, indeed! Master always wore his plain gold wedding-ring on the little finger of his left hand.* That ring with the rough nugget on it was above it, and the twisted snake-ring on the third finger. There's the nugget, and there's the snake, but the wedding-ring is gone.'

'He's right,' said Barker.

'Do you tell me,' said the sergeant, 'that the wedding-ring was *below* the other?'

'Always!'

'Then the murderer, or whoever it was, first took off this ring you call the nugget-ring, then the wedding-ring, and afterwards put the nugget-ring back again.'

'That is so.'

The worthy country policeman shook his head.

'Seems to me the sooner we get London on to this case the better,' said he. 'White Mason is a smart man. No local job has ever been too much for White Mason. It won't be long now before he is here to help us. But I expect we'll have to look to London before we are through. Anyhow, I'm not ashamed to say that it is a deal too thick for the likes of me.'

· CHAPTER 4 ·

Darkness

AT three in the morning the chief Sussex detective, obeying the urgent call from Sergeant Wilson, of Birlstone, arrived from headquarters in a light dog-cart behind a breathless trotter. By the five-forty train in the morning he had sent his message to Scotland Yard, and he was at the Birlstone station at twelve o'clock to welcome us. Mr White Mason was a quiet, comfortable-looking person, in a loose tweed suit, with a clean-shaven, ruddy face, a stoutish body, and powerful bandy legs adorned with gaiters, looking like a small farmer, a retired gamekeeper, or anything upon earth except a very favourable specimen of the provincial criminal officer.

'A real downright snorter, Mr MacDonald,' he kept repeating. 'We'll have the pressmen down like flies when they understand it. I'm hoping we will get our work done before they get poking their noses into it and messing up all the trails. There has been nothing like this that I can remember. There are some bits that will come home to you, Mr Holmes, or I am mistaken. And you also, Dr Watson, for the medicos will have a word to say before we finish. Your room is at the Westville Arms. There's no other place, but I hear that it is clean and good. The man will carry your bags. This way, gentlemen, if *you* please.'

He was a very bustling and genial person, this Sussex detective. In ten minutes we had all found our quarters. In ten more we were seated in the parlour of the inn and being treated to a rapid sketch of those events which have been outlined in the previous chapter. MacDonald made an occasional note, while Holmes sat absorbed with the expression of surprised and reverent admiration with which the botanist* surveys the rare and precious bloom.

'Remarkable!' he said, when the story was unfolded. 'Most remarkable! I can hardly recall any case where the features have been more peculiar.'

'I thought you would say so, Mr Holmes,' said White Mason, in great delight. 'We're well up with the times in Sussex. I've told you now how matters were, up to the time when I took over from Sergeant Wilson between three and four this morning. My word, I made the old mare go! But I need not have been in such a hurry as it turned out, for there was nothing immediate that I could do. Sergeant Wilson had all the facts. I checked them and considered them, and maybe added a few on my own.'

'What were they?' asked Holmes, eagerly.

'Well, I first had the hammer examined. There was Dr Wood there to help me. We found no signs of violence upon it. I was hoping that, if Mr Douglas defended himself with the hammer, he might have left his mark upon the murderer before he dropped it on the mat. But there was no stain.'

'That, of course, proves nothing at all,' remarked Inspector MacDonald. 'There has been many a hammer murder and no trace on the hammer.'

'Quite so. It doesn't prove it wasn't used. But there might have been stains, and that would have helped us. As a matter of fact, there were none. Then I examined the gun. They were buck-shot cartridges, and, as Sergeant Wilson pointed out, the triggers were wired together so that if you pulled on the hinder one both barrels were discharged. Whoever fixed that up had made up his mind that he was going to take no chances of missing his man. The sawn gun was not more than two feet long; one could carry it easily under one's coat. There was no complete maker's name, but the printed letters "P E N" were on the fluting between the barrels, and the rest of the name had been cut off by the saw.'

'A big "P" with a flourish above it—"E" and "N" smaller?' asked Holmes.

'Exactly.'

'Pennsylvania Small Arm Company*—well-known American firm,' said Holmes.

White Mason gazed at my friend as the little village practitioner looks at the Harley Street specialist who by a word can solve the difficulties that perplex him.

'That is very helpful, Mr Holmes. No doubt you are right. Wonderful—wonderful! Do you carry the names of all the gunmakers in the world in your memory?'

Holmes dismissed the subject with a wave.

'No doubt it is an American shot-gun,' White Mason continued. 'I seem to have read that a sawed-off shot-gun is a weapon used in some parts of America. Apart from the name upon the barrel, the idea had occurred to me. There is some evidence, then, that this man who entered the house and killed its master was an American.'

MacDonald shook his head. 'Man, you are surely travelling over-fast,' said he. 'I have heard no evidence yet that any stranger was ever in the house at all.'

'The open window, the blood on the sill, the queer card, marks of boots in the corner, the gun.'

'Nothing there that could not have been arranged. Mr Douglas was an American, or had lived long in America. So had Mr Barker. You don't need to import an American from outside in order to account for American doings.'

'Ames, the butler—'

'What about him? Is he reliable?'

'Ten years with Sir Charles Chandos—as solid as a rock. He has been with Douglas ever since he took the Manor House five years ago. He has never seen a gun of this sort in the house.'

'The gun was made to conceal. That's why the barrels were sawn. It would fit into any box. How could he swear there was no such gun in the house?'

'Well, anyhow he had never seen one.'

MacDonald shook his obstinate Scotch head. 'I'm not convinced yet that there was ever anyone in the house,' said he. 'I'm asking you to conseedar'—his accent became more Aberdonian as he lost himself in his argument—'I'm asking you to conseedar what it involves if you suppose that this gun was ever brought into the house and that all these strange things were done by a person from outside. Oh, man, it's just inconceivable! It's clean against common sense. I put it to you, Mr Holmes, judging it by what we have heard.'

'Well, state your case, Mr Mac,' said Holmes, in his most judicial style.

'The man is not a burglar, supposing that he ever existed. The ring business and the card point to premeditated murder for some private reason. Very good. Here is a man who slips into a house with the deliberate intention of committing murder. He knows, if he knows anything, that he will have a deeficulty in making his escape, as the house is surrounded with water. What weapon would he choose? You would say the most silent in the world. Then he could hope, when the deed was done, to slip quickly from the window, to wade the moat, and to get away at his leisure. That's understandable. But is it understandable that he should go out of his way to bring with him the most noisy weapon he could select, knowing well that it will fetch every human being in the house to the spot as quick as they can

34

run, and that it is all odds that he will be seen before he can get across the moat?* Is that credible, Mr Holmes?'

'Well, you put your case strongly,' my friend replied, thoughtfully. 'It certainly needs a good deal of justification. May I ask, Mr White Mason, whether you examined the farther side of the moat at once, to see if there were any signs of the man having climbed out from the water?'

'There were no signs, Mr Holmes. But it is a stone ledge, and one could hardly expect them.'

'No tracks or marks?'

'None.'

'Ha! Would there be any objection, Mr White Mason, to our going down to the house at once? There may possibly be some small point which might be suggestive.'

'I was going to propose it, Mr Holmes, but I thought it well to put you in touch with all the facts before we go. I suppose, if anything should strike you—' White Mason looked doubtfully at the amateur.

'I have worked with Mr Holmes before,' said Inspector MacDonald. 'He plays the game.'

'My own idea of the game, at any rate,' said Holmes, with a smile. 'I go into a case to help the ends of justice and the work of the police. If ever I have separated myself from the official force, it is because they have first separated themselves from me. I have no wish ever to score at their expense. At the same time, Mr White Mason, I claim the right to work in my own way and give my results at my own time—complete, rather than in stages.'

'I am sure we are honoured by your presence and to show you all we know,' said White Mason, cordially. 'Come along, Dr Watson, and when the time comes we'll all hope for a place in your book.'*

We walked down the quaint village street* with a row of pollarded elms on either side of it. Just beyond were two ancient stone pillars, weather-stained and lichen-blotched, bearing upon their summits a shapeless something which had once been the ramping lion of Capus of Birlstone. A short walk along the winding drive, with such sward and oaks around it as one only sees in rural England; then a sudden turn, and the long, low, Jacobean house of dingy, liver-coloured brick lay before us, with an old-fashioned garden of cut yews on either side of it.* As we approached it there were the wooden drawbridge and the beautiful broad moat, as still and luminous as quicksilver in the cold winter sunshine. Three centuries had flowed past the old Manor House, centuries of births and home-comings, of country dances and of the meetings of fox-hunters. Strange that now in its old age this dark business should have cast its shadow upon the venerable walls. And yet those strange peaked roofs and quaint overhung gables were a fitting covering to grim and terrible intrigue. As I looked at the deep-set windows and the long sweep of the dull-coloured, water-lapped front I felt that no more fitting scene could be set for such a tragedy.

'That's the window,' said White Mason: 'that one on the immediate right of the drawbridge. It's open just as it was found last night.'

'It looks rather narrow for a man to pass.'

'Well, it wasn't a fat man, anyhow. We don't need your deductions, Mr Holmes, to tell us that. But you or I could squeeze through all right.'

Holmes walked to the edge of the moat and looked across. Then he examined the stone ledge and the grass border beyond it.

'I've had a good look, Mr Holmes,' said White Mason. 'There is nothing there; no sign that anyone has landed. But why should he leave any sign?'

'Exactly. Why should he? Is the water always turbid?'

'Generally about this colour. The stream brings down the clay.'

'How deep is it?'

'About two feet at each side and three in the middle.'

'So we can put aside all idea of the man having been drowned in crossing?'

'No; a child could not be drowned in it.'

We walked across the drawbridge, and were admitted by a quaint, gnarled, dried-up person who was the butler—

Ames. The poor old fellow was white and quivering from the shock. The village sergeant, a tall, formal, melancholy man, still held his vigil in the room of fate. The doctor had departed.

'Anything fresh, Sergeant Wilson?' asked White Mason.

'No, sir.'

'Then you can go home. You've had enough. We can send for you if we want you. The butler had better wait outside. Tell him to warn Mr Cecil Barker, Mrs Douglas, and the housekeeper that we may want a word with them presently. Now, gentlemen, perhaps you will allow me to give you the views I have formed first, and then you will be able to arrive at your own.'

He impressed me, this country specialist. He had a solid grip of fact and a cool, clear, common-sense brain, which should take him some way in his profession. Holmes listened to him intently, with no sign of that impatience which the official exponent too often produced.

'Is it suicide or is it murder—that's our first question, gentlemen, is it not? If it were suicide, then we have to believe that this man began by taking off his wedding-ring and concealing it; that he then came down here in his dressing-gown, trampled mud into a corner behind the curtain in order to give the idea someone had waited for him, opened the window, put the blood on the—'

'We can surely dismiss that,' said MacDonald.

'So I think. Suicide is out of the question.* Then a murder has been done. What we have to determine is whether it was done by someone outside or inside the house.'

'Well, let's hear the argument.'

'There are considerable difficulties both ways, and yet one or the other it must be. We will suppose first that some person or persons inside the house did the crime. They got this man down here at a time when everything was still, and yet no one was asleep. They then did the deed with the queerest and noisiest weapon in the world, so as to tell every one what had happened—a weapon that was never seen in the house before. That does not seem a very likely start, does it?'

'No, it does not.'

'Well, then, everyone is agreed that after the alarm was given only a minute at the most had passed before the whole household—not Mr Cecil Barker alone, though he claims to have been the first, but Ames and all of them—were on the spot. Do you tell me that in that time the guilty person managed to make footmarks in the corner, open the window, mark the sill with blood, take the wedding-ring off the dead man's finger, and all the rest of it? It's impossible!'

'You put it very clearly,' said Holmes. 'I am inclined to agree with you.'

'Well, then, we are driven back to the theory that it was done by someone from outside. We are still faced with some big difficulties, but, anyhow, they have ceased to be impossibilities. The man got into the house between four-thirty and six—that is to say, between dusk and the time when the bridge was raised. There had been some visitors, and the door was open, so there was nothing to prevent him. He may have been a common burglar, or he may have had some private grudge against Mr Douglas. Since Mr Douglas has spent most of his life in America, and this shot-gun seems to be an American weapon, it would seem that the private grudge is the more likely theory. He slipped into this room because it was the first he came to, and he hid behind the curtain. There he remained until past eleven at night. At that time Mr Douglas entered the room. It was a short interview, if there were any interview at all, for Mrs Douglas declares that her husband had not left her more than a few minutes when she heard the shot.'

'The candle shows that,' said Holmes.

'Exactly. The candle, which was a new one, is not burned more than half an inch. He must have placed it on the table before he was attacked, otherwise, of course, it would have fallen when he fell. This shows that he was not attacked the instant that he entered the room. When Mr Barker arrived the lamp was lit and the candle put out.'

'That's all clear enough.'

'Well, now, we can reconstruct things on those lines. Mr Douglas enters the room. He puts down the candle. A man appears from behind the curtain. He is armed with this gun. He demands the wedding-ring—Heaven only knows why, but so it must have been. Mr Douglas gave it up. Then either in cold blood or in the course of a struggle—Douglas may have gripped the hammer that was found upon the mat—he shot Douglas in this horrible way. He dropped his gun and also, it would seem, this queer card, "V.V. 341", whatever that may mean, and he made his escape through the window and across the moat at the very moment when Cecil Barker was discovering the crime. How's that, Mr Holmes?'

'Very interesting, but just a little unconvincing.'

'Man, it would be absolute nonsense if it wasn't that anything else is even worse,' cried MacDonald. 'Somebody killed the man, and whoever it was I could clearly prove to you that he should have done it some other way. What does he mean by allowing his retreat to be cut off like that? What does he mean by using a shot-gun when silence was his one chance of escape? Come, Mr Holmes, it's up to you to give us a lead, since you say Mr White Mason's theory is un-convincing.'

Holmes had sat intently observant during this long discus-sion, missing no word that was said, with his keen eyes darting to right and to left, and his forehead wrinkled with speculation.

'I should like a few more facts before I get so far as a theory, Mr Mac,' said he, kneeling down beside the body. 'Dear me! these injuries are really appalling. Can we have the butler in for a moment? . . . Ames, I understand that you have often seen this very unusual mark, a branded triangle inside a circle, upon Mr Douglas's forearm?'

'Frequently, sir.'

'You never heard any speculation as to what it meant?'

'No, sir.'

'It must have caused great pain when it was inflicted. It is undoubtedly a burn. Now, I observe, Ames, that there is a small piece of plaster at the angle of Mr Douglas's jaw. Did you observe that in life?'

'Yes, sir; he cut himself in shaving yesterday morning.'

'Did you ever know him cut himself in shaving before?'

'Not for a very long time, sir.'

'Suggestive!' said Holmes. 'It may, of course, be a mere coincidence, or it may point to some nervousness which would indicate that he had reason to apprehend danger. Had you noticed anything unusual in his conduct yesterday, Ames?'

'It struck me that he was a little restless and excited, sir.'

'Ha! The attack may not have been entirely unexpected. We do seem to make a little progress, do we not? Perhaps you would rather do the questioning, Mr Mac?'

'No, Mr Holmes; it's in better hands.'

'Well, then, we will pass to this card—"V.V. 341". It is rough cardboard. Have you any of the sort in the house?'

'I don't think so.'

Holmes walked across to the desk and dabbed a little ink from each bottle on to the blotting-paper. 'It has not been printed in this room,' he said; 'this is black ink, and the other purplish. It has been done by a thick pen, and these are fine. No, it has been done elsewhere, I should say. Can you make anything of the inscription, Ames?'

'No, sir, nothing.'

'What do you think, Mr Mac?'

'It gives me the impression of a secret society of some sort. The same with this badge upon the forearm.'

'That's my idea, too,' said White Mason.

'Well, we can adopt it as a working hypothesis, and then see how far our difficulties disappear. An agent from such a society makes his way into the house, waits for Mr Douglas, blows his head nearly off with this weapon, and escapes by wading the moat, after leaving a card beside the dead man which will, when mentioned in the papers, tell other members of the society that vengeance has been done. That all hangs together. But why this gun, of all weapons?'

'Exactly.'

'And why the missing ring?'

'Quite so.'

'And why no arrest? It's past two now. I take it for granted that since dawn every constable within forty miles has been looking out for a wet stranger?'

'That is so, Mr Holmes.'

'Well, unless he has a burrow close by, or a change of clothes ready, they can hardly miss him. And yet they *have* missed him up to now.' Holmes had gone to the window and was examining with his lens the blood-mark upon the sill. 'It is clearly the tread of a shoe. It is remarkably broad—a splay foot, one would say. Curious, because, so far as one can trace any footmark in this mud-stained corner, one would say it was a more shapely sole. However, they are certainly very indistinct. What's this under the side-table?'

'Mr Douglas's dumb-bells,' said Ames.

'Dumb-bell—there's only one. Where's the other?'

'I don't know, Mr Holmes. There may have been only one. I have not noticed them for months.'

'One dumb-bell—' Holmes said, seriously, but his remarks were interrupted by a sharp knock at the door. A tall, sunburned, capable-looking, clean-shaven man looked in at us. I had no difficulty in guessing that it was the Cecil Barker of whom I had heard. His masterful eyes travelled quickly with a questioning glance from face to face.

'Sorry to interrupt your consultation,' said he, 'but you should hear the latest.'

'An arrest?'

'No such luck. But they've found his bicycle. The fellow left his bicycle behind him. Come and have a look. It is within a hundred yards of the hall door.'

We found three or four grooms and idlers standing in the drive inspecting a bicycle which had been drawn out from a clump of evergreens in which it had been concealed. It was a well-used Rudge-Whitworth, splashed as from a considerable journey. There was a saddle-bag with spanner and oil-can, but no clue as to the owner.

'It would be a grand help to the police,' said the inspector, 'if these things were numbered and registered. But we must be thankful for what we've got. If we can't find where he went to, at least we are likely to get where he came from. But what in the name of all that is wonderful made the fellow leave it behind? And how in the world has he got away without it? We don't seem to get a gleam of light in the case, Mr Holmes.'

'Don't we?' my friend answered, thoughtfully. 'I wonder!'

· CHAPTER 5 ·

The People of the Drama

'HAVE you seen all you want of the study?' asked White Mason as we re-entered the house.

'For the time,' said the inspector; and Holmes nodded.

'Then perhaps you would now like to hear the evidence of some of the people in the house? We could use the dining-room, Ames. Please come yourself first and tell us what you know.'

The butler's account was a simple and a clear one, and he gave a convincing impression of sincerity. He had been engaged five years ago when Mr Douglas first came to Birlstone. He understood that Mr Douglas was a rich gentleman who had made his money in America. He had been a kind and considerate employer—not quite what Ames was used to, perhaps, but one can't have everything. He never saw any signs of apprehension in Mr Douglas—on the contrary, he was the most fearless man he had ever known. He ordered the drawbridge to be pulled up every night because it was the ancient custom of the old house, and he liked to keep the old ways up. Mr Douglas seldom went to London or left the village, but on the day before the crime he had been shopping at Tunbridge Wells. He, Ames, had observed some restlessness and excitement on the part of Mr Douglas upon that day, for he had seemed impatient and irritable, which was unusual with him. He had not gone to bed that night, but was in the pantry at the back of the house, putting away the silver, when he heard the bell ring violently. He heard no shot, but it was hardly possible he should, as the pantry and kitchens were at the very back of the house and there were several closed doors and a long passage between. The housekeeper had come out of her room, attracted by the violent ringing of the bell. They had gone to the front of the house together. As they reached the bottom of the stair he had seen Mrs Douglas coming down it. No, she was not hurrying—it did not seem to him that she was particularly agitated. Just as she reached the bottom of the stair Mr Barker had rushed out of the study. He had stopped Mrs Douglas and begged her to go back.

'For God's sake, go back to your room!' he cried. 'Poor Jack is dead. You can do nothing. For God's sake, go back!'

After some persuasion upon the stairs Mrs Douglas had gone back. She did not scream. She made no outcry whatever. Mrs Allen, the housekeeper, had taken her upstairs and stayed with her in the bedroom. Ames and Mr Barker had then returned to the study, where they had found everything exactly as the police had seen it. The candle was not lit at that time, but the lamp was burning. They had looked out of the window, but the night was very dark and nothing could be seen or heard. They had then rushed out into the hall, where Ames had turned the windlass which had lowered the drawbridge. Mr Barker had then hurried off to get the police.

Such, in its essentials, was the evidence of the butler.

The account of Mrs Allen, the housekeeper, was, so far as it went, a corroboration of that of her fellow-servant. The housekeeper's room was rather nearer to the front of the house than the pantry in which Ames had been working. She was preparing to go to bed when the loud ringing of the bell had attracted her attention. She was a little hard of hearing. Perhaps that was why she had not heard the sound of the shot, but in any case the study was a long way off.

She remembered hearing some sound which she imagined to be the slamming of a door. That was a good deal earlier—half an hour at least before the ringing of the bell. When Mr Ames ran to the front she went with him. She saw Mr Barker, very pale and excited, come out of the study. He intercepted Mrs Douglas, who was coming down the stairs. He entreated her to go back, and she answered him, but what she said could not be heard.

'Take her up. Stay with her!' he had said to Mrs Allen.

She had therefore taken her to the bedroom and endeavoured to soothe her. She was greatly excited, trembling all over, but made no other attempt to go downstairs. She just sat in her dressing-gown by her bedroom fire with her head sunk in her hands. Mrs Allen stayed with her most of the night. As to the other servants, they had all gone to bed, and the alarm did not reach them until just before the police arrived. They slept at the extreme back of the house, and could not possibly have heard anything.

So far the housekeeper—who could add nothing on cross-examination save lamentations and expressions of amazement.

Mr Cecil Barker succeeded Mrs Allen as a witness. As to the occurrences of the night before, he had very little to add to what he had already told the police. Personally, he was convinced that the murderer had escaped by the window. The blood-stain was conclusive, in his opinion, upon that point. Besides, as the bridge was up there was no other possible way of escaping. He could not explain what had become of the assassin, or why he had not taken his bicycle, if it were indeed his. He could not possibly have been drowned in the moat, which was at no place more than three feet deep.

In his own mind he had a very definite theory about the murder. Douglas was a reticent man, and there were some chapters in his life of which he never spoke. He had emigrated to America from Ireland* when he was a very young man. He had prospered well, and Barker had first met him in California, where they had become partners in a success-

44

ful mining claim at a place called Benito Canyon.* They had done very well, but Douglas had suddenly sold out and started for England. He was a widower at that time. Barker had afterwards realized his money and come to live in London. Thus* they had renewed their friendship. Douglas had given him the impression that some danger was hanging over his head, and he had always looked upon his sudden departure from California, and also his renting a house in so quiet a place in England, as being connected with this peril. He imagined that some secret society, some implacable organization, was on Douglas's track which would never rest until it killed him. Some remarks of his had given him this idea, though he had never told him what the society was, nor how he had come to offend it. He could only suppose that the legend upon the placard had some reference to this secret society.

'How long were you with Douglas in California?' asked Inspector MacDonald.

'Five years altogether.'

'He was a bachelor, you say?'

'A widower.'

'Have you ever heard where his first wife came from?'

'No; I remember his saying that she was of German* extraction, and I have seen her portrait. She was a very beautiful woman. She died of typhoid the year before I met him.'

'You don't associate his past with any particular part of America?'

'I have heard him talk of Chicago. He knew that city well and had worked there. I have heard him talk of the coal and iron districts. He had travelled a good deal in his time.'

'Was he a politician? Had this secret society to do with politics?'

'No; he cared nothing about politics.'

'You have no reason to think it was criminal?'

'On the contrary, I never met a straighter man in my life.'

'Was there anything curious about his life in California?'

'He liked best to stay and to work at our claim in the mountains. He would never go where other men were if he could help it. That's why I first thought that someone was after him. Then when he left so suddenly for Europe I made sure that it was so. I believe that he had a warning of some sort. Within a week of his leaving half-a-dozen men were inquiring for him.'

'What sort of men?'

'Well, they were a mighty hard-looking crowd. They came up to the claim and wanted to know where he was. I told them that he was gone to Europe and that I did not know where to find him. They meant him no good—it was easy to see that.'

'Were these men Americans—Californians?'

'Well, I don't know about Californians. They were Americans all right. But they were not miners.* I don't know what they were, and was very glad to see their backs.'

'That was six years ago?'

'Nearer seven.'

'And then you were together five years in California, so that this business dates back not less than eleven years at the least?'

'That is so.'

'It must be a very serious feud that would be kept up with such earnestness for as long as that. It would be no light thing that would give rise to it.'

'I think it shadowed his whole life. It was never quite out of his mind.'

'But if a man had a danger hanging over him, and knew what it was, don't you think he would turn to the police for protection?'

'Maybe it was some danger that he could not be protected against. There's one thing you should know. He always went about armed. His revolver was never out of his pocket. But, by bad luck, he was in his dressing-gown and had left it in the bedroom last night. Once the bridge was up I guess he thought he was safe.'

'I should like these dates a little clearer,' said MacDonald. 'It is quite six years since Douglas left California. You followed him next year, did you not?'

46

'That is so.'

'And he has been married for five years. You must have returned about the time of his marriage.'

'About a month before. I was his best man.'

'Did you know Mrs Douglas before her marriage?'

'No, I did not. I had been away from England for ten years.'

'But you have seen a good deal of her since?'

Barker looked sternly at the detective.

'I have seen a good deal of *him* since,' he answered. 'If I have seen her, it is because you cannot visit a man without knowing his wife. If you imagine there is any connection—'

'I imagine nothing, Mr Barker. I am bound to make every inquiry which can bear upon the case. But I mean no offence.'

'Some inquiries are offensive,' Barker answered, angrily.

'It's only the facts that we want. It is in your interest and everyone's interests that they should be cleared up. Did Mr Douglas entirely approve your friendship with his wife?'

Barker grew paler, and his great strong hands were clasped convulsively together.

'You have no right to ask such questions!' he cried. 'What has this to do with the matter you are investigating?'

'I must repeat the question.'

'Well, I refuse to answer.'

'You can refuse to answer, but you must be aware that your refusal is in itself an answer, for you would not refuse if you had not something to conceal.'

Barker stood for a moment, with his face set grimly and his strong black eyebrows drawn low in intense thought. Then he looked up with a smile.

'Well, I guess you gentlemen are only doing your clear duty, after all, and that I have no right to stand in the way of it. I'd only ask you not to worry Mrs Douglas over this matter, for she has enough upon her just now. I may tell you that poor Douglas had just one fault in the world, and that was his jealousy. He was fond of me—no man could be fonder of a friend. And he was devoted to his wife. He loved

47

me to come here and was for ever sending for me. And yet if his wife and I talked together or there seemed any sympathy between us, a kind of wave of jealousy would pass over him and he would be off the handle and saying the wildest things in a moment. More than once I've sworn off coming for that reason, and then he would write me such penitent, imploring letters that I just had to. But you can take it from me, gentlemen, if it was my last word, that no man ever had a more loving, faithful wife—and I can say, also, no friend could be more loyal than I.'

It was spoken with fervour and feeling, and yet Inspector MacDonald could not dismiss the subject.

'You are aware,' said he, 'that the dead man's wedding-ring has been taken from his finger?'

'So it appears,' said Barker.

'What do you mean by "appears"? You know it as a fact.'

The man seemed confused and undecided.

'When I said "appears", I meant that it was conceivable that he had himself taken off the ring.'

'The mere fact that the ring should be absent, whoever may have removed it, would suggest to anyone's mind, would it not, that the marriage and the tragedy were connected?'

Barker shrugged his broad shoulders.

'I can't profess to say what it suggests,' he answered. 'But if you mean to hint that it could reflect in any way upon this lady's honour'—his eyes blazed for an instant, and then with an evident effort he got a grip upon his own emotions—'well, you are on the wrong track, that's all.'

'I don't know that I've anything else to ask you at present,' said MacDonald, coldly.

'There was one small point,' remarked Sherlock Holmes. 'When you entered the room there was only a candle lighted upon the table, was there not?'

'Yes, that was so.'

'By its light you saw that some terrible incident had occurred?'

'Exactly.'

'You at once rang for help?'

48

'Yes.'

'And it arrived very speedily?'

'Within a minute or so.'

'And yet when they arrived they found that the candle was out and that the lamp had been lighted. That seems very remarkable.'

Again Barker showed some signs of indecision.

'I don't see that it was remarkable, Mr Holmes,' he answered, after a pause. 'The candle threw a very bad light. My first thought was to get a better one. The lamp was on the table, so I lit it.'

'And blew out the candle?'

'Exactly.'

Holmes asked no further question, and Barker, with a deliberate look from one to the other of us, which had, as it seemed to me, something of defiance in it, turned and left the room.

Inspector MacDonald had sent up a note to the effect that he would wait upon Mrs Douglas in her room, but she had replied that she would meet us in the dining-room. She entered now, a tall and beautiful woman of thirty, reserved and self-possessed to a remarkable degree, very different from the tragic and distracted figure that I had pictured. It is true that her face was pale and drawn, like that of one who has endured a great shock, but her manner was composed, and the finely-moulded hand which she rested upon the edge of the table was as steady as my own. Her sad, appealing eyes travelled from one to the other of us with a curiously inquisitive expression. That questioning gaze transformed itself suddenly into abrupt speech.

'Have you found out anything yet?' she asked.

Was it my imagination that there was an undertone of fear rather than of hope in the question?

'We have taken every possible step, Mrs Douglas,' said the inspector. 'You may rest assured that nothing will be neglected.'

'Spare no money,' she said, in a dead, even tone. 'It is my desire that every possible effort should be made.'

49

'Perhaps you can tell us something which may throw some light upon the matter.'

'I fear not, but all I know is at your service.'

'We have heard from Mr Cecil Barker that you did not actually see—that you were never in the room where the tragedy occurred?'

'No; he turned me back upon the stairs. He begged me to return to my room.'

'Quite so. You had heard the shot and you had at once come down.'

'I put on my dressing-gown and then came down.'

'How long was it after hearing the shot that you were stopped on the stair by Mr Barker?'

'It may have been a couple of minutes. It is so hard to reckon time at such a moment. He implored me not to go on. He assured me that I could do nothing. Then Mrs Allen, the housekeeper, led me upstairs again. It was all like some dreadful dream.'

'Can you give us any idea how long your husband had been downstairs before you heard the shot?'

'No, I cannot say. He went from his dressing-room and I did not hear him go. He did the round of the house every night, for he was nervous of fire. It is the only thing that I have ever known him nervous of.'

'That is just the point which I want to come to, Mrs Douglas. You have only known your husband in England, have you not?'

'Yes. We have been married five years.'

'Have you heard him speak of anything which occurred in America and which might bring some danger upon him?'

Mrs Douglas thought earnestly before she answered.

'Yes,' she said at last. 'I have always felt that there was a danger hanging over him. He refused to discuss it with me. It was not from want of confidence in me—there was the most complete love and confidence between us—but it was out of his desire to keep all alarm away from me. He thought I should brood over it if I knew all, and so he was silent.'

'How did you know it, then?'

Mrs Douglas's face lit with a quick smile.

'Can a husband ever carry about a secret all his life and a woman who loves him have no suspicion of it? I knew it in many ways. I knew it by his refusal to talk about some episodes in his American life. I knew it by certain precautions he took. I knew it by certain words he let fall. I knew it by the way he looked at unexpected strangers. I was perfectly certain that he had some powerful enemies, that he believed they were on his track and that he was always on his guard against them. I was so sure of it that for years I have been terrified if ever he came home later than was expected.'

'Might I ask', said Holmes, 'what the words were which attracted your attention?'

' "The Valley of Fear," ' the lady answered. 'That was an expression he has used when I questioned him. "I have been in the Valley of Fear. I am not out of it yet." "Are we never to get out of the Valley of Fear?" I have asked him, when I have seen him more serious than usual. "Sometimes I think that we never shall," he has answered.'

'Surely you asked him what he meant by the Valley of Fear?'

'I did; but his face would become very grave and he would shake his head. "It is bad enough that one of us should have been in its shadow," he said. "Please God it shall never fall upon you." It was some real valley in which he had lived and in which something terrible had occurred to him—of that I am certain—but I can tell you no more.'

'And he never mentioned any names?'

'Yes; he was delirious with fever once when he had his hunting accident three years ago. Then I remember that there was a name that came continually to his lips. He spoke it with anger and a sort of horror. McGinty was the name— Bodymaster* McGinty. I asked him, when he recovered, who Bodymaster McGinty was, and whose body he was master of. "Never of mine, thank God!" he answered, with a laugh, and that was all I could get from him. But there is a connection between Bodymaster McGinty and the Valley of Fear.'

'There is one other point,' said Inspector MacDonald. 'You met Mr Douglas in a boarding-house in London, did you not, and became engaged to him there? Was there any romance, anything secret or mysterious, about the wedding?'

'There was romance. There is always romance.* There was nothing mysterious.'

'He had no rival?'

'No; I was quite free.'

'You have heard, no doubt, that his wedding-ring has been taken. Does that suggest anything to you? Suppose that some enemy of his old life had tracked him down and committed this crime, what possible reason could he have for taking his wedding-ring?'

For an instant I could have sworn that the faintest shadow of a smile* flickered over the woman's lips.

'I really cannot tell,' she answered. 'It is certainly a most extraordinary thing.'

'Well, we will not detain you any longer, and we are sorry to have put you to this trouble at such a time,' said the inspector. 'There are some other points, no doubt, but we can refer to you as they arise.'

She rose, and I was again conscious of that quick, questioning glance with which she had just surveyed us: 'What impression has my evidence made upon you?' The question might as well have been spoken. Then, with a bow, she swept from the room.

'She's a beautiful woman—a very beautiful woman,' said MacDonald, thoughtfully, after the door had closed behind her. 'This man Barker has certainly been down here a good deal. He is a man who might be attractive to a woman. He admits that the dead man was jealous, and maybe he knew best himself what cause he had for jealousy. Then there's that wedding-ring. You can't get past that. The man who tears a wedding-ring off a dead man's—What do you say to it, Mr Holmes?'

My friend had sat with his head upon his hands, sunk in the deepest thought. Now he rose and rang the bell.

'Ames,' he said, when the butler entered, 'where is Mr Cecil Barker now?'

'I'll see, sir.'

He came back in a moment to say that Mr Barker was in the garden.

'Can you remember, Ames, what Mr Barker had upon his feet last night when you joined him in the study?'

'Yes, Mr Holmes. He had a pair of bedroom slippers. I brought him his boots when he went for the police.'

'Where are the slippers now?'

'They are still under the chair in the hall.'

'Very good, Ames. It is, of course, important for us to know which tracks may be Mr Barker's and which from outside.'

'Yes, sir. I may say that I noticed that the slippers were stained with blood—so, indeed, were my own.'

'That is natural enough, considering the condition of the room. Very good, Ames. We will ring if we want you.'

A few minutes later we were in the study. Holmes had brought with him the carpet slippers from the hall. As Ames had observed, the soles of both were dark with blood.

'Strange!' murmured Holmes, as he stood in the light of the window and examined them minutely. 'Very strange indeed!'

Stooping with one of his quick, feline pounces he placed the slipper upon the blood-mark on the sill. It exactly corresponded. He smiled in silence at his colleagues.

The inspector was transfigured with excitement. His native accent rattled like a stick upon railings.

'Man!' he cried, 'there's not a doubt of it! Barker has just marked the window himself. It's a good deal broader than any boot-mark. I mind that you said it was a splay foot, and here's the explanation. But what's the game, Mr Holmes—what's the game?'

'Aye, what's the game?' my friend repeated, thoughtfully.

White Mason chuckled and rubbed his fat hands together in his professional satisfaction.

'I said it was a snorter!' he cried. 'And a real snorter it is!'

· CHAPTER 6 ·

A Dawning Light

THE three detectives had many matters of detail into which to inquire, so I returned alone to our modest quarters at the village inn; but before doing so I took a stroll in the curious old-world garden which flanked the house. Rows of very ancient yew trees,* cut into strange designs, girded it round. Inside was a beautiful stretch of lawn with an old sundial in the middle, the whole effect so soothing and restful that it was welcome to my somewhat jangled nerves. In that deeply peaceful atmosphere one could forget or remember only as some fantastic nightmare that darken-ed study with the sprawling, blood-stained figure upon the floor. And yet as I strolled round it and tried to steep my soul in its gentle balm, a strange incident occurred which brought me back to the tragedy and left a sinister impression on my mind.

I have said that a decoration of yew trees circled the garden. At the end which was farthest from the house they thickened into a continuous hedge. On the other side of this hedge, concealed from the eyes of any one approaching from the direction of the house, there was a stone seat. As I approached the spot I was aware of voices, some remark in the deep tones of a man, answered by a little ripple of feminine laughter. An instant later I had come round the end of the hedge, and my eyes lit upon Mrs Douglas and the man Barker before they were aware of my presence. Her appearance gave me a shock. In the dining-room she had been demure and discreet. Now all pretence of grief had passed away from her. Her eyes shone with the joy of living, and her face still quivered with amusement at some remark of her companion. He sat forward, his hands clasped and his forearms on his knees, with an answering smile upon his

54

bold, handsome face. In an instant—but it was just one instant too late—they resumed their solemn masks* as my figure came into view. A hurried word or two passed between them, and then Barker rose and came towards me.

'Excuse me, sir,' said he, 'but am I addressing Dr Watson?'

I bowed with a coldness which showed, I dare say, very plainly the impression which had been produced upon my mind.

'We thought that it was probably you, as your friendship with Mr Sherlock Holmes is so well known. Would you mind coming over and speaking to Mrs Douglas for one instant?'

I followed him with a dour face. Very clearly I could see in my mind's eye that shattered figure upon the floor. Here within a few hours of the tragedy were his wife and his nearest friend laughing together behind a bush in the garden which had been his. I greeted the lady with reserve. I had grieved with her grief in the dining-room. Now I met her appealing gaze with an unresponsive eye.

'I fear you think me callous and hard-hearted?' said she.

I shrugged my shoulders.

'It is no business of mine,' said I.

'Perhaps some day you will do me justice. If you only realized—'

'There is no need why Dr Watson should realize,' said Barker, quickly. 'As he has himself said, it is no possible business of his.'

'Exactly,' said I, 'and so I will beg leave to resume my walk.'

'One moment, Dr Watson,' cried the woman, in a pleading voice. 'There is one question which you can answer with more authority than anyone else in the world, and it may make a very great difference to me. You know Mr Holmes and his relations with the police better than anyone else can do. Supposing that a matter were brought confidentially to his knowledge, is it absolutely necessary that he should pass it on to the detectives?'

'Yes, that's it,' said Barker, eagerly. 'Is he on his own or is he entirely in with them?'

'I really don't know that I should be justified in discussing such a point.'

'I beg—I implore that you will, Dr Watson, I assure you that you will be helping us—helping me greatly if you will guide us on that point.'

There was such a ring of sincerity in the woman's voice that for the instant I forgot all about her levity and was moved only to do her will.

'Mr Holmes is an independent investigator,' I said. 'He is his own master, and would act as his own judgement directed. At the same time he would naturally feel loyalty towards the officials who were working on the same case, and he would not conceal from them anything which would help them in bringing a criminal to justice. Beyond this I can say nothing, and I would refer you to Mr Holmes himself if you want fuller information.'

So saying I raised my hat and went upon my way, leaving them still seated behind that concealing hedge. I looked back as I rounded the far end of it, and saw that they were still talking very earnestly together, and, as they were gazing after me, it was clear that it was our interview that was the subject of their debate.

'I wish none of their confidences,' said Holmes, when I reported to him what had occurred. He had spent the whole afternoon at the Manor House in consultation with his two colleagues, and returned about five with a ravenous appetite for a high tea which I had ordered for him.* 'No confidences, Watson, for they are mighty awkward if it comes to an arrest for conspiracy and murder.'

'You think it will come to that?'

He was in his most cheerful and *débonnaire* humour.

'My dear Watson, when I have exterminated that fourth egg I will be ready to put you in touch with the whole situation. I don't say that we have fathomed it—far from it—but when we have traced the missing dumb-bell—'

'The dumb-bell!'

56

'Dear me, Watson, is it possible that you have not penetrated the fact that the case hangs upon the missing dumb-bell? Well, well, you need not be downcast, for, between ourselves, I don't think that either Inspector Mac or the excellent local practitioner has grasped the overwhelming importance of this incident. One dumb-bell, Watson! Consider an athlete with one dumb-bell. Picture to yourself the unilateral development—the imminent danger of a spinal curvature. Shocking, Watson; shocking!'

He sat with his mouth full of toast and his eyes sparkling with mischief, watching my intellectual entanglement. The mere sight of his excellent appetite was an assurance of success, for I had very clear recollections of days and nights without a thought of food, when his baffled mind had chafed before some problem whilst his thin, eager features became more attenuated with the asceticism of complete mental concentration. Finally he lit his pipe and, sitting in the ingle-nook of the old village inn, he talked slowly and at random about his case, rather as one thinks aloud than as one who makes a considered statement.

'A lie, Watson—a great big, thumping, obtrusive, uncompromising lie—that's what meets us on the threshold. There is our starting point. The whole story told by Barker is a lie. But Barker's story is corroborated by Mrs Douglas. Therefore she is lying also. They are both lying and in a conspiracy. So now we have the clear problem—why are they lying, and what is the truth which they are trying so hard to conceal? Let us try, Watson, you and I, if we can get behind the lie and reconstruct the truth.

'How do I know that they are lying? Because it is a clumsy fabrication which simply *could* not be true. Consider! According to the story given to us the assassin had less than a minute after the murder had been committed to take that ring, which was under another ring, from the dead man's finger, to replace the other ring—a thing which he would surely never have done—and to put that singular card beside his victim. I say that this was obviously impossible. You may argue—but I have too much respect for your judgement, Watson, to think that you will do so—that the ring may have been taken before the man was killed. The fact that the candle had only been lit a short time shows that there had been no lengthy interview. Was Douglas, from what we hear of his fearless character, a man who would be likely to give up his wedding-ring at such short notice, or could we conceive of his giving it up at all? No, no, Watson, the assassin was alone with the dead man for some time with the lamp lit. Of that I have no doubt at all. But the gunshot was apparently the cause of death. Therefore the gunshot must have been fired some time earlier than we are told. But there could be no mistake about such a matter as that. We are in the presence, therefore, of a deliberate conspiracy upon the part of the two people who heard the gunshot—of the man Barker and of the woman Douglas. When on the top of this I am able to show that the bloodmark upon the window-sill was deliberately placed there by Barker in order to give a false clue to the police, you will admit that the case grows dark against him.

'Now we have to ask ourselves at what hour the murder actually did occur. Up to half-past ten the servants were moving about the house, so it was certainly not before that time. At a quarter to eleven they had all gone to their rooms with the exception of Ames, who was in the pantry. I have been trying some experiments after you left us this afternoon, and I find that no noise which MacDonald can make in the study can penetrate to me in the pantry when the doors are all shut. It is otherwise, however, from the housekeeper's room. It is not so far down the corridor, and from it I could vaguely hear a voice when it was very loudly raised. The sound from a shot-gun is to some extent muffled when the discharge is at very close range, as it undoubtedly was in this instance. It would not be very loud, and yet in the silence of the night it should have easily penetrated to Mrs Allen's room. She is, as she has told us, somewhat deaf, but none the less she mentioned in her evidence that she did hear something like a door slamming half an hour before the alarm was given. Half an hour before the alarm was given would be a quarter to eleven. I have no doubt that what she heard was the report of the gun, and that this was the real instant of the murder. If this is so, we have now to determine what Mr Barker and Mrs Douglas, presuming that they are not the actual murderers, could have been doing from a quarter to eleven, when the sound of the gun-shot brought them down, until a quarter past eleven, when they rang the bell and summoned the servants. What were they doing, and why did they not instantly give the alarm? That is the question which faces us, and when it has been answered we will surely have gone some way to solve our problem.'

'I am convinced myself,' said I, 'that there is an understanding between those two people. She must be a heartless creature to sit laughing at some jest within a few hours of her husband's murder.'

'Exactly. She does not shine as a wife even in her own account of what occurred. I am not a whole-souled admirer of womankind, as you are aware, Watson, but my experience of life has taught me that there are few wives having any regard for their husbands who would let any man's spoken word stand between them and that husband's dead body. Should I ever marry, Watson, I should hope to inspire my wife with some feeling which would prevent her from being walked off by a housekeeper when my corpse was lying within a few yards of her. It was badly stage-managed,* for even the rawest of investigators must be struck by the absence of the usual feminine ululation.* If there had been nothing else, this incident alone would have suggested a pre-arranged conspiracy to my mind.'

'You think, then, definitely, that Barker and Mrs Douglas are guilty of the murder?'

'There is an appalling directness about your questions, Watson,' said Holmes, shaking his pipe at me. 'They come at me like bullets. If you put it that Mrs Douglas and Barker know the truth about the murder and are conspiring to conceal it, then I can give you a whole-souled answer. I am sure they do. But your more deadly proposition is not so clear. Let us for a moment consider the difficulties which stand in the way.

'We will suppose that this couple are united by the bonds of a guilty love and that they have determined to get rid of the man who stands between them. It is a large supposition, for discreet inquiry among servants* and others has failed to corroborate it in any way. On the contrary, there is a good deal of evidence that the Douglases were very attached to each other.'

'That I am sure cannot be true,' said I, thinking of the beautiful, smiling face in the garden.

'Well, at least they gave that impression. However, we will suppose that they are an extraordinarily astute couple, who deceive everyone upon this point and who conspire to murder the husband. He happens to be a man over whose head some danger hangs—'

'We have only their word for that.'*

Holmes looked thoughtful.

'I see, Watson. You are sketching out a theory by which everything they say from the beginning is false. According to your idea, there was never any hidden menace or secret society or Valley of Fear or Boss MacSomebody* or anything else. Well, that is a good, sweeping generalization. Let us see what that brings us to. They invent this theory to account for the crime. They then play up to the idea by leaving this bicycle in the park as a proof of the existence of some outsider. The stain on the window-sill conveys the same idea. So does the card upon the body, which might have been prepared in the house. That all fits into your hypothesis, Watson. But now we come on the nasty angular, uncompromising bits which won't slip into their places. Why a cut-off shot-gun of all weapons—and an American one at that? How could they be so sure that the sound of it would not bring someone on to them? It's a mere chance, as it is, that Mrs Allen did not start out to inquire for the slamming door. Why did your guilty couple do all this, Watson?'

'I confess that I can't explain it.'

'Then, again, if a woman and her lover conspire to murder a husband, are they going to advertise their guilt by ostentatiously removing his wedding-ring after his death? Does that strike you as very probable, Watson?'

'No, it does not.'

'And once again, if the thought of leaving a bicycle concealed outside had occurred to you, would it really have seemed worth doing when the dullest detective would naturally say this is an obvious blind, as the bicycle is the first thing which the fugitive needed in order to make his escape?'

'I can conceive of no explanation.'

'And yet there should be no combination of events for which the wit of man cannot conceive an explanation. Simply as a mental exercise, without any assertion that it is true, let me indicate a possible line of thought. It is, I admit, mere imagination, but how often is imagination the mother of truth?*

'We will suppose that there *was* a guilty secret, a really shameful secret, in the life of this man Douglas.* This leads to his murder by someone who is, we will suppose, an avenger—someone from outside. This avenger, for some reason which I confess I am still at a loss to explain, took the dead man's wedding-ring. The vendetta might conceivably date back to the man's first marriage and the ring be taken for some such reason. Before this avenger got away Barker and the wife had reached the room. The assassin convinced them that any attempt to arrest him would lead to the publication of some hideous scandal. They were converted to this idea and preferred to let him go. For this purpose they probably lowered the bridge, which can be done quite noiselessly, and then raised it again. He made his escape, and for some reason thought that he could do so more safely on foot than on the bicycle. He therefore left his machine where it would not be discovered until he had got safely away. So far we are within the bounds of possibility, are we not?'

'Well, it is possible, no doubt,' said I, with some reserve.

'We have to remember, Watson, that whatever occurred is certainly something very extraordinary. Well now, to continue our supposititious case, the couple—not necessarily a guilty couple—realize after the murderer is gone that they have placed themselves in a position in which it may be difficult for them to prove that they did not themselves either do the deed or connive at it. They rapidly and rather clumsily met the situation. The mark was put by Barker's blood-stained slipper upon the window-sill to suggest how the fugitive got away. They obviously were the two who must have heard the sound of the gun, so they gave the alarm exactly as they would have done, but a good half-hour after the event.'

'And how do you propose to prove all this?'

'Well, if there were an outsider he may be traced and taken. That would be the most effective of all proofs. But if not*—well, the resources of science are far from being exhausted.* I think that an evening alone in that study would help me much.'

'An evening alone!'

'I propose to go up there presently. I have arranged it with the estimable Ames, who is by no means whole-hearted about Barker. I shall sit in that room and see if its atmosphere brings me inspiration. I'm a believer in the *genius loci.** You smile, friend Watson. Well, we shall see. By the way, you have that big umbrella* of yours, have you not?'

'It is here.'

'Well, I'll borrow that, if I may.'

'Certainly, but what a wretched weapon! If there is danger—'

'Nothing serious, my dear Watson, or I should certainly ask for your assistance. But I'll take the umbrella. At present I am only awaiting the return of our colleagues from Tunbridge Wells, where they are at present engaged in trying for a likely owner to the bicycle.'

It was nightfall before Inspector MacDonald and White Mason came back from their expedition, and they arrived exultant, reporting a great advance in our investigation.

'Man, I'll admeet that I had my doubts if there was ever an outsider,' said MacDonald, 'but that's all past now. We've had the bicycle identified, and we have a description of our man, so that's a long step on our journey.'

'It sounds to me like the beginning of the end,' said Holmes; 'I'm sure I congratulate you both with all my heart.'

'Well, I started from the fact that Mr Douglas had seemed disturbed since the day before, when he had been at Tunbridge Wells. It was at Tunbridge Wells, then, that he had become conscious of some danger. It was clear, therefore, that if a man had come over with a bicycle it was from Tunbridge Wells that he might be expected to have come. We took the bicycle over with us and showed it at the hotels. It was identified at once by the manager of the Eagle Commercial as belonging to a man named Hargrave* who had taken a room there two days before. This bicycle and a small valise were his whole belongings. He had registered his name as coming from London, but had given no address. The valise was London-made and the contents were British, but the man himself was undoubtedly an American.'

'Well, well,' said Holmes, gleefully, 'you have indeed done some solid work whilst I have been sitting spinning theories with my friend. It's a lesson in being practical, Mr Mac.'

'Aye, it's just that, Mr Holmes,' said the inspector with satisfaction.

'But this may all fit in with your theories,' I remarked.

'That may or may not be. But let us hear the end, Mr Mac. Was there nothing to identify this man?'

'So little that it was evident he had carefully guarded himself against identification. There were no papers or letters and no marking upon the clothes. A cycle-map of the county lay upon his bedroom table. He had left the hotel after breakfast yesterday morning upon his bicycle, and no more was heard of him until our inquiries.'

'That's what puzzles me, Mr Holmes,' said White Mason. 'If the fellow did not want the hue and cry raised over him, one would imagine that he would have returned and remained at the hotel as an inoffensive tourist. As it is, he must know that he will be reported to the police by the hotel manager, and that his disappearance will be connected with the murder.'

'So one would imagine. Still he has been justified of his wisdom up to date at any rate, since he has not been taken. But his description—what of that?'

MacDonald referred to his notebook.

'Here we have it so far as they could give it. They don't seem to have taken any very particular stock of him, but still the porter, the clerk, and the chambermaid are all agreed that this about covers the points. He was a man about five foot nine in height, fifty or so years of age, his hair slightly grizzled, a greyish moustache, a curved nose and a face which all of them described as fierce and forbidding.'

'Well, bar the expression, that might almost be a description of Douglas himself,' said Holmes. 'He is just over fifty, with grizzled hair and moustache and about the same height. Did you get anything else?'

'He was dressed in a heavy grey suit with a reefer jacket, and he wore a short yellow overcoat and a soft cap.'

'What about the shot-gun?'

'It is less than two feet long. It could very well have fitted into his valise. He could have carried it inside his overcoat without difficulty.'

'And how do you consider that all this bears upon the general case?'

'Well, Mr Holmes,' said MacDonald, 'when we have got our man—and you may be sure that I had his description on the wires within five minutes of hearing it—we shall be able to judge. But even as it stands, we have surely gone a long way. We know that an American calling himself Hargrave came to Tunbridge Wells two days ago with bicycle and valise. In the latter was a sawn-off shot-gun, so he came with the deliberate purpose of crime. Yesterday morning he set off for this place upon his bicycle with his gun concealed in his overcoat. No one saw him arrive, so far as we can learn, but he need not pass through the village to reach the park gates, and there are many cyclists upon the road. Presumably he at once concealed his cycle among the laurels, where it was found, and possibly lurked there himself, with his eye on the house waiting for Mr Douglas to come out. The shot-gun is a strange weapon to use inside a house, but he had intended to use it outside, and then it has very obvious advantages, as it would be impossible to miss with it, and the sound of shots is so common in an English sporting neighbourhood that no particular notice would be taken.'

'That is all very clear!' said Holmes.

'Well, Mr Douglas did not appear. What was he to do next? He left his bicycle and approached the house in the twilight. He found the bridge down and no one about. He took his chance, intending, no doubt, to make some excuse if he met anyone. He met no one. He slipped into the first room that he saw and concealed himself behind the curtain. From thence he could see the drawbridge go up and he knew that his only escape was through the moat. He waited until a quarter past eleven, when Mr Douglas, upon his usual nightly round, came into the room. He shot him and escaped, as arranged. He was aware that the bicycle would be described by the hotel people and be a clue against him, so he left it there and made his way by some other means to London or to some safe hiding-place which he had already arranged. How is that, Mr Holmes.'

'Well, Mr Mac, it is very good and very clear so far as it goes. That is your end of the story. My end is that the crime was committed half an hour earlier than reported; that Mrs Douglas and Mr Barker are both in a conspiracy to conceal something; that they aided the murderer's escape—or at least, that they reached the room before he escaped—and that they fabricated evidence of his escape through the window, whereas in all probability they had themselves let him go by lowering the bridge. That's *my* reading of the first half.'

The two detectives shook their heads.

'Well, Mr Holmes, if this is true we only tumble out of one mystery into another,' said the London inspector.

'And in some ways a worse one,' added White Mason. 'The lady has never been in America in her life. What

65

possible connection could she have with an American assassin which would cause her to shelter him?'

'I freely admit the difficulties,' said Holmes. 'I propose to make a little investigation of my own tonight, and it is just possible that it may contribute something to the common cause.'

'Can we help you, Mr Holmes?'

'No, no! Darkness and Dr Watson's umbrella. My wants are simple. And Ames—the faithful Ames—no doubt he will stretch a point for me. All my lines of thought lead me back invariably to the one basic question—why should an athletic man develop his frame upon so unnatural an instrument as a single dumb-bell?'

It was late that night when Holmes returned from his solitary excursion. We slept in a double-bedded room, which was the best that the little country inn could do for us. I was already asleep when I was partly awakened by his entrance.

'Well, Holmes,' I murmured, 'have you found out anything?'

He stood beside me in silence, his candle in his hand. Then the tall lean figure inclined towards me.

'I say, Watson,' he whispered, 'would you be afraid to sleep in the same room as a lunatic, a man with softening of the brain, an idiot whose mind has lost its grip?'*

'Not in the least,' I answered in astonishment.

'Ah, that's lucky,' he said, and not another word would he utter that night.

66

· **CHAPTER 7** ·

The Solution

NEXT morning, after breakfast,* we found Inspector MacDonald and Mr White Mason seated in close consultation in the small parlour of the local police-sergeant. Upon the table in front of them were piled a number of letters and telegrams, which they were carefully sorting and docketing. Three had been placed upon one side.

'Still on the track of the elusive bicyclist?' Holmes asked, cheerfully. 'What is the latest news of the ruffian?'

MacDonald pointed ruefully to his heap of correspondence.

'He is at present reported from Leicester, Nottingham, Southampton, Derby, East Ham, Richmond,* and fourteen other places. In three of them—East Ham, Leicester, and Liverpool—there is a clear case against him and he has actually been arrested. The country seems to be full of fugitives with yellow coats.'

'Dear me!' said Holmes, sympathetically. 'Now, Mr Mac, and you, Mr White Mason, I wish to give you a very earnest piece of advice. When I went into this case with you I bargained, as you will no doubt remember, that I should not present you with half-proved theories, but that I should retain and work out my own ideas until I had satisfied myself that they were correct. For this reason I am not at the present moment telling you all that is in my mind. On the other hand, I said that I would play the game fairly by you, and I do not think it is a fair game to allow you for one unnecessary moment to waste your energies upon a profitless task. Therefore I am here to advice you this morning, and my advice to you is summed up in three words: Abandon the case.'

MacDonald and White Mason stared in amazement at their celebrated colleague.

'You consider it hopeless?' cried the inspector.

'I consider *your* case to be hopeless. I do not consider that it is hopeless to arrive at the truth.'

'But this cyclist. He is not an invention. We have his description, his valise, his bicycle. The fellow must be somewhere. Why should we not get him?'

'Yes, yes; no doubt he is somewhere, and no doubt we shall get him, but I would not have you waste your energies in East Ham or Liverpool. I am sure that we can find some shorter cut to a result.'

'You are holding something back. It's hardly fair of you, Mr Holmes.' The inspector was annoyed.

'You know my methods of work, Mr Mac. But I will hold it back for the shortest time possible. I only wish to verify my details in one way, which can very readily be done, and then I make my bow and return to London, leaving my results entirely at your service. I owe you too much to act otherwise, for in all my experience I cannot recall any more singular and interesting study.'

'This is clean beyond me, Mr Holmes. We saw you when we returned from Tunbridge Wells last night, and you were in general agreement with our results. What has happened since then to give you a completely new idea of the case?'

'Well, since you ask me, I spent as I told you that I would, some hours last night at the Manor House.'

'Well, what happened?'

'Ah! I can only give you a very general answer to that for the moment. By the way, I have been reading a short, but clear and interesting, account of the old building, purchasable at the modest sum of one penny from the local tobacconist.' Here Holmes drew a small tract, embellished with a rude engraving of the ancient Manor House, from his waistcoat pocket. 'It immensely adds to the zest of an investigation, my dear Mr Mac, when one is in conscious sympathy with the historical atmosphere of one's surroundings. Don't look so impatient, for I assure you that even so bald an account as this raises some sort of picture of the past in one's mind. Permit me to give you a sample. "Erected in the fifth year of the reign of James I,* and standing upon the site of a much older building, the Manor House of Birlstone presents one of the finest surviving examples of the moated Jacobean residence—" '

'You are making fools of us, Mr Holmes!'*

'Tut, tut, Mr Mac!—the first sign of temper I have detected in you. Well, I won't read it verbatim, since you feel so strongly upon the subject. But when I tell you that there is some account of the taking of the place by a Parliamentary colonel in 1644, of the concealment of Charles for several days in the course of the Civil War, and finally of a visit there by the second George, you will admit that there are various associations of interest connected with this ancient house.'

'I don't doubt it, Mr Holmes, but that is no business of ours.'

'Is it not? Is it not? Breadth of view, my dear Mr Mac, is one of the essentials of our profession. The interplay of ideas and the oblique uses of knowledge are often of extraordinary interest. You will excuse these remarks from one who, though a mere connoisseur of crime, is still rather older and perhaps more experienced than yourself.'*

'I'm the first to admit that,' said the detective, heartily. 'You get to your point, I admit, but you have such a deuced round-the-corner way of doing it.'

'Well, well, I'll drop past history and get down to present-day facts. I called last night, as I have already said, at the Manor House. I did not see either Mr Barker or Mrs Douglas. I saw no necessity to disturb them, but I was pleased to hear that the lady was not visibly pining and that she had partaken of an excellent dinner. My visit was specially made to the good Mr Ames, with whom I exchanged some amiabilities which culminated in his allowing me, without reference to anyone else, to sit alone for a time in the study.'

'What! With that!' I ejaculated.

'No, no; everything is now in order. You gave permission for that, Mr Mac, as I am informed. The room was in its

69

normal state, and in it I passed an instructive quarter of an hour.'

'What were you doing?'

'Well, not to make a mystery of so simple a matter, I was looking for the missing dumb-bell. It has always bulked rather large in my estimate of the case. I ended by finding it.'

'Where?'

'Ah! There we come to the edge of the unexplored.* Let me go a little farther, a very little farther, and I will promise that you shall share everything that I know.'

'Well, we're bound to take you on your own terms,' said the inspector; 'but when it comes to telling us to abandon the case—Why, in the name of goodness, should we abandon the case?'

'For the simple reason, my dear Mr Mac, that you have not got the first idea what it is that you are investigating.'

'We are investigating the murder of Mr John Douglas, of Birlstone Manor.'

'Yes, yes; so you are. But don't trouble to trace the mysterious gentleman upon the bicycle. I assure you that it won't help you.'

'Then what do you suggest that we do?'

'I will tell you exactly what to do, if you will do it.'

'Well, I'm bound to say I've always found you had reason behind all your queer ways. I'll do what you advise.'

'And you, Mr White Mason?'

The country detective looked helplessly from one to the other. Mr Holmes and his methods were new to him.

'Well, if it is good enough for the inspector it is good enough for me,' he said, at last.

'Capital!' said Holmes. 'Well, then, I should recommend a nice, cheery, country walk for both of you. They tell me that the views from Birlstone Ridge over the Weald are very remarkable. No doubt lunch could be got at some suitable hostelry, though my ignorance of the country prevents me from recommending one. In the evening, tired but happy—'

'Man, this is getting past a joke!' cried MacDonald, rising angrily from his chair.

'Well, well, spend the day as you like,' said Holmes, patting him cheerfully on the shoulder. 'Do what you like and go where you will, but meet me here before dusk without fail—without fail, Mr Mac.'

'That sounds more like sanity.'

'All of it was excellent advice, but I don't insist, so long as you are here when I need you. But now, before we part, I want you to write a note to Mr Barker.'

'Well?'

'I'll dictate it, if you like. Ready?

' "Dear Sir,—It has struck me that it is our duty to drain the moat, in the hope that we may find some—" '

'It's impossible,' said the inspector; 'I've made inquiry.'

'Tut, tut, my dear sir! Do, please, do what I ask you.'

'Well, go on.'

' "—in the hope that we may find something which may bear upon our investigation. I have made arrangements, and the workmen will be at work early to-morrow morning diverting the stream—" '

'Impossible!'

' "—diverting the stream, so I thought it best to explain matters beforehand." Now sign that, and send it by hand about four o'clock. At that hour we shall meet again in this room. Until then we can each do what we like, for I can assure you that this inquiry has come to a definite pause.'

Evening was drawing in when we reassembled. Holmes was very serious in his manner, myself curious, and the detectives obviously critical and annoyed.

'Well, gentlemen,' said my friend, gravely, 'I am asking you now to put everything to the test with me, and you will judge for yourselves whether the observations which I have made justify the conclusions to which I have come. It is a chill evening, and I do not know how long our expedition may last, so I beg that you will wear your warmest coats. It is of the first importance that we should be in our places before it grows dark, so, with your permission, we will get started at once.'

We passed along the outer bounds of the Manor House park until we came to a place where there was a gap in the rails which fenced it. Through this we slipped, and then, in the gathering gloom, we followed Holmes until we had reached a shrubbery which lies nearly opposite to the main door and the drawbridge. The latter had not been raised. Holmes crouched down behind the screen of laurels, and we all three followed his example.

'Well, what are we to do now?' asked MacDonald, with some gruffness.

'Possess our souls in patience* and make as little noise as possible,' Holmes answered.

'What are we here for at all? I really think that you might treat us with more frankness.'

Holmes laughed.

'Watson insists that I am the dramatist in real life,'* said he. 'Some touch of the artist wells up within me and calls insistently for a well-staged performance. Surely our profession, Mr Mac, would be a drab and sordid one if we did not sometimes set the scene so as to glorify our results. The blunt accusation, the brutal tap upon the shoulder—what can one make of such a *dénouement*? But the quick inference, the subtle trap, the clever forecast of coming events, the triumphant vindication of bold theories—are these not the pride and the justification of our life's work? At the present moment you thrill with the glamour of the situation and the anticipation of the hunter. Where would be that thrill if I had been as definite as a time-table? I only ask a little patience, Mr Mac, and all will be clear to you.'

'Well, I hope the pride and justification and the rest of it will come before we all get our death of cold,' said the London detective, with comic resignation.

We all had good reason to join in the aspiration, for our vigil was a long and bitter one. Slowly the shadows darkened over the long sombre face of the old house. A cold, damp reek from the moat chilled us to the bones and set our teeth chattering. There was a single lamp over the gateway and a steady globe of light in the fatal study. Everything else was dark and still.

'How long is this to last?' asked the inspector, suddenly. 'And what is it we are watching for?'

'I have no more notion than you how long it is to last,' Holmes answered with some asperity. 'If criminals* would always schedule their movements like railway trains it would certainly be more convenient for all of us. As to what it is we—Well, *that's* what we are watching for.'

As he spoke the bright yellow light in the study was obscured by somebody passing to and fro before it. The laurels among which we lay were immediately opposite the window and not more than a hundred feet from it. Presently it was thrown open with a whining of hinges, and we could dimly see the dark outline of a man's head and shoulders looking out into the gloom. For some minutes he peered forth, in a furtive, stealthy fashion, as one who wishes to be assured that he is unobserved. Then he leaned forward, and in the intense silence we were aware of the soft lapping of agitated water. He seemed to be stirring up the moat with something which he held in his hand. Then suddenly he hauled something in as a fisherman lands a fish—some large, round object which obscured the light as it was dragged through the open casement.

'Now!' cried Holmes. 'Now!'

We were all upon our feet, staggering after him with our stiffened limbs, whilst he, with one of those outflames of nervous energy which could make him on occasion both the most active and the strongest man that I have ever known, ran swiftly across the bridge and rang violently at the bell. There was the rasping of bolts from the other side, and the amazed Ames stood in the entrance. Holmes brushed him aside without a word and, followed by all of us, rushed into the room which had been occupied by the man whom we had been watching.

The oil lamp on the table represented the glow which we had seen from outside. It was now in the hand of Cecil Barker, who held it towards us as we entered. Its light shone upon his strong, resolute, clean-shaven face and his menacing eyes.

'What the devil is the meaning of all this?' he cried. 'What are you after, anyhow?'

73

Holmes took a swift glance round and then pounced upon a sodden bundle tied together with cord which lay where it had been thrust under the writing-table.

'This is what we are after, Mr Barker. This bundle, weighted with a dumb-bell, which you have just raised from the bottom of the moat.'

Barker stared at Holmes with amazement in his face.

'How in thunder came you to know anything about it?' he asked.

'Simply that I put it there.'

'You put it there! You!'

'Perhaps I should have said "replaced it there",' said Holmes. 'You will remember, Inspector MacDonald, that I was somewhat struck by the absence of a dumb-bell. I drew your attention to it, but with the pressure of other events you had hardly the time to give it the consideration which would have enabled you to draw deductions from it. When water is near and a weight is missing it is not a very far-fetched supposition that something has been sunk in the water. The idea was at least worth testing, so with the help of Ames, who admitted me to the room, and the crook of Dr Watson's umbrella, I was able last night to fish up and inspect this bundle. It was of the first importance, however, that we should be able to prove who placed it there. This we accomplished by the very obvious device of announcing that the moat would be dried to-morrow, which had, of course, the effect that whoever had hidden the bundle would most certainly withdraw it the moment that darkness enabled him to do so. We have no fewer than four witnesses as to who it was who took advantage of the opportunity, and so, Mr Barker, I think the word lies now with you.'

Sherlock Holmes put the sopping bundle upon the table beside the lamp and undid the cord which bound it. From within he extracted a dumb-bell, which he tossed down to its fellow in the corner. Next he drew forth a pair of boots. 'American, as you perceive,' he remarked, pointing to the toes. Then he laid upon the table a long, deadly, sheathed knife. Finally he unravelled a bundle of clothing, comprising

74

a complete set of underclothes, socks, a grey tweed suit, and a short yellow overcoat.

'The clothes are commonplace,' remarked Holmes, 'save only the overcoat, which is full of suggestive touches.' He held it tenderly towards the light, whilst his long, thin fingers flickered over it. 'Here, as you perceive, is the inner pocket prolonged into the lining in such a fashion as to give ample space for the truncated fowling-piece. The tailor's tab is on the neck—Neale, Outfitter, Vermissa,* USA. I have spent an instructive afternoon in the rector's library, and have enlarged my knowledge by adding the fact that Vermissa is a flourishing little town at the head of one of the best-known coal and iron valleys in the United States. I have some recollection, Mr Barker, that you associated the coal districts with Mr Douglas's first wife, and it would surely not be too far-fetched an inference that the V. V. upon the card by the dead body might stand for Vermissa Valley, or that this very valley, which sends forth emissaries of murder, may be that Valley of Fear of which we have heard. So much is fairly clear. And now, Mr Barker, I seem to be standing rather in the way of your explanation.'

It was a sight to see Cecil Barker's expressive face during this exposition of the great detective. Anger, amazement, consternation, and indecision swept over it in turn. Finally he took refuge in a somewhat acid irony.

'You know such a lot, Mr Holmes, perhaps you had better tell us some more,' he sneered.

'I have no doubt that I could tell you a great deal more, Mr Barker, but it would come with a better grace from you.'

'Oh, you think so, do you? Well, all I can say is that if there's any secret here it is not my secret, and I am not the man to give it away.'

'Well, if you take that line, Mr Barker,' said the inspector, quietly, 'we must just keep you in sight until we have the warrant and can hold you.'

'You can do what you damn well please about that,' said Barker, defiantly.

75

The proceedings seemed to have come to a definite end so far as he was concerned, for one had only to look at that granite face to realize that no *peine forte et dure** would ever force him to plead against his will. The deadlock was broken, however, by a woman's voice. Mrs Douglas had been standing listening at the half-opened door, and now she entered the room.

'You have done enough for us, Cecil,' said she. 'Whatever comes of it in the future, you have done enough.'

'Enough and more than enough,' remarked Sherlock Holmes, gravely. 'I have every sympathy with you, madam, and I should strongly urge you to have some confidence in the common sense of our jurisdiction and to take the police voluntarily into your complete confidence. It may be that I am myself at fault for not following up the hint which you conveyed to me through my friend, Dr Watson, but at that time I had every reason to believe that you were directly concerned in the crime. Now I am assured that this is not so. At the same time, there is much that is unexplained, and I should strongly recommend that you ask *Mr Douglas* to tell us his own story.'

Mrs Douglas gave a cry of astonishment at Holmes's words. The detectives and I must have echoed it, when we were aware of a man who seemed to have emerged from the wall, and who advanced now from the gloom of the corner in which he had appeared. Mrs Douglas turned, and in an instant her arms were round him. Barker had seized his outstretched hand.

'It's best this way, Jack,' his wife repeated. 'I am sure that it is best.'

'Indeed, yes, Mr Douglas,' said Sherlock Holmes. 'I am sure that you will find it best.'

The man stood blinking at us with the dazed look of one who comes from the dark into the light. It was a remarkable face—bold grey eyes, a strong, short-clipped, grizzled moustache, a square, projecting chin, and a humorous mouth. He took a good look at us all, and then, to my amazement, he advanced to me and handed me a bundle of paper.

'I've heard of you,' said he, in a voice which was not quite English and not quite American, but was altogether mellow and pleasing. 'You are the historian of this bunch.* Well, Dr Watson, you've never had such a story as that pass through your hands before, and I'd lay my last dollar on that. Tell it your own way, but there are the facts, and you can't miss the public so long as you have those. I've been cooped up two days, and I've spent the daylight hours—as much daylight as I could get in that rat-trap—in putting the thing into words. You're welcome to them—you and your public. There's the story of the Valley of Fear.'

'That's the past, Mr Douglas,' said Sherlock Holmes, quietly. 'What we desire now is to hear your story of the present.'

'You'll have it, sir,' said Douglas. 'Can I smoke as I talk? Well, thank you, Mr Holmes; you're a smoker yourself, if I remember right, and you'll guess what it is to be sitting for two days with tobacco in your pocket and afraid that the smell will give you away.' He leaned against the mantel-piece and sucked at the cigar which Holmes had handed him. 'I've heard of you, Mr Holmes; I never guessed that I would meet you. But before you are through with that'—he nodded at my papers—'you will say I've brought you some-thing fresh.'

Inspector MacDonald had been staring at the newcomer with the greatest amazement.

'Well, this fairly beats me!' he cried at last. 'If you are Mr John Douglas, of Birlstone Manor, then whose death have we been investigating for these two days, and where in the world have you sprung from now? You seemed to me to come out of the floor like a Jack-in-the-box.'

'Ah, Mr Mac,' said Holmes, shaking a reproving fore-finger, 'you would not read that excellent local compilation which described the concealment of King Charles. People did not hide in those days without reliable hiding-places, and the hiding-place that has once been used may be again. I had persuaded myself that we should find Mr Douglas under this roof.'

'And how long have you been playing this trick upon us, Mr Holmes?' said the inspector, angrily. 'How long have you allowed us to waste ourselves upon a search that you knew to be an absurd one?'

'Not one instant, my dear Mr Mac. Only last night did I form my views of the case. As they could not be put to the proof until this evening, I invited you and your colleague to take a holiday for the day. Pray, what more could I do? When I found the suit of clothes in the moat it at once became apparent to me that the body we had found could not have been the body of Mr John Douglas at all, but must be that of the bicyclist from Tunbridge Wells. No other conclusion was possible. Therefore I had to determine where Mr John Douglas himself could be, and the balance of probability was that, with the connivance of his wife and his friend, he was concealed in a house which had such conveniences for a fugitive, and awaiting quieter times, when he could make his final escape.'

'Well, you figured it out about right,' said Mr Douglas, approvingly. 'I thought I'd dodge your British law, for I was not sure how I stood under it, and also I saw my chance to throw these hounds once for all off my track. Mind you, from first to last I have done nothing to be ashamed of, and nothing that I would not do again,* but you'll judge that for yourselves when I tell you my story. Never mind warning me, inspector; I'm ready to stand pat* upon the truth.

'I'm not going to begin at the beginning. That's all there'—he indicated my bundle of papers—'and a mighty queer yarn you'll find it. It all comes down to this: That there are some men that have good cause to hate me and would give their last dollar to know that they had got me. So long as I am alive and they are alive, there is no safety in this world for me. They hunted me from Chicago to California; then they chased me out of America; but when I married and settled down in this quiet spot I thought my last years were going to be peaceable. I never explained to my wife how things were. Why should I pull her into it? She would never have a quiet moment again, but would be always imagining trouble. I fancy she knew something, for I may have dropped a word here or a word there—but until yesterday, after you gentlemen had seen her, she never knew the rights of the matter. She told you all she knew, and so did Barker here, for on the night when this thing happened there was mighty little time for explanations. She knows everything now, and I would have been a wiser man if I had told her sooner.* But it was a hard question, dear'—he took her hand for an instant in his own—'and I acted for the best.

'Well, gentlemen, the day before these happenings I was over in Tunbridge Wells and I got a glimpse of a man in the street. It was only a glimpse, but I have a quick eye for these things, and I never doubted who it was. It was the worst enemy I had among them all—one who has been after me like a hungry wolf after a caribou* all these years. I knew there was trouble coming, and I came home and made ready for it. I guessed I'd fight through it all right on my own. There was a time when my luck was the talk of the whole United States.* I never doubted that it would be with me still.

'I was on my guard all that next day and never went out into the park. It's as well, or he'd have had the drop on me with that buck-shot gun of his before ever I could draw on him. After the bridge was up—my mind was always more restful when that bridge was up in the evenings—I put the thing clear out of my head. I never figured on his getting into the house and waiting for me. But when I made my round in my dressing-gown, as my habit was, I had no sooner entered the study than I scented danger. I guess when a man has had dangers in his life—and I've had more than most in my time—there is a kind of sixth sense that waves the red flag. I saw the signal clear enough, and yet I couldn't tell you why. Next instant I spotted a boot under the window curtain, and then I saw why plain enough.

'I'd just the one candle that was in my hand, but there was a good light from the hall lamp through the open door. I put down the candle and jumped for a hammer that I'd left on the mantel. At the same moment he sprang at me. I saw the glint of a knife and I lashed at him with the hammer. I got him somewhere, for the knife tinkled down on the floor. He dodged round the table as quick as an eel, and a moment later he'd got his gun from under his coat. I heard him cock it, but I had got hold of it before he could fire. I had it by the barrel, and we wrestled for it all ends up for a minute or more. It was death to the man that lost his grip. He never lost his grip, but he got it butt downwards for a moment too long. Maybe it was I that pulled the trigger. Maybe we just jolted it off between us. Anyhow, he got both barrels in the face, and there I was, staring down at all that was left of Ted Baldwin. I'd recognized him in the township and again when he sprang for me, but his own mother wouldn't recognize him as I saw him then. I'm used to rough work, but I fairly turned sick at the sight of him.

'I was hanging on to the side of the table when Barker came hurrying down. I heard my wife coming, and I ran to the door and stopped her. It was no sight for a woman. I promised I'd come to her soon. I said a word or two to Barker—he took it all in at a glance*—and we waited for the rest to come along. But there was no sign of them. Then we understood that they could hear nothing, and that all that had happened was only known to ourselves.

'It was at that instant that the idea came to me. I was fairly dazzled by the brilliancy of it. The man's sleeve had slipped up and there was the branded mark of the Lodge upon his forearm. See here.'

The man whom we knew as Douglas turned up his own coat and cuff to show a brown triangle within a circle exactly like that which we had seen upon the dead man.

'It was the sight of that which started me on to it. I seemed to see it all clear at a glance. There was his height and hair and figure about the same as my own. No one could swear to his face, poor devil! I brought down this suit of clothes, and in a quarter of an hour Barker and I had put my dressing-gown on him and he lay as you found him. We tied all his things into a bundle, and I weighted them with the only weight I could find and slung them through the window. The card he had meant to lay upon my body was lying beside his own. My rings were put on his finger, but when it came to the wedding-ring'—he held out his muscular hand—'you can see for yourselves that I had struck my limit. I have not moved it since the day I was married, and it would have taken a file to get it off. I don't know, anyhow, that I would have cared to part with it, but if I had wanted to I couldn't. So we just had to leave the detail to take care of itself. On the other hand, I brought a bit of plaster down and put it where I am wearing one myself at this instant. You slipped up there, Mr Holmes,* clever as you are, for if you had chanced to take off that plaster you would have found no cut underneath it.

'Well, that was the situation. If I could lie low for a while and then get away where I would be joined by my wife,* we would have a chance at last of living at peace for the rest of our lives. These devils would give me no rest so long as I was above-ground but if they saw in the papers that Baldwin had got his man there would be an end of all my troubles. I hadn't much time to make it clear to Barker and to my wife, but they understood enough to be able to help me. I knew all about this hiding-place, so did Ames, but it never entered his head to connect it with the matter. I retired into it, and it was up to Barker to do the rest.*

'I guess you can fill in for yourselves what he did. He opened the window and made the mark on the sill to give an idea of how the murderer escaped. It was a tall order, that, but as the bridge was up there was no other way. Then, when everything was fixed, he rang the bell for all he was worth. What happened afterwards you know—and so, gentlemen, you can do what you please, but I've told you the truth and the whole truth, so help me, God! What I ask you now is, how do I stand by the English law?'

There was a silence, which was broken by Sherlock Holmes.

'The English law is, in the main, a just law.* You will get no worse than your deserts* from that, Mr Douglas. But I would ask you how did this man know that you lived here, or how to get into your house, or where to hide to get you?'

'I know nothing of this.'

Holmes's face was very white and grave.

'The story is not over yet, I fear,' said he. 'You may find worse dangers than the English law, or even than your enemies from America. I see trouble before you, Mr Douglas. You'll take my advice and still be on your guard.'

And now, my long-suffering readers, I will ask you to come away with me for a time, far from the Sussex Manor House of Birlstone, and far also from the year of grace in which we made our eventful journey which ended with the strange story of the man who had been known as John Douglas. I wish you to journey back some twenty years in time,* and westward some thousands of miles in space, that I may lay before you a singular and a terrible narrative—so singular and so terrible that you may find it hard to believe that, even as I tell it, even so did it occur.

Do not think that I intrude one story before another is finished. As you read on you will find that this is not so. And when I have detailed those distant events and you have solved this mystery of the past, we shall meet once more in those rooms in Baker Street* where this, like so many other wonderful happenings, will find its end.

PART 2

*The Scowrers**

• CHAPTER 1 •

The Man

IT was the fourth of February in the year 1875.* It had been a severe winter, and the snow lay deep in the gorges of the Gilmerton Mountains.* The steam plough* had, however, kept the rail-track* open, and the evening train which connects the long line of coal-mining and iron-working settlements was slowly groaning its way up the steep gradients which lead from Stagville on the plain to Vermissa, the central township which lies at the head of the Vermissa Valley. From this point the track sweeps downwards to Barton's Crossing, Helmdale, and the purely agricultural county of Merton. It was a single-track railroad, but at every siding—and they were numerous—long lines of trucks piled with coal and with iron ore told of the hidden wealth which had brought a rude population and a bustling life to this most desolate corner of the United States of America.

For desolate it was! Little could the first pioneer who had traversed it have ever imagined that the fairest prairies and the most lush water-pastures were valueless compared with this gloomy land of black crag and tangled forest. Above the dark and often scarcely penetrable woods upon their sides, the high, bare crowns of the mountains, white snow and jagged rock, towered upon either flank, leaving a long, winding, tortuous valley in the centre. Up this the little train was slowly crawling.

The oil lamps had just been lit in the leading passenger-car, a long, bare carriage in which some twenty or thirty people were seated. The greater number of these were workmen returning from their day's toil in the lower portion of the valley. At least a dozen, by their grimed faces and the safety lanterns which they carried, proclaimed themselves as miners.* These sat smoking in a group, and conversed in

85

low voices, glancing occasionally at two men on the opposite side of the car, whose uniform and badges showed them to be policemen.*

Several women of the labouring class, and one or two travellers who might have been small local storekeepers, made up the rest of the company, with the exception of one young man in a corner by himself. It is with this man that we are concerned. Take a good look at him, for he is worth it.*

He is a fresh-complexioned, middle-sized young man, not far, one would guess, from his thirtieth year. He has large, shrewd, humorous grey eyes which twinkle inquiringly from time to time as he looks round through his spectacles at the people about him. It is easy to see that he is of a sociable and possibly simple disposition, anxious to be friendly to all men. Anyone could pick him at once as gregarious in his habits and communicative in his nature, with a quick wit and a ready smile. And yet the man who studied him more closely might discern a certain firmness of jaw and grim tightness about the lips which would warn him that there were depths beyond, and that this pleasant, brown-haired young Irishman might conceivably leave his mark for good or evil upon any society to which he was introduced.

Having made one or two tentative remarks to the nearest miner, and received only short, gruff replies, the traveller resigned himself to uncongenial silence, staring moodily out of the window at the fading landscape.

It was not a cheering prospect. Through the growing gloom there pulsed the red glow of the furnaces on the sides of the hills. Great heaps of slag and dumps of cinders loomed up on each side, with the high shafts of the collieries towering above them. Huddled groups of mean, wooden houses, the windows of which were beginning to outline themselves in light, were scattered here and there along the line, and the frequent halting-places were crowded with their swarthy inhabitants.

The iron and coal valleys of the Vermissa district were no resorts for the leisured or the cultured. Everywhere there

were stern signs of the crudest battle of life, the rude work
to be done, and the rude, strong workers who did it.

The young traveller gazed out into this dismal country
with a face of mingled repulsion and interest, which showed
that the scene was new to him. At intervals he drew from
his pocket a bulky letter to which he referred, and on the
margins of which he scribbled some notes. Once from the
back of his waist he produced something which one would
hardly have expected to find in the possession of so mild-
mannered a man. It was a navy revolver of the largest size.
As he turned it slantwise to the light, the glint upon the rims
of the copper shells within the drum showed that it was fully
loaded. He quickly restored it to his secret pocket, but not
before it had been observed by a working man who had
seated himself upon the adjoining bench.

'Hullo, Mate!' said he. 'You seem heeled and ready.'

The young man smiled with an air of embarrassment.

'Yes,' said he, 'we need them sometimes in the place I
come from.'

'And where may that be?'

'I'm last from Chicago.'

'A stranger in these parts?'

'Yes.'

'You may find you need it here,' said the workman.

'Ah! Is that so?' The young man seemed interested.

'Have you heard nothing of doings hereabouts?'

'Nothing out of the way.'

'Why, I thought the country was full of it. You'll hear
quick enough. What made you come here?'

'I heard there was always work for a willing man.'

'Are you a member of the union?'*

'Sure.'

'Then you'll get your job, I guess. Have you any friends?'

'Not yet, but I have the means of making them.'

'How's that, then?'

'I am one of the Ancient Order of Freemen. There's no
town without a lodge, and where there is a lodge I'll find
my friends.'

The remark had a singular effect upon his companion. He glanced round suspiciously at the others in the car. The miners were still whispering among themselves. The two police-officers were dozing. He came across, seated himself close to the young traveller, and held out his hand.

'Put it there,' he said.

A hand-grip passed between the two.

'I see you speak the truth. But it's well to make certain.' He raised his right hand to his right eyebrow. The traveller at once raised his left hand to his left eyebrow.*

'Dark nights are unpleasant,' said the workman.

'Yes, for strangers to travel,'* the other answered.

'That's good enough. I'm Brother Scanlan,* Lodge 341, Vermissa Valley. Glad to see you in these parts.'

'Thank you. I'm Brother John McMurdo, Lodge 29, Chicago.* Bodymaster, J. H. Scott. But I am in luck to meet a brother so early.'

'Well, there are plenty of us about. You won't find the Order more flourishing anywhere in the States than right here in Vermissa Valley. But we could do with some lads like you. I can't understand a spry man of the union finding no work to do in Chicago.'

'I found plenty of work to do,' said McMurdo.

'Then why did you leave?'

McMurdo nodded towards the policemen and smiled. 'I guess those chaps would be glad to know,' he said. Scanlan groaned sympathetically. 'In trouble?' he asked in a whisper.

'Deep.'

'A penitentiary job?'

'And the rest.'

'Not a killing!'*

'It's early days to talk of such things,' said McMurdo, with the air of a man who had been surprised into saying more than he intended. 'I've my own good reasons for leaving Chicago, and let that be enough for you. Who are you that you should take it on yourself to ask such things?' His grey eyes gleamed with sudden and dangerous anger from behind his glasses.

'All right, Mate. No offence meant. The boys will think none the worse of you whatever you may have done. Where are you bound for now?'

'Vermissa.'

'That's the third halt down the line. Where are you staying?'

McMurdo took out an envelope and held it close to the murky oil lamp. 'Here is the address—Jacob Shafter,* Sheridan Street.* It's a boarding-house that was recommended by a man I knew in Chicago.'

'Well, I don't know it, but Vermissa is out of my beat. I live at Hobson's Patch, and that's here where we are drawing up. But, say, there's one bit of advice I'll give you before we part: If you're in trouble in Vermissa, go straight to the Union House and see Boss McGinty. He is the bodymaster of Vermissa Lodge, and nothing can happen in these parts unless Black Jack McGinty* wants it. So long, Mate. Maybe we'll meet in Lodge one of these evenings. But mind my words: If you are in trouble, go to Boss McGinty.'

Scanlan descended, and McMurdo was left once again to his thoughts. Night had now fallen, and the flames of the frequent furnaces were roaring and leaping in the darkness. Against their lurid background dark figures were bending and straining, twisting, and turning, with the motion of winch or of windlass, to the rhythm of an eternal clank and roar.

'I guess hell must look something like that,' said a voice.

McMurdo turned and saw that one of the policemen had shifted in his seat and was staring out into the fiery waste.

'For that matter,' said the other policeman, 'I allow that hell must *be* something like that. If there are worse devils down yonder than some we could name, it's more than I'd expect. I guess you are new to this part, young man?'

'Well, what if I am?' McMurdo answered, in a surly voice.

'Just this, Mister; that I should advise you to be careful in choosing your friends. I don't think I'd begin with Mike* Scanlan or his gang if I were you.'

'What the hell* is it to you who are my friends?' roared McMurdo, in a voice which brought every head in the carriage round to witness the altercation. 'Did I ask you for your advice, or did you think me such a sucker that I couldn't move without it? You speak when you are spoken to, and by the Lord you'd have to wait a long time if it was me!' He thrust out his face, and grinned at the patrolmen like a snarling dog.

The two policemen, heavy, good-natured men, were taken aback by the extraordinary vehemence with which their friendly advances had been rejected.

'No offence, Stranger,' said one. 'It was a warning for your own good, seeing that you are, by your own showing, new to the place.'

'I'm new to the place; but I'm not new to you and your kind!' cried McMurdo, in a cold fury. 'I guess you're the same in all places, shoving your advice in when nobody asks for it.'

'Maybe we'll see more of you before very long,' said one of the patrolmen, with a grin. 'You're a real hand-picked one, if I am a judge.'

'I was thinking the same,' remarked the other. 'I guess we may meet again.'

'I'm not afraid of you, and don't you think it!' cried McMurdo. 'My name's Jack McMurdo—see? If you want me you'll find me at Jacob Shafter's, on* Sheridan Street, Vermissa; so I'm not hiding from you, am I? Day or night I dare to look the like of you in the face—don't make any mistake about that.'

There was a murmur of sympathy and admiration from the miners at the dauntless demeanour of the new-comer, while the two policemen shrugged their shoulders and renewed a conversation between themselves.

A few minutes later the train ran into the ill-lit station* and there was a general clearing, for Vermissa was by far the largest town* on the line. McMurdo picked up his leather grip-sack, and was about to start off into the darkness, when one of the miners accosted hi.

'By Gar,* Mate, you know how to speak to the cops,' he said, in a voice of awe. 'It was grand to hear you. Let me carry your grip* and show you the road. I'm passing Shafter's on the way to my own shack.'

There was a chorus of friendly 'Good-nights' from the other miners as they passed from the platform. Before ever he had set foot in it, McMurdo the turbulent had become a character in Vermissa.

The country had been a place of terror,* but the town was in its way even more depressing. Down that long valley there was at least a certain gloomy grandeur in the huge fires and the clouds of drifting smoke, while the strength and industry of man found fitting monuments in the hills which he had spilled by the side of his monstrous excavations. But the town showed a dead level of mean ugliness and squalor. The broad street was churned up by the traffic into a horrible rutted paste of muddy snow. The sidewalks were narrow and uneven. The numerous gas-lamps served only to show more clearly a long line of wooden houses, each with its veranda facing the street, unkempt and dirty.*

As they approached the centre of the town, the scene was brightened by a row of well-lit stores, and even more by a cluster of liquor saloons and gaming-houses, in which the miners spent their hard-earned but generous wages.*

'That's the Union House,' said the guide, pointing to one saloon which rose almost to the dignity of being an hotel.* 'Jack McGinty is the Boss there.'

'What sort of a man is he?' McMurdo asked.*

'What! Have you never heard of the Boss?'

'How could I have heard of him when you know that I am a stranger in these parts?'

'Well, I thought his name was known clear across the country.* It's been in the papers often enough.'

'What for?'

'Well'—the miner lowered his voice—'over the affairs.'

'What affairs?'

'Good Lord, Mister! you are queer,* if I must say it* without offence. There's only one set of affairs that you'll hear of in these parts, and that's the affairs of the Scowrers.'

'Why, I seem to have read of the Scowrers in Chicago. A gang of murderers,* are they not?'

'Hush, on your life!' cried the miner, standing still in his alarm, and gazing in amazement at his companion. 'Man, you won't live long in these parts if you speak in the open street like that. Many a man has had the life beaten out of him for less.'

'Well, I know nothing about them. It's only what I have read.'

'And I'm not saying that you have not read the truth.' The man looked nervously round him as he spoke, peering into the shadows as if he feared to see some lurking danger. 'If killing is murder, then God knows there is murder and to spare. But don't you dare breathe the name of Jack McGinty in connection with it, Stranger; for every whisper goes back to him, and he is not one that is likely to let it pass. Now, that's the house you're after, that one standing back from the street. You'll find old Jacob Shafter that runs it as honest a man as lives in this township.'

'I thank you,' said McMurdo, and shaking hands with his new acquaintance he plodded, his grip-sack in his hand, up the path which led to the dwelling-house, at the door of which he gave a resounding knock. It was opened at once by someone very different from what he had expected.

It was a woman, young and singularly beautiful. She was of the German type, blonde and fair-haired, with the piquant contrast of a pair of beautiful dark eyes; with which she surveyed the stranger with surprise and a pleasing embarrassment which brought a wave of colour over her pale face. Framed in the bright light of the open doorway, it seemed to McMurdo that he had never seen a more beautiful picture, the more attractive for its contrast with the sordid and gloomy surroundings. A lovely violet growing upon one of those black slag-heaps of the mines would not have seemed more surprising. So entranced was he that he stood staring without a word, and it was she who broke the silence.

'I thought it was father,' said she, with a pleasing little touch of a German accent. 'Did you come to see him? He is down town. I expect him back every minute.'

McMurdo continued to gaze at her in open admiration until her eyes dropped in confusion before this masterful visitor.

'No, miss,' he said at last; 'I'm in no hurry to see him. But your house was recommended to me for board. I thought it might suit me—and now I know it will.'

'You are quick to make up your mind,' said she, with a smile.

'Anyone but a blind man could do as much,'* the other answered.

She laughed at the compliment.

'Come right in, sir,' she said. 'I'm Miss Ettie* Shafter, Mr Shafter's daughter. My mother's dead, and I run the house. You can sit down by the stove in the front room until father comes along—Ah, here he is! So you can fix things with him right away.'

A heavy, elderly man came plodding up the path. In a few words McMurdo explained his business. A man of the name of Murphy had given him the address in Chicago. He in turn had had it from someone else. Old Shafter was quite ready. The stranger made no bones about terms, agreed at once to every condition, and was apparently fairly flush of money. For seven dollars a week,* paid in advance, he was to have board and lodging. So it was that McMurdo, the self-confessed fugitive from justice, took up his abode under the roof of the Shafters, the first step* which was to lead to so long and dark a train of events, ending in a far distant land.

· **CHAPTER 2** ·

The Bodymaster

MCMURDO was a man who made his mark quickly. Wherever he was the folk around soon knew it. Within a week he had become infinitely the most important person at Shafter's. There were ten or a dozen boarders* there, but they were honest foremen or commonplace clerks from the stores, of a very different calibre to the young Irishman.* Of an evening when they gathered together his joke was always the readiest, his conversation the brightest, and his song the best.* He was a born boon companion, with a magnetism which drew good humour from all around him.

And yet he showed again and again, as he had shown in the railway-carriage, a capacity for sudden, fierce anger which compelled the respect and even the fear of those who met him. For the law, too, and all connected with it, he exhibited a bitter contempt which delighted some and alarmed others of his fellow-boarders.

From the first he made it evident, by his open admiration, that the daughter of the house had won his heart from the instant that he had set eyes upon her beauty and her grace. He was no backward suitor. On the second day he told her that he loved her, and from then onwards he repeated the same story with an absolute disregard of what she might say to discourage him.

'Someone else?' he would cry. 'Well, the worse luck for someone else! Let him look out for himself! Am I to lose my life's chance and all my heart's desire for someone else? You can keep on saying no, Ettie! The day will come when you will say yes, and I'm young enough to wait.'*

He was a dangerous suitor, with his glib Irish tongue and his pretty, coaxing ways.* There was about him also that glamour of experience and of mystery which attracts a woman's interest and finally her love. He could talk of the sweet valleys of County Monaghan* from which he came, of the lovely distant island, the low hills and green meadows of which seemed the more beautiful when imagination viewed them from this place of grime and snow.

Then he was versed in the life of the cities of the North, of Detroit and the lumber-camps of Michigan, of Buffalo,* and finally of Chicago, where he had worked in a planing-mill.* And afterwards came the hint of romance, the feeling that strange things had happened to him in that great city, so strange and so intimate that they might not be spoken of. He spoke wistfully of a sudden leaving, a breaking of old ties, a flight into a strange world ending in this dreary valley, and Ettie listened, her dark eyes gleaming with pity and with sympathy—those two qualities which may turn so rapidly and so naturally to love.*

McMurdo had obtained a temporary job as a book-keeper, for he was a well-educated man. This kept him out most of the day, and he had not found occasion yet to report himself to the head of the Lodge of the Ancient Order of Freemen. He was reminded of his omission, however, by a visit one evening from Mike Scanlan, the fellow-member whom he had met in the train. Scanlan, a small, sharp-faced, nervous, black-eyed man, seemed glad to see him once more. After a glass or two of whiskey,* he broached the object of his visit.

'Say, McMurdo,' said he, 'I remembered your address, so I made bold to call. I'm surprised that you've not reported to the Bodymaster. Why haven't you seen* Boss McGinty yet?'

'Well, I had to find a job. I have been busy.'

'You must find time for him if you have none for anything else. Good Lord, man! you're a fool* not to have been down to the Union House and registered your name the first morning after you came here! If you run against him*—well, you *mustn't*—that's all!'

McMurdo showed mild surprise. 'I've been a member of Lodge for over two years, Scanlan, but I never heard that duties were so pressing as all that.'

'Maybe not in Chicago.'

'Well, it's the same society here.'

'Is it?' Scanlan looked at him long and fixedly. There was something sinister in his eyes.

'Isn't it?'*

'You'll tell me that in a month's time. I hear you had a talk with the patrolmen after I left the train.'

'How did you know that?'

'Oh, it got about—things do get about for good and for bad in this district.'*

'Well, yes. I told the hounds what I thought of them.'

'By the Lord, you'll be a man after McGinty's heart!'

'What—does he hate the police, too?'

Scanlan burst out laughing.

'You go and see him, my lad,' said he, as he took his leave. 'It's not the police but you that he'll hate if you don't! Now, take a friend's advice and go at once!'

It chanced that on the same evening McMurdo had another more pressing interview which urged him in the same direction. It may have been that his attentions to Ettie had been more evident than before, or that they had gradually obtruded themselves into the slow mind of his good German host; but, whatever the cause, the boarding-house keeper beckoned the young man into his private room and started on to the subject without any circumlocution.

'It seems to me, Mister,' said he, 'that you are gettin' set on my Ettie. Ain't that so, or am I wrong?'

'Yes, that is so,' the young man answered.

'Vell, I vant to tell you right now that it ain't no manner of use. There's someone slipped in afore you.'

'She told me so.'

'Vell, you can lay that she told you truth! But did she tell you who it vas?'

'No; I asked her, but she wouldn't tell.'

'I dare say not, the leetle baggage! Perhaps she did not vish to frighten you avay.'

'Frighten!' McMurdo was on fire in a moment.

96

'Ah, yes, my friend! You need not be ashamed to be frightened of him. It is Teddy Baldwin.'*

'And who the devil is he?'

'He is a Boss of Scowrers.'

'Scowrers! I've heard of them before. It's Scowrers here and Scowrers there, and always in a whisper! What are you all afraid of? Who *are* the Scowrers?'

The boarding-house keeper instinctively sank his voice, as everyone did who talked about the terrible society.

'The Scowrers,' said he, 'are the Ancient Order of Freemen.'

The young man started.* 'Why, I am a member of that Order myself.'

'You! I vould never have had you in my house if I had known it—not if you vere to pay me a hundred dollar a veek.'

'What's amiss with the Order? It's for charity and good fellowship. The rules say so.'

'Maybe in some places. Not here!'

'What is it here?'

'It's a murder society, that's vat it is.'

McMurdo laughed incredulously.

'How do you prove that?' he asked.

'Prove it! Are there not fifty murders to prove it? Vat about Milman* and Van Shorst, and the Nicholson family, and old Mr Hyam, and little Billy James, and the others? Prove it! Is there a man or a voman in this valley vhat does not know it?'

'See here!' said McMurdo earnestly. 'I want you to take back what you've said or else make it good. One or the other you must do before I quit this room. Put yourself in my place. Here am I, a stranger in the town. I belong to a society that I know only as an innocent one. You'll find it through the length and breadth of the States, but always as an innocent one. Now, when I am counting upon joining it here, you tell me that it is the same as a murder society called the "Scowrers". I guess you owe me either an apology or else an explanation, Mr Shafter.'

'I can but tell you vat the whole vorld knows, Mister. The bosses of the one are the bosses of the other. If you offend the one, it is the other vhat vill strike you. We have proved it too often.'

'That's just gossip—I want proof!' said McMurdo.

'If you live here long you vill get your proof. But I forget that you are yourself one of them. You vill soon be as bad as the rest. But you vill find other lodgings, Mister. I cannot have you he e. Is it not bad enough that one of these people come courting my Ettie, and that I dare not turn him down, but that I should have another for my boarder? Yes, indeed, you shall not sleep here after to-night!'*

So McMurdo found himself under sentence of banishment both from his comfortable quarters and from the girl whom he loved. He found her alone in the sitting-room that same evening, and he poured his troubles into her ear.

'Sure, your father is after giving me notice,' he said. 'It's little I would care if it was just my room, but indeed, Ettie, though it's only a week that I've known you, you are the very breath of life to me, and I can't live without you.'

'Oh, hush, Mr McMurdo! Don't speak so!' said the girl. 'I have told you, have I not, that you are too late? There is another, and if I have not promised to marry him at once, at least I can promise no one else.'

'Suppose I had been first, Ettie, would I have had a chance?'

The girl sank her face into her hands. 'I wish to Heaven that you *had* been first,' she sobbed.

McMurdo was down on his knees before her in an instant. 'For God's sake, Ettie, let it stand at that!' he cried. 'Will you ruin your life and my own for the sake of this promise? Follow your heart, acushla!* 'Tis a safer guide than any promise given before you knew what it was that you were saying.'

He had seized Ettie's white hand between his own strong brown ones.

'Say that you will be mine and we will face it out together!'

'Not here?'

'Yes, here.'

'No, no Jack!' His arms were round her now. 'It could not be here. Could you take me away?'

A struggle passed for a moment over McMurdo's face, but it ended by setting like granite. 'No, here,' he said. 'I'll hold you against the world, Ettie, right here where we are!'

'Why should we not leave together?'

'No, Ettie, I can't leave here.'

'But why?'

'I'd never hold my head up again if I felt that I had been driven out. Besides, what is there to be afraid of? Are we not free folks in a free country? If you love me and I you, who will dare to come between?'

'You don't know, Jack. You've been here too short a time. You don't know this Baldwin. You don't know McGinty and his Scowrers.'

'No, I don't know them, and I don't fear them, and I don't believe in them!' said McMurdo. 'I've lived among rough men, my darling, and instead of fearing them it has always ended that they have feared me—always, Ettie. It's mad on the face of it! If these men, as your father says, have done crime after crime in the valley, and if every one knows them by name, how comes it that none are brought to justice? You answer me that, Ettie!'

'Because no witness dares to appear against them. He would not live a month if he did. Also because they have always their own men to swear that the accused one was far from the scene of the crime.* But surely, Jack, you must have read all this. I had understood that every paper in the United States* was writing about it.'

'Well, I have read something, it is true, but I had thought it was a story. Maybe these men have some reason in what they do. Maybe they are wronged and have no other way to help themselves.'

'Oh, Jack, don't let me hear you speak so! That is how he speaks—the other one!'*

'Baldwin—he speaks like that, does he?'

'And that is why I loathe him so. Oh, Jack, now I can tell you the truth, I loathe him with all my heart; but I fear him

99

also. I fear him for myself, but, above all, I fear him for Father. I know that some great sorrow would come upon us if I dared to say what I really felt. That is why I have put him off with half-promises. It was in real truth our only hope. But if you would fly with me, Jack, we could take Father with us and live for ever far from the power of these wicked men.'

Again there was a struggle upon McMurdo's face, and again it set like granite. 'No harm shall come to you, Ettie—nor to your father either. As to wicked men, I expect you may find that I am as bad as the worst of them before we're through.'

'No, no, Jack! I would trust you anywhere.'

McMurdo laughed bitterly. 'Good Lord! how little you know of me! Your innocent soul, my darling, could not even guess what is passing in mine.* But, hullo, who's the visitor?'

The door had opened suddenly and a young fellow came swaggering in with the air of one who is the master. He was a handsome, dashing young man of about the same age and build as McMurdo himself. Under his broad-brimmed black felt hat, which he had not troubled to remove, a handsome face, with fierce, domineering eyes and curved hawk-bill of a nose, looked savagely at the pair who sat by the stove.

Ettie had jumped to her feet, full of confusion and alarm. 'I'm glad to see you, Mr Baldwin,' said she. 'You're earlier than I had thought. Come and sit down.'

Baldwin stood with his hands on his hips looking at McMurdo. 'Who is this?' he asked curtly.

'It's a friend of mine, Mr Baldwin, a new boarder here. Mr McMurdo, may I introduce you to Mr Baldwin?'*

The young men nodded in surly fashion to each other.

'Maybe Miss Ettie has told you how it is with us?' said Baldwin.

'I didn't understand that there was any relation between you.'

'Didn't you? Well, you can understand it now. You can take it from me that this young lady is mine, and you'll find it a very fine evening for a walk.'

'Thank you, I am in no humour for a walk.'

'Aren't you?' The man's savage eyes were blazing with anger. 'Maybe you are in a humour for a fight, Mr Boarder!'

'That I am!' cried McMurdo, springing to his feet. 'You never said a more welcome word.'

'For God's sake, Jack! Oh, for God's sake!' cried poor, distracted Ettie. 'Oh, Jack, Jack, he will hurt you!'*

'Oh, it's "Jack", is it!' said Baldwin with an oath. 'You've come to that already, have you?'

'Oh, Ted, be reasonable—be kind! For my sake, Ted, if ever you loved me, be big-hearted* and forgiving!'

'I think, Ettie, that if you were to leave us alone we could get this thing settled,' said McMurdo, quietly. 'Or maybe, Mr Baldwin, you will take a turn down the street with me. It's a fine evening, and there's some open ground beyond the next block.'

'I'll get even with you without needing to dirty my hands,' said his enemy. 'You'll wish you had never set foot in this house before I am through with you.'

'No time like the present,' cried McMurdo.

'I'll choose my own time, Mister.* You can leave the time to me. See here!' He suddenly rolled up his sleeve and showed upon his forearm a peculiar sign which appeared to have been branded there. It was a circle with a triangle within it. 'D'you know what that means?'

'I neither know nor care!'

'Well, you will know. I'll promise you that. You won't be much older, either. Perhaps Miss Ettie can tell you something about it. As to you, Ettie, you'll come back to me on your knees—D'ye hear, girl?—On your knees!—And then I'll tell you what your punishment may be. You've sowed—and by the Lord, I'll see that you reap!'* He glared* at them both in fury. Then he turned upon his heel, and an instant later the outer door had banged behind him.

For a few moments McMurdo and the girl stood in silence. Then she threw her arms around him.

'Oh, Jack, how brave you were! But it is no use—you must fly! To-night—Jack—to-night! It's your only hope. He will have your life. I read it in his horrible eyes. What chance have you against a dozen of them, with Boss McGinty and all the power of the Lodge behind them?'

McMurdo disengaged her hands, kissed her, and gently pushed her back into a chair. 'There, acushla, there! Don't be disturbed or fear for me. I'm a Freeman myself. I'm after telling your father about it. Maybe I am no better than the others; so don't make a saint of me. Perhaps you hate me too, now that I've told you as much.'

'Hate you, Jack? While life lasts I could never do that! I've heard that there is no harm in being a Freeman anywhere but here; so why should I think the worse of you for that? But if you are a Freeman, Jack, why should you not go down and make a friend of Boss McGinty? Oh, hurry, Jack, hurry!* Get your word in first, or the hounds will be on your trail.'

'I was thinking the same thing,' said McMurdo. 'I'll go right now and fix it. You can tell your father that I'll sleep here to-night and find some other quarters in the morning.'

The bar of McGinty's saloon was crowded as usual, for it was the favourite loafing place* of all the rougher elements of the town. The man was popular, for he had a rough, jovial disposition which formed a mask, covering a great deal which lay behind it. But apart from this popularity, the fear in which he was held throughout the township, and indeed down the whole thirty miles of the valley and past the mountains upon either side of it, was enough in itself to fill his bar, for none could afford to neglect his goodwill.

Besides those secret powers which it was universally believed that he exercised in so pitiless a fashion, he was a high public official, a municipal councillor, and a commissioner for roads, elected to the office through the votes of the ruffians who in turn expected to receive favours at his hands. Assessments* and taxes were enormous, the public works were notoriously neglected, the accounts were slurred over by bribed auditors, and the decent citizen was terrorized into paying public blackmail, and holding his tongue lest some worse thing befall him.

Thus it was that, year by year, Boss McGinty's diamond pins became more obtrusive, his gold chains more weighty across a more gorgeous vest, and his saloon stretched farther and farther, until it threatened to absorb one whole side of the Market Square.

McMurdo pushed open the swinging door of the saloon and made his way amid the crowd of men within, through an atmosphere which was blurred with tobacco smoke and heavy with the smell of spirits. The place was brilliantly lighted, and the huge, heavily gilt mirrors upon every wall reflected and multiplied the garish illumination. There were several bar-tenders in their shirt-sleeves hard at work, mixing drinks for the loungers who fringed the broad, brass-trimmed counter.*

At the far end, with his body resting upon the bar, and a cigar stuck at an acute angle from the corner of his mouth, there stood a tall, strong, heavily built man, who could be none other than the famous McGinty himself.* He was a black-maned giant, bearded to the cheek-bones, and with a shock of raven hair which fell to his collar. His complexion was as swarthy as that of an Italian, and his eyes were of a strange, dead black, which, combined with a slight squint, gave them a particularly sinister appearance.

All else in the man—his noble proportions, his fine features, and his frank bearing—fitted in with that jovial man-to-man manner which he affected. Here, one would say, is a bluff, honest fellow, whose heart would be sound, however rude his outspoken words might seem. It was only when those dead, dark eyes, deep and remorseless, were turned upon a man that he shrank within himself, feeling that he was face to face with an infinite possibility of latent evil, with a strength and courage and cunning behind it which made it a thousand times more deadly.

Having had a good look at his man, McMurdo elbowed his way forward with his usual careless audacity, and pushed himself through the little group of courtiers who were fawning upon the powerful Boss, laughing uproariously at the smallest of his jokes. The young stranger's bold grey eyes looked back fearlessly through their glasses at the deadly black ones which turned sharply upon him.

'Well, young man. I can't call your face to mind.'

'I'm new here, Mr McGinty.'

'You are not so new that you can't give a gentleman his proper title.'

'He's Councillor McGinty, young man,' said a voice from the group.

'I'm sorry, Councillor. I'm strange to the ways of the place. But I was advised to see you.'

'Well, you see me. This is all there is. What d'you think of me?'

'Well, it's early days. If your heart is as big as your body, and your soul as fine as your face, then I'd ask for nothing better,' said McMurdo.

'By Gar!* you've got an Irish tongue in your head, any-how,' cried the saloon-keeper, not quite certain whether to humour this audacious visitor or to stand upon his dignity. 'So you are good enough to pass my appearance?'

'Sure,' said McMurdo.

'And you were told to see me?'

'I was.'

'And who told you?'

'Brother Scanlan, of Lodge 341, Vermissa. I drink your health, Councillor, and to our better acquaintance.' He raised a glass with which he had been served to his lips and elevated his little finger as he drank it.*

McGinty, who had been watching him narrowly, raised his thick black eyebrows.

'Oh, it's like that, is it?' said he. 'I'll have to look a bit closer into this, Mister—'

'McMurdo.'

'A bit closer, Mr McMurdo; for we don't take folk on trust in these parts, nor believe all we're told neither. Come in here for a moment, behind the bar.'

There was a small room there, lined round with barrels. McGinty carefully closed the door, and then seated himself on one of them, biting thoughtfully on his cigar, and surveying his companion with those disquieting eyes. For a couple of minutes he sat in complete silence. McMurdo bore the inspection cheerfully, one hand in his coat-pocket, the other twisting his brown moustache. Suddenly McGinty stooped and produced a wicked-looking revolver.

'See here, my joker,'* said he, 'if I thought you were playing any game on us, it would be a short shrift for you.'

'This is a strange welcome,' McMurdo answered, with some dignity, 'for the bodymaster of a Lodge of Freemen to give to a stranger brother.'

'Aye, but it's just that same that you have to prove,' said McGinty, 'and God help you if you fail. Where were you made?'

'Lodge 29, Chicago.'

'When?'

'June 24th, 1872.'

'What bodymaster?'

'James H. Scott.'

'Who is your district ruler?'

'Bartholomew Wilson.'

'Hum! You seem glib enough in your tests. What are you doing here?'

'Working, the same as you—but a poorer job.'

'You have your back answer quick enough.'

'Yes, I was always quick of speech.'

'Are you quick of action?'

'I have had that name among those who knew me best.'

'Well, we may try you sooner than you think. Have you heard anything of the Lodge in these parts?'

'I've heard that it takes a man to be a brother.'

'True for you, Mr McMurdo. Why did you leave Chicago?'

'I'm damned* if I tell you that.'

McGinty opened his eyes. He was not used to being answered in such fashion, and it amused him. 'Why won't you tell me?'

'Because no brother may tell another a lie.'

'Then the truth is too bad to tell?'

'You can put it that way if you like.'

'See here, Mister, you can't expect me, as Bodymaster, to pass into the Lodge a man for whose past he can't answer.'

McMurdo looked puzzled. Then he took a worn newspaper-cutting from an inner pocket.

'You wouldn't squeal on a fellow?' said he.

'I'll wipe my hand across your face if you say such words to me!' cried McGinty hotly.

'You are right, Councillor,' said McMurdo meekly. 'I should apologize. I spoke without thought. Well, I know that I am safe in your hands. Look at that clipping.'*

McGinty glanced his eyes over the account of the shooting of one Jonas Pinto, in the Lake Saloon, Market Street, Chicago, in the New Year week of 1874.

'Your work?' he asked, as he handed back the paper.

McMurdo nodded.

'Why did you shoot him?'

'I was helping Uncle Sam to make dollars. Maybe mine were not as good gold as his, but they looked as well and were cheaper to make. This man Pinto helped me to shove the queer—'

'To do what?'

'Well, it means to pass the dollars out into circulation. Then he said he would split. Maybe he did split. I didn't wait to see. I just killed him and lighted out for the coal country.'

'Why the coal country?'

' 'Cause I'd read in the papers that they weren't too particular in those parts.'

McGinty laughed. 'You were first a coiner and then a murderer, and you came to these parts because you thought you'd be welcome?'

'That's about the size of it,' McMurdo answered.

'Well, I guess you'll go far. Say, can you make those dollars yet?'

McMurdo took half a dozen from his pocket. 'Those never passed the Philadelphia mint,'* said he.

'You don't say!' McGinty held them to the light in his enormous hand, which was as hairy as a gorilla's. 'I can see no difference! Gar! you'll be a mighty useful brother, I'm thinking! We can do with a bad man or two among us, Friend McMurdo, for there are times when we have to take our own part.* We'd soon be against the wall if we didn't shove back at those that were pushing us.'

'Well, I guess I'll do my share of shoving with the rest of the boys.'

'You seem to have a good nerve. You didn't squirm* when I put this pistol on you.'

'It was not me that was in danger.'

'Who, then?'

'It was you, Councillor.' McMurdo drew a cocked pistol from the side-pocket of his pea-jacket. 'I was covering you all the time. I guess my shot would have been as quick as yours.'

'By Gar!' McGinty flushed* an angry red and then burst into a roar of laughter.

'Say, we've had no such holy terror come to hand this many a year. I reckon the Lodge will learn to be proud of you . . . Well, what the hell* do you want? And can't I speak alone with a gentleman for five minutes but you must butt in upon us?'

The bar-tender stood abashed.

'I'm sorry, Councillor, but it's Ted Baldwin.* He says he must see you this very minute.'

The message was unnecessary, for the set, cruel face of the man himself was looking over the servant's shoulder. He pushed the bar-tender out and closed the door on him.

'So,' said he, with a furious glance at McMurdo, 'you got here first, did you? I've a word to say to you, Councillor, about this man.'

'Then say it here and now before my face,' cried McMurdo.

'I'll say it at my own time, in my own way.'

'Tut, tut!'* said McGinty getting off his barrel. 'This will never do. We have a new brother here, Baldwin, and it's not for us to greet him in such a fashion. Hold out your hand, man, and make it up!'

'Never!' cried Baldwin in a fury.

107

'I've offered to fight him if he thinks I have wronged him,' said McMurdo. 'I'll fight him with fists, or, if that won't satisfy him, I'll fight him any other way he chooses. Now I'll leave it to you, Councillor,* to judge between us as a Bodymaster should.'

'What is it, then?'

'A young lady. She's free to choose for herself.'

'Is she?' cried Baldwin.

'As between two brothers of the Lodge, I should say that she was,' said the Boss.

'Oh, that's your ruling, is it?'

'Yes, it is, Ted Baldwin,' said McGinty, with a wicked stare. 'Is it you that would dispute it?'*

'You would throw over one that has stood by you this five years in favour of a man that you never saw before in your life? You're not Bodymaster for life, Jack McGinty, and, by God!* when next it comes to a vote—'

The Councillor sprang at him like a tiger. His hand closed round the other's neck and he hurled him back across one of the barrels. In his mad fury he would have squeezed the life out of him if McMurdo had not interfered.*

'Easy, Councillor! For Heaven's sake, go easy!' he cried, as he dragged him back.

McGinty released his hold, and Baldwin, cowed and shaken, gasping for breath, and shivering in every limb as one who has looked over the very edge of death, sat up on the barrel over which he had been hurled.

'You've been asking for it this many a day, Ted Baldwin—now you've got it!' cried McGinty, his huge chest rising and falling. 'Maybe you think if I were voted down* from Bodymaster you would find yourself in my shoes. It's for the Lodge to say that. But so long as I am the chief I'll have no man lift his voice against me or my rulings.'

'I have nothing against you,' mumbled Baldwin, feeling his throat.

'Well, then,' cried the other, relapsing in a moment into a bluff joviality, 'we are all good friends again and there's an end of the matter.'

He took a bottle of champagne down from the shelf and twisted out the cork.

'See now,' he continued, as he filled three high glasses 'Let us drink the quarrelling toast of the Lodge. After that, as you know, there can be no bad blood between us. Now, then, the left hand on the apple of my throat, I say to you, Ted Baldwin, what is the offence, sir?'

'The clouds are heavy,' answered Baldwin.

'But they will for ever brighten.'

'And this I swear!'*

The men drank their wine, and the same ceremony was performed between Baldwin and McMurdo.

'There,' cried McGinty, rubbing his hands, 'that's the end of the black blood. You come under Lodge discipline if it goes farther, and that's a heavy hand in these parts, as Brother Baldwin knows—and as you will damn* soon find out, Brother McMurdo, if you ask for trouble.'

'Faith, I'd be slow to do that,' said McMurdo. He held out his hand to Baldwin. 'I'm quick to quarrel and quick to forgive. It's my hot Irish blood, they tell me. But it's over for me, and I bear no grudge.'

Baldwin had to take the proffered hand; for the baleful eye of the terrible Boss was upon him. But his sullen face showed how little the words of the other had moved him.

McGinty clapped them both on the shoulders. 'Tut! These girls, these girls!' he cried. 'To think that the same petticoats should come between two of my boys. It's the devil's own luck. Well, it's the colleen inside of them* that must settle the question, for it's outside the jurisdiction of a Bodymaster, and the Lord be praised for that. We have enough on us, without the women as well. You'll have to be affiliated to Lodge 341, Brother McMurdo. We have our own ways and methods, different from Chicago.* Saturday night is our meeting, and if you come then we'll make you free for ever of the Vermissa Valley.'

· CHAPTER 3 ·

Lodge 341, Vermissa

ON the day following the evening which had contained
so many exciting events, McMurdo moved his lodgings
from old Jacob Shafter's and took up his quarters at the
Widow MacNamara's,* on the extreme outskirts of the town.
Scanlan, his original acquaintance aboard the train, had
occasion shortly afterwards to move into Vermissa, and the
two lodged together. There was no other boarder, and
the hostess was an easy-going old Irish woman who left
them to themselves, so that they had a freedom for speech
and action welcome to men who had secrets in common.

Shafter had relented to the extent of letting McMurdo
come to his meals there when he liked, so that his intercourse* with Ettie was by no means broken. On the contrary,
it drew closer and more intimate as the weeks went by.

In his bedroom at his new abode McMurdo felt it to be
safe to take out the coining moulds, and under many a
pledge of secrecy a number of the brothers from the Lodge
were allowed to come in and see them, each of them
carrying away in his pocket some examples of the false
money, so cunningly struck that there was never the slightest
difficulty or danger in passing it. Why, with such a wonderful art at his command, McMurdo should condescend to
work at all was a perpetual mystery to his companions,
though he made it clear to any one who asked him that if
he lived without any visible means it would very quickly
bring the police on his track.

One policeman was, indeed, after him already; but the
incident, as luck would have it, did the adventurer a great
deal more good than harm. After the first introduction
there were few evenings when he did not find his way to
McGinty's saloon, there to make closer acquaintance with

'the boys',* which was the jovial title by which the dangerous gang who infested the place were known to each other.
His dashing manner and fearlessness of speech made him
a favourite with them all, while the rapid and scientific way
in which he polished off his antagonist in an 'all-in' bar-room
scrap* earned the respect of that rough community. Another incident, however, raised him even higher in their
estimation.

Just at the crowded hour one night, the door opened and
a man entered with the quiet blue uniform and peaked cap
of the Coal and Iron Police.* This was a special body raised
by the railways and colliery owners to supplement the efforts
of the ordinary civil police, who were perfectly helpless in
the face of the organized ruffianism which terrorized the
district. There was a hush as he entered, and many a curious
glance was cast at him; but the relations between policemen
and criminals are peculiar in the States,* and McGinty himself, standing behind his counter, showed no surprise when
the policeman* enrolled himself among his customers.

'A straight whiskey; for the night is bitter,' said the
police-officer. 'I don't think we have met before, Councillor?'

'You'll be the new captain?' said McGinty.

'That's so. We're looking to you, Councillor, and to the
other leading citizens, to help us in upholding law and order
in this township. Captain Marvin is my name*—of the Coal
and Iron.'

'We'd do better without you, Captain Marvin,' said
McGinty, coldly. 'For we have our own police* of the township, and no need for any imported goods. What are you
but the paid tool of the capitalists,* hired by them to club*
or to shoot your poorer fellow-citizen?'*

'Well, well, we won't argue about that,'* said the police-
officer, good-humouredly. 'I expect we all do our duty same
as we see it, but we can't all see it the same.' He had drunk
off his glass and had turned to go, when his eyes fell upon
the face of Jack McMurdo, who was scowling at his elbow.
'Hullo! Hullo!' he cried, looking him up and down. 'Here's
an old acquaintance!'*

McMurdo shrank away from him. 'I was never a friend to you nor any other cursed copper in my life,' said he.

'An acquaintance isn't always a friend,' said the police-captain, grinning. 'You're Jack McMurdo of Chicago, right enough, and don't you deny it!'

McMurdo shrugged his shoulders. 'I'm not denying it,'* said he. 'D'ye think I'm ashamed of my own name?'

'You've got good cause to be, anyhow.'

'What the devil d'you mean by that?' he roared with his fists clenched.

'No, no, Jack; bluster won't do with me. I was an officer in Chicago before ever I came to this darned coal-bunker, and I know a Chicago crook when I see one.'

McMurdo's face fell. 'Don't tell me that you're Marvin of the Chicago Central!' he cried.

'Just the same old Teddy Marvin at your service. We haven't forgotten the shooting of Jonas Pinto* up there.'

'I never shot him.'

'Did you not? That's good impartial evidence, ain't it? Well, his death came in uncommon handy for you, or they would have had you for shoving the queer. Well, we can let that be bygones, for, between you and me—and perhaps I'm going further than my duty in saying it—they could get no clear case against you, and Chicago's open to you tomorrow.'

'I'm very well where I am.'

'Well, I've given you the pointer,* and you're a sulky dog not to thank me for it.'

'Well, I suppose you mean well, and I do thank you,' said McMurdo in no very gracious manner.

'It's mum with me so long as I see you living on the straight,'* said the captain. 'But, by the Lord!* if you get off on the cross after this it's another story! So good night to you—and good night, Councillor.'

He left the bar-room; but not before he had created a local hero. McMurdo's deeds in far Chicago had been whispered before. He had put off all questions with a smile as one who did not wish to have greatness thrust upon him.* But now the thing was officially confirmed. The bar-loafers crowded round him and shook him heartily by the hand. He was free of the community from that time on. He could drink hard and show little trace of it, but that evening, had his mate Scanlan not been at hand to lead him home, the fêted hero would surely have spent his night under the bar.*

On a Saturday night McMurdo was introduced to the Lodge. He had thought to pass in without ceremony as being an initiate of Chicago; but there were particular rites in Vermissa of which they were proud, and these had to be undergone by every postulant.* The assembly met in a large room reserved for such purposes at the Union House. Some sixty members assembled at Vermissa; but that by no means represented the full strength of the organization, for there were several other lodges in the valley, and others across the mountains on either side, who exchanged members when any serious business was afoot, so that a crime might be done by men who were strangers to the locality.* Altogether, there were not less than five hundred scattered over the coal district.

In the bare assembly room the men were gathered round a long table. At the side was a second one laden with bottles and glasses, on which some members of the company were already turning their eyes. McGinty sat at the head with a flat black velvet cap upon his shock of tangled black hair and a coloured purple stole round his neck, so that he seemed to be a priest presiding over some diabolical ritual. To right and left of him were the higher Lodge officials, the cruel, handsome face of Ted Baldwin among them. Each of these wore some scarf or medallion as emblem of his office.

They were, for the most part, men of mature age; but the rest of the company consisted of young fellows from eighteen to twenty-five, the ready and capable agents who carried out the commands of their seniors. Among the older men were many whose features showed the tigerish, lawless souls within; but looking at the rank and file it was difficult to believe that these eager and open-faced young fellows were in very truth a dangerous gang of murderers, whose minds had suffered such complete moral perversion that they took a horrible pride in their proficiency at the business, and looked with the deepest respect at the man who had the reputation for making what they called a 'clean job'.

To their contorted natures it had become a spirited and chivalrous thing to volunteer for service against some man who had never injured them, and whom, in many cases, they had never seen in their lives. The crime committed, they quarrelled as to who had actually struck the fatal blow, and amused each other and the company by describing the cries and contortions of the murdered man.

At first they had shown some secrecy in their arrangements; but at the time which this narrative describes their proceedings were extraordinarily open, for the repeated failures of the law had proved to them that, on the one hand, no one would dare to witness against them, and, on the other, they had an unlimited number of staunch witnesses upon whom they could call, and a well-filled treasure chest* from which they could draw the funds to engage the best legal talent in the State. In ten long years of outrage there had been no single conviction, and the only danger that ever threatened the Scowrers* lay in the victim himself, who, however outnumbered and taken by surprise, might, and occasionally did, leave his mark upon his assailants.

McMurdo had been warned that some ordeal lay before him, but no one would tell him in what it consisted. He was led now into an outer room by two solemn brothers. Through the plank partition he could hear the murmur of many voices from the assembly within. Once or twice he caught the sound of his own name, and he knew that they were discussing his candidature. Then there entered an inner guard with a green and gold sash across his chest.

'The Bodymaster orders that he shall be trussed, blinded, and entered,' said he. The three of them then removed his coat, turned up the sleeve of his right arm, and finally passed a rope round above the elbows and made it fast. They next placed a thick black cap right over his head and the upper part of his face, so that he could see nothing. He was then led into the assembly hall.

It was pitch-dark and very oppressive under his hood. He heard the rustle and murmur of the people round him, and then the voice of McGinty sounded, dull and distant, through the covering of his ears.

'John McMurdo,' said the voice, 'are you already a member of the Ancient Order of Freemen?'

He bowed in assent.

'Is your lodge No. 29, Chicago?'

He bowed again.

'Dark nights are unpleasant,' said the voice.

'Yes, for strangers to travel,' he answered.

'The clouds are heavy.'

'Yes, a storm is approaching.'

'Are the brethren satisfied?' asked the Bodymaster.

There was a general murmur of assent.

'We know, brother, by your sign and by your counter sign, that you are indeed one of us,' said McGinty. 'We would have you know, however, that in this county and in other counties of these parts we have certain rites,* and also certain duties of our own, which call for good men. Are you ready to be tested?'

'I am.'

'Are you of stout heart?'

'I am.'

'Take a stride forward to prove it.'

As the words were said he felt two hard points in front of his eyes, pressing upon them so that it appeared as if he could not move forward without a danger of losing them. None the less, he nerved himself to step resolutely out, and as he did so the pressure melted away. There was a low murmur of applause.

'He is of stout heart,' said the voice. 'Can you bear pain?'

'As well as another,' he answered.

'Test him!'

It was all he could do to keep himself from screaming out, for an agonizing pain shot through his forearm. He nearly fainted at the sudden shock of it; but he bit his lip and clenched his hands to hide his agony.

'I can take more than that,' said he.

This time there was loud applause. A finer first appearance had never been made in the Lodge. Hands clapped him on the back, and the hood was plucked from his head. He stood blinking and smiling amid the congratulations of the brothers.

'One last word, Brother McMurdo,' said McGinty. 'You have already sworn the oath of secrecy and fidelity, and you are aware that the punishment for any breach of it is instant and inevitable death?'

'I am,' said McMurdo.

'And you accept the rule of the Bodymaster for the time being under all circumstances?'

'I do.'

'Then, in the name of Lodge 341, Vermissa, I welcome you to its privileges and debates. You will put the liquor on the table, Brother Scanlan, and we will drink to our worthy brother.'

McMurdo's coat had been brought to him; but before putting it on he examined his right arm, which still smarted heavily. There, on the flesh of the forearm, was a clear-cut circle with a triangle within it, deep and red, as the branding-iron had left it. One or two of his neighbours pulled up their sleeves and showed their own Lodge marks.

'We've all had it,' said one, 'but not all as brave as you over it.'

'Tut! It was nothing,' said he; but it burned and ached all the same.

When the drinks which followed the ceremony of initiation had all been disposed of, the business of the Lodge proceeded. McMurdo, accustomed only to the prosaic performances of Chicago, listened with open ears, and more surprise than he ventured to show, to what followed.

'The first business on the agenda paper',* said McGinty, 'is to read the following letter from Division Master Windle, of Merton County, Lodge 249. He says:

Dear Sir,—There is a job to be done on Andrew Rae, of Rae and Sturmash, coal-owners near this place. You will remember that your Lodge owes us a return, having had the services of two brethren in the matter of the patrolman last fall. If you will send two good men they will be taken charge of by Treasurer Higgins of this Lodge, whose address you know. He will show them when to act and where.—Yours in freedom. J. W. Windle, DMAOF*

Windle has never refused us when we have had occasion to ask for the loan of a man or two, and it is not for us to refuse him.' McGinty paused and looked round the room with his dull, malevolent eyes. 'Who will volunteer for the job?'

Several young fellows held up their hands. The Bodymaster looked at them with an approving smile.

'You'll do, Tiger Cormac. If you handle it as well as you did the last, you won't be wrong.* And you, Wilson.'

'I've no pistol,' said the volunteer, a mere boy in his teens.

'It's your first, is it not? Well, you have to be blooded some time.* It will be a great start for you. As to the pistol, you'll find it waiting for you, or I'm mistaken. If you report yourselves on Monday it will be time enough. You'll get a great welcome when you return.'

'Any reward this time?' asked Cormac, a thick-set, dark-faced, brutal-looking young man, whose ferocity had earned him the nickname of 'Tiger'.

'Never mind the reward. You just do it for the honour of the thing. Maybe when it is done there will be a few odd dollars at the bottom of the box.'

'What has the man done?' asked young Wilson.

'Sure, it's not for the likes of you to ask what the man has done. He has been judged over there. That's no business of ours. All we have to do is to carry it out for them, same as they would for us. Speaking of that, two brothers from the Merton lodge are coming over to us next week to do some business in this quarter.'

'Who are they?' asked someone.

'Faith, it is wiser not to ask. If you know nothing you can testify nothing, and no trouble can come of it. But they are men who will make a clean job when they are about it.'

'And time, too!' cried Ted Baldwin. 'Folk are gettin' out of hand in these parts. It was only last week that three of our men were turned off by Foreman Blaker. It's been owing him a long time, and he'll get it full and proper.'

'Get what?' McMurdo whispered to his neighbour.

'The business end of a buck-shot cartridge,' cried the man, with a loud laugh. 'What think you of our ways, Brother?'

McMurdo's criminal soul seemed to have already absorbed the spirit of the vile association of which he was now a member. 'I like it well,' said he. ' 'Tis a proper place for a lad of mettle.'

Several of those who sat around heard his words and applauded them.

'What's that?' cried the black-maned Bodymaster, from the end of the table.

' 'Tis our new brother, sir, who finds our ways to his taste.'

McMurdo rose to his feet for an instant. 'I would say, Eminent Bodymaster,* that if a man should be wanted I should take it as an honour to be chosen to help the Lodge.'

There was great applause at this. It was felt that a new sun was pushing its rim above the horizon. To some of the elders it seemed that the progress was a little too rapid.

'I would move,' said the secretary, Harraway, a vulture-faced old greybeard who sat near the chairman, 'that Brother McMurdo should wait until it is the good pleasure of the Lodge to employ him.'*

'Sure, that was what I meant; I'm in your hands,' said McMurdo.

'Your time will come, Brother,' said the chairman. 'We have marked you down as a willing man, and we believe that you will do good work in these parts. There is a small matter to-night in which you may take a hand, if it so please you.'

'I will wait for something that is worth while.'

'You can come to-night, anyhow, and it will help you to know what we stand for in this community. I will make the announcement later. Meanwhile'—he glanced at his agenda paper—'I have one or two more points to bring before the meeting. First of all, I will ask the treasurer as to our bank balance. There is the pension to Jim Carnaway's widow. He was struck down doing the work of the Lodge, and it is for us to see that she is not the loser.'

'Jim was shot last month when they tried to kill Chester Wilcox, of Marley Creek,' McMurdo's neighbour informed him.

'The funds are good at the moment,' said the treasurer, with the bank-book in front of him. 'The firms have been generous of late. Max Linder and Co. paid five hundred to be left alone. Walker Brothers sent in a hundred, but I took it on myself to return it and ask for five. If I do not hear by Wednesday their winding gear* may get out of order. We had to burn their breaker* last year before they became reasonable. Then the West Section Coaling Company has paid its annual contribution.* We have enough in hand to meet any obligations.'

'What about Archie Swindon?' asked a brother.

'He has sold out and left the district. The old devil left a note for us to say that he had rather be a free crossing-sweeper in New York than a large mine-owner under the power of a ring of blackmailers. By Gar! it was as well that he made a break for it before the note reached us! I guess he won't* show his face in this valley again.'

An elderly, clean-shaven man with a kindly face and a good brow rose from the end of the table which faced the chairman. 'Mr Treasurer,' he asked, 'may I ask who has bought the property of this man that we have driven out of the district?'

'Yes, Brother Morris. It has been bought by the State and Merton County Railroad Company.'*

'And who bought the mines of Todman and of Lee that came into the market in the same way last year?'

'The same company, Brother Morris.'

'And who bought the ironworks of Manson and of Shuman and of Van Deher and of Atwood, which have all been given up of late?'

'They were all bought by the West Gilmerton General Mining Company.'

'I don't see, Brother Morris,' said the chairman, 'that it matters a nickel to us who buys them, since they can't carry them out of the district.'

'With all respect to you, Eminent Bodymaster, I think that it may matter very much to us. This process has been going on now for ten long years. We are gradually driving all the small men out of trade. What is the result? We find in their places great companies like the Railroad or the General Iron,* who have their directors in New York or Philadelphia, and care nothing for our threats. We can take it out of their local bosses, but it only means that others will be sent in their stead. And we are making it dangerous for ourselves. The small men could not harm us. They had not the money nor the power. So long as we did not squeeze them too dry, they would stay on under our power. But if these big companies find that we stand between them and their profits, they will spare no pains and no expense to hunt us down and bring us to court.'

There was a hush at these ominous words, and every face darkened as gloomy looks were exchanged. So omnipotent and unchallenged had they been that the very thought that there was possible retribution in the background had been banished from their minds. And yet the idea struck a chill to the most reckless of them.

'It is my advice', the speaker continued, 'that we go easier* upon the small men. On the day that they have all been driven out the power of this society will have been broken.'

Unwelcome truths are not popular. There were angry cries as the speaker resumed his seat. McGinty rose with gloom upon his brow.

'Brother Morris,' said he, 'you were always a croaker.* So long as the members of this Lodge stand together there is no power in the United States that can touch them. Sure, have we not tried it often enough in the law courts? I expect the big companies will find it easier to pay than to fight,

same as the little companies do. And now, brethren'—
McGinty took off his black velvet cap and his stole as he
spoke—'this Lodge has finished its business for the evening
save for one small matter which may be mentioned when we
are parting. The time has now come for fraternal refresh-
ment and for harmony.'

Strange indeed is human nature. Here were these men to
whom murder was familiar, who again and again had struck
down the father of the family, some man against whom they
had no personal feeling, without one thought of compunc-
tion or of compassion for his weeping wife or helpless
children, and yet the tender or pathetic in music could move
them to tears. McMurdo had a fine tenor voice, and if he
had failed to gain the goodwill of the Lodge before, it could
no longer have been withheld after he had thrilled them
with 'I'm Sitting on the Stile, Mary',* and 'On the Banks of
Allan Water'. In his very first night the new recruit had
made himself one of the most popular of the brethren,
marked already for advancement and high office. There
were other qualities, however, besides those of good fellowship, to make a worthy Freeman, and of these he was given
an example before the evening was over. The whiskey bottle
had passed round many times, and the men were flushed
and ripe for mischief, when their Bodymaster rose once
more to address them.

'Boys,' said he, 'there's one man in this town that wants
trimming up, and it's for you to see that he gets it. I'm
speaking of James Stanger, of the *Herald*.* You've seen how
he's been opening his mouth against us again?'

There was a murmur of assent, with many a muttered
oath. McGinty took a slip of paper from his waistcoat
pocket.

' "Law and Order!" That's how he heads it. "Reign of
Terror in the Coal and Iron District. Twelve years have now
elapsed since the first assassinations which proved the existence of a criminal organization in our midst. From that day
these outrages have never ceased, until now they have
reached a pitch which makes us the opprobrium of the

civilized world. Is it for such results as this that our great country welcomes to its bosom the alien who flies from the despotisms of Europe? Is it that they shall themselves become tyrants over the very men who have given them shelter, and that a state of terrorism and lawlessness should be established under the very shadow of the sacred folds of the starry flag of freedom which would raise horror in our minds if we read of it as existing under the most effete monarchy of the East? The men are known. The organization is patent and public. How long are we to endure it? Can we for ever live——" Sure, I've read enough of the slush!' cried the chairman, tossing the paper down upon the table. 'That's what he says of us. The question I'm asking you is, What shall we say to him?'

'Kill him!' cried a dozen fierce voices.

'I protest against that,' said Brother Morris, the man of the good brow and shaven face. 'I tell you, brethren, that our hand is too heavy in this valley, and that there will come a point where, in self-defence, every man will unite to crush us out. James Stanger is an old man. He is respected in the township and the district. His paper stands for all that is solid in the valley. If that man is struck down, there will be a stir through this State that will only end with our destruction.'

'And how would they bring about our destruction, Mister Stand-back?' cried McGinty. 'Is it by the police? Sure, half of them are in our pay and half of them afraid of us. Or is it by the law courts and the judge? Haven't we tried that before now, and what ever came of it?'

'There is a Judge Lynch* that might try the case,' said Brother Morris.

A general shout of anger greeted the suggestion.

'I have but to raise my finger,' cried McGinty, 'and I could put two hundred men into this town that would clear it out from end to end.' Then, suddenly raising his voice and bending his huge black brows into a terrible frown, 'See here, Brother Morris, I have my eye on you, and have had for some time! You've no heart yourself, and you try to take

122

the heart out of others. It will be an ill day for you, Brother Morris, when your own name comes on our agenda paper, and I'm thinking that it's just there that I ought to place it.'

Morris had turned deadly pale, and his knees seemed to give way under him as he fell back into his chair. He raised his glass in his trembling hand and drank before he could answer. 'I apologize, Eminent Bodymaster, to you and to every brother in this Lodge if I have said more than I should. I am a faithful member—you all know that—and it is my fear lest evil come to the Lodge which makes me speak in anxious words. But I have greater trust in your judgment than in my own, Eminent Bodymaster, and I promise you that I will not offend again.'

The Bodymaster's scowl relaxed as he listened to the humble words. 'Very good, Brother Morris. It's myself that would be sorry if it were needful to give you a lesson. But so long as I am in this chair we shall be a united Lodge in word and in deed. And now, boys,' he continued, looking round at the company, 'I'll say this much, that if Stanger got his full deserts there would be more trouble than we need ask for. These editors hang together, and every journal in the state would be crying out for police and troops. But I guess you can give him a pretty severe warning. Will you fix it, Brother Baldwin?'

'Sure!' said the young man, eagerly.

'How many will you take?'

'Half-a-dozen, and two to guard to door. You'll come, Gower, and you, Mansel, and you, Scanlan, and the two Willabys.'

'I promised the new brother he should go,' said the chairman.

Ted Baldwin looked at McMurdo with eyes which showed that he had not forgotten nor forgiven. 'Well, he can come if he wants,' he said, in a surly voice. 'That's enough. The sooner we get to work the better.'

The company broke up with shouts and yells and snatches of drunken song. The bar was still crowded with revellers, and many of the brethren remained there. The little band who had been told off for duty passed out into the street, proceeding in twos and threes along the side-walk so as not to provoke attention. It was a bitterly cold night, with a half-moon shining brilliantly in a frosty, star-spangled sky. The men stopped and gathered in a yard which faced a high building. The words 'Vermissa Herald' were printed in gold lettering between the brightly-lit windows. From within came the clanking of the printing-press.

'Here, you,' said Baldwin to McMurdo; 'you can stand below at the door and see that the road is kept open for us. Arthur Willaby can stay with you. You others come with me. Have no fear, boys, for we have a dozen witnesses that we are in the Union Bar at this very moment.'

It was nearly midnight, and the street was deserted save for one or two revellers upon their way home. The party crossed the road and, pushing open the door of the newspaper office, Baldwin and his men rushed in and up the stair which faced them. McMurdo and another remained below. From the room above came a shout, a cry for help, and then the sound of trampling feet and of falling chairs. An instant later a grey-haired man rushed out on to the landing.

He was seized before he could get farther, and his spectacles came tinkling down to McMurdo's feet. There was a thud and a groan. He was on his face and half-a-dozen sticks were clattering together as they fell upon him. He writhed, and his long, thin limbs quivered under the blows. The others ceased at last; but Baldwin, his cruel face set in an infernal smile, was hacking at the man's head, which he vainly endeavoured to defend with his arms. His white hair was dabbled with patches of blood. Baldwin was still stooping over his victim, putting in a short, vicious blow whenever he could see a part exposed, when McMurdo dashed up the stair and pushed him back.

'You'll kill the man,' said he. 'Drop it!'

Baldwin looked at him in amazement. 'Curse you!' he cried. 'Who are you to interfere—you that are new to the Lodge? Stand back!' He raised his stick; but McMurdo had whipped his pistol out of his hip pocket.

'Stand back yourself!' he cried. 'I'll blow your face in if you lay a hand on me.* As to the Lodge, wasn't it the order of the Bodymaster that the man was not to be killed—and what are you doing but killing him?'

'It's truth he says,' remarked one of the men.

'By Gar! you'd best hurry yourselves!' cried the man below. 'The windows are all lighting up and you'll have the whole town here* inside of five minutes.'

There was indeed the sound of shouting in the street, and a little group of compositors and typesetters was forming in the hall below and nerving itself to action. Leaving the limp and motionless body of the editor at the head of the stair, the criminals rushed down and made their way swiftly along the street. Having reached the Union House, some of them mixed with the crowd in McGinty's saloon, whispering across the bar to the Boss that the job had been well carried through. Others, and among them McMurdo, broke away into side-streets, and so by devious paths to their own homes.

· **CHAPTER 4** ·

The Valley of Fear

WHEN McMurdo awoke next morning he had good reason to remember his initiation into the Lodge. His head ached with the effect of the drink, and his arm, where he had been branded, was hot and swollen. Having his own peculiar source of income,* he was irregular in his attendance at his work; so he had a late breakfast and remained at home for the morning, writing a long letter to a friend.* Afterwards he read the *Daily Herald*. In a special column, put in at the last moment, he read, 'OUTRAGE AT THE *HERALD* OFFICE. EDITOR SERIOUSLY INJURED.' It was a short account of the facts with which he was himself more familiar than the writer could have been. It ended with the statement:

The matter is now in the hands of the police, but it can hardly be hoped that their exertions will be attended by any better results than in the past. Some of the men were recognized, and there is hope that a conviction may be obtained. The source of the outrage was, it need hardly be said, that infamous society which has held this community in bondage for so long a period, and against which the *Herald* has taken so uncompromising a stand. Mr Stanger's many friends will rejoice to hear that, though he has been cruelly and brutally beaten, and has sustained severe injuries about the head, there is no immediate danger to his life.

Below, it stated that a guard of Coal and Iron Police, armed with Winchester rifles, had been requisitioned for the defence of the office.

McMurdo had laid down the paper, and was lighting his pipe with a hand which was shaky from the excesses of the previous evening, when there was a knock outside, and his landlady brought to him a note which had just been handed in by a lad. It was unsigned, and ran thus:

I should wish to speak to you, but had rather not do so in your house. You will find me beside the flagstaff upon Miller Hill. If you will come there now I have something which it is important for you to hear and for me to say.

McMurdo read the note twice with the utmost surprise; for he could not imagine what it meant or who was the author of it. Had it been in a feminine hand he might have imagined that it was the beginning of one of those adventures which had been familiar enough in his past life.* But it was the writing of a man, and of a well-educated one, too. Finally, after some hesitation, he determined to see the matter through.

Miller Hill is an ill-kept public park in the very centre of the town. In summer it is a favourite resort of the people, but in winter it is desolate enough. From the top of it one has a view not only of the whole grimy, straggling town, but of the winding valley beneath, with its scattered mines and factories blackening the snow on either side of it, and of the wooded and white-capped ranges flanking it.

McMurdo strolled up the winding path hedged in with evergreens until he reached the deserted restaurant which forms the centre of summer gaiety. Beside it was a bare flagstaff, and underneath it a man, his hat drawn down and the collar of his overcoat raised up. When he turned his face McMurdo saw that it was Brother Morris, he who had incurred the anger of the Bodymaster the night before. The Lodge sign was given and exchanged as they met.

'I wanted to have a word with you, Mr McMurdo,' said the older man, speaking with a hesitation which showed that he was on delicate ground. 'It was kind of you to come.'

'Why did you not put your name to the note?'

'One has to be cautious, Mister. One never knows in times like these how a thing may come back to one. One never knows either who to trust or who not to trust.'

'Surely one may trust brothers of the Lodge?'

'No, no; not always,' cried Morris with vehemence. 'Whatever we say, even what we think, seems to go back to that man McGinty.'

'Look here,' said McMurdo sternly; 'it was only last night, as you know well, that I swore good faith to our Bodymaster. Would you be asking me to break my oath?'

'If that is the view you take,' said Morris, sadly, 'I can only say that I am sorry I gave you the trouble to come and meet me. Things have come to a bad pass when two free citizens cannot speak their thoughts to each other.'

McMurdo, who had been watching his companion very narrowly, relaxed somewhat in his bearing. 'Sure, I spoke for myself only,' said he. 'I am a new-comer, as you know, and I am strange to it all. It is not for me to open my mouth, Mr Morris, and if you think well to say anything to me I am here to hear it.'

'And to take it back to Boss McGinty,' said Morris bitterly.

'Indeed, then, you do me injustice there,' cried McMurdo. 'For myself I am loyal to the Lodge, and so I tell you straight; but I would be a poor creature if I were to repeat to any other what you might say to me in confidence. It will go no further than me; though I warn you that you may get neither help nor sympathy.'

'I have given up looking for either the one or the other,' said Morris. 'I may be putting my very life in your hands by what I say, but, bad as you are—and it seemed to me last night that you were shaping* to be as bad as the worst—still you are new to it, and your conscience cannot yet be as hardened as theirs. That was why I thought to speak with you.'

'Well, what have you to say?'

'If you give me away, may a curse be on you!'*

'Sure, I said I would not.'

'I would ask you, then, when you joined the Freemen's Society in Chicago, and swore vows of charity and fidelity, did ever it cross your mind that you might find it would lead you to crime?'

'If you call it crime,' McMurdo answered.

'Call it crime!' cried Morris, his voice vibrating with passion. 'You have seen little of it if you can call it anything else. Was it crime last night when a man old enough to be your father was beaten till the blood dripped from his white hairs? Was that crime—or what else would you call it?'

'There are some would say it was war,' said McMurdo. 'A war of two classes with all in, so that each struck as best it could.'

'Well, did you think of such a thing when you joined the Freemen's Society in Chicago?'

'No, I'm bound to say I did not.'

'Nor did I when I joined it at Philadelphia. It was just a benefit club and a meeting-place for one's fellows. Then I heard of this place—curse the hour that the name first fell upon my ears!—and I came to better myself. My God! to better myself! My wife and three children came with me. I started a dry-goods store in Market Square, and I prospered well. The word had gone round that I was a Freeman, and I was forced to join the local lodge, same as you did last night. I've the badge of shame on my forearm, and something worse branded on my heart. I found that I was under the orders of a black villain, and caught in a meshwork of crime. What could I do? Every word I said to make things better was taken as treason, same as it was last night. I can't get away, for all I have in the world is in my store. If I leave the society, I know well that it means murder to me, and God knows what to my wife and children. Oh, man, it is awful—awful!' He put his hands to his face, and his body shook with convulsive sobs.

McMurdo shrugged his shoulders. 'You were too soft for the job,' said he. 'You are the wrong sort for such work.'

'I had a conscience and a religion, but they made me a criminal among them. I was chosen for a job. If I backed down I knew well what would come to me. Maybe I'm a coward. Maybe it's the thought of my poor little woman and the children that makes me one. Anyhow, I went. I guess it will haunt me for ever.

'It was a lonely house, twenty miles from here, over the range yonder. I was told off for the door, same as you were last night. They could not trust me with the job. The others went in. When they came out their hands were crimson to the wrists. As we turned away a child was screaming out of the house behind us. It was a boy of five who had seen his father murdered. I nearly fainted with the horror of it, and yet I had to keep a bold and smiling face; for well I knew that if I did not it would be out of my house that they would come next with their bloody hands, and it would be my little Fred that would be screaming for his father.

'But I was a criminal then—part sharer in a murder, lost for ever in this world, and lost also in the next. I am a good Catholic, but the priest would have no word with me when he heard I was a Scowrer, and I am excommunicated from my faith. That's how it stands with me. And I see you going down the same road, and I ask you what the end is to be? Are you ready to be a cold-blooded murderer also, or can we do anything to stop it?'

'What would you do?' asked McMurdo, abruptly. 'You would not inform?'

'God forbid!' cried Morris. 'Sure, the very thought would cost me my life.'

'That's well,' said McMurdo. 'I'm thinking that you are a weak man, and that you make too much of the matter.'

'Too much! Wait till you have lived here longer. Look down the valley! See the cloud of a hundred chimneys that over-shadows it. I tell you that the cloud of murder hangs thicker and lower than that over the heads of the people. It is the Valley of Fear—the Valley of Death. The terror is in the hearts of the people from the dusk to the dawn. Wait, young man, and you will learn for yourself.'

'Well, I'll let you know what I think when I have seen more,' said McMurdo carelessly. 'What is very clear is that you are not the man for the place, and that the sooner you sell out—if you only get a dime a dollar for what the business is worth—the better it will be for you. What you have said is safe with me, but, by Gar! if I thought you were an informer—'

'No, no!' cried Morris piteously.

'Well, let it rest at that. I'll bear what you have said in mind, and maybe some day I'll come back to it. I expect you meant kindly by speaking to me like this. Now I'll be getting home.'

'One word before you go,' said Morris. 'We may have been seen together. They may want to know what we have spoken about.'

'Ah! that's well thought of.'

'I offer you a clerkship in my store.'

'And I refuse it. That's our business. Well, so long, Brother Morris, and may you find things go better with you in the future.'*

That same afternoon, as McMurdo sat smoking, lost in thought, beside the stove of his sitting-room, the door swung open, and its framework was filled with the huge figure of Boss McGinty. He passed the sign, and then, seating himself opposite to the young man, he looked at him steadily for some time, a look which was as steadily returned.

'I'm not much of a visitor, Brother McMurdo,' he said at last. 'I guess I am too busy over the folk that visit me. But

I thought I'd stretch a point and drop down to see you in your own house.'

'I'm proud to see you here, Councillor,' McMurdo answered, heartily, bringing his whiskey-bottle out of the cupboard. 'It's an honour that I had not expected.'

'How's the arm?' asked the Boss.

McMurdo made a wry face. 'Well, I'm not forgetting it,' he said. 'But it's worth it.'

'Yes, it's worth it,' the other answered, 'to those that are loyal, and go through with it, and are a help to the Lodge. What were you speaking to Brother Morris about on Miller Hill this morning?'

The question came so suddenly that it was well that he had his answer prepared. He burst into a hearty laugh. 'Morris didn't know I could earn a living here at home. He sha'n't know either, for he has got too much conscience for the likes of me. But he's a good-hearted old chap. It was his idea that I was at a loose end, and that he would do me a good turn by offering me a clerkship in a dry-goods store.'

'Oh, that was it?'

'Yes, that was it.'

'And you refused it?'

'Sure. Couldn't I earn ten times as much in my own bedroom with four hours' work?'

'That's so. But I wouldn't get about too much with Morris.'

'Why not?'

'Well, I guess because I tell you not. That's enough for most folk in these parts.'

'It may be enough for most folks; but it ain't enough for me, Councillor,' said McMurdo boldly. 'If you are a judge of men you'll know that.'

The swarthy giant glared at him, and his hairy paw closed for an instant round the glass as though he would hurl it at the head of his companion. Then he laughed in his loud, boisterous, insincere fashion.

'You're a queer card, for sure,' said he. 'Well, if you want reasons, I'll give them. Did Morris say nothing to you against the Lodge?'

'No.'

'Nor against me?'

'No.'

'Well, that's because he daren't trust you. But in his heart he is not a loyal brother. We know that well. So we watch him, and we wait for the time to admonish him. I'm thinking that the time is drawing near. There's no room for scabby sheep in our pen. But if you keep company with a disloyal man, we might think that you were disloyal, too.* See?'

'There's no chance of my keeping company with him; for I dislike the man,' McMurdo answered. 'As to being disloyal, if it was any man but you, he would not use the word to me twice.'

'Well, that's enough,' said McGinty, draining off his glass. 'I came down to give you a word in season, and you've had it.'

'I'd like to know,' said McMurdo, 'how you ever came to learn that I had spoken with Morris at all.'

McGinty laughed. 'It's my business to know what goes on in this township,' said he. 'I guess you'd best reckon on my hearing all that passes. Well, time's up, and I'll just say—'

But his leave-taking was cut short in a very unexpected fashion. With a sudden crash the door flew open, and three frowning, intent faces glared in at them from under the peaks of police caps. McMurdo sprang to his feet and half drew his revolver; but his arm stopped midway as he became conscious that two Winchester rifles were levelled at his head. A man in uniform advanced into the room, a six-shooter in his hand. It was Captain Marvin, once of Chicago, and now of the Coal and Iron Constabulary.* He shook his head with a half smile at McMurdo.

'I thought you'd be getting into trouble, Mr Crooked McMurdo of Chicago,' said he. 'Can't keep out of it, can you? Take your hat and come along with us.'

'I guess you'll pay for this, Captain Marvin,' said McGinty. 'Who are you, I'd like to know, to break into a house in this fashion and molest honest, law-abiding men?'

'You're standing out in this deal, Councillor McGinty,' said the police captain. 'We are not out after you, but after this man McMurdo. It is for you to help, not to hinder us in our duty.'

'He is a friend of mine, and I'll answer for his conduct,' said the Boss.

'By all accounts, Mr McGinty, you may have to answer for your own conduct some of these days,' the police captain answered. 'This man McMurdo was a crook before ever he came here, and he's a crook still. Cover him, Patrolman, while I disarm him.'

'There's my pistol,' said McMurdo, coolly. 'Maybe, Captain Marvin, if you and I were alone and face to face, you would not take me so easily.'

'Where's your warrant?' asked McGinty. 'By Gar! a man might as well live in Russia* as in Vermissa while folk like you are running the police. It's a capitalist outrage, and you'll hear more of it, I reckon.'

'You do what you think is your duty the best way you can, Councillor. We'll look after ours.'

'What am I accused of?' asked McMurdo.

'Of being concerned in the beating of old Editor Stanger at the *Herald* office. It wasn't your fault that it isn't a murder charge.'

'Well, if that's all you have against him,' cried McGinty with a laugh, 'you can save yourself a deal of trouble by dropping it right now. This man was with me in my saloon playing poker up to midnight, and I can bring a dozen to prove it.'

'That's your affair, and I guess you can settle it in court tomorrow. Meanwhile, come on, McMurdo, and come quietly if you don't want a gun* across your head. You stand wide, Mr McGinty; for I warn you I will brook no resistance when I am on duty!'

So determined was the appearance of the captain that both McMurdo and his Boss were forced to accept the situation. The latter managed to have a few whispered words with the prisoner before they parted.

'What about—' He jerked his thumb upwards to signify the coining plant.

'All right,' whispered McMurdo, who had devised a safe hiding-place under the floor.*

'I'll bid you good-bye,' said the Boss, shaking hands. 'I'll see Reilly,* the lawyer, and take the defence upon myself. Take my word for it that they won't be able to hold you.'

'I wouldn't bet on that. Guard the prisoner, you two, and shoot him if he tries any games. I'll search the house before I leave.'

Marvin did so, but apparently found no trace of the concealed plant. When he had descended he and his men escorted McMurdo to headquarters. Darkness had fallen, and a keen blizzard was blowing, so that the streets were nearly deserted; but a few loiterers followed the group and emboldened by invisibility shouted imprecations at the prisoner.

'Lynch the cursed Scowrer!'* they cried. 'Lynch him!' They laughed and jeered as he was pushed into the police station.* After a short formal examination from the inspector-in-charge, he was handed on to the common cell. Here he found Baldwin and three other criminals of the night before, all arrested that afternoon, and waiting their trial next morning.

But even within this inner fortress of the law the long arm of the Freemen was able to extend. Late at night there came a jailer with a straw bundle for their bedding, out of which he extracted two bottles of whiskey, some glasses, and a pack of cards.* They spent a hilarious night without an anxious thought as to the ordeal of the morning.

Nor had they cause, as the result was to show. The magistrate could not possibly, on the evidence, have held them for* a higher court. On the one hand, the compositors and pressmen were forced to admit that the light was uncertain, that they were themselves much perturbed, and that it was difficult for them to swear to the identity of the assailants, although they believed that the accused were among them. Cross-examined by the clever attorney who had been engaged by McGinty, they were even more nebulous in their evidence.

The injured man had already deposed that he was so taken by surprise by the suddenness of the attack that he could state nothing beyond the fact that the first man who struck him wore a moustache. He added that he knew them to be Scowrers, since no one else in the community could possibly have any enmity to him, and he had long been threatened on account of his outspoken editorials. On the other hand, it was clearly shown by the united and unfaltering evidence of six citizens, including that high municipal official Councillor McGinty, that the men had been at a card party at the Union House until an hour very much later than the commission of the outrage.

Needless to say that they were discharged with something very near to an apology from the Bench for the inconvenience to which they had been put, together with an implied censure of Captain Marvin and the police for their officious zeal.

The verdict was greeted with loud applause by a Court in which McMurdo saw many familiar faces. Brothers of the Lodge smiled and waved. But there were others who sat with compressed lips and brooding eyes as the men filed out of the dock. One of them, a little dark-bearded, resolute fellow, put the thoughts of himself and comrades into words as the ex-prisoners passed him.

'You damned murderers!' he said. 'We'll fix you yet.'*

· CHAPTER 5 ·

The Darkest Hour

I F anything had been needed to give an impetus to Jack McMurdo's popularity among his fellows, it would have been his arrest and acquittal. That a man on the very night of joining the Lodge should have done something which brought him before the magistrate was a new record in the annals of the society. Already he had earned the reputation of a good boon companion, a cheery reveller, and withal a man of high temper, who would not take an insult even from the all-powerful Boss himself. But, in addition to this, he impressed his comrades with the idea that among them all there was not one whose brain was so ready to devise a bloodthirsty scheme, or whose hand would be more capable of carrying it out. 'He'll be the boy for the clean job,' said the oldsters to each other, and waited their time until they could set him to his work.

McGinty had instruments enough already but he recognized that this was a supremely able one. He felt like a man holding a fierce bloodhound in leash. There were curs to do the smaller work, but some day he would slip this creature upon its prey. A few members of the Lodge, Ted Baldwin among them, resented the rapid rise of the stranger, and hated him for it, but they kept clear of him, for he was as ready to fight as to laugh.

But if he gained favour with his fellows, there was another quarter, one which had become even more vital to him, in which he lost it. Ettie Shafter's father would have nothing more to do with him, nor would he allow him to enter the house. Ettie herself was too deeply in love to give him up altogether, and yet her own good sense warned her of what would come from a marriage with a man who was regarded as a criminal.

One morning after a sleepless night she determined to see him, possibly for the last time, and make one strong endeavour to draw him from those evil influences which were sucking him down. She went to his house, as he had often begged her to do, and made her way into the room which he used as his sitting-room. He was seated at a table with his back turned and a letter in front of him. A sudden spirit of girlish mischief came over her—she was still only nineteen. He had not heard her when she pushed open the door. Now she tip-toed forward, and laid her hand lightly upon his bended shoulders.

If she had expected to startle him, she certainly succeeded; but only in turn to be startled herself. With a tiger spring he turned on her, and his right hand was feeling for her throat. At the same instant, with the other hand he crumpled up the paper that lay before him. For an instant he stood glaring. Then astonishment and joy took the place of the ferocity which had convulsed his features—a ferocity which had sent her shrinking back in horror as from something which had never before intruded into her gentle life.*

'It's you!' said he, mopping his brow. 'And to think that you should come to me, heart of my heart, and I should find nothing better to do than to want to strangle you! Come then, darling,' and he held out his arms 'let me make it up to you.'

But she had not recovered from that sudden glimpse of guilty fear which she had read in the man's face. All her woman's instinct told her that it was not the mere fright of a man who is startled. Guilt—that was it—guilt and fear.

'What's come over you, Jack?' she cried. 'Why were you so scared of me? Oh, Jack, if your conscience was at ease, you would not have looked at me like that!'

'Sure, I was thinking of other things, and when you came tripping so lightly on those fairy feet of yours—'

'No, no; it was more than that, Jack.' Then a sudden suspicion seized her. 'Let me see that letter you were writing.'*

'Ah, Ettie, I couldn't do that.'

Her suspicions became certainties.

'It's to another woman!' she cried. 'I know it. Why else should you hold it from me? Was it to your wife that you were writing? How am I to know that you are not a married man—you, a stranger, that nobody knows?'

'I am not married, Ettie. See now, I swear it. You're the only one woman on earth to me.* By the Cross of Christ, I swear it!'

He was so white with passionate earnestness that she could not but believe him.

'Well, then,' she cried, 'why will you not show me the letter?'

'I'll tell you, acushla,' said he. 'I'm under oath not to show it, and just as I wouldn't break my word to you, so I would keep it to those who hold my promise. It's the business of the Lodge,* and even to you it's secret. And if I was scared when a hand fell on me, can't you understand it when it might have been the hand of a detective?'

She felt that he was telling the truth. He gathered her into his arms, and kissed away her fears and doubts.

'Sit here by me, then. It's a queer throne for such a queen, but it's the best your poor lover can find. He'll do better for you some of these days, I'm thinking. Now your mind is easy once again, is it not?'

'How can it ever be at ease, Jack, when I know that you are a criminal among criminals—when I never know the day that I may hear that you are in the dock for murder?* McMurdo the Scowrer—that was what one of our boarders called you yesterday. It went through my heart like a knife.'

'Sure, hard words break no bones.'

'But they were true.'

'Well, dear, it's not as bad as you think. We are but poor men that are trying in our own way to get our rights.'

Ettie threw her arms round her lover's neck. 'Give it up, Jack! For my sake—for God's sake, give it up! It was to ask you that I came here today. Oh, Jack, see—I beg it of you on my bended knees. Kneeling here before you, I implore you to give it up!'*

He raised her, and soothed her with her head against his breast.

'Sure, my darlin', you don't know what it is you are asking. How could I give it up when it would be to break my oath and to desert my comrades? If you could see how things stand with me, you could never ask it of me. Besides, if I wanted to, how could I do it? You don't suppose that the Lodge would let a man go free with all its secrets?'

'I've thought of that, Jack. I've planned it all. Father has saved some money. He is weary of this place, where the fear of these people darkens our lives. He is ready to go. We would fly together to Philadelphia or New York, where we would be safe from them.'

McMurdo laughed. 'The Lodge has a long arm. Do you think it could not stretch from here to Philadelphia or New York?'

'Well, then, to the West, or to England, or to Germany whence father came.* Anywhere to get away from this Valley of Fear!'

McMurdo thought of old Brother Morris. 'Sure, it is the second time I have heard the valley so named,' said he. 'The shadow does indeed seem to lie heavy on some of you.'

'It darkens every moment of our lives. Do you suppose that Ted Baldwin has ever forgiven us? If it were not that he fears you, what do you suppose that our chances would be? If you saw the look in those dark, hungry eyes of his when they fall on me!'*

'By Gar! I'd teach him better manners if I caught him at it! But see here, little girl. I can't leave here. I can't. Take that from me once and for all. But if you will leave me to find my own way, I will try to prepare a way of getting honourably out of it.'

'There is no honour in such a matter.'

'Well, well, it's just how you look at it. But if you'll give me six months I'll work it so as I can leave without being ashamed to look others in the face.'

The girl laughed with joy. 'Six months!' she cried. 'Is it a promise?'

'Well, it may be seven or eight. But within a year at the farthest we will leave the valley behind us.'*

It was the most that Ettie could obtain, and yet it was something. There was this distant light to illuminate the gloom of the immediate future. She returned to her father's house more lighthearted than she had ever been since Jack McMurdo had come into her life.

It might be thought that as a member all the doings of the society would be told to him, but he was soon to discover that the organization was wider and more complex than the simple Lodge. Even Boss McGinty was ignorant as to many things, for there was an official named the County Delegate, living at Hobson's Patch, farther down the line, who had power over several different lodges, which he wielded in a sudden and arbitrary way. Only once did McMurdo see him, a sly little grey-haired rat of a man with a slinking gait and a sidelong glance which was charged with malice. Evans Pott was his name, and even the great Boss of Vermissa felt towards him something of the repulsion and fear which the huge Danton may have felt for the puny but dangerous Robespierre.*

One day Scanlan, who was McMurdo's fellow-boarder, received a note from McGinty enclosing one from Evans Pott, which informed him that he was sending over two good men, Lawler and Andrews,* who had instructions to act in the neighbourhood; though it was best for the cause that no particulars as to their objects should be given. Would the Bodymaster see to it that suitable arrangements be made for their lodgings and comfort until the time for action should arrive? McGinty added that it was impossible for anyone to remain secret at the Union House, and that, therefore, he would be obliged if McMurdo and Scanlan would put the strangers up for a few days in their boarding-house.

The same evening the two men arrived, each carrying his grip-sack. Lawler was an elderly man, shrewd, silent, and self-contained, clad in an old black frock-coat, which, with his soft felt hat and ragged, grizzled beard, gave him a general resemblance to an itinerant preacher. His companion, Andrews, was little more than a boy, frank-faced and cheerful, with the breezy manner of one who is out for a holiday, and means to enjoy every minute of it. Both of the men were total abstainers, and behaved in all ways as exemplary members of society, with the one single exception that they were assassins who had often proved themselves to be most capable instruments for this Association of murder. Lawler had already carried out fourteen commissions of the kind, and Andrews three.

They were, as McMurdo found, quite ready to converse about their deeds in the past, which they recounted with the half-bashful pride of men who had done good and unselfish service for the community.* They were reticent, however, as to the immediate job in hand.

'They chose us because neither I nor the boy here drink,' Lawler explained. 'They can count on us saying no more than we should. You must not take it amiss, but it is the orders of the County Delegate that we obey.'

'Sure, we are all in it together,' said Scanlan, McMurdo's mate, as the four sat together at supper.

'That's true enough, and we'll talk till the cows come home of the killing of Charlie Williams, or of Simon Bird, or any other job in the past. But till the work is done we say nothing.'

'There are half a dozen about here that I have a word to say to,' said McMurdo, with an oath. 'I suppose it isn't Jack Knox, of Ironhill, that you are after? I'd go some way to see him get his deserts.'

'No; it's not him yet.'

'Or Herman Strauss?'

'No, nor him either.'

'Well, if you won't tell us, we can't make you; but I'd be glad to know.'

Lawler smiled, and shook his head. He was not to be drawn.

In spite of the reticence of their guests, Scanlan and McMurdo were quite determined to be present at what they called the 'fun'. When, therefore, at an early hour one morning McMurdo heard them creeping down the stairs, he awakened Scanlan, and the two hurried on their clothes. When they were dressed they found that the others had stolen out, leaving the door open behind them. It was not yet dawn, and by the light of the lamps they could see the two men some distance down the street. They followed them warily, treading noiselessly in the deep snow.

The boarding-house was near the edge of the town, and soon they were at the crossroads which is beyond its boundary. Here three men were waiting, with whom Lawler and Andrews held a short, eager conversation. Then they all moved on together. It was clearly some notable job which needed numbers. At this point there are several trails which lead to various mines. The strangers took that which led to the Crow Hill, a huge business which was in strong hands, who had been able, thanks to their energetic and fearless New England manager, Josiah H. Dunn, to keep some order and discipline during the long reign of terror.

Day was breaking now, and a line of workmen were slowly making their way, singly and in groups, along the blackened path.

McMurdo and Scanlan strolled on with the others, keeping in sight of the men whom they followed. A thick mist lay over them, and from the heart of it there came the sudden scream of a steam whistle. It was the ten-minute signal before the cages descended and the day's labour began.

When they reached the open space round the mineshaft there were a hundred miners waiting, stamping their feet and blowing on their fingers; for it was bitterly cold. The strangers stood in a little group under the shadow of the engine-house. Scanlan and McMurdo climbed a heap of slag from which the whole scene lay before them. They saw the mine engineer, a great bearded Scotchman named Menzies, come out of the engine-house and blow his whistle for the cages to be lowered.

At the same instant a tall, loose-framed young man with a clean-shaven, earnest face, advanced eagerly towards the pit-head. As he came forward his eyes fell upon the group, silent and motionless, under the engine-house. The men had drawn down their hats and turned up their collars to screen their faces. For a moment the presentiment of Death laid its cold hand upon the manager's heart. At the next he had shaken it off and saw only his duty towards intrusive strangers.

'Who are you?' he asked, as he advanced. 'What are you loitering there for?'

There was no answer, but the lad Andrews stepped forward and shot him in the stomach. The hundred waiting miners stood as motionless and helpless as if they were paralysed. The manager clapped his two hands to the wound and doubled himself up. Then he staggered away, but another of the assassins fired, and he went down sideways, kicking and clawing among a heap of clinkers. Menzies, the

Scotchman, gave a roar of rage at the sight and rushed with an iron spanner at the murderers; but was met by two balls in the face, which dropped him dead at their very feet.

There was a surge forward of some of the miners, and an inarticulate cry of pity and of anger; but a couple of the strangers emptied their six-shooters over the heads of the crowd, and they broke and scattered, some of them rushing wildly back to their homes in Vermissa.

When a few of the bravest had rallied, and there was a return to the mine, the murderous gang had vanished in the mists of the morning, without a single witness being able to swear to the identity of these men who in front of a hundred spectators had wrought this double crime.

Scanlan and McMurdo made their way back, Scanlan somewhat subdued, for it was the first murder job that he had seen with his own eyes, and it appeared less funny than he had been led to believe. The horrible screams of the dead manager's wife pursued them as they hurried to the town. McMurdo was absorbed and silent; but he showed no sympathy for the weakening of his companion.

'Sure, it is like a war,' he repeated. 'What is it but a war between us and them, and we hit back where we best can?'*

There was high revel in the Lodge room at the Union House that night, not only over the killing of the manager and engineer of the Crow Hill mine, which would bring this organization into line with the other blackmailed and terror-stricken companies of the district, but also over a distant triumph which had been wrought by the hands of the Lodge itself. It would appear that when the County Delegate had sent over five good men to strike a blow in Vermissa, he had demanded that, in return, three Vermissa men should be secretly selected and sent across to kill William Hales, of Stake Royal, one of the best-known and most popular mine-owners in the Gilmerton district, a man who was believed not to have an enemy in the world, for he was in all ways a pattern employer. He had insisted, however, upon efficiency in the work, and had therefore paid off certain drunken and idle *employés* who were members of the all-powerful society.

Coffin notices hung outside his door had not weakened his resolution, and so in a free, civilized country he found himself condemned to death.*

The execution had now been duly carried out. Ted Baldwin, who sprawled in the seat of honour beside the Bodymaster, had been the chief of the party. His flushed face and glazed, bloodshot eyes told of sleeplessness and drink. He and his two comrades had spent the night before among the mountains. They were unkempt and weather-stained. But no heroes, returning from a forlorn hope, could have had a warmer welcome from their comrades.

The story was told and retold amid cries of delight and shouts of laughter. They had waited for their man as he drove home at nightfall, taking their station at the top of a steep hill, where his horse must be at a walk. He was so furred to keep out the cold that he could not lay his hand on his pistol. They had pulled him out and shot him again and again.*

He had screamed for mercy. The screams were repeated for the amusement of the lodge. 'Let's hear again how he squealed,' they cried.

None of them knew the man, but there is eternal drama in a killing, and they had shown the Scowrers of Gilmerton that the Vermissa men were to be relied upon.

There had been one *contretemps*, for a man and his wife had driven up while they were still emptying their revolvers into the silent body. It had been suggested that they should shoot them both; but they were harmless folk who were not connected with the mines, so they were sternly bidden to drive on and keep silent, lest a worse thing befall them. And so the blood-mottled figure had been left as a warning to all such hard-hearted employers, and the three noble avengers had hurried off into the mountains where unbroken Nature comes down to the very edge of the furnaces and the slag-heaps.* Here they were safe and sound, their work well done, and the plaudits of their companions in their ears.

It had been a great day for the Scowrers. The shadow had fallen even darker over the valley. But as the wise general chooses the moment of victory in which to redouble his

efforts, so that his foes may have no time to steady themselves after disaster, so Boss McGinty, looking out upon the
scene of his operations with his brooding and malicious eyes,
had devised a new attack upon those who opposed him.
That very night, as the half-drunken company broke up, he
touched McMurdo on the arm and led him aside into the
inner room where they had their first interview.

'See here, my lad,' said he, 'I've got a job that's worthy
of you at last. You'll have the doing of it in your own hands.'

'Proud I am to hear it,' McMurdo answered.

'You can take two men with you—Manders and Reilly.
They have been warned for service. We'll never be right in
this district until Chester Wilcox has been settled,* and
you'll have the thanks of every Lodge in the coalfields if you
can down him.'

'I'll do my best, anyhow. Who is he, and where shall I find
him?'

McGinty took his eternal half-chewed, half-smoked cigar
from the corner of his mouth, and proceeded to draw a
rough diagram on a page torn from his notebook.

'He's the chief foreman of the Iron Dyke Company. He's
a hard citizen, an old colour-sergeant of the war, all scars
and grizzle. We've had two tries at him, but had no luck,
and Jim Carnaway lost his life over it. Now it's for you to
take it over. That's the house, all alone at the Iron Dyke
cross-road, same as you see here in the map, without another
within earshot. It's no good by day. He's armed, and shoots
quick and straight, with no questions asked. But at night—
well, there he is, with his wife, three children, and a hired
help. You can't pick or choose. It's all or none. If you could
get a bag of blasting powder at the front door with a slow
match to it—'

'What's the man done?'

'Didn't I tell you he shot Jim Carnaway?'

'Why did he shoot him?'*

'What in thunder has that to do with you? Carnaway was
about his house at night, and he shot him. That's enough
for me and you. You've got to set the thing right.'

'There's these two women and the children. Do they go up, too?'

'They have to—else how can we get him?'

'It seems hard on them, for they've done nothing.'*

'What sort of talk is this? Do you back out?'*

'Easy, Councillor, easy. What have I ever said or done that you should think I would be after standing back from an order of the Bodymaster of my own Lodge? If it's right or if it's wrong it's for you to decide.'

'You'll do it, then?'

'Of course I will do it.'

'When?'

'Well, you had best give me a night or two that I may see the house and make my plans. Then—'

'Very good,' said McGinty, shaking him by the hand. 'I leave it with you. It will be a great day when you bring us the news. It's just the last stroke that will bring them all to their knees.'

McMurdo thought long and deeply over the commission which had been so suddenly placed in his hands. The isolated house in which Chester Wilcox lived was about five miles off in an adjacent valley. That very night he started off all alone to prepare for the attempt. It was daylight before he returned from his reconnaissance. Next day he interviewed his two subordinates, Manders and Reilly, reckless youngsters, who were as elated as if it were a deer hunt.

Two nights later they met outside the town, all three armed, and one of them carrying a sack stuffed with the powder which was used in the quarries. It was two in the morning before they came to the lonely house. The night was a windy one, with broken clouds drifting swiftly across the face of a three-quarter moon. They had been warned to be on their guard against bloodhounds; so they moved forward cautiously, with their pistols cocked in their hands. But there was no sound save the howling of the wind and no movement but the swaying branches above them. McMurdo listened at the door of the lonely house; but all was still within. Then he leaned the powder bag against it, ripped a hole in it with his knife, and attached the fuse. When it was well alight, he and his two companions took to their heels, and were some distance off, safe and snug in a sheltering ditch, before the shattering roar of the explosion, with the low, deep rumble of the collapsing building, told them that their work was done. No cleaner job* had ever been carried out in the blood-stained annals of the society.

But alas that work so well organized and boldly conceived should all have gone for nothing! Warned by the fate of the various victims, and knowing that he was marked down for destruction, Chester Wilcox had moved himself and his family only the day before to some safer and less known quarters, where a guard of police should watch over them. It was an empty house which had been torn down by the gunpowder, and the grim old colour-sergeant of the war was still teaching discipline to the miners of Iron Dyke.

'Leave him to me,' said McMurdo. 'He's my man, and I'll get him sure, if I have to wait a year for him.'

A vote of thanks and confidence was passed in full Lodge, and so for the time the matter ended. When a few weeks later it was reported in the papers that Wilcox had been shot at from an ambuscade, it was an open secret that McMurdo was still at work upon his unfinished job.*

Such were the methods of the Society of Freemen, and such were the deeds of the Scowrers by which they spread their rule of fear over the great and rich district which was for so long a period haunted by their terrible presence. Why should these pages be stained by further crimes? Have I not said enough to show the men and their methods?

These deeds are written in history, and there are records wherein one may read the details of them. There one may learn of the shooting of Policemen Hunt and Evans* because they had ventured to arrest two members of the society—a double outrage planned at the Vermissa Lodge, and carried out in cold blood upon two helpless and disarmed men. There also one may read of the shooting of Mrs Larbey* whilst she was nursing her husband, who had been beaten almost to death by orders of Boss McGinty.

The killing of the elder Jenkins,* shortly followed by that of his brother, the mutilation of James Murdoch,* the blowing-up of the Staphouse* family, and the murder of the Stendals* all followed hard upon each other in the same terrible winter.

Darkly the shadow lay upon the Valley of Fear. The spring had come with running brooks and blossoming trees. There was hope for all Nature, bound so long in an iron grip; but nowhere was there any hope for the men and women who lived under the yoke of the terror. Never had the cloud above them been so dark and hopeless as in the early summer of the year 1875.

· **CHAPTER 6** ·

Danger

IT was the height of the reign of terror. McMurdo, who had already been appointed Inner Deacon,* with every prospect of some day succeeding McGinty as Bodymaster, was now so necessary to the councils of his comrades that nothing was done without his help and advice. The more popular he became, however, with the Freemen, the blacker were the scowls which greeted him as he passed along the streets of Vermissa. In spite of their terror the citizens were taking heart to bind themselves together against their oppressors. Rumours had reached the Lodge of secret gatherings in the *Herald* office and of distribution of firearms among the law-abiding people. But McGinty and his men were undisturbed by such reports. They were numerous, resolute, and well armed. Their opponents were scattered and powerless. It would all end, as it had done in the past, in aimless talk, and possibly in impotent arrests. So said McGinty, McMurdo, and all the bolder spirits.

It was a Saturday evening in May. Saturday was always the Lodge night, and McMurdo was leaving his house to attend it when Morris, the weaker brother of the Order, came to see him. His brow was creased with care, and his kindly face was drawn and haggard.

'Can I speak with you freely, Mr McMurdo?'

'Sure.'

'I can't forget that I spoke my heart to you once, and that you kept it to yourself, even though the Boss himself came to ask you about it.'

'What else could I do if you trusted me? It wasn't that I agreed with what you said.'

'I know that well. But you are the one here I can speak to and be safe. I've a secret here'—he put his hand to his breast—'and it is just burning the life out of me. I wish it had come to any one of you but me. If I tell it, it will mean murder, for sure. If I don't, it may bring the end of us all. God help me, but I am near out of my wits over it!'

McMurdo looked at the man earnestly. He was trembling in every limb. He poured some whiskey into a glass and handed it to him. 'That's the physic for the likes of you,' said he. 'Now let me hear of it.'

Morris drank, and his white face took a tinge of colour. 'I can tell it you all in one sentence,' said he. 'There's a detective on our trail.'

McMurdo stared at him in astonishment. 'Why, man, you're crazy!' he said. 'Isn't the place full of police and detectives, and what harm did they ever do us?'

'No, no, it's no man of the district. As you say, we know them, and it is little that they can do. But you've heard of Pinkerton's?'

'I've read of some folk of that name.'

'Well, you can take it from me you've no show when they are on your trail. It's not a take-it-or-miss-it Government concern. It's a dead earnest business proposition that's out for results and keeps out till, by hook or by crook, it gets them. If a Pinkerton man is deep in this business we are all destroyed.'

149

'We must kill him.'

'Ah, it's the first thought that came to you! So it will be up at the Lodge. Didn't I say to you that it would end in murder?'

'Sure, what is murder? Isn't it common enough in these parts?'

'It is indeed, but it's not for me to point out the man that is to be murdered. I'd never rest easy again. And yet it's our own necks that may be at stake. In God's name what shall I do?' He rocked to and fro in his agony of indecision.

But his words had moved McMurdo deeply. It was easy to see that he shared the other's opinion as to the danger, and the need for meeting it. He gripped Morris's shoulder, and shook him in his earnestness.

'See here, man,' he cried, and he almost screeched the words in his excitement, 'you won't gain anything by sitting keening like an old wife at a wake. Let's have the facts. Who is the fellow? Where is he? How did you hear of him? Why did you come to me?'

'I came to you, for you are the one man that would advise me. I told you that I had a store in the East before I came here. I left good friends behind me, and one of them is in the telegraph service. Here's a letter that I had from him yesterday. It's this part from the top of the page. You can read it for yourself.'

This was what McMurdo read:

How are the Scowrers getting on in your parts? We read plenty of them in the papers. Between you and me I expect to hear news from you before long. Five big corporations and the two railroads have taken the thing up in dead earnest. They mean it, and you can bet they'll get there. They are right deep down into it. Pinkerton* has taken hold under their orders, and his best man, Birdy Edwards,* is operating. The thing has got to be stopped right now.

'Now read the postscript.'

Of course, what I give you is what I learned in business, so it goes no further. It's a queer cipher that you handle by the yard every day and can get no meaning from.

McMurdo sat in silence for some time with the letter in his listless* hands. The mist had lifted for a moment, and there was the abyss before him.

'Does anyone else know of this?' he asked.

'I have told no one else.'

'But this man—your friend—has he any other person that he would be likely to write to?'

'Well, I dare say he knows one or two more.'

'Of the Lodge?'

'It's likely enough.'

'I was asking because it is likely that he may have given some description of this fellow Birdy Edwards—then we could get on his trail.'

'Well, it's possible. But I should not think he knew him. He is just telling me the news that came to him by way of business. How would he know this Pinkerton man?'

McMurdo gave a violent start.

'By Gar!' he cried, 'I've got him. What a fool I was not to know it! Lord but we're in luck! We will fix him before he can do any harm. See here, Morris, will you leave this thing in my hands?'

'Sure, if you will only take it off mine.'

'I'll do that. You can stand right back and let me run it. Even your name need not be mentioned. I'll take it all on myself as if it were to me that this letter has come. Will that content you?'

'It's just what I would ask.'

'Then leave it at that and keep your head shut. Now I'll get down to the Lodge, and we'll soon make old man Pinkerton sorry for himself.'

'You wouldn't kill this man?'

'The less you know, Friend Morris, the easier your conscience will be and the better you will sleep. Ask no questions, and let things settle themselves. I have hold of it now.'

Morris shook his head sadly as he left. 'I feel that his blood is on my hands,' he groaned.

'Self-protection is no murder, anyhow,' said McMurdo, smiling grimly. 'It's him or us. I guess this man would destroy us all if we left him long in the valley. Why, Brother Morris, we'll have to elect you Bodymaster yet; for you've surely saved the Lodge.'

And yet it was clear from his actions that he thought more seriously of this new intrusion than his words would show. It may have been his guilty conscience; it may have been the reputation of the Pinkerton organization; it may have been the knowledge that great rich corporations had set themselves the task of clearing out the Scowrers; but, whatever his reason, his actions were those of a man who is preparing for the worst. Every paper which could incriminate him* was destroyed before he left the house. After that he gave a long sigh of satisfaction; for it seemed to him that he was safe. And yet the danger must still have pressed somewhat upon him, for on his way to the Lodge he stopped at old man Shafter's. The house was forbidden him, but when he tapped at the window Ettie came out to him. The dancing Irish devilry had gone from her lover's eyes. She read his danger in his earnest face.

'Something has happened!' she cried. 'Oh Jack, you are in danger!'

'Sure, it is not very bad, my sweetheart. And yet it may be wise that we make a move before it is worse.'

'Make a move?'

'I promised you once that I would go some day. I think the time is coming. I had news to-night, bad news, and I see trouble coming.'

'The police?'

'Well, a Pinkerton. But, sure, you wouldn't know what that is, acushla, nor what it may mean to the likes of me. I'm too deep in this thing, and I may have to get out of it quick. You said you would come with me if I went.'

'Oh, Jack, it would be the saving of you.'

'I'm an honest man in some things, Ettie. I wouldn't hurt a hair of your bonnie head for all that the world can give, nor ever pull you down one inch from the golden throne above the clouds where I always see you. Would you trust me?'

She put her hand in his without a word.

'Well, then, listen to what I say and do as I order you; for indeed it's the only way for us. Things are going to happen in this valley. I feel it in my bones. There may be many of us that will have to look out for ourselves. I'm one, anyhow. If I go, by day or night, it's you that must come with me!'

'I'd come after you, Jack.'

'No, no; you shall come *with* me. If this valley is closed to me and I can never come back, how can I leave you behind, and me perhaps in hiding from the police with never a chance of a message? It's with me you must come. I know a good woman in the place I come from, and it's there I'd leave you till we can get married. Will you come?'

'Yes, Jack, I will come.'

'God bless you for your trust in me! It's a fiend out of hell that I should be if I abused it. Now, mark you, Ettie, it will be just a word to you, and when it reaches you you will drop everything and come right down to the waiting room* at the depot and stay there till I come for you.'

'Day or night, I'll come at the word, Jack.'

Somewhat eased in mind now that his own preparations for escape had been begun, McMurdo went on to the Lodge. It had already assembled, and only by complicated signs and counter signs could he pass through the outer guard and inner guard who close-tiled* it. A buzz of pleasure and welcome greeted him as he entered. The long room was crowded, and through the haze of tobacco-smoke he saw the tangled black mane of the Bodymaster, the cruel, unfriendly features of Baldwin, the vulture face of Harraway, the secretary, and a dozen more who were among the leaders of the Lodge. He rejoiced that they should all be there* to take counsel over his news.

'Indeed, it's glad we are to see you, Brother!' cried the chairman. 'There's business here that wants a Solomon in judgment* to set it right.'

'It's Lander and Egan,' explained his neighbour, as he took his seat. 'They both claim the head-money given by the Lodge for the shooting of old man Crabbe over at Styles-town, and who's to say which fired the bullet?'*

153

McMurdo rose in his place and raised his hand. The expression of his face froze the attention of the audience. There was a dead hush of expectation.

'Eminent Bodymaster,' he said, in a solemn voice, 'I claim urgency.'

'Brother McMurdo claims urgency,' said McGinty. 'It's a claim that by the rules of this Lodge takes precedence. Now, Brother, we attend you.'

McMurdo took the letter from his pocket.

'Eminent Bodymaster and Brethren,'* he said, 'I am the bearer of ill news this day, but it is better that it should be known and discussed than that a blow should fall upon us without warning which would destroy us all. I have information that the most powerful and richest organizations in this State have bound themselves together for our destruction, and that at this very moment there is a Pinkerton detective, one Birdy Edwards, at work in the valley collecting the evidence which may put a rope round the neck of many of us, and send every man in this room into a felon's cell. That is the situation for the discussion of which I have made a claim of urgency.'

There was a dead silence in the room. It was broken by the chairman.

'What is your evidence for this, Brother McMurdo?' he asked.

'It is in this letter which has come into my hands,' said McMurdo. He read the passage aloud. 'It is a matter of honour with me that I can give no further particulars about the letter, nor put it into your hands, but I assure you that there is nothing else in it which can affect the interests of the Lodge. I put the case before you as it has reached me.'

'Let me say, Mr Chairman,' said one of the older brethren, 'that I have heard of Birdy Edwards, and that he has the name of being the best man in the Pinkerton service.'*

'Does any one know him by sight?' asked McGinty.

'Yes,' said McMurdo, 'I do.'

There was a murmur of astonishment through the hall.

'I believe we hold him in the hollow of our hands,' he continued with an exulting smile upon his face. 'If we

act quickly and wisely, we can cut this thing short. If I have
your confidence and your help, it is little that we have to
fear.'*

'What have we to fear anyhow? What can he know of our
affairs?'

'You might say so if all were as stanch as you, Councillor.
But this man has all the millions of the capitalists at his
back.* Do you think there is no weaker brother among all
our Lodges that could not be bought? He will get at our
secrets—maybe has got them already. There's only one sure
cure.'

'That he never leaves the valley,' said Baldwin.

McMurdo nodded. 'Good for you, Brother Baldwin,' he
said. 'You and I have had our differences, but you have said
the true word tonight.'

'Where is he, then? Where shall we know him?'*

'Eminent Bodymaster,' said McMurdo, earnestly, 'I would
put it to you that this is too vital a thing for us to discuss in
open Lodge.* God forbid that I should throw a doubt on
anyone here, but if so much as a word of gossip got to the
ears of this man, there would be an end of any chance of
our getting him. I would ask the Lodge to choose a trusty
committee, Mr Chairman—yourself, if I might suggest it,
and Brother Baldwin here, and five more. Then I can talk
freely of what I know and of what I would advise should be
done.'

The proposition was at once adopted and the committee
chosen. Besides the chairman and Baldwin, there were the
vulture-faced secretary, Harraway; Tiger Cormac, the brutal
young assassin; Carter, the treasurer; and the brothers
Willaby,* who were fearless and desperate men who would
stick at nothing.

The usual revelry of the Lodge was short and subdued,
for there was a cloud upon the men's spirits, and many there
for the first time began to see the cloud of avenging Law
drifting up in that serene sky under which they had dwelled
so long. The horrors which they had dealt out to others had
been so much a part of their settled lives that the thought of

retribution had become a remote one, and so seemed the more startling now that it came so closely upon them. They broke up early and left their leaders to their council.

'Now, McMurdo,' said McGinty, when they were alone. The seven men sat frozen in their seats.

'I said just now that I knew Birdy Edwards,' McMurdo explained. 'I need not tell you that he is not here under that name. He's a brave man, I dare bet, but not a crazy one. He passes under the name of Steve Wilson, and he is lodging at Hobson's Patch.'

'How do you know this?'

'Because I fell into talk with him. I thought little of it at the time, nor would have given it a second thought but for this letter; but now I'm sure it's the man. I met him on the cars* when I went down the line on Wednesday—a hard case if ever there was one. He said he was a reporter.* I believed it for the moment. Wanted to know all he could get about the Scowrers and what he called "the outrages" for a New York Paper.* Asked me every kind of question so as to get something.* You bet I was giving nothing away. "I'd pay for it, and pay well," said he, "if I could get some stuff that would suit my editor." I said what I thought would please him best, and he handed me a twenty-dollar bill for my information. "There's ten times that for you," said he, "if you can find me all that I want." '

'What did you tell him, then?'

'Any stuff I could make up.'

'How do you know he wasn't a newspaper man?'

'I'll tell you. He got out at Hobson's Patch, and so did I. I chanced into the telegraph bureau, and he was leaving it.

' "See here," said the operator, after he'd gone out, "I guess we should charge double rates for this," "I guess you should," said I. He had filled the form with stuff that might have been Chinese for all we could make of it. "He fires a sheet of this off every day," said the clerk. "Yes," said I; "it's special news for his paper, and he's scared that the others should tap it." That was what the operator thought and what I thought at the time; but I think different now.'

'By Gar! I believe you are right,' said McGinty. 'But what do you allow that we should do about it?'

'Why not go right down now and fix him?' someone suggested.

'Aye, the sooner the better.'

'I'd start this next minute if I knew where we could find him,' said McMurdo. 'He's in Hobson's Patch; but I don't know the house. I've got a plan, though, if you'll only take my advice.'

'Well, what is it?'

'I'll go to the Patch tomorrow morning. I'll find him through the operator. He can locate him, I guess. Well, then, I'll tell him that I'm a Freeman myself. I'll offer him all the secrets of the Lodge for a price. You bet he'll tumble to it. I'll tell him the papers are at my house, and that it's as much as my life would be worth to let him come while folk were about. He'll see that that's horse sense. Let him come at ten o'clock at night, and he shall see everything. That will fetch him, sure.'

'Well?'

'You can plan the rest for yourselves. Widow MacNamara's is a lonely house. She's as true as steel and as deaf as a post.* There's only Scanlan and me in the house. If I get his promise—and I'll let you know if I do—I'd have the whole seven of you come to me by nine o'clock. We'll get him in. If ever he gets out alive—well, he can talk of Birdy Edward's luck for the rest of his days.'

'There's going to be a vacancy at Pinkerton's or I'm mistaken,' said McGinty. 'Leave it at that, McMurdo. At nine tomorrow we shall be with you. You once get the door shut behind him, and you can leave the rest with us.'*

157

· CHAPTER 7 ·

The Trapping of Birdy Edwards

As McMurdo had said, the house in which he lived was a lonely one and very well suited for such a crime as they had planned. It was on the extreme fringe of the town, and stood well back from the road. In any other case the conspirators would have simply called out their man, as they had many a time before, and emptied their pistols into his body; but in this instance it was very necessary to find out how much he knew, how he knew it, and what had been passed on to his employers.

It was possible that they were already too late and that the work had been done. If that were indeed so, they could at least have their revenge upon the man who had done it. But they were hopeful that nothing of great importance had yet come to the detective's knowledge, as otherwise, they argued, he would not have troubled to write down and forward such trivial information as McMurdo claimed to have given him. However, all this they would learn from his own lips. Once in their power they would find a way to make him speak. It was not the first time they had handled an unwilling witness.

McMurdo went to Hobson's Patch as agreed. The police seemed to take a particular interest in him that morning, and Captain Marvin—he who had claimed the old acquaintance with him at Chicago—actually addressed him as he waited at the station. McMurdo turned away and refused to speak with him.* He was back from his mission in the afternoon, and saw McGinty at the Union House.

'He is coming,' he said.

'Good!' said McGinty. The giant was in his shirtsleeves, with chains and seals gleaming athwart his ample waistcoat and a diamond twinkling through the fringe of his bristling beard. Drink and politics had made the Boss a very rich as well as powerful man.* The more terrible, therefore, seemed that glimpse of the prison or the gallows which had risen before him the night before.

'Do you reckon he knows much?' he asked anxiously.

McMurdo shook his head gloomily. 'He's been here some time—six weeks at the least. I guess he didn't come into these parts to look at the prospect. If he has been working among us all that time with the railroad money at his back, I should expect that he has got results, and that he has passed them on.'

'There's not a weak man in the Lodge,' cried McGinty. 'True as steel, every man of them. And yet, by the Lord! there is that skunk Morris. What about him? If any man gives us away it would be he. I've a mind to send a couple of the boys round before evening to give him a beating up and see what they can get from him.'

'Well, there would be no harm in that,' McMurdo answered. 'I won't deny that I have a liking for Morris and would be sorry to see him come to harm. He has spoken to me once or twice over Lodge matters, and though he may not see them the same as you or I, he never seemed the sort that squeals.* But still, it is not for me to stand between him and you.'

'I'll fix the old devil,' said McGinty with an oath. 'I've had my eye on him this year past.'

'Well, you know best about that,' McMurdo answered. 'But whatever you do must be to-morrow, for we must lie low until the Pinkerton affair is settled up. We can't afford to set the police buzzing to-day of all days.'

'True for you,' said McGinty. 'And we'll learn from Birdy Edwards himself where he got his news, if we have to cut his heart out first. Did he seem to scent a trap?'

McMurdo laughed. 'I guess I took him on his weak point,' he said. 'If he could get on a good trail of the Scowrers, he's ready to follow it into hell.* I took his money'—McMurdo grinned as he produced a wad of dollar notes—'and as much more when he has seen all my papers.'

'What papers?'

'Well, there are no papers. But I filled him up about constitutions and books of rules and forms of membership. He expects to get right down to the end of everything before he leaves.'

'Faith, he's right there,' said McGinty grimly. 'Didn't he ask you why you didn't bring him the papers?'

'As if I would carry such things, and me a suspected man, and Captain Marvin after speaking to me this very day at the depot!'

'Aye, I heard of that,' said McGinty. 'I guess the heavy end of this business is coming on to you. We could put him down an old shaft when we've done with him; but however we work it we can't get past the man living at Hobson's Patch and you being there to-day.'

McMurdo shrugged his shoulders. 'If we handle it right, they can never prove the killing,' said he. 'No one can see him come to the house after dark, and I'll lay to it that no one will see him go. Now, see here, Councillor, I'll show you my plan, and I'll ask you to fit the others into it. You will all come in good time. Very well. He comes at ten. He is to tap three times, and me to open the door for him. Then I'll get behind him and shut it. He's our man then.'

'That's all easy and plain.'

'Yes; but the next step wants considering. He's a hard proposition. He's heavily armed. I've fooled him proper, and yet he is likely to be on his guard. Suppose I show him right into a room with seven men in it where he expected to find me alone. There is going to be shooting and somebody is going to be hurt.'

'That's so.'

'And the noise is going to bring every damned copper in the township on top of it.'*

'I guess you are right.'

'This is how I should work it. You will all be in the big room—same as you saw when you had a chat with me. I'll open the door for him, show him into the parlour beside the door, and leave him there while I get the papers. That will give me the chance of telling you how things are shaping. Then I will go back to him with some faked papers. As he is reading them I will jump for him and get my grip on his pistol arm. You'll hear me call and in you will rush. The quicker the better; for he is as strong a man as I, and I may have more than I can manage. But I allow that I can hold him till you come.'

'It's a good plan,' said McGinty. 'The Lodge will owe you a debt for this. I guess when I move out of the chair I can put a name to the man that's coming after me.'

'Sure, Councillor, I am little more than a recruit,' said McMurdo, but his face showed what he thought of the great man's compliment.*

When he had returned home he made his own preparations for the grim evening in front of him. First he cleaned, oiled, and loaded his Smith & Wesson revolver. Then he surveyed the room in which the detective was to be trapped. It was a large apartment, with a long deal table in the centre, and the big stove at one side. At each of the other sides were windows. There were no shutters to these: only light curtains which drew across. McMurdo examined these attentively. No doubt it must have struck him that the apartment was very exposed for so secret a meeting. Yet its distance from the road made it of less consequence. Finally he discussed the matter with his fellow-lodger. Scanlan, though a Scowrer, was an inoffensive little man who was too weak to stand against the opinion of his comrades, but was secretly horrified by the deeds of blood at which he had sometimes been forced to assist. McMurdo told him shortly what was intended.

'And if I were you, Mike Scanlan, I would take a night off and keep clear of it. There will be bloody work here before morning.'

'Well, indeed, then, Mac,' Scanlan answered, 'it's not the will but the nerve that is wanting in me. When I saw Manager Dunn go down at the colliery yonder it was just more than I could stand. I'm not made for it, same as you or McGinty. If the Lodge will think none the worse of me,

I'll just do as you advise, and leave you to yourselves for the evening.'

The men came in good time as arranged. They were outwardly respectable citizens, well-clad and cleanly; but a judge of faces would have read little hope for Birdy Edwards in those hard mouths and remorseless eyes. There was not a man in the room whose hands had not been reddened a dozen times before.* They were as hardened to human murder as a butcher to sheep.

Foremost, of course, both in appearance and in guilt, was the formidable Boss. Harraway, the secretary, was a lean, bitter man, with a long, scraggy neck and nervous, jerky limbs—a man of incorruptible fidelity where the finances of the Order were concerned, and with no notion of justice or honesty to anyone beyond. The treasurer,* Carter, was a middle-aged man with an impassive, rather sulky expression and a yellow parchment skin. He was a capable organizer, and the actual details of nearly every outrage had sprung from his plotting brain. The two Willabys were men of action, tall, lithe young fellows with determined faces, while their companion, Tiger Cormac, a heavy, dark youth, was feared even by his own comrades for the ferocity of his disposition. These were the men who assembled that night under the roof of McMurdo for the killing of the Pinkerton detective.

Their host had placed whiskey upon the table, and they had hastened to prime themselves for the work before them. Baldwin and Cormac were already half drunk, and the liquor had brought out all their ferocity. Cormac placed his hands on the stove for an instant—it had been lighted, for the nights* were still cold.

'That will do,' said he, with an oath.

'Aye,' said Baldwin, catching his meaning. 'If he is strapped to that we will have the truth out of him.'

'We'll have the truth out of him, never fear,' said McMurdo. He had nerves of steel, this man, for, though the whole weight of the affair was on him, his manner was as cool and unconcerned as ever. The others marked it and applauded.

'You are the one to handle him,' said the Boss, approvingly. 'Not a warning will he get till your hand is on his throat. It's a pity there are no shutters to your windows.'

McMurdo went from one to the other and drew the curtain tighter. 'Sure, no one can spy upon us now. It's close upon the hour.'

'Maybe he won't come. Maybe he'll get a sniff of danger,' said the secretary.

'He'll come, never fear,' McMurdo answered. 'He is as eager to come as you can be to see him. Hark to that!'

They all sat like wax figures, some with their glasses arrested halfway to their lips. Three loud knocks had sounded at the door.

'Hush!' McMurdo raised his hand in caution. An exulting glance went round the circle and hands were laid upon hidden weapons.

'Not a sound, for your lives!' McMurdo whispered, as he went from the room, closing the door carefully behind him.

With strained ears the murderers waited. They counted the steps of their comrade down the passage. Then they heard him open the outer door. There were a few words as of greeting. Then they were aware of a strange step inside and of an unfamiliar voice. An instant later came the slam of the door and the turning of the key in the lock. Their prey was safe within the trap. Tiger Cormac laughed horribly,* and Boss McGinty clapped his great hand across his mouth.

'Be quiet, you fool!' he whispered. 'You'll be the undoing of us yet!'

There was a mutter of conversation from the next room. It seemed interminable. Then the door opened, and McMurdo appeared, his finger upon his lip.

He came to the end of the table and looked round at them. A subtle change had come over him. His manner was as of one who has great work to do. His face had set into granite firmness. His eyes shone with a fierce excitement behind his spectacles. He had become a visible leader of men. They stared at him with eager interest; but he said nothing. Still with the same singular gaze, he looked from man to man.

'Well,' cried Boss McGinty at last, 'is he here? Is Birdy Edwards here?'

'Yes,' McMurdo answered slowly. 'Birdy Edwards is here. I am Birdy Edwards!'

There were ten seconds after that brief speech during which the room might have been empty, so profound was the silence. The hissing of a kettle upon the stove rose sharp and strident to the ear. Seven white faces, all turned upwards to this man who dominated them, were set motionless with utter terror. Then, with a sudden shivering of glass, a bristle of glistening rifle-barrels broke through each window, while the curtains were torn from their hangings.

At the sight Boss McGinty gave the roar of a wounded bear and plunged for the half-opened door. A levelled revolver met him there, with the stern blue eyes of Captain Marvin of the Coal and Iron Police gleaming behind the sights. The Boss recoiled and fell back into his chair.

'You're safer there, Councillor,' said the man whom they had known as McMurdo. 'And you, Baldwin, if you don't take your hand off your gun you'll cheat the hangman yet.* Pull it out, or, by the Lord that made me—There, that will do. There are forty armed men round this house,* and you can figure it out for yourselves what chance you have. Take their pistols,* Marvin!'

There was no possible resistance under the menace of those rifles. The men were disarmed. Sulky, sheepish, and amazed,* they still sat round the table.

'I'd like to say a word to you before we separate,' said the man who had trapped them. 'I guess we may not meet again until you see me on the stand in the court-house. I'll give you something to think over between* now and then. You know me now for what I am. At last I can put my cards on the table. I am Birdy Edwards of Pinkerton's. I was chosen to break up your gang. I had a hard and a dangerous game to play. Not a soul, not one soul, not my nearest and dearest, knew that I was playing it. Only Captain Marvin here and my employers knew that.* But it's over to-night, thank God, and I am the winner!'

The seven pale, rigid faces looked up at him. There was an unappeasable hatred in their eyes. He read the relentless threat.

'Maybe you think that the game is not over yet. Well, I take my chance on that. Anyhow, some of you will take no further hand, and there are sixty more besides yourselves that will see a jail this night.* I'll tell you this, that when I was put upon this job I never believed there was such a society as yours. I thought it was paper talk, and that I would prove it so. They told me it was to do with the Freemen, so I went to Chicago and was made one. Then I was surer than ever that it was just paper talk; for I found no harm in the society, but a deal of good.

'Still, I had to carry out my job, and I came to the coal valleys. When I reached this place I learned that I was wrong and that it wasn't a dime novel after all. So I stayed to look after it. I never killed a man in Chicago. I never minted a dollar in my life. Those I gave you were as good as any others; but I never spent money better. But I knew the way* into your good wishes, and so I pretended to you that the law was after me. It all worked just as I thought.

'So I joined your infernal Lodge and I took my share in your councils. Maybe they will say that I was as bad as you. They can say what they like, so long as I get you. But what is the truth? The night I joined, you beat up old man Stanger. I could not warn him, for there was no time; but I held your hand, Baldwin, when you would have killed him. If ever I have suggested things, so as to keep my place among you, they were things which I knew I could prevent.* I could not save Dunn and Menzies, for I did not know enough; but I will see that their murderers are hanged.* I gave Chester Wilcox warning,* so that when I blew his house in he and his folk were in hiding. There was many a crime that I could not stop, but if you look back and think how often your man came home the other road, or was down in town when you went for him, or stayed indoors when you thought that he would come out, you'll see my work.'*

'You blasted traitor!'* hissed McGinty, through his closed teeth.

'Aye, John McGinty, you may call me that if it eases your smart. You and your like have been the enemy of God and man in these parts. It took a man to get between you and the poor devils of men and women that you held under your grip. There was just one way of doing it, and I did it. You call me a "traitor", but I guess there's many a thousand will call me a "deliverer" that went down into hell to save them. I've had three months of it.* I wouldn't have three such months again if they let me loose in the Treasury at Washington for it. I had to stay till I had it all, every man and every secret, right here in this hand. I'd have waited a little longer if it hadn't come to my knowledge that my secret was coming out. A letter had come into the town that would have set you wise to it all. Then I had to act, and act quickly.

'I've nothing more to say to you, except that when my time comes I'll die the easier when I think of the work I have done in this valley. Now, Marvin, I'll keep you no more. Take* them in and get it over.'

There is little more to tell. Scanlan* had been given a sealed note to be left at the address of Miss Ettie Shafter*—a mission which he had accepted with a wink and a knowing smile. In the early hours of the morning a beautiful woman and a much-muffled man boarded a special train* which had been sent by the railroad company, and made a swift, unbroken journey out of the land of danger. It was the last time that ever either Ettie or her lover set foot in the Valley of Fear. Ten days later they were married in Chicago, with old Jacob Shafter as witness of the wedding.*

The trial of the Scowrers was held far from the place where their adherents might have terrified the guardians of the law. In vain they struggled. In vain the money of the lodge—money squeezed by blackmail* out of the whole countryside—was spent like water in the attempt to save them.* That cold, clear, unimpassioned statement from one who knew every detail of their lives, their organization, and their crimes was unshaken by all the wiles of their defenders. At last, after so many years, they were broken and scattered. The cloud was lifted for ever from the valley. McGinty met his fate upon the scaffold, cringing and whining when the last hour came.* Eight of his chief followers* shared his fate. Fifty-odd had various degrees of imprisonment. The work of Birdy Edwards was complete.

And yet, as he had guessed, the game was not over yet. There was another hand to be played, and yet another and another. Ted Baldwin, for one, had escaped the scaffold;* so had the Willabys; so had several other of the fiercest spirits of the gang. For ten years they were out of the world, and then came a day when they were free once more—a day which Edwards, who knew his men, was very sure would be an end of his life of peace. They had sworn an oath on all that they thought holy to have his blood as a vengeance for their comrades. And well they strove to keep their vow!*

From Chicago he was chased, after two attempts so near to success that it was sure that the third would get him. From Chicago he went under a changed name to California, and it was there that the light went for a time out of his life when Ettie Edwards died. Once again he was nearly killed, and once again under the name of Douglas he worked in a lonely canyon, where, with an English partner named Barker, he amassed a fortune. At last there came a warning to him that the bloodhounds were on his track once more, and he cleared—only just in time—for England. And thence* came the John Douglas who for a second time married a worthy mate and lived for five years as a Sussex country gentleman*—a life which ended with the strange happenings of which we have heard.*

Epilogue

THE police-court proceedings* had passed, in which the case of John Douglas was referred to a higher court. So had the Assizes, at which he was acquitted as having acted in self-defence.

'Get him out of England at any cost,' wrote Holmes to the wife. 'There are forces here which may be more dangerous than those he has escaped. There is no safety for your husband in England.'

Two months had gone by, and the case had to some extent passed from our minds. Then one morning there came an enigmatic note slipped into our letter-box. 'Dear me, Mr Holmes! Dear me!' said this singular epistle. There was neither superscription nor signature. I laughed at the quaint message, but Holmes showed an unwonted seriousness.

'Devilry, Watson!' he remarked, and sat long with a clouded brow.

Late that night* Mrs Hudson, our landlady, brought up a message that a gentleman wished to see Holmes, and that the matter was of the utmost importance. Close at the heels of his messenger came Mr Cecil Barker, our friend of the moated Manor House. His face was drawn and haggard.

'I've had bad news—terrible news, Mr Holmes,' said he.

'I feared as much,' said Holmes.

'You have not had a cable, have you?'

'I have had a note from someone who has.'

'It's poor Douglas. They tell me his name is Edwards, but he will always be Jack Douglas of Benito Canyon to me. I told you that they started together for South Africa in the *Palmyra* three weeks ago.'

'Exactly.'

'The ship reached Cape Town last night. I received this cable from Mrs Douglas this morning:

' "Jack has been lost overboard in gale off St Helena. No one knows how accident occurred—Ivy Douglas." '

'Ha! It came like that, did it?' said Holmes, thoughtfully. 'Well, I've no doubt it was well stage-managed.'

'You mean that you think there was no accident?'

'None in the world.'

'He was murdered?'*

'Surely!'

'So I think also. These infernal Scowrers, this cursed vindictive nest of criminals—'

'No, no, my good sir,' said Holmes. 'There is a master hand here. It is no case of sawed-off shot-guns and clumsy six-shooters. You can tell an old master by the sweep of his brush. I can tell a Moriarty when I see one. This crime is from London, not from America.'

'But for what motive?'

'Because it is done by a man who cannot afford to fail—one whose whole unique position depends upon the fact that all he does must succeed. A great brain and a huge organization have been turned to the extinction of one man. It is crushing the nut with the hammer—an absurd extravagance of energy—but the nut is very effectually crushed all the same.'

'How came this man to have anything to do with it?'

'I can only say that the first word that ever came to us of the business was from one of his lieutenants. These Americans were well advised. Having an English job to do, they took into partnership, as any foreign criminal could do, this great consultant in crime. From that moment their man was doomed. At first he would content himself by using his machinery in order to find their victim. Then he would indicate how the matter might be treated. Finally, when he read in the reports of the failure of this agent, he would step in himself with a master touch. You heard me warn this man at Birlstone Manor House that the coming danger was greater than the past. Was I right?'

Barker beat his head with his clenched fist in his impotent anger.

'Do you tell me that we have to sit down under this? Do you say that no one can ever get level with this king-devil?'

'No, I don't say that,' said Holmes, and his eyes seemed to be looking far into the future. 'I don't say that he can't be beat. But you must give me time—you must give me time!'

We all sat in silence for some minutes, while those fateful eyes still strained to pierce the veil.*

EXPLANATORY NOTES

The Valley of Fear was first serialized in the *Strand Magazine*, 48–9 (Sept. 1914–May 1915), with 31 illustrations by Frank Wiles, as follows:

Vol. 48

Sept. 1914 (pp. 241–52): Part 1, Chs. 1 and 2.

Oct. 1914 (pp. 363–75): synopsis of previous Chs.; Part 1, Chs. 3 and 4.

Nov. 1914 (pp. 483–91): synopsis of previous Chs.; Part 1, Ch. 5.

Dec. 1914 (pp. 602–13): synopsis of previous Chs.; Part 1, Ch. 6 and Ch. 7 to 'this inquiry has come to a definite pause'.

Vol. 49

Jan. 1915 (pp. 2–15): synopsis of previous Chs.; Part 1, Ch. 7 from 'Evening was drawing in when we reassembled' to end, and Part 2, Ch. 1.

Feb. 1915 (pp. 176–87): synopsis of previous Chs.; Part 2, Ch. 2.

Mar. 1915 (pp. 257–67): [no further synopses] Part 2, Ch. 3.

Apr. 1915 (pp. 449–61): Part 2, Chs. 4 and 5.

May 1915 (pp. 543–56): Part 2, Chs. 6, 7, and Epilogue.

All instalments carried the subtitle 'A NEW SHERLOCK HOLMES STORY' except the last two, for which the subtitle was used as a pre-titular cross-head. Serialized in the USA by Associated Sunday Magazines (see Green and Gibson, *Bibliography*, 143), with illustrations by Arthur I. Keller, in ten weekly instalments from 20 Sept. to 22 Nov. 1914. Newspaper locations where ASM syndicated that are relevant to Part 2 include *Philadelphia Press*, *Pittsburgh Post* (both Pennsylvania); *Boston Post*, *New York Tribune* (Irish-American centres); *Chicago Record-Herald* (McParlan/McMurdo take-off point); Denver *Rocky Mountain Tribune* (McParlan residence at publication date); *Baltimore Sun* (where Hammett lived); *Washington Star* (Gowen's suicide).

The first book edn. was published on 3 June 1915, in an edn. of 6,000 copies, by Smith, Elder & Co.; a second impression was published in 1915; John Murray reissued the volume, with an inserted title-page, in 1917. First American edn. had been published on 27 Feb. 1915 by the George H. Doran Co. of New York (while the *Strand* still had Part 2, Chs. 3–7, and the Epilogue, to run).

The American edn. varied in many small particulars from the British, some ACD's earlier work prior to *Strand* sub-editing, some conceivably the work of a staff editor acting for Associated Sunday Magazines or even one of the magazines (to have influence on Doran, a New York publisher, it would almost certainly have had to be the *New York Tribune*). Those emendations made to increase the authenticity of the American material are usually sensible and were not repudiated by ACD; most are accepted here. ACD could well have looked at some American serial proofs and taken local advice while he was there, and then failed to adopt these changes in the London proofs for publication because of absorption in the war. The outbreak of war with Germany in August 1914 induced pressure from Greenhough Smith of the *Strand* on the author to change the ethnicity of the American heroine from German-American; ACD accordingly made her and her father Swedish-American. But German-Americans are among the oldest white settlers of Pennsylvania (the Pennsylvania 'Dutch' from the original *Deutscher*, a German) although those still living in such valleys as 'Vermissa' in the late 19th century after 200 years continued to speak with strong German accents, 'v' for 'w', and so on, while Swedish immigration (apart from the abortive foundation of Delaware in the mid-17th century) is largely 19th-century in time and Midwestern (especially Great Lakes) in location; so in this edn. the Shafters are German. The American figure of over £40,000 for the 1865 sale price of a Greuze was in the *Strand* and was joined there to the French price of over 1 million francs listed in the *Encyclopaedia Britannica* (11th edn.) article on Greuze by using the equivalents of its article on 'Money'; but presumably the author thought better of 1865 prices reckoned by 1911 encyclopaedists, and his London book-publication revision '£4,000' is retained here. The American substitution of 'Eminent' for 'Ancient' in the fictitious 'Order of Freemen', the Scowrers' benevolent national organization, was in deference to the susceptibilities of the Ancient Order of Hibernians: that correction arose from considerations of fear rather than fact and is not accepted here. Neither are Doran's corrections of English usages in English contexts such as Holmes's 'Devilry', and 'hammer' in the Epilogue (Americanized as 'deviltry' and 'triphammer').

The MS (in private hands, apart from the Epilogue, which has vanished) has not been studied for this edn. The *Strand* (Aug. 1914), advertising the forthcoming serial a month before its beginning, reproduced the opening lines of the MS (p. 227), corrected to the present text from the original, viz.: 'The Tragedy of Birlstone' [title of Part 1] originally 'The Manorhouse [*or possibly* The Manor house] of Birlstone'; 'said I' originally 'said Dr Watson'; 'Sherlock Holmes remarked' originally 'Sherlock Holmes interrupted'; 'I believe that I am' originally 'Dr Watson was'; 'I admit that I was annoyed at the sardonic interruption' originally 'a flush of annoyance came to his cheeks'; 'said I, severely' originally 'said he'; 'trying at times' originally 'annoying at times'; 'He was too much absorbed' originally 'Holmes was too much absorbed'; 'to my remonstrance' not present in original.

[Title]: 'Yea, though I walk through the valley of the shadow of death, I will fear no evil' (Psalm 23: 4). Another point of origin, this time from ACD's infancy or school-days, may be in the Roman Catholic prayer to the Blessed Virgin Mary 'Hail, Holy Queen' (*Salve Regina*): 'To thee do we send up our sighs, mourning and weeping in this valley of tears.'

5 *remonstrance*: strong protest on grounds of integrity, notably directed to the Pope.

untasted breakfast: Ronald Knox noted in 'Studies in the Literature of Sherlock Holmes', sent to ACD on its first publication (*The Blue Book*, July 1912), that the 'false' (post-Reichenbach) Holmes 'deliberately abstains from food while at work: the real Holmes only does so through absent-mindedness'. ACD shows occasional signs of sardonically confuting this essay in subsequent work: it is impossible to say whether Holmes's fasting here is deliberate or absent-minded, but it certainly betokens absorption after 'a long series of sterile weeks'.

Porlock's: Porlock is a town in Somerset, famous for providing Coleridge's excuse for the sudden ending of his 'Kubla Khan', a poem he asserted was the realization of a dream-vision whose composition was interrupted 'by a person on business from Porlock', after which recollection, and hence inspiration, were gone. The poem was popularly believed to have been induced by Coleridge's opium dependence. Conan Doyle had Watson assert in 'The Missing Three-Quarter' (*Return*) that he had weaned Holmes from cocaine, but *The Valley of Fear* is set in the late 1880s. ACD might defer to his second wife, Jean, in ostensibly keeping Holmes off drugs, having met her demand to take him off them, but the implication is present for interested cipher-readers that 'Porlock' has interrupted the kind of Holmes drug-trip we might expect sterile weeks to induce in the period of *The Sign of the Four*.

5 *The Greek 'e'*: the short 'e', epsilon, as opposed to the long. In handwriting it was subject to irregular flourish, as Holmes said, where in print it is often rendered symmetrically. Lower-case is meant (capitals being the same as the Roman form). Scholars and aesthetes often used it, ACD's *Lippincott's* stable-mate Oscar Wilde among them. Porlock's ostentatious deployment of his skill in Greek script and English literary biography argue a Moriarty recruit from academic life. ACD's use of academic rivalry in *The Lost World* suggests he may have seen Porlock's tale-bearing as typical scholarly readiness to put surreptitious spokes in the wheel of an overbearing colleague heading their professional activity and not to be openly defied.

nom de plume: literally name of pen, and here meaning, simply, a name to cover the activities of this penmanship.

6 *Professor Moriarty*: Holmes's Napoleonic adversary, originally invented (in 'The Final Problem', *Memoirs*) as a diabolic master-mind whose destruction would merit self-sacrifice. Apparently based on several originals, among them two eponymous fellow-students at Stonyhurst, one an infant prodigy in mathematics, the other a future Irish Lord Justice of notable lack of scruple (respectively Michael and John).

The famous . . . blushes:
> 'Let humble Allen, with an awkward shame,
> Do good by stealth, and blush to find it fame.
>
> (Alexander Pope, *Epilogue to the Satires* (1738),
> i. 135–6).

A touch: Hamlet. Come.—[*They play.*] Another hit, what say you?
> Laertes. A touch, a touch, I do confess.
>
> (Shakespeare, *Hamlet*, V. ii. 284–5)

See also *The Hound of the Baskervilles*, Ch. 5:

'Did he say anything more?'
'He mentioned his name.'
Holmes cast a swift glance of triumph at me.
'Oh, he mentioned his name, did he? That was imprudent. What was the name that he mentioned?'
'His name', said the cabman, 'was Mr Sherlock Holmes.'

Never have I seen my friend more completely taken aback than by the cabman's reply. For an instant he sat in silent amazement. Then he burst into a hearty laugh:

'A touch, Watson—an undeniable touch!' said he. 'I feel a foil as quick and supple as my own. He got home upon me very prettily that time . . .'

Naturally, Holmes would quote the energetic Laertes rather than the posturing Osric ('A hit, a very palpable hit').

pawky: more correctly 'pawkie' (Scots) but usually found as 'pawky' in English: wily, crafty, shrewd, astute, matter-of-fact while being humorously critical. As an undertone, it is much more characteristic of Watson than is generally realized, but is seldom as explicit as here.

uttering libel: in English law a libel can be uttered only in writing or some form of enduring mechanism such as a recording, or possibly its being taught to a parrot. That Watson is presumed to have written it here makes it libel unless Moriarty is dead at the time of writing (*Regina* v. *Ensor* (1887)). As the subsequent allusion to 'the end of the 'eighties' in the context of Mac-Donald implies narration long after the events, Moriarty's decease at Reichenbach on 4 May 1891 seems presumed to have taken place before the writing of *The Valley of Fear* and Holmes's allusion to libel is therefore erroneous.

there lies: *Strand* and later British edns.; 'there lie' Doran (1915) and subsequent MS edns.

the glory and the wonder of it: Charles Darwin (1809–82) in *The Descent of Man* (1871) states that from the 'Old World monkeys . . . at a remote period, Man, the wonder and the glory of the universe, proceeded' (Ch. 6). Holmes's description of Moriarty's organization sometimes seems as intricate as the Darwinian relationships of species, and the irony of the professor's place in the criminal world seems intentionally paralleled with man among the monkeys. But in 'The Final Problem' (*Memoirs*) Holmes speaks of the universal ignorance of Moriarty's existence (which Watson in that story shares) as 'the genius and the wonder of the thing'.

your year's pension: Watson receives a pension for his service, severe wound(s?) and near-fatal illness in the Second Afghan War (1880). Libel damages could prove as severe as this even in those days, though slander damages would be much less.

6 *solatium*: damages for injury to feelings or for pain and suffering; a more Scottish usage than seems appropriate to Holmes and Watson, though natural for ACD. (Scots law recognizes defamation without division of libel and slander, though the proof of the latter and of its effects would also be more problematic there.)

The Dynamics of an Asteroid: yet another origin of Moriarty surfaces here, the multifaceted and formidable Major-General Alfred Wilks Drayson, FRAS (1827–1901), ACD's mentor and medical client at Southsea in the mid- and late 1880s. The young doctor spoke at the Portsmouth Literary and Scientific Society on 12 Feb. 1884 after Drayson's paper 'Our Earth and its Movements' and attended Drayson's lectures on 'Thirty Thousand Years of the Earth's History, read by the aid of Astronomy' and 'The Discovery of the Second Rotation of the Earth' (23 Nov. and 21 Dec. 1886). The private joke here is that Moriarty's Asteroid is Earth. Drayson's bitter complaint that the professional astronomers refused to take his theory of the Earth's second rotation seriously is elegantly turned by ACD into the inability of the scientific press to review Moriarty. Bradley E. Schaefer in 'Sherlock Holmes and Some Astronomical Connections' (*Journal of the British Astronomical Association*, 103/1 (1993), 30–4), notes that the great American astronomer Simon Newcomb (1835–1909) had published on the dynamics of single asteroids. His nearest title to Moriarty's was 'On the Dynamics of the Earth's Rotation' (1892), given in London at the Royal Astronomical Society. His views were antithetical to those of Drayson, whom Schaefer argues would have brought his work to ACD's attention.

slandered: for Moriarty to have recovered slander damages against Watson, all would have turned on satisfactory evidence from Holmes.

if I am spared . . . come: possibly a satirical recollection from the new convert to Irish Home Rule, ACD, of his former support for Joseph Chamberlain (1836–1914) who said at Birmingham on 12 May 1904, 'The day of small nations has long passed away. The day of Empires has come.'

May I be there to see:
> And when his stout retainers had brought him to his door
> His face and neck were all one cake of filth and clotted gore.

As Appius Claudius was that day, so may his grandson be!
God send Rome one such other sight, and send me there to see!
(T. B. Macaulay, 'Virginia', *The Lays of Ancient
Rome* (1842))

7 *unused plate*: Holmes and Watson had their breakfast brought
to them on covered dishes containing curried fowl, eggs, and
so on (see 'The Naval Treaty', *Memoirs*), whence they helped
themselves on to their plates. The plate had presumably
cooled off, having been sent to the table hot.

Douglas: The choice of name acknowledges the inspiration of
Sir Walter Scott's *Marmion* (1808):

On the Earl's cheek the flush of rage
O'ercame the ashen hue of age:
Fierce he broke forth:—'And darest thou then
To beard the lion in his den,
The Douglas in his hall?
And hopest thou hence unscathed to go?—
No, by Saint Bryde of Bothwell, no!—
Up drawbridge, grooms—what, Warder, ho!
Let the portcullis fall!'

(VI. xiv)

Scott and Macaulay were probably ACD's two favourite
sources of inspiration: in this instance the idea of bearding the
Douglas in his hall, obvious enough in the context of the
story, perhaps induced from the original verse the decision to
make a drawbridge affect plot.

Birlstone: 'birl' (Scots) = 'a turn, twist, revolving movement'
(late 19th century). ACD spoke street Scots in boyhood and
wrote in it in *The Mystery of Cloomber* and other early work.
The meaning here would be as in the English 'the tables
are turned': there may also be an echo of the Irish cursing-stone,
turned against pursuers.

the apocrypha of the agony column: apocrypha being the uncanon-
ical or artificial masquerading as the genuine, agony apocrypha
would be coded messages presented as anguished heart-cries.
Holmes would have conned each day's agony column for
secret communications much as crossword addicts follow their
daily ration of clues.

8 *Billy, the page*: as a young doctor in Southsea, ACD for a time used his brother Innes (1873–1919), who had been domiciled with him since 1882 after their father's institutionalization, as page. An unnamed page-boy is in office in 'A Case of Identity' and 'The Noble Bachelor' (*Adventures*), and 'The Yellow Face' (*Memoirs*); thence nothing is heard of him other than as an off-stage messenger ('Wisteria Lodge', *His Last Bow*). Holmes had used youthful assistants in the shape of the Baker Street Irregulars in the first two (long) stories and the messenger-boy Cartwright in *The Hound*. Despite the family status of the young Dr Conan Doyle's own page, Billy acquires a name and an assistantship only in *The Valley of Fear* and *The Case-Book*, both written after he had become a stock item in Holmes plays, notably as performed by the young Charles Chaplin (1889–1977). Curiously, the name Billy was first given to Holmes's page-boy in the wholly unauthorized play *Sherlock Holmes* (1894) by Charles Rogers, and later in William Gillette's *Sherlock Holmes* (1899), for which ACD wrote the first (and perhaps Billy-less) draft. ACD's ultimate acceptance of him in the canon by name probably owed something to his own children.

Dear me: in retrospect, the symbolism of this mild expletive becomes chilling. In the Epilogue Moriarty uses it to announce the demise of Douglas. By inference Holmes's use of it here would seem to imply the death of Porlock.

I will go no further in this matter: presumably derived from Shakespeare, concerning the murder of Duncan, in *Macbeth*: 'We will proceed no further in this business' (I. vii. 30).

suspicion in his eyes:
>*Worcester.* He will suspect us still, and find a time
>To punish this offence in other faults:
>Suspicion all our lives shall be stuck full of eyes.
>
>(Shakespeare, 1 *Henry IV*, V. ii. 6–8)

Fred: induced by thinking of the great jurist Sir Frederick Pollock (1845–1937), by this time famous for his *History of English Law* (1895), and a fellow-resident of Hindhead (1897–1907). But it is surely coincidence that he is today also remembered for *The Holmes–Pollock Letters* (1942), a correspondence with Oliver Wendell Holmes Jr., from 1874 to 1932. If there is a connection between Sherlock and Oliver Wendell, it is with OWH senior, not junior, from what ACD said.

all the powers of darkness: a reminder that Moriarty will ultimately embody those powers against which Holmes will apparently sacrifice his life. The Christ-like Holmes is not conspicuous in *The Valley of Fear*, but is not to be forgotten.

9 *Machiavellian*: ironic, but affectionately so. Niccolo Machiavelli (1469–1527), the formal advocate of the cause of statesmanship justifying unscrupulous means, is in essence Watson's antithesis, and Holmes, lacking innocence in himself, here celebrates it in Watson.

a large 534: not conspicuously large either in the *Strand* or other printings, or in Frank Wiles's illustration of Holmes brooding over it. But the largeness of the number and its separation from the others by 'C2' seems to imply one page only, where other codes might depend on page/word, page/word, and so on to the end.

editions of Holy Writ are so numerous: a topical allusion, for the period, to the publication of the Revised Version of the Bible in May 1885. As an ex-Catholic ACD was also very conscious of the Donai as well as the Authorised Version, and used both in his writings.

10 *Bradshaw*: George Bradshaw (1801–53), a Manchester printer, produced *Railway Time-Tables* (1839), which developed into *Bradshaw's Monthly Railway Guide* (1841). Newton Deane, 'The Story of "Bradshaw"', which appeared in the *Strand* (Feb. 1904) in the same covers as 'The Priory School' (*Return*), began: ' "What books do you consult most?" a political adherent once asked John Bright in the midst of an arduous campaign. "The Bible and Bradshaw" was the reply of the great Quaker' (p. 156).

The dictionary: Holmes is correct for a cipher based on one page, but the dictionary is an excellent cipher-basis if one is not so restricted. But which is 'the' dictionary? By 1888–9 the quantity might have invalidated any one candidate, as with the Bible. Alas, the *Concise Oxford Dictionary of Current English* (1911) could be the choice only by anachronism, whether or not it had become *the* dictionary by the time of writing. The same applies to the product of the first publishers to print an ACD story, *Chambers's Twentieth-Century Dictionary* (1901). Robert Winthrop Adams (*Baker Street Journal*, 4 (Apr. 1954)) argues for the work of the Aberdonian mathematician John Ogilvie

(1797–1867), which would link by idea association with Mac-Donald's origin and Moriarty's profession, as well as with ACD's youth; but his *Students' English Dictionary* (1865) seems more probable, at least in ACD's mind, than his *Comprehensive* (1862–4).

11 *Whitaker's Almanack*: annual publication commenced 1868 by Joseph Whitaker (1820–95), bookseller's apprentice turned theological publisher who founded the *Bookseller* (1858). The *Almanack* continued after his death as by him. In 1909, 1910, and 1911 p. 534 was on 'The Indian Empire: Native States', an article which had changed very little in the preceding quarter-century. In column 2, 'Mahratta' was the fourth word in 1909 (fifth if you count numbers), and the ninth (or eleventh) in 1910 and 1911; 'government' appeared much lower down the same column although it was not the 127th word; unsurprisingly, there are no pigs'-bristles. (It is good for an editor to know his author is laughing at him.) ACD might quite well have read p. 534 in 1888 or 1889 since in both years it concerned different aspects of astronomy of importance to General Drayson, and hence, perhaps, to his doctor. In 1912, p. 534 discussed the London Metropolitan Police, as also in 1913. In 1914, it examined 'Ireland: Government, Religion, &c'.

We are undone: 'Then said I, Woe is me! for I am undone; because I am a man of unclean lips, and I dwell in the midst of a people of unclean lips' (Isaiah 6: 5).

It is finished: 'When Jesus therefore had received the vinegar, he said, It is finished: and he bowed his head, and gave up the ghost' (John 19: 30). A slightly blasphemous Christ-identification, even granting Holmes's disappointment.

'danger'. Ha! Ha! Capital!: 'He mocketh at fear, and is not affrighted; neither turneth he back from the sword. ... He saith among the trumpets, Ha, ha; and he smelleth the battle afar off, the thunder of the captains, and the shouting' (Job 39: 22, 25).

12 *Inspector MacDonald*: as though in preparation for his most Irish book, ACD is surrounding himself with symbolism of the land of his birth, Scotland. MacDonald never appears again: arguably he is the most human of all the policemen in the canon and seems to arouse more genuine affection in Holmes even than Stanley Hopkins of *The Return*, or, save at supreme moments, the old sparring-partner Lestrade.

Scotland Yard: a Scottish policeman from Scotland Yard, apart from its obvious music-hall implications, seems derived from the leading adversary faced by his brother-in-law E. W. Hornung's Raffles—'Mackenzie, o' Scoteland Yarrd an' Scoteland itsel'!' (*The Amateur Cracksman*, 1899); but in character the two Macs are very different, as Hornung's original derivations from ACD, Raffles and Bunny, are very different in character from Holmes and Watson, their inspirations.

Aberdonian accent: MacDonald will do very well as a type of Aberdeen professional, but ACD has made no attempt to produce an Aberdeen accent, fortunately for his non-Scottish readers. The Aberdeen accent renders 'w' as 'f', 'a' as 'i', and 'o' as 'a', so that a waitress or pot-boy enquiring the customer's choice would be 'fit are ye far?' ('what are you for?').

13 *a wee nip*: this is, unusually in the Holmes saga, an Edinburgh joke—on the fishing capital of north Scotland, Aberdeen, whose pubs in the fish market necessarily opened very early so that a quick whisky before a journey, however early in the morning, was supposedly commonplace for an Aberdonian.

this morning: pedants have pointed out that the murder was announced at 11.45 p.m. the previous night. But, as stated above, morning begins early in Aberdeen.

15 *a wee bit of a bee in your bonnet*: Holmes at this point is fifteen years before retirement to a bee farm, but readers had known of that destiny since 'The Second Stain' (*Return*), in the *Strand* of Dec. 1904. The term, shorn of its affectionate Scottish diminution, implies its subject is obsessed on the subject beyond the norm of sanity. The CID is the Criminal Investigation Department housed in Scotland Yard.

a grand meenister: there is a particularly delicious private joke here since in physical description Moriarty was instantly recognizable to the surviving Jesuit priests at Stonyhurst as the Revd Thomas Kay, SJ, Prefect of Discipline when ACD was a wayward pupil under his charge.

16 *keeking at you sideways*: good description of Greuze's *Girl with Arms Folded*, which ACD's father, the artist Charles Altamont Doyle, must surely have shown him on visits to the Scottish National Gallery on the Edinburgh Mound. Together with better-known Greuze masterpieces, *Girl with Dead Canary* and *Boy with Lesson Book*, it formed part of the great bequest by

Lady Murray of Henderland to the gallery in 1861; it had previously been part of the collection of the family of the Scots painter Allan Ramsay (1713–84). For Moriarty to have somehow become the owner of the Greuze girl is a charming joke, together with the implication that it is perfectly legal ownership. The painting is, of course, still in the SNG although—by pure coincidence—at the time of writing it is in Bute House.

16 *Jean Baptise Greuze*: Holmes is correct in speaking of Greuze's (1725–1805) high reputation, although it did not prevent his death in poverty and obloquy. His *Young Girl of the Lamb* obtained its high price at the 1865 sale of the privately owned Portales Gallery of Art in Paris, though no doubt a few hard bargains could have been struck during the Siege of Paris five years later.

17 *four thousand pounds*: 'fetched one million two hundred thousand francs—more than forty thousand pounds' (*Strand*). The editor of *The World of Art* wrote at once to ACD when this appeared in the *Strand* (Sept. 1914), pointing out that no work of art had hitherto fetched such a price. ACD cited Lady Dilke's notice of Greuze in the *Encyclopaedia Britannica* (11th edn., vol. 12, 1910): ' "La Jeune Fille à l'agneau" fetched, indeed, at the Pourtale's sale in 1865, no less than 1,000,200 francs.' The error was acknowledged and the price corrected in American and British book texts. (Thanks are due to Richard Lancelyn Green for MS evidence for this note.)

seven hundred a year: a very good salary for the late 1880s. If we are to retain the information given in 'The Final Problem', Moriarty was deprived of it before he died (although Watson's ignorance of him until a couple of weeks before his death, is now revealed as spurious).

His younger brother is a station-master: first name unknown, whereas both the professor and his other brother, the colonel, are first-named James: 'My hand has been forced . . . by the recent letters in which Colonel James Moriarty defends the memory of his brother . . . an absolute perversion of the facts' ('The Final Problem'); 'if I remember aright, you had not heard the name of Professor James Moriarty' ('The Empty House', *Return*). Dakin (p. 209) says of the station-master, 'His comparatively humble position makes it likely that he was the poor but respectable member of the family.'

18 *Jonathan Wild wasn't a detective . . . novel*: since ACD knew perfectly well he was both, being a 'thief-taker' by profession
although for criminal purposes, and an eponymous subject
(1743) for Henry Fielding (1707–54), why make Holmes so
overbearingly inaccurate? Evidently, we are to conclude that
frustration at Moriarty's triumph and immunity at the hands
of immovable authorities is affecting Holmes. And for all his
preaching about studying the annals of crime, MacDonald
would be unwise to follow his chronology. Far from living in
1750, Wild was hanged in 1725, as could 'be ascertained in
several trustworthy books of reference'.

The old wheel turns: another usage of the Birlstone symbol.

Colonel Sebastian Moran: unmentioned (and presumably uncre-
ated) in 'The Final Problem' save for his beloved airgun,
Holmes turns on him his own tiger-trapping methods in 'The
Empty House', using a Holmes bust as bait. Later references
indicate Moran was not hanged, although his most recent
murder begins 'The Empty House'.

19 *the Prime Minister gets*: i.e. as a salary in his official capacity. But
Robert Arthur Talbot Gascoyne-Cecil, third Marquess of
Salisbury (1830–1903), then in his second administration
(1886–92), as heir to the generations of Cecil wealth accumulated since Queen Elizabeth's minister Burleigh, was in little
danger of being cast into the financial shade by the colonel.
And Holmes's 'paying for brains' as an American business
principle relates to this: in Britain an aristocrat's lineage might
ensure him a salary denied to a commoner of superior
intellect. Compare 'The Musgrave Ritual' (*Memoirs*): ' "You
will excuse me, Musgrave, if I say that your butler appears to
me to have been a very clever man, and to have had a clearer
insight than ten generations of his masters." "I hardly follow
you", said Musgrave.'

20 *A long series of sterile weeks*: the theme of the struggling professional usually in dire financial straits searching for recognition
haunts 'The Red-Headed League', 'The Engineer's Thumb',
and 'The Copper Beeches' in *Adventures*, and 'The Stock-
broker's Clerk', 'The Musgrave Ritual', 'The Resident Patient', and 'The Crooked Man' in *Memoirs*. 'The Solitary
Cyclist' (*Return*) seems the last formal instance, although it has
an undertone in Moriarty's career ('The Final Problem' more
than here). It derives from ACD's own long wait for patients

when starting up as general practitioner in Southsea in 1882 and his failure to find any when he came to London to specialize in 1891. Holmes supposedly has recognition and money by now, although a few years earlier he needed a fellow-lodger to help pay for Baker Street and thus met Watson. His taking to drugs during unemployment parallels underused doctors taking to drink, however he might rationalize it. The next sentences are as close to saying Holmes had gone back to the drugs as Lady Conan Doyle would now permit.

21 *White Mason*: MacDonald's Aberdonianism is too finely judged to be regarded simply as stage Scots, although Holmes's 'Mr Mac' recalls the music-hall act 'the Two Macs'; but White Mason seems a deliberate, if kindly, introduction of a stage Englishman. Both White Mason (a name from the Anglophile Henry James), and MacDonald are characters whose voices seem unusually audible to the reader, partly because of Mason's signature-tune 'a snorter!' (i.e. a 'knotty problem', what in more recent times, or more informal prose, would be termed 'a stinker'). For another aspect of the Metropolitan v. provincial police see 'Wisteria Lodge' (*His Last Bow*): the medical basis of these conclusions may be studied in *A Pox on the Provinces: Proceedings of the 12th Annual Congress of the British Society for the History of Medicine*, ed. Roger Rolls, Jean Guy, and John R. Guy (1990) which contains discussion of ACD in the context.

you would think . . . no fool: here White Mason solves the case.

a recognized official term: given its Scots speaker, this sounds like a reminiscence of a professorial rebuke from ACD's days as an Edinburgh medical student.

22 *my own insignificant personality*: obviously a late interpolation during the alteration of Part 1 and Epilogue to Watsonian from third-person narrative, and a trifle Uriah Heepish for Watson who otherwise never loses dignity as narrator, but is necessary, to keep this chapter in the original oblique style. Initially, the chapter would seem to have begun with what is now its second paragraph.

ten or twelve miles to the eastward: Baring-Gould citing James Montgomery, quoted ACD's inscription on a presentation copy of *The Valley of Fear*: 'With all kind [*sic*] of remembrance from Arthur Conan Doyle who hopes you have pleasant memories of Groombridge House which is the old house herein described. June 22/21' (ii. 482), but the village is given as only 3 miles from Tunbridge Wells. Dakin (pp. 213–15) notes some contrasts between the imaginary Birlstone Manor and Groombridge Place. Higham (p. 246) sees the descriptive passage 'Douglas . . . society of Sussex' as 'none other than Conan Doyle in very thin disguise', but Douglas turns out to be 'middle-sized' (a very obvious real-life original for his Part 2 persona being 5 feet 7 inches) where ACD was well over 6 feet. In fact, Crowborough, Windlesham, and the Conan Doyle adults provided both conscious and unconscious inspiration as the narrative proceeded, with Groombridge and Groombridge Place used when the author needed them. Crowborough, not Groombridge, became a town. Groombridge Place is older than Birlstone, taking its name from Gromen the Saxon. We are at liberty to conjecture that Douglas's situation in Sussex society reflected ACD's; the relevant passages, while courteous, are cool.

the first Crusade: captured Jerusalem from the Turks (1095–9) and founded the Latin Kingdom under Baldwin I in 1100. A reference to Ted Baldwin, given the next note.

Hugo de Capus: the Norman conquest of England (1066) brought spoil to various Hugos including a nephew whom William I made Earl of Chester (1071) with lands in twenty shires. 'Capus' is a joke, combining the Latin words for head (*caput*) and body (*corpus*), thus 'headbody', or 'bodymaster'.

the Red King: William II, who succeeded his eponymous father in 1087 and met doubtful death in 1100. But the faint note of illusion hinted with Hugo is increased here: the sleeping Red King in Lewis Carroll's *Through the Looking Glass, and What Alice Found There* (1871) is dreaming Alice while she is dreaming him, much as Douglas and Holmes are part of one another's cases. Hence possibly the choice of 'fortalice' in place of the more lucid 'small fortress'.

23 *some far lower horizon*: the life of a Pinkerton detective disguised as a fugitive forger, and employed as a union plug-ugly, may be so described in relation to Sussex county society. So might that of the boy champion of an Edinburgh gang of street-fighters.

24 *with an excellent song*: Douglas's drawing-room repertoire shows slight signs of invading his earlier existence (see Part 2, Ch. 3 and note 'I'm Sitting on the Stile, Mary', p. 214).

24 *after the English fashion*: one of the few formal expressions of ACD's alien consciousness.

26 *Dr Wood*: ACD's secretary was Alfred Wood, occasionally if anachronistically identified by family members with Dr Watson.

30 *brand cattle*: a proceeding more likely to take place among Texan cowboys than Pennsylvanian miners. This brand symbolizes that the bearer is a slave (from Δοῦλος, a Greek capital D, Δ, used by the ancient Greeks to brand their slaves) within the circle (or division of a secret society which has received him). It seems to have no basis in fact.

plain gold wedding-ring . . . left hand: the wearing of wedding-rings by men was more favoured in the USA than in Britain, and the subsequent revelations as to its immobility suggest it is from Douglas's first (American) marriage, allegedly twenty years earlier, rather than his second (English) one, five years old. This reworks the ring motif of *A Study in Scarlet* where Jefferson Hope initially snatches Lucy Ferrier's wedding-ring from her corpse in contempt of her forced marriage and then cannot bear to be separated from it as his only relic of her. Ted Baldwin, as a former lover of Douglas's late wife, might actually have wished to dishonour the marriage-band that symbolizes her preference for the man who betrayed and destroyed his organization.

32 *botanist*: botany was one of the subjects in which ACD was trained in the science of deduction at Edinburgh, where it was greatly influenced by Professor Sir Robert Christison's (1797–1882) use of it for toxicological study.

33 *Pennsylvania Small Arm Company*: 'Arms' in some late reprints.

35 *get across the moat*: *The Valley of Fear* is distinguished by the excellence of the points made by MacDonald, White Mason, and Watson, instead of the usual police fatuity and Watsonian incomprehension, which strengthens the detective-story element. Much is also made of mutual respect and co-operation, and the story demands the virtual assertion of a contract between Holmes and the police in the investigation. Contrast the rivalry with a policeman he respects in 'Wisteria Lodge', (*His Last Bow*) and the abandonment of some of those who in other stories reject his conclusions.

in your book: *The Valley of Fear* is unique in the canon in the Pirandello-like procedure of characters virtually discussing their place in the book, with Douglas himself proclaiming the principle at his epiphany (or resurrection); it is interrelated to the sense of the book as Holmes's critique of Barker's staging of Douglas's play, followed by Watson's staging of Douglas's other play, written just after he designed the tragedy of Birlstone, though concerning events twenty years earlier, and ending with Holmes's vain attempt to foresee another story published twenty years earlier.

We walked down . . . cut yews on either side of it: see note on *The country had been . . . unkempt and dirty* (p. 199).

37 *Suicide is out of the question*: but not in its symbolic form of a man planning his own murder.

44 *to America from Ireland*: a significant assertion, since Douglas's Irishness in Part 2 might simply be a disguise. It is important for him and for ACD that he be part of the ethnic world of which he is so critical.

45 *Benito Canyon*: a silent tribute from ACD to Herman Melville (1819–91), author of 'Benito Cereno', *Moby-Dick*, and other works still badly undervalued in 1914 but championed by ACD. Douglas and Barker were highly fortunate in their gold-mining, California's annual gold-production having declined from the reliable £3 million sterling worth up to 1876. 'Canyon' is, correctly, 'Cañon' in the later American texts.

Thus: it is never made clear how much more Douglas told Barker about his background than is stated here, but we are evidently to assume in retrospect that he said considerably more than Barker here alleges. Otherwise his disclosure of his Birlstone refuge to a man he has trusted so little seems incomprehensible, all the more when he has left that man to face pursuing avengers without warning and with no guarantee he might not be suborned by them. It would also mean that Douglas's explanations to Barker in the sequel to his killing of Baldwin involved automatic conscription as an accessory to conspiracy to obstruct justice, of a man hitherto deemed unworthy of confidence and aware of it. The same logic, with less background, applies to Ivy Douglas; but it seems likely we are to accept Douglas's statement of her ignorance, since ACD evidently wished to drive home a lesson about husbands trusting wives and Douglas's self-reproach on the point after coming out of his closet is better genuine. (His endorsement of

Barker's version in the same passage is fleeting and valueless. He could not know the details of Barker's statement in Ch. 5.)

45 *German*: 'Swedish' in British texts.

46 *miners*: i.e. not gold-miners. In theory the Scowrers were coal-miners, though the officials seldom seem to be.

51 *Bodymaster*: quasi-Masonic term adopted by the Molly Maguires on their affiliation with the Ancient Order of Hibernians to denote the head of a lodge. Bodymasters encountered by McKenna (alias McParlan: see introduction) included Patrick Butler of Lost Creek, Alexander Campbell of Storm Hill, Dennis Canning of Locust Gap, Lawrence Crean of Girardville, Patrick Dolan of Big Mine Run, Yellow Jack Donahue of Tuscarora, Dennis ('Bucky') Donnelly of Raven Run, Black Jack Kehoe of Girardville, James Kerrigan of Tamaqua, Michael ('Muff') Lawler of Shenandoah, Frank McAndrew of Shenandoah, Peter McManus of Coal Run, Michael O'Brien of Mahanoy City, Francis O'Neil of St Clair, and James Roarity of Coaldale; McKenna narrowly escaped becoming Bodymaster of Shenandoah himself. Campbell, Donahue, Donnelly, Kehoe, McManus, and Roarity were hanged; Butler, Kerrigan, and Lawler turned state's evidence; Canning, Dolan, O'Brien, and O'Neil were convicted of conspiracy to murder or to reward for murder; McAndrew saved McKenna's life and was protected by him. By focusing the novel on one Bodymaster, ACD invested the term with greater authority and horror.

52 *There is always romance*: Another Edinburgh celebration of hard-bitten Aberdeen.

of a smile: the ironies of a second wife, possibly with one eye on a second husband, smiling at her first husband's inability to separate himself from the ring of his first wife, may be savoured. Watson is brought back into the front row of observers to do so, for the first time since Ch. 2: Ivy Douglas requires a connoisseur's appraisal, and would hardly get it from MacDonald, White Mason, or Holmes.

54 *ancient yew trees*: the yew alley in *The Hound* (originally courtesy of Stonyhurst College) radiates antiquity, terror, and doom. The yew garden here, also bespeaking antiquity, simply declares its own artificiality by its strange designs.

55 *solemn masks*: the theatrical metaphor, Wildean and Yeatsian, continues. The mask may have the greater truth.

56 *which I had ordered for him*: Watson is Holmes's attendant physician, guarding his sole patient after the manner of doctors superintending wealthy lunatics, as demonstrated in his last sentence in this chapter.

59 *stage-managed*: an unintentional tribute to the sincerity of Ivy Douglas, a poor actress.

ululation: one of Holmes's few self-revelations as the brain-child of an Irish-descended author, but this is the book for it. See Charles Lever, *Charles O'Malley, the Irish Dragoon* (1841), Ch. 17, 'Trinity College—a Lecture'. ' "Not one of you capable of translating a chorus from Euripides—ou, ou, papai, papai, &c.; which, after all, means no more than, 'Oh whilleleu, murder, why did you die! &c?" '

60 *discreet inquiry among servants*: the ambiguity of this is kept in play by Holmes's note a few paragraphs later that 'Ames . . . is by no means whole-hearted about Barker'.

We have only their word for that: there is Moriarty, but Barker and Ivy Douglas might be his clients.

Boss MacSomebody: Holmes is not privy to the equation of Bodymaster and Boss in McGinty's case. The previous comic use of 'Boss MacSomebody' proves a herald to the menace of the Bodymaster when we make his acquaintance, a joke suddenly proving horribly real, and frightening accordingly.

61 *imagination the mother of truth*: 'I am certain of nothing but . . . the truth of Imagination—What the imagination seizes as Beauty must be truth—whether it existed before or not' (John Keats to Benjamin Bailey, 22 Nov. 1817).

there was a guilty secret . . . Douglas: a supposition never fully tested, and hence left hanging over the story. At the same time, the hypothesis would hold good for Enoch Drebber in *A Study in Scarlet*, with a murderer envisaged by Holmes like Jefferson Hope. (Italic not used in American edn.)

62 *But if not*: presumably meaning, if not, the outsider may be already dead, killed by Barker, perhaps with the assistance and certainly with the knowledge of Ivy Douglas, and with the body then concealed in the moat until the investigation is ended. It is difficult otherwise to see why Holmes would search the moat and yet be surprised by what he actually found there.

62 *the resources of science . . . exhausted*: the undercurrent of identification of theme with Ireland in Land League times is asserted here by reminiscence of the speech of W. E. Gladstone (1809–98) in his second premiership, at Leeds on 7 Oct. 1881: 'the resources of civilization are not yet exhausted.' This proved preliminary to his order of the arrest of the Land League president and Home Rule Party chairman, Charles Stewart Parnell.

genius loci: Latin for the spirit of a place, or the inspiration of an environment.

big umbrella: a curve-handled walking-stick would have done as well but they were not in much use at this time, and even the normal right-angled grasping-end used by Holmes and Watson in the early *Strand* illustrations would not be a natural candidate to take on a journey as well as the umbrella dictated by an English January.

63 *Hargrave*: ACD did not make much use of symbolic surnames in the manner of Dickens or Trollope, but an alias might elicit one, e.g. 'Robinson' (robbing-son) used by the thief Ryder in 'The Blue Carbuncle' (*Adventures*), 'Darbyshire' (rural-dwelling racehorse-man), thus giving the dishonest trainer Straker in 'Silver Blaze' (*Memoirs*) his bigamous identity. 'Hargrave' seems to be 'harry-to-the-grave', a harrier being synonymous with a scowrer as used in this book.

66 *lost its grip*: commentators have been puzzled by the reason for this question, among them Dakin (p. 216) and Ian McQueen, *Sherlock Holmes Detected* (p. 190). Dakin rightly compares it with 'You are now standing in the presence of one of the most absolute fools in Europe' ('The Man with the Twisted Lip', *Adventures*) at his delay in working out the solution; the dumb-bell makes Holmes conclude something has been sunk in the moat, and he later denounces himself for not having deduced it to be the missing cyclist's clothing and hence argue for Douglas's survival. ACD evidently thought Holmes's disproved solution too obvious to state.

67 *Next morning, after breakfast*: Holmes must have purchased the penny guide to the Manor House before breakfast, or else on his way to the house itself the previous night. But he had less reason to study it then, and the local tobacconist is more likely to have opened early than closed late.

East Ham, Richmond: nowadays identified with Newham, East Ham is north of Woolwich, remote (now disused) dockland, west of Barking. Richmond is presumably that of the noble park at the polar opposite end of London, not the north Yorkshire retreat. East Ham and Liverpool as possible embarkation points would (with Southampton) be the obvious places for investigation.

69 *fifth year of the reign of James I*: i.e. 1607, James VI of Scotland having become James I of England on 28 Apr. 1603. As James (1566–1625) had less than a quarter-century for his English reign, 'the moated Jacobean residence' is unlikely to have many competitors in quality. Holmes's wicked enjoyment of the inflated style characteristic of such descriptions makes this little caricature a probable origin for 'The Stately Homes of England' by Sir Noël Coward (1899–1973), at least in its remarks on the lavatory used by Charles I (quite informally) during the Civil War. One stately Holmes suggests another.

Mr Holmes!: the English printings do not carry the exclamation-mark, but the context demands a rising, angry Scots voice, as the American editors designated.

than yourself: a significant repudiation of the specialist reductionism proclaimed in *A Study in Scarlet*, Ch. 2.

70 *the edge of the unexplored*: ACD's last book, published two weeks before his death, was *The Edge of the Unknown*. Its devout Spiritualist content is admirably served by a title similar to a phrase of Holmes at his most ironically scientific. Sceptic and priest remained in harmony to the end, in their literary expression, however much they irritated one another in the process of its creation.

72 *I am the dramatist . . . life's work*: McQueen says of this passage: 'Strangely enough, it might as well have been the doctrine that inspired Birdy Edwards, himself in his assumed identity of Douglas now about to be trapped by Sherlock Holmes' (p. 194).

Possess our souls in patience: 'In your patience possess ye your souls' (Luke 21: 19).

73 *criminals*: Holmes now knows Barker is innocent of the murder of Douglas, but he also knows him guilty of the crime of obstruction of justice. This is the last moment of comedy, the removal of which darkens all that follows.

75 *Vermissa*: no doubt Baldwin is to be taken as setting forth on his mission of vengeance after a return to Vermissa to form plans with other surviving Scowrers, although the overcoat might quite well be a relic of his pre-prison life as his ten years out of the world would keep it unused. As for the name, 'Vermissa' seems derived from 'vermis' (Latin for worm), implying a valley of corpses. It does not directly correspond to a real valley, but has features in common with Schuylkill River valley in Schuylkill county. The coal in question is anthracite. 'Neal' is so spelled in American texts.

76 *peine forte et dure*: an allusion to the practice of crushing prisoners to death who would not plead guilty or otherwise, a 'strong and hard punishment'. For example, Giles Corey of Salem, Mass., elected to be crushed to death during the witchcraft hysteria of 1692, rather than plead not guilty, be found guilty, and have his lands confiscated to the enrichment of rivals who had engineered his accusation; as he made no plea, his lands remained his family's after his death. Barker is both guilty and not guilty, in relation to the cover-up for Douglas, and perhaps to courtship of Ivy Douglas.

77 *You are the historian of this bunch*: characteristic of the world Douglas comes from, this declares to be fact what it calls into being. Watson, as editor of Douglas's MS and narrator of the case (whether—as first drafted—in third-person narrative or, as amended, partly in first-person), will be far more a 'historian' than ever before, his previous work (before either 1888 or 1914) being as a memorialist or Boswellian. The Sherlockians' question—How did Douglas know? To which they answered he must have read *A Study in Scarlet* (just published in *Beeton's Christmas Annual* 1887 if the case is 1888 (see Dakin, 210)), making this the most startling reader's response any first-time author can ever have enjoyed—is less important than the sense of history and of theatre his words display. It is an assertion of art for art's sake as fully as Holmes's quotation of Flaubert ending 'The Red-Headed League' (*Adventures*): '*L'homme c'est rien, l'œuvre c'est tout*'.

78 *nothing to be ashamed of . . . again*: he does not say 'nothing wrong', still less 'nothing unlawful'.

to stand pat: Americanism popularized in the 1896 presidential campaign by Senator Mark Hanna (1837–1904), Republican leader of the McKinley forces, who summed up party policy by saying 'We'll stand pat' (i.e. make no changes).

79 *I would have been . . . sooner*: the folly of marital partners not giving one another full confidence concerning their previous histories and present preoccupations is implied, though often not stated, in 'The Man With the Twisted Lip' (*Adventures*), 'The Yellow Face' (*Memoirs*), 'The Dancing Men', 'Charles Augustus Milverton', and 'The Second Stain' (*Return*). (It does not apply to 'The Crooked Man' (*Memoirs*) where the marriage could hardly have survived the knowledge that the husband had betrayed a comrade into death or torture and slavery to advance himself and obtain his wife.) This statement seems explicit also for clarification of the ambiguities on the point in the earlier cases. See note on 'Thus' (p. 187).

caribou: North American reindeer, a startlingly peaceable analogy for someone with Douglas's record and attainments. But Baldwin certainly exhibited the perseverance with which a wolf would pursue a weak or wounded member of a reindeer pack for days. One might imagine such imagery from a former resident of Alaska or Canada rather than an Irishman whose experience was limited chiefly to Chicago, Buffalo, Pennsylvania, and California. As the dating in the story is notoriously self-contradictory, it may be that from time to time ACD vaguely thought of the Birlstone setting as early 20th-century and the Douglas–Barker gold-mining as the Klondike in 1897.

my own. There was a time . . . United States: 'my own, my luck was a proverb in the States about '76' (American edns.).

80 *I said a word . . . glance*: ACD intends us by this to realize that Barker was well briefed in advance (otherwise the 'word or two' would have been the most brilliant and drastic synopsis in history) and that Douglas's previous 'so did Barker here', as an assurance that Barker had not concealed his prior knowledge from the police, is paper-thin cover for the veracity of a statement Douglas himself had not heard. (We do not know how much of the proceedings in the death-chamber Douglas heard in his priest's-hole, but Barker talked to the police in another room.)

81 *You slipped up there, Mr Holmes*: Douglas now finds himself yet another detective humiliated by Holmes's superiority and

reduced to scoring such trivial points as he can. McQueen (p. 186) points out that the plaster would have had to be disfigured by the head-wounds and powder-burns in order for it not to elicit immediate investigation for its purity from Dr Wood and Sergeant Wilson, let alone the ensuing detectives: so Douglas and Barker must have affixed it after previously blackening and bloodying its upper side. The virginity of the underside masking practically the sole unblemished portion of Ted Baldwin's face was certainly unnoticed by Holmes: no doubt the trouble in dirtying the bandage and fixing it right palliates Douglas's pedantry.

81 *wife*: 'widow' in American texts.

I retired into it . . . rest: 'Our rulers will best promote the improvement of the nation by strictly confining themselves . . . the People will assuredly do the rest' (Macaulay, 'Southey's Colloquies of Society', conclusion, in *Critical and Historical Essays*—a book, ACD said, which 'opened up a new world for me' as a schoolboy (*Through the Magic Door*, 11)).

The English law . . . just law: here Holmes speaks for his creator, the reservation being important.

your deserts: Holmes neither here nor elsewhere gives his opinion as to what these are. 'From that, Mr Douglas' in American edns. becomes 'from it' in British edns.

82 *twenty years in time*: i.e. to 1868. Obviously inconsistent with the first sentence of the next chapter, but twelve chapters were written between them, by the end of which ACD was worried that the Scowrers were too clearly the Molly Maguires. The result is a story in double-track time, involuntarily adding to the element of creative recollection in Douglas, Ivy Douglas, and Barker. McQueen points out (p. 196) that more than twenty years seems to be involved, allowing ten years for Baldwin to serve his sentence, five for Douglas and Barker to prospect in California, five for the Birlstone squirearchy, all as stated, to which we must allow time for two assassination attempts in Chicago, removal to California, followed by the illness and death of Douglas's first wife. Barker—credible at least on this point—says that it was nearer seven than six years since Douglas fled California. Historical sources of inspiration cover events as early as 1866 (Schuylkill murder of Henry H. Dunne) and as late as 1913 (Big Jim Larkin's labour

leadership in the Dublin labour disputes). As the Scowrers might point out, double-track time is appropriate for a story of two-timing.

in Baker Street: 'on Baker Street' (American texts).

83 *Scowrers*: The word 'scour' in Scots could mean, apart from the obvious 'cleanse' or 'purge', to flush out with liquid (especially oneself with alcoholic liquid), and to drive off enemies, cattle, and so on; also to reprimand. ACD's choice of the name was certainly affected by Macaulay's *History of England*:

> It was a favourite amusement of dissolute young gentlemen to swagger by night about the town, breaking windows, upsetting sedans, beating quiet men, and offering rude caresses to pretty women. Several dynasties of these tyrants had, since the Restoration, domineered over the streets . . . [By 1685] the Hectors had been recently succeeded by the Scourers . . . The machinery for keeping the peace was utterly contemptible (ch. 3, 'Police of London').

In a footnote Macaulay suggests such gangs had inspired Milton's famous lines in *Paradise Lost*, 'then wander forth the sons | Of Belial, flown with insolence and wine' (I. 501–2). ACD described such a ruffian of around 1800 in his 'The Fall of Lord Barrymore' (*Strand*, Dec. 1912). This pattern explains the oddly classless quality of most of the Scowrers, despite McGinty's and Morris's forays into socialist rhetoric.

ACD may have chosen his secret society's name on hearing that the principal county involved, Schuylkill, was probably pronounced 'Scowlkill' by its first settlers, the early-17th-century Dutch (real Dutch in these early years): modern Pennsylvanians pronounce it 'Schoolkill', 'Scougall', 'Skykill', and 'Skullykill'.

85 *the fourth of February 1875*: James McParlan left Philadelphia on 27 Oct. 1873, arriving in Port Clinton, Pa., as James McKenna, a tramp, and after some inconclusive adventures to the west, established himself in Molly Maguire circles in Pottsville, Girardville, Mahanoy City, and from 30 Jan. 1874 Shenandoah, where he remained, being admitted on 14 Apr. 1874 to the Shenandoah Lodge by its Bodymaster, Muff Lawler. By the summer the county delegate, Barney Dolan (predecessor to Black Jack Kehoe), was proposing him for Bodymaster in

succession to Lawler; a compromise was made in favour of
Frank McAndrew with McKenna as secretary (to compensate
for McAndrew's illiteracy) on 15 July 1874. The speed of
McMurdo's rise is therefore authentic.

85 *Gilmerton Mountains*: Gilmerton is a district in south Edinburgh;
ACD lived for a time with John Hill Burton's sister Mary on
what is now the corner of Liberton Dams and Gilmerton
Road during a family break-up before he was 9 years of age.
It is flat country between Arthur's Seat and the Braid Hills.
There is no obviously intended range in the anthracite
country of Pennsylvania, unless it is the entire Allegheny
Mountains, a watershed between the Atlantic and the Missis-
sippi. The name was assigned because of the town of Gilber-
ton near Shenandoah; slightly west of both is Mahanoy
Mountain. But it is clear that Vermissa Valley is not a
replication of Schuylkill county, however impressively its boldly sketched terrain may approximate to it, and the prolifera-
tion of names has no obvious reference to any real-life
originals. Vermissa as a town has to do duty for Port Clinton,
where McKenna made his landfall, also Pottsville, Girardville,
Shenandoah, and Tamaqua (where McKenna's sweetheart
lived).

plough: 'plow' in the Doran text (1915), though not in the
Doubleday Doran *Complete Sherlock Holmes*, which has 'ploughs'.

rail-track: American revision 'railroad' (and 'flanks' for 'sides'
in the following paragraph) makes for repetition and is
unnecessary.

as miners: 'as' deleted in American printings but in English this
is a formal act without it.

86 *policemen*: these may not be the Coal and Iron Police run for
the Railroad from Pinkerton's, but it is in McMurdo's interest
to denounce all police in hopes of winning credibility among
criminals.

he is worth it: 'Thou wilt show my head to the people; it is
worth showing' (Georges Jacques Danton (1759–94), Jacobin
leader, about to be guillotined, quoted by Thomas Carlyle
(1795–1881), *The French Revolution* (1837)). 'Danton was brave
and resolute, fond of pleasure, of power, and of distinction,
with vehement passions with lax principles, but with some
kind and manly feelings, capable of great crimes, but capable

also of friendship and of compassion. He, therefore, naturally finds admirers among persons of bold and sanguine dispositions' (Macaulay, 'Barère' (1844), *Miscellaneous Writings*).

87 *Are you a member of the union?*: American version of English 'Are you one of the Labour Union?' (which seems to demand 'Are you one too?').

88 *his left eyebrow*: these signs, like the varieties of password, were not determined by the Molly Maguires, i.e. the anthracite coalfield lodges of Pennsylvania, but were sent down apparently four times a year from Ireland as orders of the Board of Erin, head body of the Ancient Order of Hibernians, and transmitted by ship stewards. This may well have been an AOH signal (any gesture has a sporting chance of having been one at some stage, as they were constantly being changed). One example of a sign in use by the coal-miner brethren in the 1870s was two first fingers of the right hand downward on the apple of the throat, to be answered by two first fingers of the left hand to the side of the nose. As a Mason ACD no doubt was familiar with Craft equivalents. (The brand may also have a Masonic origin, at least in design.)

strangers to travel: same origin. This is not a normal password, but a night one. In use among the Molly Maguires were: '*Q.* The nights are very dark. *A.* I hope they will soon end.' Also, '*Q.* The nights are getting short. *A.* We'll soon have the Spring.' These ran some danger of receiving correct answers from innocents. In formal daytime passwords the Board of Erin went in for sophisticated chat about current affairs which must have bewildered the more parochial Pennsylvanians (e.g. 'What do you think of the European war?' 'The Turks will lose'). ACD very carefully removed all Anglophobic, Home Rule, or Fenian rhetoric in adapting Molly Maguire material.

Brother Scanlan: there was a Molly named Patrick Scanlan, but this is not he. ACD mixed the names around, and at no point seems to have kept name and identity together when using Molly names. Scanlan has touches of McAndrew, with whom McKenna would form a very close friendship. As McMurdo's later room-mate, Scanlan shares a role with Michael Doyle, but where Scanlan goes innocently to witness what proves to be the murders of Dunn and Menzies, Doyle participated in the corresponding slaughter. He disappeared and was never brought to trial. Scanlan may seem doomed to inconsistency in a story deriving from two such contrasting figures, but ACD's psychology was sound; the tough talk of some Mollies occasionally gave way to humane instincts.

88 *Lodge 29, Chicago*: McKenna was not in the AOH in Chicago (whence he had come) or anywhere else, though he tried to pretend he had been. McKenna's employers were to try to incriminate the AOH at large in the criminal activities in the anthracite country. ACD is very anxious to clear them and their equivalent, the easily recognizable 'Freemen': they were now his colleagues in the Home Rule cause.

a killing: Scanlan is conceived in the spirit of Pegeen Mike in *The Playboy of the Western World* (1907) by John Millington Synge (1871–1909), ready to condone or applaud murder until confronted by it ('there's a great gap between a gallous story and a dirty deed').

89 *Jacob Shafter*: obvious Americanization of Schafter, and the name may be chosen as an abbreviation of *Brüderschaft* to show that in him McMurdo found true brotherhood while himself masquerading in false brotherhood.

Sheridan Street: another mix. Patrick Dormer, the first of the several sources of Bodymaster McGinty, called his saloon 'Sheridan House'. He would probably have been ill advised to call it 'Union House'. The Molly Maguires had been opponents of the draft in the Civil War and may have been manipulated by Confederate agents. But Dormer's Sheridan was probably the Union general Philip Sheridan (1831–88), the most distinguished Irish-descended Civil War commander. Even so, the Mollies thought Dormer insufficiently ethnocentric.

Black Jack McGinty: the nickname and power apply not to Pat Dormer but to Black Jack Kehoe, Bodymaster of Girardville and afterwards County Delegate of the AOH.

Mike: Scanlan receives the first name of the homicidal roommate Doyle.

the hell: 'in thunder' (*Strand* and later British edns.).

90 *on*: English edns. 'at'.

station: English edns. 'depot'.

by far the largest town: English edns. have 'far the largest township'. In Pennsylvania a township is a political division, whence a school board etc. could be elected; American edns. sometimes alter the English 'township' to 'town' and sometimes retain the original, depending on which seems appropriate.

By Gar: American version used here throughout for what in English edns. appears as 'By gosh' (which implied a level of delicacy somewhat unusual among Pennsylvania miners and hoodlums). That was doubtless subediting under the rules of Sir George Newnes (1851–1910) who insisted on such substitutes for 'By God'; his prejudices apparently persisted in this respect after his death, although some relaxation is evident in respect of other former taboos. But the meaning of 'By Gar' itself is in dispute. Slang lexicography relates it to American pronunciation of 'By God' as 'By Gard', with resultant clipping of the final consonant for bowdlerization. But it actually links with agrarian faction-fighting in ACD's maternal country on the Waterford–Tipperary border, where Paudeen Gar Connors was the 'Shanavest' leader in 1808 when William Foley, ACD's grandfather, was born. When ACD visited Lismore in 1881 he might have stumbled on some invocation of Paudeen Gar, who had certainly been a symbolic name to rally faction stalwarts far beyond the geographical and chronological confines of his personal authority. 'Gar' is an adjective, dispute again existing as to whether Paudeen was *'gear'* (short) or *'géar'* (sharp); but nicknames easily subordinate real names, as is common practice with American gangsters. It is possible that 'By Gar' was ACD's choice of an Irish-American oath, censored by the Newnes editors on general if ignorant principles. Hammett, no doubt satirically, has a detective-sergeant with the unknown name O'Gar: an ACD legacy?

90 *grip*: English edns. continue the narrator's 'grip-sack' (travelling-bag) but a late 19th-century American would have said 'grip'.

91 *The country had been . . . unkempt and dirty*: this paragraph is singled out by Dennis Porter as a *genriste* example of the naturalistic detective story symbolized by the work of Dashiell Hammett—in contrast to the classical village of the English murder famous in the as yet unwritten works of Agatha Christie (1890–1976) described in Part 1, Ch. 4, 'We walked down . . . cut yews on either side of it' (see pp. 35–6). *The Valley of Fear* anticipates both schools but, Porter points out, is unique

in incorporating both in obviously deliberate contrast (*The Pursuit of Crime* (1981), 191–2.)

91 *hard-earned but generous wages*: less insensitive than it sounds, though unimaginative. 'The anthracite laborers, who at the beginning of the decade were as poorly paid as any in the United States, had become [by 1864] perhaps the best paid' (G. O. Virtue, 'The Anthracite Mine Laborer', US Bureau of Labor *Bulletin* (Nov. 1897), 731). ACD may have relied on this official source—it is clear his researches were wide—or else drew on works it fed. But wages plummeted after the Civil War and were badly forced down in the early 1870s by a complex of factors including the American depression of 1873–7 (see Wayne G. Broehl, *The Molly Maguires* (1965), parts 2 and 3). In bad times miners got 50 cents a day and men with large families would work fourteen hours to get that; there was seldom more than thirty-six weeks' work a year for a miner.

dignity of being a hotel: 'The Sheridan House, Patrick Dormer proprietor, situated in Centre Street, Pottsville . . . was neither private residence nor hotel, but a compound of the two. Three stories in height, having a low long extension in its rear, lighted by a sky light, and in which was located the well-patronized ten pin alley; the basement of the main structure was employed as dining room, kitchen, and laundry, and the first, or business floor, front, for saloon purposes. Just back of the latter was a card playing and bagatelle division' (Allan Pinkerton, *The Mollie Maguires and the Detectives* (1877), 73). It may be that Pinkerton's ghost-writer (or even Pinkerton himself) had seen it; it was open to view with no danger, as it played no part in events subsequent to McParlan's meeting with Dormer and his departure from Pottsville a few days later, bar a brief return at the end of Jan. 1874 before final settlement in Shenandoah.

McMurdo asked: 'asked McMurdo' in English edns.

clear across the country: 'right across the Union' in English edns. which, apart from causing confusion between labour and federal unions, is an instructive instance of British striving for the right voice without quite getting it. The phrase is too inflated, a common error in British attempts at American speech.

you are queer: 'you are queer goods' in English edns.

must say it: 'may say it' in English edns.

A gang of murderers: McMurdo tells McGinty and company in Ch. 7 he did not believe in the existence of a murder-gang when he joined the Freemen and before he came to Vermissa. The present tactic seems to have been to elicit attention and induce a response. The relevant chapter-title in Allan Pinkerton, *The Mollie Maguires and the Detectives* (1877) is 'The Detective Sings, Fights, and Dances Himself into Popularity.'

93 *a blind man could do as much*: presumably not intended as Irish-American lack of appreciation of German-American intonation. McMurdo's technique in courtship from the starting-line may seem a trifle professional, since he is not credited with the promiscuity of McKenna or the experience he had accumulated as McParlan.

Ettie: probably a diminutive of Dorothea, as ACD's sister Lottie for Charlotte or his first wife Touie (surely in his mind in writing) for Louisa.

seven dollars a week: 'twelve dollars a week' in English edns. The American adjustment reminds us of the unreality of ACD's notion of living standards in Schuylkill County in 1875. (McKenna got $12 per week and expenses; ACD may absent-mindedly have taken the figure from there).

the first step: not in McMurdo's investigation of the Scowrers but in the feud with Baldwin, whose hatred at his humiliation over Ettie kept him in pursuit. This implies that the Willabys and other survivors would have given up, but once McMurdo's second victory over Baldwin was blazed to the world, and Moriarty's prestige was at stake, his death was inevitable.

94 *boarders*: Lawler's family of eight (with whom Mr Kenna first lodged at Shenandoah) and adjoining tavern (as with so many Molly Maguire Bodymasters) is the equivalent of Shafter's ten or a dozen boarders.

Irishman: ACD's distancing of the story from ethnic rivalry allows McMurdo to lodge with a rival ethnic group. American edns. have 'different from'.

his song the best: a link with McKenna's conquest of Schuylkill but the accent from the first is on lace-curtain rather than bar-room song.

94 *I'm young enough to wait*: 'I am young and can wait' (Charles Stewart Parnell, quoted in Richard Barry O'Brien, *Life of Charles Stewart Parnell* (1899)). McMurdo's taciturnity and passion do suggest Parnell, which enhances the book's place in the Irish Renaissance.

pretty coaxing ways: in Scots 'pretty' is courageous, gallant, manly. Yet here it may have an androgynous character also: the Duke of Holdernesse ('The Priory School', *Return*) speaks of his late mistress's 'pretty ways' being inherited by their illegitimate son (invisibly to the reader). There was also something slightly androgynous about McKenna, especially in the affection he seemed to arouse in men.

95 *sweet valleys of County Monaghan*: next county westward from McKenna/McParlan's native Armagh, albeit now divided from it by the boundary sundering Northern Ireland from the Republic.

of Buffalo: omitted in American edns. Buffalo had played a crucial part in James McKenna's imaginary autobiography, released by stages for the benefit of the Molly Maguires. It was there that he had supposedly 'killed his man', as the historian James Ford Rhodes put it genially (in 'The Molly Maguires in the Anthracite Region of Pennsylvania', *American Historical Review*, 15 (Apr. 1910)). Rhodes's faint note of approval registers a significant common human note of the time: the imaginary Buffalo killing had a touch of winning spurs about it, in cultures supposedly much more civilized than the Molly Maguires. McMurdo's allusions to the murder of Jonas Pinto in Chicago play the same part. The American publisher's anxiety to remove any reference to Buffalo may have had something to do with McParlan still being alive, and some anxiety that the McMurdo character should not be permitted to grow too close to his public image.

planing-mill: 'saw-mill' in English edns.

to love: cf. Shakespeare, *Othello*, I. iii. 128–70.

whiskey: so spelled by Irish and Americans (including some editors); the Scowrers were not very likely to drink Scotch, whose spelling 'whisky' is the English printing.

Why haven't you seen: curiously academic English version 'What's amiss that you've not seen'. McKenna's incessant efforts to find Molly Maguires, let alone Bodymasters, took time to find harbour, but *The Valley of Fear* supposes the Scowrers as part Tammany Hall, part union, part benevolent society, part Murder Inc., a far from impossible mix. So McMurdo can sit and wait. We are apparently to assume Pinkerton's has given him the Shafter address as a house frequented by suspected Scowrers (i.e. Ted Baldwin): the counterpart here is McKenna's subsequent fear his Molly Maguire girl (sister-in-law, not fiancée, to Bodymaster Jim Kerrigan) must have thought, as she watched him giving evidence in the final court trials, that he had courted her only to collect ammunition. She never saw him again. Ettie might well have asked McMurdo after their marriage if he had first commenced his siege in order to gain attention in the Scowrers as Baldwin's rival.

you're a fool: 'you're mad' in English edns., which in American normally means 'you're very angry'.

run against him: 'fall foul of him' in English version.

96 *Isn't it?*: 'Is it not?' (English edns.).

in this district: ACD testifies here to the Irish closeness of the community, for good or ill. The Valley of Fear in part earns that name from being, in the words of another novel's title, the valley of the squinting windows (1918)—by Brinsley Mac-Namara (1890–1963), probably influenced by ACD's *Valley*.

97 *Teddy Baldwin*: the German-accented speech of Shafter natur-ally says 'Teddy' as in 'Fritzi', or 'Putzi', where the crisp American usually says 'Ted'. ACD may not have had much experience among the Pennsylvania Dutch, but he had lived in Germany for a year as a schoolboy.

started: 'stared' in the American edns. McMurdo virtually practises deceit for its own sake, and is certainly pretending ignorance: is a start not a more obvious means of counterfeit-ing surprise than a stare? Shafter's response to McMurdo's being a Freeman perhaps owes something to Roman Catholic reactions to ACD becoming a Freemason.

Milman: this litany is self-sustaining and requires no efforts to translate into the real roster of murders before McKenna's arrival in Schuylkill (the total rose dramatically after it, coincidentally or otherwise).

98 *after tonight*: old Shafter was taking risks (much worse than McMurdo's street bravado exposed *him* to), for a loud-mouthed stranger was not worth punishing unless he kept up abuse or

looked like being a spy. On 26 Apr. 1872 a boss carpenter of Mahanoy City had his skull fractured, both arms broken, and his tongue torn out by the roots for refusing to hire Irishmen as 'all a bunch of God-damned Mollies', and on 5 May 1872 a Centralia schoolteacher had both ears cut off for having disparaged the Mollies at a teachers' meeting a few days previously. Shafter's permitting Baldwin to court his daughter gave him a kind of insurance. Baldwin certainly behaves as if this was the case.

98 *acushla*: the Irish language does not seem to have been one of ACD's many fields of conquest. 'A' is the vocative particle, the archaic English 'O'; 'cuisle' is translated by the great lexicographer the Revd Patrick S. Dinneen as 'diarrhoea' which as an endearment seems a little excessive, even for a former Edinburgh medical student. He also defines it (amongst other things) as a vein, a pulse, an artery, and a pipe. 'Cuisle mo chroidhe' (crudely pronounced 'kishla macree' (the c as in 'loch')) means 'my heart's pulse' and therefore, acknowledges Father Dinneen genially, 'my darling'. Music-hall had picked up the phrase and ignorantly shortened it. Possibly McMurdo was wise to keep his romantic pursuits outside his own ethnic group after all: many of the older Molly Maguires, emigrants from the Great Famine, knew some Irish.

99 *scene of the crime*: this is standard Irish landlord propaganda against the Land League and against secret agrarian societies.

United States: 'States' in English edns, which while good American is bad German-American. As ACD's instincts on Ettie's German constructions are sound in general, some errors may be the result of English editorial intervention and American maintenance of the author's text. Shafter, too, speaks in good, if more traditional, German-American, once the last-minute Swedifications (which almost certainly were by *Strand* subeditors) have been removed from the English text (they are not in the American).

the other one: asserting Baldwin's role as antithetical double to be climaxed in the killing at Birlstone.

100 *Your innocent soul . . . mine*: replete with irony in content and source. The sentiment is traditional for predatory male and innocent female, even if it is often thought rather than spoken, but McMurdo means his agenda as spy and profession as

detective. His chief original, McKenna, also fell in love, but his promiscuity (whose only counterparts here are the two marriages of McMurdo/Edwards/Douglas) resulted in his bedding a Polish servant while flirting with Mary Ann Higgins *chez* Kerrigan; and he seems to have been in far more terror that this would come to the ears of Black Jack Kehoe than that he should be discovered to be a detective.

may I introduce you to Mr Baldwin?: 'can I' (for some reason) in English edns. A good question, but not one she would have asked. This may remotely have inspired Sue Brown's introduction of the detective Pilbeam to Ronnie Fish in Wodehouse's *Summer Lightning* (1929), also a cause of considerable slaughter.

101 *he will hurt you*: 'he will do you a mischief' in English edns, which is legalistic (rather than Teutonic) formality.

big-hearted: 'great-hearted' in English edns, but neither Baldwin nor Ettie was likely to be a constant reader of John Bunyan's *Pilgrim's Progress*.

I'll choose my own time, Mister: as Part I proves to be his choice, this has its own charm. But it is traditional in Irish quarrels: 'I will meet you in the place and the time of my choosing' or 'in my own place and my own time'.

that you reap: 'Whatsoever a man soweth, that shall he also reap' (Galatians 6: 7); Miss Prism quotes it in Wilde's *The Importance of Being Earnest* (1895) on the supposed death of Ernest. The coolly observed male chauvinism here needs no comment, but it should be noted that the last word would have been pronounced 'rape', as the author knew.

He glared: 'He glanced' in American edns, obviously a misprint.

102 *hurry, Jack, hurry!*: 'hasten, Jack, hasten!' in English edns.

loafing place: English edns. read 'lounge'. 'Loafing' will be familiar to readers of Mark Twain, as idle strolling, chatting, time-wasting, dreaming. 'Lounge' was then used as the place for the same sort of thing, whereas it now means a place of slightly snobbish social pretensions in a public-house, small hotel, or suburban residence.

Assessments: 'rates' in English edns. None of the Molly Maguire leaders occupied such a position, the nearest to it being Black Jack Kehoe's post as High Constable. ACD is obviously thinking of the Tammany Hall bosses, notably the American-born William Marcy Tweed (1823–78), arrested in 1872, convicted in 1873, or the Irish-born Richard Croker (1841–1922), Protestant convert to Roman Catholicism and cousin of the Earl of Limerick, who after final defeat in 1901 returned to Ireland, bought a castle and won the Derby. Croker was spectacularly, if temporarily, routed by reformers in Nov. 1894 during ACD's US tour. These were Democrats; in fact the Mollies were mostly Republicans, including Kehoe.

102 *brass-trimmed counter*: 'heavily metalled counter' in English edns.

the famous McGinty himself: this whole episode is based on McKenna's visit to Big Pat Dormer at Sheridan House. In physical bulk, McGinty is based on Dormer. But while McKenna had heard rumours of Dormer's being a Molly, and the tavern was the Pottsville Molly Mecca, Dormer was in bad standing with the order for what was regarded as unduly good relations with the Protestant Odd Fellows: in fact he was glad to ingratiate himself with the Mollies by passing McKenna to Lawler. With that, McKenna goes to Shenandoah and Dormer is out of the story. It made good artistic sense to draw the portrait of the master-villain from the one major local figure in the original story against whom no crime was ever alleged.

104 *By Gar!*: 'By gosh', again, in English edns. The McKenna original for all this was a drunken entry, an accompaniment of a jig then being played on a fiddle by highly skilled dancing, and the rendition of the Molly Maguire song duly printed in Allan Pinkerton, *The Mollie Maguires and the Detectives* (1877), and presumably of particular interest to the creator of Sherlock Holmes in its description of the singer's supposed murder of one Bell. McKenna was assured of good support in the chorus:

> So let the toast go merrily round,
> Each Irish heart conspire;
> Those tyrant hounds will be crushed down
> By matchless Molly Maguire.

Dormer then drew McKenna into a euchre game which ended with McKenna proving another player was cheating them both. The Pinkerton book calls the cheat Frazer and says McKenna then took him on and defeated him in five boxing rounds, leaving no hard feelings (it is significant that so accomplished a boxing fictionist as ACD ignored this, McMurdo's challenge to Baldwin being the closest he gets to it). Another version of the story, quoted by Arthur H. Lewis in *Lament for the Molly Maguires*, and based on the recollection given by McKenna many years later to a Schuylkill journalist, Jake Haas, simply (and more plausibly) says that Dormer told attendant heavies regarding the cheat (here called Joey Clarke): 'Take him outside, boys. You know what to do.' In both stories Dormer then took McKenna to a private room.

elevated his little finger as he drank it: this was a notorious genteelism creeping into London society at the time of writing. ACD would have been quite capable of inventing it as a Molly Maguire signal simply as a private joke.

105 *my joker*: recognition that the original McKenna story actually suggests the joker of old Irish folklore. McGinty's use of the term means that a joker is inherently unreliable and may double-cross his hosts and erstwhile friends at any point, in the old stories. (He is also usually a supernatural figure.)

I'm damned: 'I'm hanged' in the *Strand*, with other English edns. following suit.

106 *clipping*: 'cutting' in English edns.

Philadelphia mint: the United States Mint was established in Philadelphia in 1792, and stayed there. English edns. read 'Washington'.

107 *take our own part*: 'Fear God, and take your own part' (George Borrow (1803–88), *The Romany Rye* (1857)). The anti-Catholic Borrow would have been furious about being quoted by McGinty, as ACD, who admired and affectionately lampooned his work, would have relished.

squirm: 'flinch' in English edns.

'By Gar!' McGinty flushed: 'By gosh, said he' in English edns.

. . . Well, what the hell: 'Well, what the deuce', with no preceding pause, in English edns.

Ted Baldwin: 'Mr Ted Baldwin' in the English texts. The preceding interview has origins in McKenna's recollections to Jake Haas of his interviews with Dormer and later with Kehoe. The Kehoe first interview (a very different first interview appearing in the Pinkerton book), put as late as 1 Mar. 1874 in McKenna's reminiscences to Haas, featured Kehoe, McKenna, and Muff Lawler (later to admit McKenna to the Mollies) in the back room of Kehoe's saloon, Hibernian House, at Girardville.

> *Kehoe.* I hear you killed a man in Buffalo.
> *McKenna.* That's none of your God-damned business, Kehoe. I don't have to account to you for anything.
> *Kehoe.* Cocky bantam you brought with you, Muff, ain't he?
> *Lawler.* He's all right, Jack. I told you that.
> *Kehoe.* Sit down, McKenna. If your story's straight you've got nothing to worry about.
> *McKenna.* You're the one who should be worried. You were the one on the wrong end of the pistol, not me.
> *Kehoe smiles.*

It may be inferred that McKenna/McParlan liked and respected Kehoe. He did not know if Kehoe ever reciprocated, and it seems unlikely that he did. McMurdo dislikes and despises McGinty. McGinty likes and admires McMurdo. The McKenna–Haas disclosures might possibly follow a reading of *The Valley of Fear*, but if, as seems probable, they preceded it ACD was privy to some version of them, possibly through communication with McKenna/McParlan himself.

107 *Tut, tut*: not pronounced as spelled (though a schoolmasterly McGinty is a cunning symbol, anarchy mockingly imitating order). The 'tch, tch' of a tongue quickly pulled back from behind the upper teeth is the sound in question. It cannot be reproduced in writing, but these ejaculations were comprehended as such in their time.

108 *Now I'll leave it to you, Councillor*: McGinty's insistence on his title melds with that title being one applied in common Irish speech to a barrister, a local representative, or an unspecified dignitary in general, with an implication of advocacy and conciliation about it.

Is it you that would dispute it?: McGinty's language here and elsewhere is remarkably Gaelic in construction, appropriately but with the likelihood of an Irish origin in ACD's memory.

by God!: given the vagaries of censorship, it is impossible to make too much of this, but as the text stands Baldwin characteristically takes the name of the Lord, his God, in vain, where his fellows bowdlerize.

if McMurdo had not interfered: but why on earth did he interfere? Had McGinty killed Baldwin, it would have removed a very dangerous Scowrer, and possibly two. It is by now clear that McGinty is the ringleader in whatever is going on; it is probable that the Scowrers are a murder-gang; and it is certain that McGinty himself is a murderer. The effect on the organization would be cataclysmic, forces for McGinty's defence would be divided, and an excellent chance to snuff the whole thing out was obviously present. The only answer has to be that McMurdo would lose both kudos and cash—expenses unlimited, as evidenced by the bogus forged notes—and so, on his own showing, much horror has yet to be caused in his own self-interest.

if I were voted down: Muff Lawler was removed as Bodymaster of Shenandoah soon after McKenna was sworn in by him, although this arose from representations to the County Delegate Barney Dolan. McKenna was proposed by Dolan as a compromise between Lawler and McAndrew, but McKenna ducked thus throwing it to McAndrew. McMurdo as mediator between Baldwin and McGinty recalls McKenna between Lawler and McAndrew, and in both cases this assists the advancement of the newcomer.

109 *And this I swear!*: McGinty is spelling out what convention would normally perform without description, but McMurdo is of uncertain provenance (and in any case the reader needs to be told). The 'quarrelling' exchange was, like the rest of the paraphernalia, universal among the Hibernians, and was intended to enable Brothers about to quarrel know that each was in the organization and so prohibited from mutual conflict: Baldwin and McMurdo should have had the exchange when they first began ruderies at Shafter's. But no doubt it was used after quarrel had been knowingly opened between Brothers now forced to be reconciled.

damn: 'very' in English edns. There is a touch of McGinty turning on McMurdo here, to indicate he is not completely sold on the new man even if he has almost murdered one of his own stalwarts in his honour.

the colleen inside of them: '*cailín*' (Irish-Gaelic) is a girl. McGinty's coy male chauvinism is as repulsive as the rest of him, but is authentic all-male conversation at the time, even among some

puritanical Catholics, the underwear also accurately designated ('shift' being inadmissable, as the Synge *Playboy* riots
proved). It seems probable Black Jack Kehoe would not have
tolerated such conversation.

109 *different from Chicago*: 'different to Chicago' in English edns.
McKenna's vague allusions to earlier induction had to be
swept aside by himself in order to make sure he was finally
admitted among the Molly Maguires.

110 *Widow McNamara*: name probably derived from the McNamara
brothers investigated by William John Burns. When Muff
Lawler's wife became ill, McKenna moved to Fenton Cooney's,
drawing Michael Doyle as an intermittent room-mate.

intercourse: the word had no sexual implication at that time.

the boys: Irish euphemism for physical force activists, Protestant or Catholic.

111 *'all-in' bar-room scrap*: the McKenna Sheridan House fights
inspiring this line seem to have had rounds and rules, as
opposed to being 'all-in'.

Coal and Iron Police: 'mine police' in American edns., Doran
being careful about undue identification with the Molly
Maguire case where the victorious capitalist organization
might prove to have long memories. 'Historians have debated
whether the Mollies were hardened criminals or innocent
labor leaders; many, in the heat of argument, have completely
neglected the episode's true significance. The Molly Maguire
investigation and trials were one of the most astounding
surrenders of sovereignty in American history. A private
corporation initiated the investigation through a private detective agency; a private police force arrested the alleged
offenders; and coal company attorneys prosecuted them. The
state provided only the courtroom and hangman. The fate of
the Molly Maguires taught the people of the anthracite regions
that the Coal and Iron Police were supreme within the area'
(Harold Aurand, *From the Molly Maguires to the United Mine
Workers: The Social Ecology of an Industrial Union 1869–1897* (1971),
quoted (approvingly) in Philip S. Klein and Ari Hoogenboom,
A History of Pennsylvania (1980 [1973]).

in the States: American edns. read 'in some parts of the States';
again a defensive publishing manœuvre, but ACD seems to
have been alluding to the electoral principle in the selection

of guardians of law and order, local judges, sheriffs, and police commissioners being elected, or chosen by elected officials.

policeman: 'inspector' in English edns.

Captain Marvin is my name: the ensuing words deleted from the American texts. Robert J. Linden of Pinkerton's (then about forty and ten years McKenna's senior) took up the post of Captain of the Reading Railroad's Coal and Iron Police on 4 May 1875, after a preliminary secret meeting with McKenna at Schuylkill Haven: Linden in fact commanded a secret squadron of seven Pinkerton men, also styling themselves police. He returned to head the Pinkerton Office in Philadelphia and ended up as a real policeman, becoming head of the Philadelphia police department in 1896. (He is a possible, though remote, further personal source for ACD.) The Linden arrival is therefore eighteen months after McKenna's, and over a year after McKenna's admission as Molly. A few days after Linden's arrival, McKenna found himself Acting Bodymaster of Shenandoah in the absence of McAndrew.

our own police: apart from High Constable Black Jack Kehoe, there seem to have been a number of police in the Mollies, not always in good standing for dues payment.

capitalists: 'men of capital' in English edns.

to club: this rhetoric is not particularly anachronistic, but is certainly prompted by Big Jim Larkin's comments on the Dublin Metropolitan Police in 1913. Cf. G. K. Chesterton, 'A Song of Swords' on the same subject, addressing the Dublin employers (Nov. 1913):

> You gave the good Irish blood to grease
> The clubs of your country's enemies;
> You saw the brave man beat to the knees:
> And you saw that it was good.

fellow-citizen: 'fellow-citizens' in English edns.

we won't argue about that: ironical, meaning that they agreed about it. Marvin then argues with the person with whom he really agrees, patterns of illusion and deception replicating Baldwin's and McMurdo's illusions of reconciliation.

old acquaintance: satirical quotation from Robert Burns, 'Auld Lang Syne'.

112 *the shooting of Jonas Pinto*: one recurrent piece of fabrication in tenth-hand regurgitations of the McKenna story years afterwards was that of a mine watchman bribed to disappear so that McKenna could boast of having beaten the man to death; the police then ostentatiously found (but could not produce) the body. This is a judicious piece of apparently independent corroboration requiring no body.

pointer: 'direction'. English edns. have 'office', i.e. kind attention, but a very ornate mode of expression, as Macdonald or Lestrade might agree. One can imagine it from White Mason.

on the straight: abbreviation for 'on the straight and narrow path', and contrast to 'on the cross' (which for some reason dropped out of American edns., making Marvin sound as though he would forgive anything except acquittal).

by the Lord!: 'by gum' in English edns.

greatness thrust upon him: 'some men are born great, some achieve greatness, and some have greatness thrust upon them' (Shakespeare, *Twelfth Night*, II. v. 158). Like Malvolio's, McMurdo's is a forged greatness and the context of the quotation is a clue: it uses the greatness McKenna feared being thrust on him in the shape of responsible office to implicate him inescapably in murder or make its avoidance proof of falseness.

113 *under the bar*: 'Remember your mothers and sisters, / Let Annie sleep under the bar' (old sentimental song, satirically perpetuated at student symposia in ACD's Edinburgh). The alternative, a bed shared with the Bodymaster, sounds gruesome, although McKenna sometimes woke up to find Michael Doyle beside him. How either McKenna or McMurdo could be so sure they held their tongues in drink is a nice question: McKenna claimed he extricated himself from assassination-duty by intoxication.

postulant: candidate for admission to holy orders, or to a religious community. One of the few hints to the Catholic background of the activists.

strangers to the locality: ACD was drawing on his knowledge of Irish agrarian violence and its traditions here. The Molly Maguires seem to have made some use of the principle, but their proceedings were frequently far more random, haphazard, and spontaneous than the Scowrers'. The novel pictures the valley by focusing on one lodge. It leaves the problem at the close that the concentration on McGinty and his associates loses sight of the multitude. Sixty or sixty-seven from Vermissa are arrested at the end; but not the 'five hundred scattered over the coal district'.

114 *well-filled treasure chest*: not true of the Molly Maguires, for whom McKenna ended as chief fund-raiser as the first arrests arising from his investigations began to be made; he was reduced to singing and dancing to accumulate about $200 so that those against whom he was building the case for the prosecution could pay for the defence.

danger that ever threatened the Scowrers: here again the Molly Maguires were far more vulnerable, what with opposition from vigilante groups, opposing secret societies from other ethnic groups, and the hideous mine conditions themselves. McKenna in a few weeks' mine work had some ugly hand injuries.

115 *we have certain rites*: McKenna's admission to the Molly Maguires, in his version, was an orthodox admission to the Ancient Order of Hibernians, at which Lawler, McAndrew, and three other miners were present. McKenna was told to remain downstairs with McAndrew while his case was discussed by the others, and when the two came upstairs McKenna was told to kneel, promise to promote friendships between Irish Catholics, assist other members at all times, and maintain secret the society's doings. He swore an oath and paid $3 as initiation fee, being given the sign and passwords. (ACD may have seen an exaggerated version of the oath in one book.) McKenna would certainly have reported to Pinkerton any brutality of the kind used by the Scowrers. What McKenna might *not* have reported was some transvestite shenanigans, of which the Molly Maguires showed occasional examples: Masonic and quasi-Masonic organizations go in for dressing up. The McGinty–McMurdo admission dialogue sounds Masonic: the eye ordeal is probably drawn from ACD's brief period as an ophthalmic specialist.

116 *agenda paper*: McKenna's first lodge meeting was not until five days after his initiation, with seven others present, convened by Lawler with the sign of the cross. Later McKenna wrote to Pinkerton, (30 Apr. 1874): 'When there is a job to be done (men to be beaten or murdered) the question or matter is never brought up in open Lodge—but the Bodymaster receives the

grievance and complaint and appoints the man or men privately and secretly notifies them of what they are required to do and then the "job" is done, and the very members of the Lodge are never made aware of the transaction or who the 'avengers' are, which must be kept a profound secret . . . If any member is caught in a fuss and arrested, he can always prove an alibi' (Broehl, 168).

117 *DMAOF*: Division Master Ancient Order of Freemen. The American editor forgot to alter 'A' to 'E' as efforts to distance the text from the Hibernians had led him to require.

wrong: 'amiss' in English edns., but one hardly likes to think of Tiger Cormac's response if anyone, even McGinty, suggested he might be 'amiss'. Cormac seems to have no obvious counterpart in the Mollies, though such a figure seems eminently plausible and is a natural product of such societies. There was a mad Molly nicknamed 'Cat', named for his burglary skills. Cormac seems intended to reveal insanity (see Ch. 7).

you have to be blooded some time: cf. ACD's autobiographical story of medical life 'His First Operation'.

118 *Eminent Bodymaster*: 'Worshipful Master' in English edns, which sounds a little too close to the Masonic usage. Admittedly, the novel is creating association of ideas between them.

to employ him: ACD has McMurdo slapped down by the bearer of the office McKenna would ultimately occupy in his lodge.

119 *winding gear*: mine hauling mechanism.

breaker: machine to crush iron ore before it is heated.

annual contribution: protection rackets are natural fund-raisers for secret societies but seem to have been only slightly practised by the Molly Maguires.

won't: 'dare not' in English edns, but the dry understatement is more probable.

State and Merton County Railroad Company: although there was a (very different-natured) Molly Maguire named Morris, the fact that Morris is obviously an honest socialist makes the name a symbolic salute to William Morris (1834–96). His analysis is excellent: the Mollies enabled the Philadelphia and Reading Railroad and its 'front', the Laurel Run Improvement Company, to gain massive control in the anthracite counties, while the Mollies' excesses resulted in the Reading Railroad President,

Franklin Benjamin Gowen (1836–89), calling in Pinkerton's. The nascent labour union, the Workingmen's Benevolent Association, under the idealistic John Siney (a figure not unlike Brother Morris), was made a scapegoat by capitalists, journalists, Church, and state. Yet Brother Morris's protest is *The Valley of Fear*'s credential for having seen more to the story of the anthracite coalfield violence than simply a murder society. It inaugurated the role of Pinkerton's as strike-breakers. Whatever their pretensions either as labour leaders or embryo capitalists, the Scowrers are simply lethal pawns.

120   *the Railroad or the General Iron*: here Morris shows an awareness of capitalism devouring its own vanguard, as indeed was the case. Gowen, product of the anthracite field, established himself outside it, but, having obsessively smashed the Mollies, crippled the WBA, and outflanked his rivals, he lost control over the Reading Railroad and was driven out of it. It went bankrupt, to be picked up by J. Pierpont Morgan. The future lay with much larger enterprises and men without local obsessions. 'General Iron' is intended as a transparent allusion to Morgan's United States Steel (though this was not formed till 1901).

go easier: 'bear less heavily' in English edns.

croaker: from the supposedly doom-laden note of a raven, with particular reference to Edgar Allan Poe's 'The Raven' (which a saloon-keeper like McGinty, accustomed to bar-room entertainment, would be likely to know).

121   *'I'm Sitting on the Stile, Mary'*: an Irish emigrant tear-jerker (the widowed young poet bids farewell to his wife's grave before departure); its gentility would not too severely outweigh what would be seen as its redeeming sentimentality, especially since neither McMurdo nor his hearers would know the real poet was Helen Selina Sheridan (1807–67), Countess of Dufferin and then Countess of Gifford. In similar circumstances McKenna performed 'The Wedding of Ballyporeen', of considerably lower social antecedent. Both McKenna and McMurdo sang Burns as an encore, very acceptable to any Irish audience at home or abroad. ACD meant McMurdo to sing 'Allan Water' whose first line is in fact 'By Allan-side I chanc'd to rove'. Burns filled the vacuum in Irish popular song caused by erosion of the Irish language.

121 *James Stanger, of the Herald*: apparently based on Thomas Jefferson Foster of the Shenandoah *Herald*, an outspoken young opponent of the Mollies, although pro-labour. ACD's Stanger in person, however, is an elderly pressman similar to the New York *Tribune*'s Horace Greeley (1811–72), the very type of editor being swept aside in the Gilded Age of the 1870s. Foster received at least four fruitless death-warnings (for such editorials as 'It is evidence of a rotten condition of affairs that desperate characters of this kind are at large and that the law has no terrors for them. We believe our judges' hands are tied by timid or dishonest jurors who perjure themselves by refusing to bring in guilty men . . . because they fear the vengeance of the friends of the prisoner. It is about time that law abiding citizens of the area organize posses and take over the functions of officials and jurors too cowardly to act on their own.')

122 *Judge Lynch*: Morris is pointing to the probable rise of vigilant- ism and 'Lynch law'. The original Judge Lynch was supposed- ly a Galway magistrate who hanged his own son 'out of the window for defrauding and killing strangers, without martial or common law, to show a good example to posterity' (Broehl, 238).

I'll blow your face in . . . me: a remarkable quotation for McMurdo to authenticate when preparing his narrative as Douglas after he has done so.

125 *the whole town here*: 'the whole township on your back' in English edns.

peculiar source of income: forgery (if you haven't read the story before), Pinkerton's (if you have).

to a friend: presumably the Pinkerton superintendent in Philadel- phia, to whom McKenna reported regularly.

126 *familiar enough in his past life*: but of which we know nothing more *except* Douglas's jealousy of his wife (a frequent side- effect of male promiscuity).

128 *shaping*: used in active and passive senses here—i.e. that McMurdo contrives to be as bad as the worse, and that he will end up by being so.

may a curse be on you!: Schuylkill county folklore in fact credited one of the Mollies' most courageous enemies among the

Roman Catholic clergy with having cursed two Mollies in the congregation for murders and concluding with the prayer that if, as they stated, they were not murderers the curse would become a blessing on them: both came to very unpleasant ends shortly afterwards. There is a sanctity about Morris which makes this no idle threat.

130   *in the future*: Morris, as a genuine socialist, a family man, a devout Catholic, and with an Irish horror of being an informer, is eminently credible; but he has no obvious real counterpart in character other than Siney, for the Molly Maguire principle—also the principle of violent agrarian agitators in Ireland and violent Irish separatists—was to have a secret organization for violent work in the midst of the much larger non-violent body, or popular front. Even so, the Mollies were a secret society in a secret AOH, but the mass of Hibernians in the anthracite country do not seem to have been privy to what was going on, much less under pressure to take part in it. McKenna found himself pressurized to commit murder, but that was because he had deliberately insinuated himself into the inner circle whose business was murder. Where the Morris–McMurdo conversations have a McKenna–Molly origin is McKenna's relationship with a very different figure from Morris: Powderkeg Jim Kerrigan. There is no suggestion that Morris suspects McMurdo, and his interest seems to lie in saving McMurdo's soul; but McKenna became very worried that Kerrigan suspected him of being a detective, and Kerrigan was the only Molly he feared in that respect until the very end, when several began to doubt him. Kerrigan, 4 foot 11 inches, but homicidally dangerous, seemed to be sounding McKenna out, grinning at him derisively, implying something both of them knew. He got drunk, for instance, and sang in parody of Molly Maguire toasts: 'Here's to every honest squealer that went upon the stand, / That swore the truth, and nothing more, may he prosper in the land!' What he was evidently looking for was insurance against prosecution, and when he was arrested for murder he informed without waiting further for revelations from McKenna. His revolted wife, and her sister Mary Ann (McKenna's sweetheart), then tried to fix the legal guilt on Kerrigan for the murder on which he was informing against his colleagues. Mary Ann's nominal 'relation' with Kerrigan and her unexpected revelation of loathing

for him has an echo in Ettie Shafter's admission to McMurdo that, despite their understanding, she loathes Baldwin.

132 *you were disloyal, too*: this reflects McKenna's problems in maintaining friendships with Bodymaster Muff Lawler and would-be Bodymaster Frank McAndrew of Shenandoah simultaneously during their power struggle; McKenna had already been thankful to get out of Pottsville as tension between Dormer and the Mollies put an increasingly difficult strain on loyalties there. Lawler ultimately informed on his former comrades also.

Coal and Iron Constabulary: 'Mine Constabulary' in American edns., here and hereafter.

133 *might as well live in Russia*: socialists, real or false, execrated the tsarist regime for its repression, although matters in 1875 were not as bad as they would become when Alexander II was assassinated in 1881 and succeeded by the brutal Alexander III. The power and ruthlessness of the secret police are noted in several of ACD's stories (including 'The Golden Pince-Nez', *Return*).

gun: 'gun-butt' in English edns.

134 *hiding-place under the floor*: for purposes not necessarily those assumed by McGinty.

Reilly: also used for a Scowrer, the homage occasioned by a tavern-owner named Jeremiah Reilly starting what evolved into the Molly Maguires in his saloon about 1850, against a gang of Protestant toughs who upset a sleigh on which Reilly's daughter was bringing a priest to say Mass to the Catholic folk of Cass Township. Neither Reilly nor the daughter (nor the priest) seems to have had anything to do with the later organization; but the Molly Maguires continued to revolve around taverns usually owned by Bodymasters (or butty-masters), the inner circle largely consisting of publicans and their sidekicks. The growth of the society was intimately related to the encouragement of sales of alcohol.

'Lynch the cursed Scowrer!': Pinkerton says Linden wrote to McKenna after the killings of Sanger and Uren (see note on, *'we hit back where we best can?'*, p. 221) that McKenna's visits to Tamaqua to see Bodymaster Kerrigan and, more urgently, Mary Ann, induced many cries of 'shame that such a fellow

218

is allowed to live! He ought to be strung up!' (Pinkerton, *Mollie Maguires*, 442).

police station: 'police depot' in English edns.

a pack of cards: not altogether unsound, since by no means all the Coal and Iron Police were Pinkertons, but not very plausible either, since few of them were Irish Catholics. It was quite true that sympathizers in police, army, and the prison service could give some transient comfort to Irish prisoners (usually political rather than agrarian, since the latter were less influential in the towns where gaols would be). The classic instance is the Fenian Chief, James Stephens (1824–1901) whose escape from Dublin's Richmond gaol in 1865 was enabled by supporters among the officials on duty. ACD wrote a youthful story in which Stephens, continuing the escape by sea, makes a dramatic appearance ('Touch and Go', *Uncollected Stories*).

held them for: 'brought in the sentence which would have carried the matter to' (English edns.).

135   *We'll fix you yet*: as the use of names such as Evans Pott indicates, the Scowrers have some basis in the Schuylkill county Welshmen's gang, the Modocs, and in the anti-Molly vigilantes, as well as in the Mollies themselves. On 11 Aug. 1873 Gomer James, a Welshman, apparently killed an Irishman, Edward Cosgrove, in Shenandoah; James was later acquitted, but later murdered. Lawler's failure to have James murdered earlier was the main cause of his being ousted as Bodymaster and his subsequent brutal beating-up by Shenandoah Mollies.

137   *into her gentle life*: yet she had known Ted Baldwin. This, therefore, expressed an emotion more dreadful than Ted Baldwin's threats of sexual sadism.

that letter you were writing: ACD's experience in Plymouth as partner of the half-mad George Turnavine Budd (1855–89)—who secretly read his letters and then sought covertly to destroy ACD professionally in revenge for conspiracies Budd deduced from them—made him particularly alert on this score. (See Edwards, *The Quest for Sherlock Holmes*, ch. 10).

You're the only one woman . . . me: Mary Ann Higgins was not, as the Polish servant could have borne witness, the only woman on earth to McKenna, but his recollection of his feelings giving courtroom evidence is, in a bleak way, akin to this: 'Only once during the whole time did I feel bad. That was when I looked down and saw Mary Ann sitting there. She was a fine, decent girl, and maybe if I'd been the marryin' type, or if we'd met under different circumstances, something would have come of it. As it was I hate to think of what I did to her pride. She must have thought all I wanted out of her was to use her to trap Kerrigan. She looked at me, oh so sadly, and then I felt I really was a proper Molly' (Lewis, *Lament*, 250).

138 *It's the business of the Lodge*: true, of course, but a cynic might suggest ACD was giving McMurdo the benefit of his own Jesuit education—appropriately, since at Stonyhurst ACD heard a great deal about Jesuit secret service work in Elizabethan England, involving comparable diplomatic replies to avert torture and death.

I never know the day . . . murder: 'I never know the day that I may read in the paper "Richard Murphy up for Murder" ' is a traditional Irish female expression of want of confidence in male relatives.

give it up!: if this passage seems less German than Irish, its origin may well be ACD's memory of pleas using exactly these words from his mother to his father—the 'it' being not murder, but drink. The excuse that he must not 'desert my comrades' also seems in keeping with what is known of that tragedy.

139 *Germany, whence father came*: 'Sweden' in the last-minute English alterations and 'where father came from' in American edns. Since the family, and its spelling, seem originally designed as 'Pennsylvania Dutch' of several generations, 'whence father came' (good German syntax) would seem to mean father's people. No doubt there was some first-generation German immigration to the Pennsylvania coalfield, but it would have consisted of miners.

when they fall on me!: the horror of Baldwin's intentions toward Ettie are circumscribed by contemporary convention, yet we are intended to be in no doubt about them. McMurdo, the protective male's only response, too, is a patronizing one rather than a sense of the woman's terror. A doctor is no good place to witness these things.

we will leave the valley behind us: the timetable promise is characteristic of the Doyle family alcohol debate. ACD may have thought of his youth as a valley of fear.

140 *puny but dangerous Robespierre*: this passage is *The Valley of Fear*'s qualification in its presentation of the entire anthracite country under the metaphor of Vermissa Valley. We do not see Evans Pott again, and at the conclusion he is left hanging in what, from the author's viewpoint, is the wrong sense. If McGinty, in authority and power, is closest to Black Jack Kehoe, Pott in *his* authority and power and actual title is Kehoe again: and Kehoe embodied qualities of both Danton and Robespierre. (It is suggestive, in any case, that McMurdo, as Douglas, should be producing such analogies when what seems his own self-portrait on the train is Dantonesque in the unveiling. McMurdo could be a younger McGinty, as McGinty with his half-infuriated, half-delighted response to McMurdo's spirit wants to believe.) Physically, Pinkerton says Kehoe was 'fox-like', which may have encouraged ACD in making Pott rat-like. But Kehoe became County Delegate only after the overthrow of Barney Dolan, who at a special meeting of all Schuylkill county Bodymasters (around Aug.–Sept. 1874) was fined $500 and expelled from the AOH for life for stealing the funds and publicly cursing the Roman Catholic Church; and this was done at the instance of the State Delegate, Captain John Gallagher, who was not a Molly Maguire and nearly deprived Schuylkill county lodges of their affiliation and passwords. ACD was wise in leaving hierarchial topics where he did.

Lawler and Andrews: the names obviously come from Muff Lawler and Frank McAndrew, but the men are wholly unlike them. Andrews is probably based on Hugh McGehan, a non-drinker, hanged (21 June 1877) for the murder of the policeman Charles Yost in Tamaqua on 5 July 1875.

we hit back where we best can: 'Josiah H. Dunn' was clearly prompted by Henry H. Dunne, 'Holly murder victim' (1866), but the murders of Dunn and Menzies derive from those of Englishmen Thomas Sanger, superintendent of Heaton's colliery at Raven Run, and his boyhood friend William Uren, who lodged with the Sangers and worked as a miner in the colliery (1 Sept. 1875). Five men took part, McKenna's room-mate Michael Doyle, the O'Donnell brothers, James

McAllister, and Thomas Munley, each armed with two pistols. James ('Friday') O'Donnell drew Sanger across to their group with a cry 'Is there any work around here for some good men?' Munley fired a shot into Sanger's groin. Then Uren shoved Munley aside to aid Sanger and was shot in the stomach by McAllister. Charles O'Donnell fired two shots in Sanger's back and ran. The murderers fled, pursued by Heaton, the colliery owner, urged on by Sanger who as he crawled away gasped 'Never mind me, Bob, give it to them'. Heaton could not hit or catch the fugitives, one of whom was seen fleeing past by Mrs Jeannette Williams; she dramatically identified Munley as the man when she saw him in the dock. Sanger was carried to his wife, managing to say 'Sarah, come and kiss me, I am dying'. Sanger had five children all under ten and had been married for twelve years; Uren was a childless widower. McKenna could never account for the decision to murder Sager and took it to be a 'return favour'; but when Doyle entered the bar he announced, 'Well, me boyos, we got one English bastard and we nailed another just for good luck.' No doubt one Doyle paid particular attention to the words of another: and this led ACD in *The Valley of Fear* to give reasons for the murder, to state the nationalities of Dunn and Menzies, and to make neither of them English— another example of his anxiety to distance the Scowrers from Irish identification and Anglophobia.

144 *condemned to death*: very few crimes were followed as closely by *The Valley of Fear* as the Sanger–Uren murders. William Hales of Stake Royal sounds like John P. Jones of Lansford, the mine superintendent who blacklisted McGehan, and who seems to have been marked down for death so that McGehan and Boyle would murder Yost. Jones was killed on the station platform at Lansford on 3 Sept. 1875. The matter was arranged by Bodymaster Kerrigan of adjoining Tamaqua, and carried out under his direction by Edward Kelly and yet another Doyle, Michael J. Doyle of Mount Laffee. Kelly and Doyle were hanged on 21 June 1877, thanks in part to Kerrigan's evidence.

again and again: the next three sentences do not appear in the *Strand*, or subsequent English edns. This was the penultimate instalment of the serial and what with pressure of war-related material in need of space even ACD's prose was not so sacrosanct as to be immune to last-minute subeditorial cut

The story may have lost little by the exclusion of these sentences, but their selection for cutting is interesting, as they are both repulsive and realistic. Presumably ACD was asked to accept the cuts, but by this time (early 1915) he would have been far too preoccupied with the war to become greatly exercised. The cut could be his; it seems more likely to be Greenhough Smith's. In any case, ACD felt it was rough luck on the *Strand* to be stuck with so trivial a work as a Sherlock Holmes serial in the middle of stern matters of war, though it is doubtful if the circulation managers agreed with him.

the slag-heaps: the next sentence also was cut from the *Strand* and later English edns. As a result, the *Strand* instalment finished very neatly at the end of the page.

145 *Chester Wilcox has been settled*: Chester Wilcox is based primarily on Bully Bill Thomas, with facets of Gomer James, George Jesse, and William Major, and certain other cases. Chester, the English town on the north-east Welsh frontier, symbolizes the marginal Welsh ethnocentricity of these cases and the Welsh Modocs. ('Major' was considered a name as Welsh as Lloyd George.)

Why did he shoot him?: even with the extortion factor heavily added to *The Valley of Fear*, it is important that the question is there to be asked, and McGinty's failure to answer it may not be for a clear reason (with so much known, why conceal?). ACD is picking out the impression of certain murders arising from apparently forgotten principles (which for the antecedent Molly Maguires would be ethnic).

146 *they've done nothing*: 'nothing amiss' concludes the line in English edn.

Do you back out?: English edns. 'Do you stand back from it?'

147 *No cleaner job*: ironic pun. The Molly Maguires and the Scowrers used the term 'clean' to mean 'well-finished'; here it means that no job has had less bloodshed.

his unfinished job: reflective of the continued attempts on Gomer James and Bully Bill Thomas.

Hunt and Evans: Benjamin Yost, murdered on 5 July 1875, and Barney McCarron, Tamaqua's only two policemen, whom Bodymaster Jim Kerrigan's wife was said (by Kerrigan when she turned state's evidence) to have denounced. Yost was an old soldier, hence possibly the origin of Chester Wilcox's colour-sergeantship.

147 *Mrs Larbey*: adaption of a vigilante killing of Mrs Ellen McAllister at Wiggans Patch on 10 Dec. 1875. Her brother Charles O'Donnell, one of the Sanger–Uren murderers, was then killed by a ring of men who pumped bullets into him. Two of the other assassins of Sanger and Uren, the other brother 'Friday' O'Donnell and Charles McAllister's brother James, fled, and eluded subsequent search from vigilantes or trial prosecutors.

148 *Jenkins*: this name and Policeman Evans are as close as *The Valley of Fear* comes to admitting an anti-Welsh vendetta. 'Jenkins' is probably William Major.

Murdoch: possibly one of the mutilations of 1872 is in mind.

Staphouse: the Scots language simile 'like staps and stairs' means a large family born in quick succession, like the Edinburgh Doyles, to whom no doubt the elder son Arthur often heard the term applied by his street playmates.

Stendals: the pattern of blood and black deeds naturally suggested the title *Le Rouge et le noire* by Stendhal, otherwise Henri Marie Beyle (1783–1842).

Inner Deacon: a more formal celebration of the ecclesiastical apparatus limited among the Molly Maguires to the sign of the cross, which Muff Lawler, and no doubt other Bodymasters, employed for opening normal lodge meetings. It alludes to McKenna's secretaryship and acting Bodymastership in the absence of Frank McAndrew. A deacon is an aspirant priest in minor orders, the 'inner' part is a symbol of his access to the altar or his distinction from the next, and now abolished, church rank 'subdeacon'. ACD would have been naturally familiar with these ranks from his days as acolyte at Stonyhurst, and would probably have smiled with other schoolboys as at the unintentional joke in the Roman Missal 'the priest is then incensed by the deacon'.

150 *Pinkerton*: the Scots-born Allan Pinkerton (1819–84) founded his detective agency in 1850, foiled an assassination plot against President-elect Lincoln in 1861, and reached the zenith of his career with the Molly Maguires. Five years later he had lost control both of the agency and of himself.

Birdy Edwards: Edwards is not an Irish name, although McMurdo alias Edwards is quite exceptionally Irish in speech (e.g. the automatic analogy of Morris with an old woman 'keening' [professionally lamenting]) as well as in birth. The name has been found among Irish Catholic persons, none known to ACD in his lifetime, so far as we can judge. 'Birdy' would serve as a diminutive for 'Bernard', a name favoured by Irish Catholics; 'Bernard' in America is often rendered as 'Bud'; Bud's diminutive is 'Buddy', an American address as standard as 'Jimmy' to a Glaswegian or 'Paddy' to a London Irishman, regardless of the real name; 'Buddy' might seem related to the Molly Maguire 'butty' for 'comrade' or 'mate'; ACD may have thought these connections stronger and more widely made than they were. 'Birdy' could have been memory of an Edinburgh street-gang nickname. Or there may be a thought of one of Boss Croker's more intellectual political opponents, the Comptroller of New York City Bird S. Coler, whom Croker blocked for the Democratic nomination for state governor in 1901 only to have Coler play a critical part in his final overthrow—in part by his essay 'Commercialism in Politics' (*Independent*, 31 Oct. 1901), which ACD may have known.

151 *listless*: 'restless' in English edns.

152 *Every paper which could incriminate him*: American edns. have 'would', but here the English seems wise in retaining the ambiguity as to McMurdo's possible guilt in the eyes of the law, of the Scowrers, and of public morality.

153 *waiting room*: 'waiting-hall' in English edns. But their departure was accomplished by special train laid on by McMurdo's employer's clients, the Railroad, and a company 'room' rather than the common 'hall' would be needed.

close-tiled: closely guarded. A 'tiler' is the name given to a symbolic guard or doorkeeper at meetings of Masonic lodges, giving us evidence that ACD had, as might be expected, partly based the (non-violent) ritual of the Scowrers on his own experiences as a Freemason.

rejoiced that they should all be there: Harraway may owe something to Alexander Campbell, tavern-owner and Bodymaster of Storm Hill, whose suspicions of McKenna seem to have been hardening just before his own arrest. He was hanged for the murder of John P. Jones.

153 *a Solomon in judgment*: a flash of surprising but characteristically schoolmasterly humour from McGinty. The allusion is to the famous story—one which McGinty (and ACD) might be expected to encounter in Roman Catholic sermons—told in 1 Kings 3: 16–28 in which two harlots dispute as to which of them own a baby surviving from two newly born; Solomon demands the child be cut in two, to which the false mother agrees, but the real one withdraws her claim in order to save her child's life and thus is given the living child; the conclusion 'they feared the king: for they saw that the wisdom of God was in him, to do judgment' is all too appropriate to McMurdo's immediate situation, though not to McGinty. Presumably, in the present case, a Solomon would prove the real murderer was anxious that it should have been a murder, whereas a false one would only want the money. There is a touch of this logic about McGinty. Solomon is also fundamental to Masonic symbolism.

which fired the bullet: such disputes sometimes divided the Mollies. At a convention at Tamaqua on 26 Aug. 1875 Tom Hurley's claim for the reward money in shooting Gomer James across James's own bar was disputed by Bodymaster Pat Butler of Lost Creek on behalf of one of his own men, John McClain. Kehoe withheld payment until McKenna and Butler had adjudicated; they decided in Hurley's favour when McClain failed to turn up at their hearing at Shenandoah two or three days later.

154 *Eminent Bodymaster and Brethren*: as usual replacing the English 'Worshipful Master and brethren'.

he has the name . . . service: Douglas's report, or Watsonian hyperbole? There would have been no such comment in the Molly Maguire antecedent. If James McParlan was the best man in the Pinkerton service it was because he had no name at all, especially one so close to 'James McKenna'.

155 *it is little that we have to fear*: another nice Jesuitical sentence; the audience not realizing who 'we' are.

the capitalists at his back: presumably, a warning (to be remembered by the smaller fry) that there may be advantages in informing (as so many did in the Molly Maguire trials, though for little material reward).

Where shall we know him?: 'How' for 'Where' in English edns., but 'Where' seems more menacing, especially taken in conjunction

226

with Genesis 19: 5 ('... the men of Sodom ... called unto Lot, and said unto him, Where are the men which came in to thee this night? bring them out to us that we may know them').

open Lodge: the only use made here of the Molly Maguire restriction of discussing murder at secret meetings; but the trial of himself proposed by McKenna to Kehoe was as exceptional an arrangement as that now put forward for the Scowrers.

the brothers Willaby: they play virtually no part in the story, yet we are left with them as the only persons known to have survived the trials other than Baldwin, and hence as those commissioning the ultimate killing. The name seems the most uncommon in ACD's fiction apart from 'Garrideb' ('The Three Garridebs', *Case-Book*). There is a remote possibility that when ACD visited Land League Ireland his landlord cousins might have referred to followers of the great agrarian journalist William O'Brien (1852–1928), whose incendiary weekly *United Ireland* began publication on 13 Aug. 1881, during or just after ACD's visit, as 'Will O'B.'s'. ACD wanted to denote the repetitive incidence of brothers in violence without producing too many Irish names.

156 *on the cars*: on the railroad-cars or coaches, again symbolic as Edwards's actual employers are the railroad, supposed masters of Wilson and real masters of McMurdo.

reporter: 'pressman' in English edns. Titles like 'the Philadelphia *Press*' (which serialized *The Valley of Fear*) ensured that the collective noun 'press' was used, but not 'pressman'. Like many another modern term, the American usage vanquished the British.

a New York paper: English edns. have 'the *New York Press*' so that the earlier 'pressman' should have been obviously superfluous. There was no such paper and it would have invited useless speculation as to the one intended.

something: 'for his paper' deleted after this from American edns.

157 *deaf as a post*: when Kerrigan was arranging the murder of John P. Jones, an elderly man was in the bar with Doyle and Kelly; when they remonstrated at Kerrigan's indiscretion, he said it was 'only old man Lutz. Deaf as a lamp-post' and hailed him, 'How are you, you miserable Dutch son-of-a-bitch?' The German-American did not even look up.

157 *leave the rest with us*: 'Somehow the boyos in Shenandoah and Tamaqua had a feeling a detective had joined the Order. Nobody suspected me, except maybe Kerrigan. But it gave me a damned uneasy feeling to be sitting in on a meeting taking notes, and hear the Brothers talk about what they'd do to the "son-of-a-bitch" if they ever caught him, and then wondering out loud who he could be' (Lewis, *Lament*, 193), quoting McKenna's oral recollection as reported.

158 *refusal to speak with him*: possibly inspired by McKenna's refusal to listen to Captain Linden's insistence that he leave the Valley at the end of Feb. 1876.

159 *a very rich as well as powerful man*: none of the tavern-keeping Bodymasters of the Molly Maguires seem to have been particularly affluent; but drink clearly gave them incomes and independence well in excess of those of the average miner. At the same time they were dependent on public opinion, especially when organized; hence they needed to show themselves orthodox concerning ethnic rivalries, sectarian hostility, and tough measures against opponents, for fear they be victimized by boycotts.

the sort that squeals: Morris is clearly not drawn from the numerous Mollies who squealed, since of the many who informed out of interest none seemed actuated also by principle; but it is Morris's principle which inflames McGinty against him.

into hell: 'home' in English edns.

160 *every damned copper in the township on top of it*: the English edns. have 'every blamed copper in the township on to the top of us'. Both versions show ACD's hand, the 'damned' being the natural word and his first thought, the 'blamed' an obvious Mark-Twainism in response to editorial censorship, while American edns. keep the first thoughts. We cannot know in how many other cases the American text enshrines the author's original idea, but it is certainly another mark in its favour.

161 *what he thought of the great man's compliment*: i.e. he was delighted by it as proof of his success and his exultation showed strong and fierce. There was no question of a delicate emotion like disgust, such as Morris, Dr Watson, or (by now) Scanlan might register.

162 *a dozen times before*: McMurdo among them—the clearest admission in the narrative.

treasurer: secretary and treasurer are important offices, but one hears little of them in most Molly Maguire material. It suggests that ACD may here have been drawing on, among other sources of inspiration, the Irish Land League in 1879–82, where secretaries and treasurers were of overwhelming importance in strategic capacities; the foremost of the latter, Patrick Egan (1841–1919), was strongly suspected of involvement in the Invincibles, who perpetrated the Phoenix Park Murders in 1882.

nights: 'spring nights' in English edns. But it has already been called 'early summer'.

163 *Tiger Cormac laughed horribly*: granted that Cormac is drunk, as is Baldwin—a piece of good fortune for McMurdo, who might otherwise have faced unstoppable murderous reaction from either at the moment of truth—this laugh asserts his mental disorder.

164 *if you don't take your hand . . . yet*: not an absolute guarantee that this was what ultimately happened to Ted Baldwin, but certainly what McMurdo/Edwards/Douglas wished to be thought as having happened.

forty armed men round this house: 'Then I had a grand idea. I figured I'd get all the boys together at one meeting. I'd send the word to Captain Linden in time and tell him to pull a raid with a hundred policemen and take the Brothers all at once. It was a long shot but I figured it'd be worth the gamble' (McKenna, reminiscing on his unfulfilled design to have himself put on trial, quoted in Lewis, *Lament*).

pistols: 'guns' in English edns.; 'pistols' carries with it instructions to make a search of the persons, not simply what may be visible.

amazed: 'very amazed' in English edns.

between: 'betwixt' in English edns.

165 *Only Captain Marvin . . . that*: English edns. have the previous sentence ending 'except Captain Marvin here and my employers.'

a jail this night: six Molly Maguires were taken by the Coal and Iron Police in night raids on 4 Feb. 1876, but it went off much less smoothly. Alexander Campbell, for instance, at 3 a.m. was dragged from his bed beside his screaming wife (who obviously feared a repeat of the vigilante murders of Ellen McAllister and Charles O'Donnell at Wiggans Patch). These six arrests were for the Yost killing; and on 10 Feb. Thomas Munley and Charles (in error for James) McAllister were taken for the Sanger–Uren murders. McKenna now began to realize he was being targeted as the detective in the coalfield; on 24 Feb. Kehoe told McKenna at Girardville that a conductor on the Reading Railroad had told him McKenna was a detective (hence McMurdo meeting Edwards 'on the cars' and discovering his identity from a telegraph-operator's evidence). McKenna did not leave the coalfield until 7 Mar. 1876, with the Mollies still unsure as to his being a detective. On 5 May Kehoe and ten others, including the wretched Muff Lawler, were arrested and McKenna's identity as James McParlan announced in court on 6 May.

165 *But I knew the way*: 'But' not in English edns.

I knew I could prevent: 'I knew that I could prevent' in English edns.

their murderers are hanged: none present. Of the Sanger–Uren murderers, only Thomas Munley was brought to trial; he was hanged on 21 June 1877.

I gave Chester Wilcox warning: the implication seems to be that McMurdo somehow convinced Wilcox to take himself and his family away from his house and leave it to be dynamited without disclosing his own identity, but presumably he told Marvin, and Marvin and his men got the Wilcoxes away into protective custody. Just before McKenna's final departure one priest—hostile to the Mollies—told him 'I know you're a detective, McKenna, and a stool pigeon beside. If you had knowledge of crimes before, why didn't you prevent them?'

you'll see my work: it is Kehoe who was quoted by McKenna as having given something like this speech to him, on 8 Feb. 1876, after the six night arrests of Campbell and company: 'Too many things are goin' wrong. There's always somethin' happens when you go out on a job. The guy we're gonna take care of ain't around or when our lads get there he's being covered by the damned police. You're good at singin' and dancin' and keepin' the boyos happy. And when you collected all that money we needed to pay the lawyers I was willin' to admit I was wrong' (Lewis, *Lament*, 228–9).

166 *You blasted traitor!*: Kehoe's last word to McKenna (after telling him there would be no trial) was later quoted by McKenna as: 'I don't know what the hell you are, McKenna. Maybe you are what you say—a Buffalo killer—and maybe not. I can't figure you out. Go 'way, man, and if you're a wrong one, a spy or a dirty informer, think how you betrayed your friends and all the poor people of the region and took the gold of the bosses and see if you can face the priests with what you've got on your conscience, McKenna.' This would have been shortly before 7 Mar. McKenna said he turned his back on Kehoe and walked out; 'I knew there'd be no bullet in my back. Kehoe was a man even if he was a bad one. He really believed he was a kind of Robin Hood.'

three months of it: McKenna was in the anthracite coalfield two years and six months.

Take: 'Have' in English edns.

Scanlan: What did Scanlan know? His conversation with McMurdo before the meeting to trap Birdy Edwards could be interpreted both ways: the ambiguity is probably intentional. It is also striking, and moving, in McKenna's conversation with McAndrew when the proposed trial mysteriously fell through about 1/2 March 1876. 'I asked McAndrew how this thing was. He said "Look here, you had better look out, for that man who is riding in that sleigh behind you calculates to take your life". He told me Dennis Dowling was the man with Monaghan. He said, "Have you got your pistols?" I said "Yes". He said "So have I, and I will lose my life for you. I do not know whether you are a detective or not, but I do not know anything against you, I always knew you were doing right, and I will stand by you. Why don't they try you fair?" I made up my mind that I would keep my eye upon Dowling, and I did as well as I could. We stopped at Danny Munley's and had a drink, and after we came out McAndrew informed me positively that he had saved my life.' And later 'I said "I will go to my boarding-house". He says "You will not go to your boarding-house". I said "What is the matter?" He said, "It makes no difference you will sleep with me." And I did, and I was very glad of the chance . . . I met McAndrew, and

McAndrew told me he was going to see the thing through. He took me aside and said, "It was a pretty lucky thing that you did not go home last night" . . . He stated that on the night previous—the night I slept with him—there came two or three men around by my boarding-house, and kept knocking about all night, but they did not manage to get the game, and they left an old carpet sack, so that they would be thought to be tramps. Of course, I had a different opinion as to their being tramps' (McParlan testifying on 10 Aug. 1876, quoted in Broehl, 283, 285–6). The latter part of this sounds like an inspiration for Barker's story about the hard-faced crowd pursuing Douglas after his departure from the gold-prospecting claim in California.

166 *Miss Ettie Shafter*: her faith in McMurdo, whatever he is, also strongly resembles McAndrew's attitude to McKenna.

a special train: one of the few indications of the railroad's decisive role in the coming of McMurdo. McKenna, very definitely the railroad's man, seems to have got out by ordinary train, shadowed by Captain Linden. The contrast between arrival and departure is conspicuous, in the McMurdo railway journeys: he arrives on a common railroad car as a free man, apparently the freest on the train in his independence of the Scowrers, the police, and normal human constraints; he leaves as a pampered guest in the company's finest luxury, marked in body and soul for life.

with old Jacob Shafter . . . wedding: ACD's odd habit of assuming one witness may be enough for a wedding (cf. 'A Scandal in Bohemia', *Adventures*) may derive from his own exceptional situation as a child baptized with but one godparent (his grand-uncle Michael Conan).

blackmail: used almost continuously in *The Valley of Fear* to mean 'protection money', as it is used in Scott's *Waverley*, with special reference to the exactions of the Gaelic-speaking Highlanders led by Fergus Mac Ivor Vich Iain Mhor.

attempt to save them: apart from the $200 raised more or less personally by McKenna from singing and dancing, the Molly Maguires seem to have had pathetically little in their funds for legal defence.

167 *cringing and whining when the last hour came*: it was the unhanged who cringed and whined, in the Molly Maguire story. The Mollies died with such nobility that the New York *Times* in its

rage declared no good was to be obtained from executions when the victims conducted themselves with such courage, contrition, and forgiveness: 'a cheap tragic show' (22 June 1877).

Eight of his chief followers: twenty Mollies were hanged, with McKenna's testimony having condemned twelve. Even of the first ten, Broehl (p. 339) suggests a wide feeling must have existed 'that all of the ten were not equally guilty'. Over the other two there was considerable doubt, one being only peripherally relevant to McKenna's testimony (and hence hanged on informers' evidence), the other—Black Jack Kehoe—indicted and hanged for a murder he almost certainly did not commit, fifteen years before his trial: he has since (1979) received a posthumous pardon.

Ted Baldwin, for one, had escaped the scaffold: it is difficult to see how, since McMurdo had his full account of his murder of Hales of Stake Royal; but presumably the lodge members were all silent and the passing couple stayed away. But the Molly Maguire murderers who received imprisonment rather than hanging were in most cases informers and of these the comparable case to Baldwin was Powderkeg Jim Kerrigan, who seems at least to have contributed a stroke or two to the brushwork on Baldwin. He was connected with McKenna's beloved, if not by cause of rival love; and he seems to have had a touch of sadism, his wife in testifying against him at the first trial for Yost's murder calling him 'liar, cheat, drunkard, wife-beater, coward, and killer'.

keep their vow: there is no sign that the Molly Maguires pursued McKenna, now again McParlan (and later McParland). While rumours circulated of post-trial murders and attacks on witnesses, some of which ACD may have heard, there was no basis to them. The sworn vengeance against a spy is drawn from the Le Caron story where the still existing Clan-na-Gael had its *amour propre* to consider (though it did not make any conspicuous effort to get its man).

thence: 'here' in English edns.

Sussex country gentleman: 'Sussex county gentleman' in American edns.

happenings of which we have heard: on 13 Dec. 1889 Franklin Benjamin Gowen (1836–89), former president of the Reading

Railroad, at whose instance James McParlan had been originally sent as James McKenna to the Schuylkill county anthracite field and who himself led the courtroom prosecution of the Molly Maguires, was found dead in his hotel room in Washington, DC with a bullet in his head and an evident suicide gun at hand. Rumours of murder by the Mollies proliferated. Linden was called in; McParlan, in Denver, thought suicide unlikely. The story may have helped bring ACD to his idea of the first part of *The Valley of Fear*.

168 *The police-court proceedings*: 'The police trial' in *Strand* and American edns. 'Quarter Sessions' in both for 'Assizes'.

Late that night: 'Late last night' in American edns., probably a printer's error.

169 *He was murdered?*: from his early (as child and student) awareness of the Burke and Hare (1828) case in Edinburgh, ACD was always fascinated by the fate of an informer from whose testimony men died, and embodied such figures in his youthful 'My Friend the Murderer', and later in 'The Resident Patient' (*Memoirs*). The sensational case in his own lifetime, occurring after the first of these stories, was that of James Carey (1845–83), leader of the Irish National Invincibles, who directed their assassination of Chief Secretary Lord Frederick Cavendish (1836–82) and Under-secretary Thomas Burke (1829–82) in Phoenix Park. Carey, having sworn away the lives of associates who were in some cases less guilty than he and under his influence, was pardoned and got away to South Africa, but he was shot and killed on the *Melrose Castle en route* from Cape Town to Natal on 29 July 1883 by Patrick O'Donnell, a fellow-passenger with Carey on the voyage to the Cape but who had learned Carey's identity only at Cape Town. Curiously enough, O'Donnell is said to have been a cousin of the Molly Maguires Charles and James ('Friday') O'Donnell involved in the Sanger–Uren murder.

170 *the veil*:

There was the Door to which I found no Key;
There was the Veil through which I might not see:
Some little talk awhile of ME and THEE
There was—and then no more of ME and THEE.

(Edward Fitzgerald, *Rubáiyát of Omar Khayyám*, 15th (final) edn., 1894, verse 32)